LOVE SHOOK MY HEART 2

Other Books by Jess Wells

Fiction

The Price of Passion
Lip Service (editor)
AfterShocks
Two Willow Chairs
The Dress, the Cry, and a Shirt With No Seams
The Sharda Stories
Run

Nonfiction

Home Fronts: Controversies in Nontraditional
Parenting (editor)
Lesbians Raising Sons (editor)
A Herstory of Prostitution in Western Europe

LOVE SHOOK MY HEART 2

lesbian love stories

edited by jess wells

alyson books
los angeles | new york

MANUFACTURED IN THE UNITED STATES OF AMERICA.

THIS TRADE PAPERBACK ORIGINAL IS PUBLISHED BY
ALYSON PUBLICATIONS, P.O. BOX 4371, LOS ANGELES, CA 90078-4371.
DISTRIBUTION IN THE UNITED KINGDOM BY
TURNAROUND PUBLISHER SERVICES LTD.,
UNIT 3, OLYMPIA TRADING ESTATE, COBURG ROAD, WOOD GREEN,
LONDON N22 6TZ ENGLAND.

FIRST EDITION: DECEMBER 2001

01 02 03 04 05 a 10 9 8 7 6 5 4 3 2 1

ISBN 1-55583-617-8

LIBRARY OF CONGRESS CATALOGING-IN-PUBLICATION DATA
LOVE SHOOK MY HEART 2 : LESBIAN LOVE STORIES / EDITED BY JESS WELLS.
    ISBN 1-55583-617-8
    1. LESBIANS—FICTION. 2. LOVE STORIES, AMERICAN. I. WELLS, JESS.
PS648.L47 L69 2001
813'.01089206643—DC21   2001046221

CREDITS

•"KISS OF DEATH, INC." BY KATHY ANDERSON FIRST APPEARED IN THE *HARRINGTON LESBIAN FICTION QUARTERLY*, 2001. "THE GIRLSCLUB" BY SALLY BELLEROSE FIRST APPEARED IN *THE SUN*, SEPTEMBER 1993. "GOOMBAY SMASH" BY JANE EATON HAMILTON APPEARED IN *PRISM INTERNATIONAL '98* AND *BEST CANADIAN SHORT STORIES* (1999), BY OBERON. "INVISIBLE" BY MARY SHARRATT APPEARED IN THE JOURNALS *HURRICANE ALICE* (1997) AND *WRITING FOR OUR LIVES* (1998). "MY SON JAKE" BY MARNIE WEBB FIRST APPEARED IN *VISIBILITIES* (WWW.WOWWOMEN.COM), SEPTEMBER 1999. "JACQUELINE" BY JESS WELLS IS AN EXCERPT FROM THE UNPUBLISHED NOVEL *THE MANDRAKE BROOM*.
•COVER DESIGN BY MATT SAMS.
•COVER PHOTOGRAPHY BY DINO DINCO.

dedicated to Joanne, cut of my cloth

Contents

Acknowledgments

Many thanks to Angela Brown, a fine editor and friend; to Michele Karlsberg, publicist, manager, and cohort; to Billie June Damon and Nora McDermott, Birdie Yusba and Leslie McKitrick, Barb Levine and Ruby Trauner and John Stover; to my son Evan and his godmother Michelle Weston; to Ellen Geiger; Rachel Wahba; the Sangha of the Tse Chen Ling temple; to my literary friends Jewelle Gomez, Elana D., Judith Katz, Sarah Schulman, Deborah Peifer, Susie Bright, Dan Biddle, Katherine Forrest, Felice Picano, Judy Grahn, Paul Willis, Greg Herren, and Jim Marks; and my beloved Joanne Horn.

Introduction

Love—the bane and boon of it, the endless feast of it. The hide and seek of love, the crash and burn of love.

The warm and contented feeling of being loved just right. We love love.

And we love women's stories of love.

In the footsteps of the best-selling *Love Shook My Heart,* here is its sequel, as good for the heart as the first volume.

But don't think this is a book of butterfly kisses and snoring outcomes. Some of lesbian fiction's most talented writers offer complex stories of love that transcends trouble, love that nearly misses, love that grows past bitterness into amusement, love that thrives in the midst of jiltings and transformations. Stories of long relationships and one-nighters; stories by and about older women, women of color, women with disabilities, first-time writers, urban pioneers, and women with an ax to grind.

You'll see yourself, now or in the past, in these stories. Better yet, you'll see your ex and be able to laugh about it now.

We offer these stories for their craft and for the love and lesbian desire they celebrate. Enjoy.

—Jess Wells

At Fourteen
Deborah J. Archer

We bobbled with the waves, our arms hooked over the sides of the enormous inner tube. Who knows what we talked about: boys, parents, our first year of high school, which would commence in three months. We probably talked about sex or what little we knew about sex at age 14 in 1973. I thought I knew nothing, and I was certain Rebecca knew plenty.

We hoisted ourselves onto opposite sides of the tube, sort of sitting-leaning back, with our loosely parted legs dangling inside, lilting to the rhythm of the salty gulf. I poked my freckled arms to check for sunburn. Rebecca was already tan. I tried to force my eyes out across the horizon or to follow the roll and peak of a particular wave. Anything to prevent myself from staring.

The geometry of her woman's body amazed me. I could share T-shirts and jeans with my 12-year-old brother but not with Rebecca. From the broad, gentle slope of her shoulders, perfect lines planed inward to her waist. From her waist, luscious quarter-moons fleshed out into hips then receded into taut, ample thighs. For a moment, it occurred to me that I might lift my foot, stretch forward, and rest my toes on the rubber just beneath her crotch. But in my 14th summer, I was about eight months away from any idea of why. So my toes stayed themselves—placid, hidden—and dallied only with the water and a brief surge of instinct.

"OK, Devvie C., which world are you in today?" Rebecca scooped a clump of drifting seaweed and tossed it into my face.

"Gross!"

"Well, I got your attention! I want you here with me today, OK?"

"Oh, yeah?"

I threw the seaweed back, and the water wrestle was on. First hands and feet, splashing, tangling. We toppled the tube in seconds. Just bodies in water then; the lift and pull of the waves slow-motioned our movements. What on land would have looked like sparring became in water a dance. Hands coupled, fingers laced, legs bumped and swayed between legs. Bellies brushed then pressed, backs arching. Each of us flexing, giggling, posturing to take the other down.

I felt Rebecca's foot hook behind my right ankle and pull up hard. I held her shoulders, swiveled my feet into the grainy bottom, and stayed my ground. She curled my calf and tugged, her whole body pressing forward, hands spread flat upon my chest. I barely budged, boldly smiled, my hands riding her hips, relishing. I was teasing her, and she knew it. When her foot dropped back to my ankle for the final pull, I locked my arms around her waist and let her have me. Under we went, rippling an entire ocean with the weight of our embrace.

Rebecca had been the most popular girl in our large junior high school, homecoming queen two years in a row, and winner of assorted beauty pageants and talent contests all over Texas. A bevy of boys—and men—trailed her constantly. Not salaciously—no, not really. They wanted mostly just to be in her presence. It seems to me, even now, everyone did. I guess if I went looking for it, I'd recall some girl rolling her eyes or strewing gossip. At 14, how could such defining moments of adolescent angst be absent? But something about Rebecca's radiance enhanced rather than detracted from those around her. Consummately charming and attractive, yes—and at 14, already gracious.

Boys from other schools, other states, some of whom had

met her only once, sent her poems and long-stemmed roses. She sang opera—for real—and wore Givenchy perfume. Yet the few boys she chose to "go with" were prototypical geeks. I remember her teaching shy, bespectacled, gangly Cory Wilson to dance. She ushered him smoothly onto the crowded, gawking dance floor, his face and neck red with terror. Rebecca just smiled at him, lifted his right hand to her waist while gently clasping his left, and began to slowly rock him. When she surrendered her cheek to his narrow chest, Cory Wilson became a dancer.

Rebecca saw the inside and drew people out.

We slept that night in a tent on the beach, Rebecca's parents in a separate tent. I sprawled onto the cool white sheets of my cot—sunned, sanded, and salted—muscles limp from the day in water, body still rolling in waves. Rebecca pushed her cot against mine, stretched herself into cotton, and took my hand. "I love you, Devon," she whispered, as she curled one whole hand around my little finger. *Hold my finger forever*, I prayed, then slipped low into hot sleep.

At 14, most of the girls I knew said "I love you" a lot, mostly to one another. They were practicing, tasting the magic words in their mouths, for what would surely come later. Easy for me to look back now and say infatuation, rehearsal, hormones, youth. Easy but untrue. I was in love with Rebecca. As full and deep and subtle as any love I've known in adulthood.

I *wanted* her—whatever that meant. My body vibrated images, told itself stories in moving pictures of me and Rebecca: an empty stairwell in our junior high school, the park we sneaked to in the middle of the night. Familiar scenes transformed by my brave imagination. I would hold her, as we had hugged many times before, but it would be different. I would kiss her, as we had kissed before, but longer, mouths open, lips moving. And there were other things I would do—I could feel them—but the images always blurred. All emotion and sensation, no vocabulary.

Drowsing on the ride home from the beach, Rebecca and I draped ourselves across the ample backseat of her parents' Continental, her head on a pillow in my lap. She played with my hands and fingers, transforming them first into dancing spiders, then into five kissing couples who smacked in unison ("boys" on the left, "girls" on the right). She slid the girl fingers between the boy fingers, pressed my palms together, then held it all tightly in both her hands. "This is us," she said.

Our naked thighs stuck to the metal bleachers as Rebecca and I watched boys play baseball on a thick August evening. Beautiful Brett Hanson, second baseman for the Mustangs, had an irrepressible crush on me. Not that I tried to repress it. Sinewy and soft-faced, lavish dark eyes with enviable lashes, Brett Hanson was just fine with me. He sauntered over after the game, then somehow we trailed off to a little merry-go-round. Away from the glaring field lights and people. Away from Rebecca.

We made plans to go to the movies on Saturday, then we kissed. His kiss surprised me: smooth, fluid; unlike the other boys I'd kissed, he didn't seem to be thinking ahead. Exciting, on a certain level, the way simple sexual dexterity is exciting. And what girl wouldn't want to kiss beautiful Brett Hanson?

Brett left for pizza with his teammates, and I caught up with Rebecca.

"Ooh la la, Devvie C.! Or should I say Mrs. Hanson?"

She kissed the air, poked my ribs, and took off running. I pretended to chase her, both of us laughing, tripping, weaving through swing-sets and jungle gyms. Finally, Rebecca collapsed near a line of trees, and I dropped down beside her. I shivered as the dry grass prickled my legs, and I realized it was dark. Rebecca stroked a shaft of grass between her thumb and index finger, her face absolutely still.

4

"What's going to happen, Devon?"

"What do you mean?" All I could answer because I knew exactly what she meant. In three weeks Rebecca would be going to Richmond High. I was going to Westfield. At 14, different schools might as well be different states. We'd made a pact not to talk about it till the end of the summer. Here it was.

"Everything's going to change. We're not going to see each other."

"We're gonna see each other plenty. Just not at school, that's all. And, I mean, we probably wouldn't get classes together anyway, so it's no big deal. We'll still do all the stuff we do now, totally. You're my best friend, Rebecca. It's not gonna change." I was truly believing and trying to convince myself simultaneously.

Rebecca stood up, offered her hands to pull me to my feet, and smiled.

"I know what your hair looks like in the morning, Devon. And when you wet your pants at that Chinese restaurant. You try to find some new best friend at Westfield and I might have to tell the whole school."

"Yeah? And what about you and Special Ed under the pool table at Amy's? Or that time at the Astrodome when you—"

She cupped her hand over my mouth and lowered her head to my shoulder. I closed my eyes and inhaled: soft creamy clean with a hint of cinnamon, Rebecca.

"Hold me," she murmured. And I did. Letting my palms press, rising and dipping, driving the small of her back. Letting my cheek brush her hair and the crest of her forehead. For the first time out of the hundreds we'd touched, letting myself *feel* Rebecca's body.

"I love you," trembled from my lips, more breath than words, as my body opened into a long, hot smile, and Rebecca wrapped me closer.

A car horn blasted in the parking lot, and I swear we jumped ten feet. We turned toward the sound, dazed, glassy-eyed, bereft of all bearings. We just stood for a moment, staring at shapes, waiting for life to return familiar.

"We should go," I offered, barely lifting my eyes to her. "All the games are over."

"Oh…yeah…I guess they are." She faced the field but seemed to be seeing something else. Moonlight, deft behind the trees, captured one dark eyebrow, one brash cheekbone, one sleeveless shoulder. I wanted to lick that light, to roll it around my tongue and swallow the glow into my body.

"So, did you and Brett-Baby make a date? It looked pretty *cozy* over on that merry-go-round." Rebecca spoke to me over her shoulder, slowly beginning the walk out of the park.

"We're going to the movies on Saturday," I stated blankly. Rebecca and I had always talked openly, I thought, about the various boys in our lives—what we "did," what they "tried," the usual 14-year-old stuff. But not now, not this moment. My body still vibrated Rebecca, smoldered and sweated 10,000 inarticulable questions. Impossible for me to shift, even if I'd wanted to.

So we walked in silence, darkness illuminated at the anticipated intervals of street corners, passed manicured lawns and brick houses beckoning "happily ever after." Each of us in her own thoughts, inadvertently brushing hands; worlds, it seemed, apart.

We lay that night in Rebecca's twin beds, opposite sides of her room, Chicago crooning "Color My World," radio low to lull us to sleep. Her room, "my" bed to her right, as familiar to me now as the one I'd grown up in; yet quickened, secured by the double breathing.

I love Rebecca. The words repeated—pumping my heart, lifting my lungs, dancing down the walls in darkness. I swooned in silence, feet and ears burning; couldn't tell if the

room was large or small, if Rebecca was close or far. Body—
love—stretched to—*Rebecca*—pulse. Strange. Terrifying.
Wonderful. And while I did not yet realize all that I'd told
Rebecca with those words—nor all that I'd told myself—I
knew I meant them.

"Devon?" Rebecca called softly, but I jumped anyway.

"Yeah?" My voice cracked.

"Sleep with me."

My belly fluttered. Not that the request was uncommon;
Rebecca and I had shared a bed often during the past year:
when she and Cory broke up, when my mom was in the hospital, after her brother's wedding, the night her mom busted us
getting sick and giddy on her dad's cigarettes. Times we needed the comfort of proximity, more than a single room; to
breathe under one blanket, unmistakably not alone. We held
hands, plotted revenges, made each other laugh; reassured
each other in all of 14's uncertainty that we were OK, that
someone understood, exactly.

But suddenly it felt different. I felt different: shy, awkward,
hesitant.

"Devon?"

I don't remember moving, but Rebecca scooched toward
the wall, drew back her covers, and I was lying beside her.
Familiar: the Downy-scented sheets, warm with my best
friend's body; the perfect fit of our lines and curves; the soft
scratch of Cory's old basketball jersey–turned–nightshirt. And
I began to relax, to slacken away from my strange new body.

"What are you thinking about?" Rebecca asked gently,
more comment than question, and my body tightened.

"I don't know. About next year, I guess."

She took my hand.

"I was thinking that I love you," I opened.

She nuzzled her head into my shoulder, cheek under my
chin, eyelashes resting lightly upon my neck.

"I was thinking about when we danced at my brother's wedding. Remember?"

"Yeah," I chuckled a little nervously as the images flashed back. The champagne toast—my first taste of alcohol—had lit me to neon. I had done the twist with her dad, and some kind of giggling, shimmy jerk-bop with the curly-haired groomsman. I had just been scooped into the balmy palms of her Uncle Ted when Rebecca tapped him on the arm, said, "She's spoken for," and slid herself between me and Uncle Ted's isn't-that-cute smile. Rebecca and I held each other gently and slow-spun to "Cherish," lilting the lyrics till they belonged to us.

"I really liked dancing with you, Devon. Slow dancing."

"I liked it too," I murmured as the pulse of my neck beat quickly against her lashes.

"Sometimes I think about...like that night, like right now...how we are. I wish you could be my boyfriend."

I flushed. Cold heat beading my palms. Overwhelmed by the spin of nameless emotions rolling one into another, lapping overlapping, I struggled to make meaning. At 14, in 1973, I had no map, no model for that moment. I understood "boyfriend" and something of what it meant to be one. And I was stuttering into the realization that how I felt about Rebecca and some of what I wanted with her were "boyfriend-like" things. I didn't know the other words and only vaguely sensed their possibilities. I just wanted Rebecca, and I thought I'd heard her say the same.

I was about to tell her yes, like a boyfriend, I want that too, when I noticed her ragged breathing, her body shaking against mine, the wetness rolling down my neck and ringing the top of my T-shirt.

"Why are you sad?" I whispered across her cheek.

"Because you're not a boy."

A jolt of inexplicable queasiness quaked my muscles, but Rebecca held me in place, pressed her face deep into my neck and squeezed my shoulder to the bed. She knew: that there was an unbreachable line between best friend and boyfriend, love and love; that our feelings threatened to spill her over that line; that I would willingly spill. She may have known more. She knew enough to cry.

I pretended to be sleeping when Rebecca's mother opened the door on us, wrapped together.

"Hey, sleepyheads! Come help me make French toast!" She closed the door behind her and padded down the hallway.

"Good morning, Devvie C.!"

"Good morning."

"Well, let's get to the kitchen before Harriette has a fit."

I wanted to say something about the long night before; to ask her, tell her how a body becomes an ocean. I sat on the bed I didn't sleep in, near her bathroom door, and watched Rebecca wash her face. The tender skin around her eyes was raw, puffy. Her lips were dry, bitten. There was nothing else to say.

School started, and Rebecca and I tried—long phone calls and pestering parents for rides. But other people beckoned, new parties, different ballgames. And I would meet the just-enough-older woman in whose body I would recognize my own. I would learn my language, with a vocabulary I knew Rebecca and I would never share.

Eight years later my parents mailed me the newspaper photo and briefing of Rebecca's wedding. White satin and pearls, properly demure, infinitely elegant. I smiled into the photo for a long while, fingering the flimsy paper till the print began to smudge. Yes, I had loved her. Before knowing. Before learning tongues and teeth and the tug of a woman's hips. The first woman I took into my body came by breath, scent; offered herself as heat, light. Taught me well.

The Grand Union
Ruthann Robson

It isn't exactly anonymous.

This is a small town, a village really, a place where everybody may not know everybody but everybody has seen everybody else around. Perhaps at the village post office made of brick or the village library formed from stone or the village community center fashioned from an old wooden Dutch Reformed Church. When I wander the streets, pretending I'm doing important errands, I notice the women mostly, as we walk past the restaurants and antique shops, recognizing one another from the performances of the experimental theater or the drumming group, nodding our heads at familiar strangers. Some afternoons it seems everyone is at the grocery store, the Grand Union, which is perched on a hill at the western edge of the village, farthest from the river.

It isn't precisely public.

Outdoors is public. Even if crouched in the hedges—I imagine boxwoods would be best, thick but not too scratchy—outdoors is what is meant by public space. At least that's what I mean. Under the brilliant dome of the sky, shredded at the borders with clouds, a slight breeze sifting through my skin. Though I know there are public places that are not outdoors; there are theaters and libraries, antique shops and restaurants. And the grocery store. But everyone would agree that a bathroom is not a public place. It has a door and the door locks. It's even called a privy sometimes, as in private.

It is sex.

I have no argument to offer that it isn't. Maybe it's not the kind of sex we like to think about when we think of women, but there's no denying it's sex.

I know some people would think I'm not the type for anonymous public sex, even if it's not exactly anonymous and only semipublic; they might even think it's a miracle I even have sex. Some of it is age; young dykes can act like the rest of us were dried up during what they consider the fuddy-duddy feminist movement. I don't bother to tell these kids that the feminists were anything but dry. I mean women-loving-women was a political act, sure, but what that meant was there was an awful lot of fucking going on. There was also no way to reject someone's sexual advances—it opened us up to accusations of being racist or anti-Semitic or classist or lookist or fatphobic. And in the rare case that none of those could be made to apply, there was always internalized homophobia. Yes, there was a lot of fucking going on.

Though we didn't call it "fucking," at least not out loud. It was whispered, in our own heads and in each other's ears. A word used so indiscriminately—the all-purpose noun, verb, and adjective—suddenly had such a throaty power when it actually referred to what it meant, to sex.

Gina would put her hands around my neck until I said it. She would press on my windpipe with the back of her hand, her eyes bulging and watery, completely focused on me and yet somehow unfocused. I liked to wait as long as I could, preferring to prolong passion. It was Gina who was the get-it-over-with girl then. Though I never complained. Mostly because once Gina got it over with, she'd want to start all over again.

These days it's neither long and languid nor repeat performances until dawn. When I get desperate, I go food shopping at the Grand Union.

I live close enough to walk, but wouldn't want to lug the groceries home, even in my special canvas bags from Save the Earth!

or in the Grand Union's brown paper bags with handles. (I never get plastic. Even though there's a spot right inside the automatic door to recycle the plastic bags, I still think it's worse for the environment.) So I drive the station wagon. I would have preferred something sexier, maybe a Miata, as impractical as that seems. Yellow, although I've never seen one that color, not even in the catalog I picked up from the showroom across the river one day, when I just happened to be driving our old falling-apart car on the strip where all the dealers display their shiny wares. But when we traded in the clunker, it was for a blue Subaru Outback. Gina was thrilled by four-wheel drive for the snow and the mountains. But we never got to go skiing, as it turned out.

Parking is simple this time of day. The Grand Union is flanked by a liquor store and a drugstore, and the parking lot divides itself similarly. It's my habit to switch the side where I park every year on my birthday, just so I don't get in a rut. I'm the type of person who's always worried about being complacent and boring. Though I live in a little village and have a safe job as a Web designer, a part of me always craves excitement and adventure. I'm not the most likely girl to go off hiking the Himalayas or anything (Gina told me there is frozen shit and urine along the trails—apparently it never decomposes; I think I'd find this unpleasant), but I've had my share of exciting vacations. Gina and I saved one year and went kayaking in New Zealand, which we learned is more correctly called by its Maori name, Aotearoa. Now, *there* is a small country, like a village really, and everyone seemed to know one another. Or at least the white people knew the white people and the Maori people knew the Maori people. The volcanoes didn't erupt while we were there, which was a bit of a disappointment, but everything else was gorgeous, just as the lesbian kayak-tour promoter had promised.

I drop off a prescription at the Drug Emporium, then head through the automatic doors, straight for the carts. The carts here usually have wheels that work, which is no small thing, I think. Or maybe it is a small thing, but it's the small things that can make or break my afternoons these days.

I don't have a list, either in my mind or in my pocket. So I stroll the aisles, hopeful that some food item will call out to me, *Choose me, I'm perfect*, hopeful that I could hear such a call if it were uttered.

It happens at the frozen foods. I hate frozen foods, I do, but sometimes I can see a red packet with a picture on it and get an idea. Lasagna. Fish with mashed potatoes. Sliced turkey and cranberries. Fried rice and snow peas. Burritos. Though all of these seem to be too much work. Who wants to take such trouble to eat alone? Nothing entices.

Except her.

She's leaning into a freezer compartment, the brick red of her shirt sliding up her back, exposing a swash of flesh above her black jeans. Gap jeans, according to the label. I'd estimate a size 14 or maybe even 16. I'd guess the reverse cut, ample in the hips and thighs, slimmer at the ankles. A mess of dark hair, curly, obscures her face. She seems ample everywhere. Like Gina; like Gina was.

When she stands up, her face is flushed and her arms are filled with frozen pizzas. *Don't buy those*, I want to warn her. Too many chemicals and preservatives. The pizza parlor downtown makes much better pizza, and the guys who work there have sworn to me that they use only fresh ingredients. Sure, these frozen pizzas are cheaper, but not in the long run.

As if she can read my thoughts, she says, "For the kids." I think I recognize her from somewhere around town; maybe she was in the women's drumming group. Or did she work at that new restaurant for a while, the one with the poetry readings on Friday nights that went out of business after three months? She's pulling her shirt down, smiling, smoothing her hair away from her forehead. A high forehead, I like that. I try to focus on

13

her hands—a sex organ if it comes to that—and they seem slight in relation to the rest of her body, although not too smooth, which I admire. Her nails are short but slightly jagged; she doesn't seem to be the persnickety type. I follow her left hand as it travels to her hair again, revealing her left ear, with its row of silver earrings, rings getting smaller and smaller and they ascend from the lobe around the helix. Her white face is a bit flushed—whether from bending over or from my stare, I don't know.

"Sorry," I tell her, moving my cart out of her way.

"No problem." That nice almost-composed-now smile. In control, with her frozen pizzas and no stomach exposed, she looks at me straight on, an unassailable trajectory between her eyes and mine. It's that direct gaze that dykes have when they look at other women—forget dress and walk and all those other telltale signs that change with the times and trends. It's the gaze that is the giveaway. And I know how to look back. Unflinchingly into her light brown eyes, darker than hazel, lighter than espresso. Sort of like the pelt of the deer that sometimes wander into the village in winter, or the fur of a coyote found frozen on Main Street after that blizzard several years ago.

I feel a shimmer of sweat start on my back, despite the fact that I'm getting cold in this aisle.

She's the one to break contact, twisting her cart too fast, unbalancing the display of colorful paper plates behind her. The paperware cascades to the floor in a rainbow waterfall, puddling between us.

I laugh. Then, to be generous, I say something about these narrow aisles. Although they are quite wide, really. Plenty of room for just the two of us, and our carts, and even the paper plate display.

She's bending down, her shirt slipping up again, scooping up the plates. The display, cardboard itself, doesn't seem sturdy enough to support them again—if it ever was—and she's stacking them near the freezer case with the bagels and waffles. There's a perfectly good bagel shop in our village; I don't know why anyone would ever buy these things. And that's what I say to her.

Not the most romantic line, but perhaps I'll earn points for originality.

Though perhaps not. She seems overly flustered. Her neck a lovely red and her eyes averted. I help her with the plates, leaving a few for her to finish, and then head the other way up the aisle.

Around the corner, near the ice cream, I see Claire. A woman I actually know. Gina and I were invited to her commitment ceremony, with her then-girlfriend—was it Anne? Anna? Joann?—and we went, mostly because Gina worked with the girlfriend, whatever her name was.

The ceremony was performed by a lesbian Presbyterian minister, a white woman with white hair who wove New Age Goddess with God the Father and a bit of Jesus the Holy Son thrown in for good measure. Claire and the girlfriend wanted to have a kid, which I guess accounted for the Holy Son and maybe even for the ceremony itself. Like straight couples, it seems more and more that having a kid means getting married, even if the marriage doesn't mean anything legal. At the cere-mony, the New Age minister kept saying what a "grand union" the ceremony commemorated, until finally Gina leaned over to me and whispered, "Why does she keep talking about the fucking grocery store?" Of course, I had to laugh. And not a slight giggle, but a very impolite—and impolitic—guffaw. The girlfriend told Gina that Gina and I were rude and smug, and I guess we were, not believing we needed any public acclaim or toaster gifts or even magic to preserve the miracle that was our love. I don't think Claire has ever forgiven me, even though she and the girlfriend didn't last a year. She cer-tainly isn't overly friendly to me now, feigning a tight smile. I give her my eye-to-eye direct-dyke look, though I have less than no interest in her. What she returns is a similar blankness, which is hurtfully tinged with pity. "Take care," I wave, and don't mean it.

Coffee, I think. Pasta. Some fresh produce—organic broccoli. Maybe there is lemongrass today. My objective is simply to put a few things—respectable items—in my cart before I go to the deli counter.

The deli section is toward the back of the store. I'm not sure how the delicatessen became the next stop in this play. But it seems to have become the standard. It's a difficult maneuver for me. I don't eat what my mother always called "lunch meat." And I haven't eaten cheese in years. The rice pudding is unmentionable except in the same sentence as the word "glue." Potato salad and all its more urbane variations remind me of soggy paper plates in summer and the smell of rancid mayonnaise, though perhaps I can convince myself that the string-bean-and-sesame "Oriental" salad is palatable. But of course I'm not going to the back of the store for vegetables.

I am going to the delicatessen section for her.

The woman with the brick-red shirt and the cart of frozen pizzas and the fleshy stomach.

She's there. Looking longingly, or so it seems to me, at the garlic-roasted chickens. *This woman must hate to cook,* I think. *But I'm not going to marry her,* I remind myself.

"They look good today, don't they?" She's no longer flushed, but slightly haughty, confident now that I've appeared at the deli counter.

"Yes," I agree. "I think I'll get one myself." I don't mention that I've been a vegetarian for 20 years, even before I met Gina.

"Oh, so you'll be here a moment?" She doesn't wait for my nod. "Would you watch my cart? I just have to run to the ladies' room."

Ladies' room, I like that. Sort of sweet. I can tell a lot about a woman by how she refers to the place. *Bathroom* is common, though there's no bath. *Restroom* also, though she's certainly not going there to rest. *Loo* is good, though a bit pretentious in the United States, and one runs the risk of not being understood. I always struggle for a moment about what to say myself, usually settling on *women's room,* glad today that she was the one who took the initiative.

I wait 30 seconds, squeezing some of the gourmet breads that rest on the deli counter.

"Did you want a chicken?" the young man behind the counter asks me.

"I'm not sure," I answer truthfully. I'm too distracted to make a decision about dinner, let alone whether or not to cease my commitment to vegetarianism.

I push my cart away from the rice pudding and breads and lunch meats. Slide it near the cereals. Abandon it there. And walk toward what she called the ladies' room.

I try not to think "moment of truth" as my fingers reach toward the handle. I hate clichés, even when they are apt. The sweat is collecting on my back again, I feel my spine straighten, and I try to push my shoulders down. *Casual, casual,* I caution myself. The handle turns.

"Hello," she says, when I'm in the bathroom with her. I lock the door behind me.

"Hi." Casual, casual. The moment of truth is not over. It could be a mistake. One never knows. It could be a coincidence. This is not a bathroom in some gay bar after all; it's the fucking Grand Union in a small town.

A small town with a sizable lesbian population, I remind myself.

And even straight women have been known to like a little lesbianism between the applesauce and seltzer.

"Fancy meeting you here," she says. I decide to forgive

such tiredness, but I don't want to endure any more of her blunders. So I move toward her, less than a step, and I'm breathing on her, pushing her against the wall, my face on the shoulder of her brick-red shirt, my fingers wild in her wild hair.

She's breathing hard already, short stabs through her nose, like a sweaty horse.

"No marks or toys," I say. That's what someone always says. That's what was said to me the first time I found myself in the Grand Union bathroom with a woman, not more than a year ago. The poor thing practically had to give me a road map before I followed her here; I'd never done anything like this before—well, at least not in a grocery store. Gina had always done the shopping, and now I wonder, though of course I can't ask her.

The second time the woman also said "No marks or toys," so the third time I said it myself. The fourth time was with the same woman as the first time, so I let her say it, just to be friendly. I started to understand that there was a pattern here. The glances and meetings. The tumble of some cardboard display. The rendezvous near the lunch meats and puddings, the "watch my cart" line, the unlocked door of the women's room. It doesn't always work, I'll admit, and I've stood in the bathroom more than a few times waiting for the handle to move. And once I walked in on someone who forgot to lock the door—both of us embarrassed by the piece of toilet paper in her hand and her pants bunched at her knees. Still, there is definitely something going on here at the Grand Union. Does the manager know? He's a nice guy, named Walter or Wilbur, I think; I assume he'd be shocked. Knowing I'm silly to assume this. He could have a little peephole or something right in the wall.

I pull her shirt up over her head, to give Wilbur or Walter a better view. I would have preferred buttons, but my compensation is her lack of bra or camisole. Her chest is long, her breasts as large and soft as Gina's were. I squeeze my mouth to the right one; opening my eye I can see a small scar—neat and surgical—gracing her rib cage. I'm kissing and slurping and biting just a bit, careful not to leave a mark.

Her hand, that small not-so-smooth hand with the jagged nails, is in my pants. She doesn't bother to unzip me; I'm glad I wore my black stretch pants instead of my jeans.

I pull her impossibly closer.

A small gurgle escapes her mouth, like a bubble.

I put my finger to her lips. Then the back of my hand against her throat.

My other hand digs around her crotch as if I could burrow through her Gap jeans. I finally unzip them, wrestle them down. Her organic-beige cotton underpants are wet. Inside them, her wonderfully coarse and damp hair does not disappoint and graciously consents to being shoved out of the way by my clumsiness.

Her elbow is in my face as I try to pull her pants down lower.

"Sorry," she whispers.

"Shut up," I say, pushing her harder against the wall. Her small hand is no longer in my pants, and I try to pin her arms above her head with my free hand, but I am not that strong, or she is too large. After a few seconds she cooperates, or maybe she just doesn't care anymore, jutting and pushing against her own pleasure.

As she is clenching and unclenching, faster, and I imagine spiraling, her knee—bare now—pushes between my own thighs and hard against me. I have to steady myself against the wall behind her, because I feel as if I am going to tumble and go crashing into the toilet.

"Gina," I want to scream. And nearly do.

I pull away from the woman, who is red-faced but combing her luxurious hair with her fingers after slipping her brick-red shirt back over her head. I kiss her on the forehead then, her beautiful shiny forehead. She touches my cheek with her hand. She leaves the bathroom first, as is the protocol.

I follow her but don't follow her. My grocery cart can stay by the cereal. There was no lemongrass in the produce section anyway.

I'm in my car, the keys in the ignition, when I recall the prescription. Shit. My black stretch pants are where they should be every time I check, but as I wait in line I'm desperately hoping the woman from the bathroom doesn't have any business in the Drug Emporium.

The three-minute drive home is uneventful. At the back door I'm rewarded by the bulbs I planted in a sprint of optimism last October; the Asiatic lilies are tall and gawky and smell sort of sickening. I compose myself in the kitchen, suppressing the impulse to shout, "Hey, baby, I'm home," and bound downstairs into the basement where Gina should be, sawing or sanding something, or just "puttering" as she used to say, which meant she was coming up with some scheme to pull me away from my computer and put me to work on home improvements.

Instead I take my little bag from the drugstore to the bathroom, wash my hands, and get out the little vial of clear liquid and the syringe. I take it to the bedroom.

"Baby," I say, "time for your shot."

She mumbles, opening her eyes. After everything, they are still that sky-blue blue.

"I hate to do this," I say to the only woman I've ever loved, still love. Touching her thigh as she flinches away, trying to find even a bit of flesh I can pinch and then insert the subcutaneous needle full of G-CSF under her skin. Her oncologist called G-CSF—the granulocyte colony stimulating factor—a miracle drug, supposed to keep her white blood counts up and ward off the infections that could annihilate her while she's so weak, so she can receive even more of the chemotherapy that has burned away 50 pounds and scoured the hair from every follicle on her body, even those that anchored those adorable little wisps on her toes. But this expensive drug doesn't seem miraculous to me. A miracle would be if Gina kissed me back when I kissed the air above her lips, so careful not to hurt her; a miracle would be if Gina grabbed me down to her with the passion of all those years I thought the Grand Union was only for groceries which I made into beautiful dinners that Gina ate, complaining about her waistline, when Gina's hair was the only hair that tumbled through my fingers and Gina's plumpness the only flesh I pulled close.

Yes, that would be a miracle.

Girls
Lu Vickers

If someone asked you about your sexuality then, you
would've said, "I don't know what you're talking about," just
like you did when you were 15 and your mama cornered you
in the hot yellow kitchen and shouted in your face, "Are you?
Are you a goddamned queer?" She'd heard stories about you
from other girls' mothers, how you were seen riding around
town, hair whipping out the window of the jacked-up VW
owned by Pat Reed, a bulldyke, her dykeness known to everyone but you, of course, even though you let her kiss you and
rub her body up against yours. When your friend Sue warned
you that Pat was queer, that she liked girls, you shrugged and
said, "Everybody likes girls." You looked past your mama's
bobbing head, out the window into your backyard where red-
orange tiger lilies grew beneath giant green elephant ears, and
even though you knew you weren't, you felt like you were
underwater, it was so humid in that room.

You told your mama you just liked girls. But deep down
you knew it was more than that—you had read the nervous
letters to Ann Landers—*What does it mean, Ann? What does
it mean when your heart flutters at the touch of your best
friend? What does it mean?* Ann said it probably meant you
were homosexual. But *sex* was something boys did, not girls.
Bathed in the colored light of stained-glass windows, girls sat
upright in church, their legs crossed, their dotted Swiss dresses
tucked in close. Girls carried their schoolbooks close to their
hearts, like the babies they would have later. Girls held hands

palm to palm and skipped down gray sidewalks together, avoiding the weed-filled cracks. And if they did do something in the dark, if they French-kissed or gave each other hickeys, they were just practicing for when it would really count, for doing it with boys.

Funny how you didn't think of what they meant until later, those brushes against sun-warmed skin, those pine-straw houses built with other girls, one playing the husband, the other the wife, those seesaw days and hide-and-go-seek nights, those moments piled up behind you like the splintered husks of seeds. You dreamed of saving the neighbor girls from fire, let them kiss thank-yous on your cheek, and thought yourself as sexless as Doris Day, as Sunday-school-pure as soap bubbles. You tried to pee standing up, practiced shaving your face with your father's dull razors. You dreamed of being a cowboy, spitting in your sleep. When your mama took you to the Florida Theater to see Faulkner's *The Reivers,* you fell in love with Corrie, the whore.

If you had known what those moments meant when they were happening, you would've thought yourself the youngest dyke in the world. When you were six years old you got on your knobby knees and begged your gorgeous blond baby-sitter to marry you, but she just squeezed your hand and laughed because you were a little girl. Marriage and boys went together, and anything else was pine-straw silly. You stared at her perfect white teeth and felt left out, like you were missing something.

In grammar school lunchrooms your little friends drank milk from tiny wax cartons and choreographed perfect weddings for faraway June days, pastel bridesmaids and flower girls, sunny getaways in sleek black cars slathered in shaving cream. Alone at home, coated in a thin layer of sweat, they dreamed of boys while they hugged their pillows, cuddled their lumpy teddy bears. While Tiffany Hall was humping the leather armrest of her father's La-Z-Boy and thinking of a boy named Tony, 11-year-old you were stretched out in the bed next to Stacey Beck, stroking her sleeping face with the back of your hand, while you watched with dreamy eyes the clouds drift by the open window. Mrs. Beck stuck her head in the room and said, "Oh, honey, you're so sweet. Can you wake Stacey? Y'all need to get dressed for church."

Girl, you were a slut and nobody knew it. Throwing a fit at Marcia Harrison's tenth-birthday slumber party because you didn't get to dance the Pony with Becky Gomez, and some other girl was going to sleep next to Rosie Stuart, a thin 11-year-old with blond peach fuzz on her skinny brown arms.

Once, on a hot spring day by the lake, Jonathan Rich's 16-year-old sister looked at you, really looked at you, with slitted eyes, and said in her husky voice, "You woulda made a good-looking boy," but you were 12 and too stupid to say, "Come on, baby. I'll show you some good-looking."

Red-faced, you turned away and stared at the green surface of the lake, rippled now by a gust of wind.

One summer under a blazing white sun, Diane Wasokowski told you her boyfriend's come looked like the Crisco y'all smeared on your 13-year-old bodies instead of suntan lotion. You didn't say anything, but you never looked at Crisco or Diane Wasokowski in the same way again. Two weeks later you went to cheerleader camp, where you fell in love on a Monday with some 14-year-old blond girl from Haines City, and y'all slept together the whole sweaty week in the top bunk, curled around each other like sleek cats, and nobody said a thing because y'all were girls. Just like sisters.

Then there was that fall you walked in on your 15-year-old brother wonking his prom-queen girlfriend, and you thought you were such a prude for being shocked, but you had forgotten about that double date when you were 15, the one where you ditched your boy, Jonathan, and ended up in the blue backseat of his Electra 225 kissing Michael Ryder's girlfriend, and Michael and Jonathan stood outside the car, hands in their pockets, their breath fogging the air, saying, Y'all shoulda gone out together. Of course, you were drunk then and so was Michael Ryder's girlfriend, so nothing y'all did counted, even if all you did was kiss—it didn't count. In fact, you could do practically anything you wanted, because nothing you did counted. This went for the girls you did it with as well. Nobody did anything. Nothing happened.

You came to understand there was a certain convenience in being invisible. Years later when they were too old to get away with girly hand-holding, the beautiful straight girls who lay skin to skin with you in damp heat beneath open windows would say they didn't mean it, they didn't know what you were talking about when you whispered, "You are, you are, you are" in their ears, but really you knew better. The way they breathed out of slightly open mouths when you kissed their necks, the way their eyelids fluttered, the way their bodies moved beneath your hands, the way they spread their legs slowly, so slowly you felt like you were underwater, even though you knew you weren't.

Antelope
Elana Dykewomon

Between the streaks of dirt on the Greyhound bus window, Esther could see the mottled western landscape, as if the ground were the face of a warthog turned upward, loving its reflection in the sky. A small group of running animals—not deer, what?—streaked through the grayish-green stubble. Antelope? She pressed as close to the greasy window as she dared. Too small to be elk, and definitely not deer—she had seen enough deer through the chain-link fences of zoo parks her father had taken her to as a child to know what deer looked like. They must be antelope. "Where the deer and the antelope play…" The antelope disappeared behind what would be a mesa in a couple hundred or a thousand years. She leaned back against the headrest and turned to look at her sleeping lover.

No, they were in the car, that first Chevy wagon they owned, on their way to Chicago from Portland, passing Little America, the world's biggest truck stop, and it was 1968. Her lover was driving, and Esther turned to see the antelope herd. Angry as she was—no, she was not angry yet, that was another trip—young as she was (yes, she was definitely young; they were eating peanut butter and jelly sandwiches, listening to AM radio, stopping at campgrounds and listening to the stories of women who washed their children's clothes in the campground bathrooms, grateful they could not see their own fate in those moody white faces), she was just learning to appreciate this sense of hooves across a vast space, this quick grazing leap that promised wilderness somewhere just beyond what she could see. In the after-image of the antelope, America was still a country with a network of tribes who had not tracked every river and valley, who knew enough not to build highways, whose maps were songs and petroglyphs. America—the world—was an expanse that was not parceled and owned, and in it the animals thrived without schedule.

She did not mind that now, 31 years later, although she had crossed the country maybe ten times, she remembered the journey rolling out on the other side of dirty bus windows. It's easy to remember stopping at night in some small station, the way you note the travelers on the way with you—how poverty and fear, certain kinds of loss mark them. Once she had been on the bus from New Orleans to Biloxi, before Biloxi had casinos, and a man said to the bus driver, "I had a wife and kids, a job. Now I just go from bus to bus." He was a white man in dark clothes that were too big for him, too hot for the weather. He didn't smell, or she was far enough away not to notice the smell, although she could hear him as clearly as Woody Guthrie songs on the old 50-buck phonograph she had in high school, scratchy, the treble too high.

So long, so long, gotta travel on—isn't this what happens to people in the U.S.? So much country without borders—it gives us all a sense of entitled motion. What was she doing going to Biloxi anyway? Their motel was on the Gulf of Mexico—at night the crabbers went out at low tide, with nets and lights held high. The lights moved among black pillars over the sheen of dark water. Esther drew something in the sand. Her 13th lover rubbed it out. "Who asked you for romance?" Then her lover laughed, as if it were a joke, nothing to worry about.

They had stolen the plane tickets. Scammed them. In the 1970s various fringe communities passed around ways to get things for free: corporate calling-card accounts, ways to order tickets from the airlines as Dr. Jones—some name close enough to your own that if photo ID was asked for at the airport (which it wasn't then, but just in case it was), you could say there was a typo, some small mistake. You ordered the tickets sent to the address of someone who was about to move (and everyone knew someone about to move in the '70s), so that when the bill came, no one had a clue who it was for. The airlines wised up. Everyone got credit cards or had to go down with cash to their local office. Wasn't it coming anyway? Small-town courtesies extended by corporations were a momentary aberration. Esther and her lover Thorn went to New Orleans by seizing the moment of aberration. They congratulated each other on their daring, the way they made their luck by simply believing in it.

They stayed in a gay guesthouse and drank Bloody Marys; they met some local dykes in a bar who were both hospitable and suspicious of northerners, but Esther was slightly infamous at the time as the author of quirky radical articles, and they were invited to spend a night or two in someone's home. Esther and Thorn hadn't been lovers for more than two months, originally attracted to each other by the seriousness of work they did for a big lesbian conference. They are white lesbians; Esther is a Jew, Thorn is an atheist from Christian background. They were both locked up in mental institutions: Esther managed to get out with only minor residual drug damage to her nervous system, but Thorn had been shocked out of half her memory.

She thinks about Thorn. It's been more than 20 years since she even heard her voice, got a letter. Is Thorn alive? At the end Thorn said: If you ever use my story I swear I'll track you down and—. But it's Esther's story that she wants to tell, to remember. Half of the story is hers. Can you rip the story in two, like an old photograph, removing the one you don't want, cutting the torn edge to a smooth strip: It was just me? I was the one watching the crabbers out on the Gulf; I went back to New Orleans after we had an argument on the bus about the wisdom of age. I was three years older, which meant a lot to me for reasons Thorn hated. She was right. We lay together on a mattress on the floor in a lesbian's home in New Orleans, and I thought: Here is the place where the seed of our end is planted.

Can she say that? She was looking out the bus windows as they came back into New Orleans. A man had given everything up and couldn't go back; his grief was a light leaking out toward the horizon. Esther had an analysis of men, of men's privilege, even in giving things up, walking away from their homes and families, following some vision of personal tragedy. It was never safe for women to renounce their lives, unless they could go to nunneries or had money. The few women on the streets die faster than men. Everyone knows that.

She had always been puzzled by the people who do studies to prove what everyone knows. Everyone knows: that racism destroys lives, that men oppress women, that the antelope are almost gone in the United States. As she got older, she conceded the wisdom of entering arguments with statistics. Usually people like to believe that things are better, that progress is good for them, that time is on their side, and individuals can do anything with their lives. Your life is a dollar, everyone gets the same dollar; you can save it, spend it, teach it to turn cartwheels in the air, mesmerizing your audiences while you pick their pockets. Often enough, you find yourself arguing with the pickpockets, so it's good to always know where your wallet is and have some statistics memorized to back you up.

Everyone knows lesbian relationships don't last long. She knows this even though she's been with her current lover 12 years. But before that, two and a half years was average, if you don't count the short affairs, a day to about three months. Sex is, after all, not a relationship. But not sex is not not a relationship either. (Esther loves the double negative, the sideways affirmation. Thorn despised that about her, which years after the fact Esther decided was anti-Semitism on Thorn's part.) She still E-mails her first lover, the one with whom she ate peanut butter and jelly and watched the antelopes. They have been friends for 33 years now, dating from when they first knew each other in high school.

Thorn said, "If you think you're going to get that from me after we break up, you're wrong. I'm not sitting around some diner reading the daily paper with you in companionable silence." She said "companionable" with a sneer. Esther stayed friends with almost everyone, certainly with everyone she'd been with for more or less two and a half years, except for Thorn, who disappeared. It has often seemed to her that the whole point of the drama—getting into sex and then ending it—is to be able to read the paper, the books, the articles, the poems together, fitting the interesting bits into a mosaic of what's said out loud. It's possible that what she was searching for at 25 was not love but language. Thorn would have said, "Then why don't you say something worthwhile?"

Somewhere she has a photograph of the first morning they were in New Orleans, drinking Bloody Marys at a patio café in the French Quarter. Thorn has a dark streak through her left eyelid, a visible blue vein. It was the pulsing of that vein that Esther found so attractive in Thorn's long, serious face. Thorn believed that if Esther only concentrated, she could control her power. If she could control her power, there was no telling what she might be able to do. She might be able to stretch her hands over Thorn's shocked head and restore the burnt connections.

Once—is this her own memory? She believes it is but is not sure. Perhaps she saw a photograph of it in a magazine: fingers with a spark of blue light arcing across them. That happened when they first got together, once. Or else, of course, it never

happened, and they each had read about it and thought if anyone could perform this feat, it had to be them, representatives
of the greatest emotional intelligences to ever grace the planet,
lesbians. Esther found herself backing down, unsure she was
up to what Thorn wanted, nervous about what Thorn would
want next if she could perform the first miracle. Miracles are,
after all, only ideas, and both of them had the idea that Esther
could heal Thorn. She had strong, blunt hands, and she put
them to use between Thorn's legs. What men have damaged,
lesbians can fix, can't they? When will, intuition, and patience
failed Esther, she decided only money would work: a regular
job, a mortgage, weekends in the Green Mountains.

First Thorn was scornful, then she started to hit. Esther was
bigger; she had been in Dyke Patrol. Thorn smashed her in the
arm, the side of the neck. Only after three or four blows did
Esther remember she had learned how to block. She blocked,
and Thorn punched her arm. "Leave me alone," Thorn said,
and slammed her door. Sometimes Esther would leave for a
couple hours or drive to Marblehead for the weekend. This was
five or six years before battering was talked about among lesbians. Esther believed that Thorn's violence came from the
physical damage that had been done to her, so she tried to
ignore it. Likely that infuriated Thorn, but this is not Thorn's
story, is it? In Esther's story a friend says to her, years later, "She
never hit anyone else, did she? She never hit you in public. She
had more aim than you're giving her credit for." Thorn said, "I
know you're selfish, I know you're limited, I know you're
afraid. Later, women will love you again, but only I will know
what a fake you are, how you refuse to live up to what you
know you can be."

Esther wept. They were driving away from somewhere
and she glanced over at the map after Thorn gave her directions. "That's what I mean—you don't trust me. You can't
trust me. If you were really my partner, you'd never check up

on me, you'd never want to see the map. You're bullshit."

Esther pulled over to the side of the road. "I only—" no way to say, no way to know, then, that she'd do the same thing at 40, at 50—glance over her right shoulder even when her lover says, "All clear on the right." Is it only a question of getting the right lover, the one who is only minimally annoyed by this, who brings it up to share a joke about control, not shame her about trust?

How did it end up being this story? Esther had a first lover and she has a last lover, and with both of them she has driven across America twice. She meant to keep on about the antelopes, how once she had seen a whole herd of them from the highway. Now, at the turn of the millennium, if you drive back roads in Nevada or Texas, places where dry country dips and stretches its upper arms in the sun, you might see one or two.

She saw a deer once, with a full rack of antlers, staring into her face from an icy ledge in the Cascade Mountains. She was on the cross-country train, going to Portland, where Thorn believed a doctor offered hope. Esther stared at the deer, at the ledge, the fir branches holding the snow in their arms like gifts, until it was out of sight. The deer do not run after the train, waving. When you take the train, the bus, the car, you enter into hundreds of lives on every trip: a child by the tracks moving her doll's arm to salute, a snake, a busload from the senior center coming back from bingo, an old man in a derby holding up traffic near the Canadian border, the hard-hat woman bouncing the SLOW sign on her hips in the mountains. That must be why people prefer the interstates, 20 miles between exits, only rock and trees and gas stations, the same gas stations, the same Denny's, the same McDonald's. It's not news that this sameness comforts Americans, makes them forget they never see antelope anymore, or buffalo, unless they drive way up into Montana or Yellowstone, where buffalo are conveniently stored.

The doctor they took the train to see ran tests. For some reason, they had to stay up all night at a bowling alley. Esther had been in Portland before, and now (or then) she realized that cities you've lived in get cobbled together to become a dream landscape—here's the curve of rock as you come out of the Portland hills merging with Clark Street in Chicago, where the 23-hour-a-day movie theater was that only closed to change the double feature around 5 A.M. and clear the seats of drunks. For a quarter extra you could sit in the ladies' balcony, no men allowed. Esther liked to sit up close at the movies, so she learned the hard way about the move she called "the Chicago feel," even though she knew men do it in every city; her father had done it too, just once, when she was 16, and because he didn't have the requisite raincoat, she was almost unsure what his hand on her knee meant.

Often she is in this collage landscape, Chicago, Portland, New Orleans, Northampton, Old San Juan, Atlanta, Boulder, and it's just a short walk to the beach where a tidal wave is coming in. Sometimes, before the tidal wave, she's lucky: Otters, whales, seals with their cautious black eyes looking sideways fill the water. She knows then that she's been blessed. Animals come to her in dreams: The deer watches from its ledge; the owl spreads its wings when she is alone in the forest; a bear cub stares at her and her new lover the morning they wake up on the Elk River, stares, and is gone. These sightings have no consequences besides a full heart.

Thorn said to the doctor, "Your technician raped me."

"What did you say?"

"He raped me. He stuck that tube up my nose at 4 A.M., and when I said it hurt, he shoved harder."

The doctor was relieved. The ordinary sadism of lab technicians is not rape. He tried to get Thorn to see her exaggeration for what it was.

Thorn walked out.

Esther stared at the doctor. They had come all this way. When they crossed the plains, the compartment they were in had no heat, and only a handful of blankets. Thorn gave her blanket to a young girl. The deer had looked Esther in the eye. "But you can see how it was an abuse of power?" she asked tentatively. Suppose Thorn wanted to come back, suppose this doctor did have an answer?

Thorn came back in and grabbed her hand. "Traitor," she said in the hall. Esther said something to defend herself, but she knew Thorn was right. She was slow to react to men, to anyone, who had blown their chance. Esther was always going around giving people the benefit of the doubt, looking for the other side, as if that would somehow insulate her from brutality.

Later they were at the beach, that place on the Oregon coast where a surviving remnant island not more than 20 irregular feet wide sits in a lagoon and a small cypress tree grows out of its craggy top. Anytime it appears in a dream, you'd recognize it. They were in a motel and Thorn made love to Esther and she let Thorn do it, even though she didn't want to. She was angry, disappointed. She suffered touch and pretended it was a sufficient apology, because she could not ask, and Thorn could not say: Sorry. *This is where I have finally done you wrong*, Esther thought, *and you don't know it.*

And you don't know it. But what if she did? It's not Thorn's story. It's Esther's. One day not long after they got back to the East Coast, they were going to the races at the county fair, and they argued before they left the house about betting. It was Thorn's position that if they concentrated, they could not fail. "Haven't we been failing?" Esther wanted to know. Thorn hauled off and punched her in the eye. Esther turned at the last minute and caught the blow on the bone instead of in the soft socket, otherwise that eye would be gone.

Later, when Esther was living alone in the old bread truck that had been converted into a homemade RV by a shop teacher, she would sometimes stop at county fairs and make $2 bets. She rarely lost more than 20 bucks. She likes county fairs, likes to wander the aisles where the sheep, goats and baby pigs are, and now they have llamas too, around which you have to be careful, because they like to spit. The cattle stalls disturb her, with the young white kids brushing the heifers, talking about how much they can get for them, a pound.

She had a first lover, she has a lasting lover, she had lovers in between. In the middle of the list she sometimes goes over, Thorn leans back, relaxed, at a table in the sunlight in New Orleans, laughing. The antelope kick up dust and are mostly gone. She knows there's an easy way out of this—blame the enemy, who is man. Man who lays asphalt on the sweating brow of the Mojave desert and sucks the Colorado River dry, man who decides the brain is a pair of dice and you can shock it sideways in a gamble for a better roll.

Who wouldn't want an answer that places the blame squarely outside of the way you behaved? Some things can't be resolved, not by living long enough, not by art. Children leave home and don't come back; a foot is lost to frostbite or gangrene; it's possible to glue broken pieces back together, but you will always see the crack. The fact is when Esther imagines the photograph torn in half, she's the one who's missing, not Thorn. The refuge of a battered dyke is to believe that your lover was right; you could have been: more honest, clear, brave, trusting, intuitive, sincere. You were given a chance to have true love, but what you did instead was grow up, accepting that it would not be you who'd save the antelope, only tell their story.

The One I Left Behind
M. Christian

The Seaside Café was a secret. Just four Formica tables ringed with strips of cheap, peeling chrome. Steel napkin holders, rarely holding any napkins. Salt and pepper. Industrial ketchup and bright yellow mustard. Behind a counter with seven red-plastic-cushioned stools, a menu of plastic letters on stained, warped plastic: hamburger, cheeseburger, fish and chips, hot dog, and sodas. Above the antique weight of the cash register, a 7-Up clock that was four minutes slow.

The café was always turgid with steam from the kitchen; hell on hot days, stifling on cold ones. Its surfaces were covered with a perpetual patina of greases and oils. The food was bad at best, but with an honesty that still made it tasty—the same way going home is never a good idea but walking familiar roads can be a thrill. It was loud, hot, and dirty, but it was special, sacred, because it was hers and hers alone.

Alice would walk the half mile from their place on Highton Road after doing her chores, arriving around 12:30 or so. Everyday she'd order fish and chips—two big pieces of unknown bottom-feeder and two dozen or so fat, glistening slabs of potato—and read her book of the week and eat. There was always something thrilling about that first taste of fish, the way the breading crackled between her teeth, the way the rich juices and grease made her mouth water with forbidden pleasure.

She'd eat and read. Sometimes something lurid, with cowboys or spaceships on the cover; sometimes something serious, books with bold covers proclaiming just the title and author. The Seaside Café rarely had more than three or four other people in it at lunchtime. It was always filled with the sounds of kitchen clatter and the scratchy, distant sounds of the invisible cook's Spanish-language baseball game. Everyday the same older heavyset woman left her stool behind the cash register and slowly made her way over to Alice's table to take her order; and everyday Alice felt a faint flash of shame at never having asked her name.

It was good. Not just because she liked the guilty thrill of the fish or the salt and oil of the chips, but because it was hers. The house on Highton Road was theirs, as was the old yellow Volvo in the drive, the various appliances, and the furniture. It was a good home: warm, safe, and always there. The paint wasn't peeling, the garden was surprisingly large, and the plumbing was solid. But it was theirs, not hers.

It was Thursday. That morning she'd done the laundry, weeded the front yard, and put away the dishes from last night. This afternoon she had to take the Volvo in for a fluid change and stop by the market to pick up groceries. And water, yeah, she had to call about getting some more bottles delivered. The local stuff tasted OK to Alice, maybe a bit metallic, but it always gave Deborah headaches.

That was before and after, but right now it was 12:45 in the Seaside Café. She'd taken her first bite of fish and was relishing the grease, fat, and her first swallow of icy 7-Up. On the linoleum table off to the side, pages slightly resting against the condensation-dotted can of soft drink, was *Apollo's Moon*. It was a tale about a bunch of brilliant young scientists who discovered an ancient Roman temple buried under the Sea of Tranquility. It wasn't a good book, but the author had a knack for descriptive narration that kept her turning the pages, even when she'd already figured out the ending.

"Mind if I sit?" said someone standing by Alice's elbow.

Two years—two years of fish and chips and 7-Up—and no one, not even once, had asked that question. Alice turned quickly, to the source of the voice. Before she looked, she knew what she wanted to say: "No, I don't want you to sit here." Final. Nothing else in her life was certain and absolute; it was all various shades of negotiation. "No" had a firm, sharp feeling, like she imagined a shot of bourbon might taste if she ever had the bravery to sample it.

But she did look up. The woman beside her was slender and long like herself, with hair the warm color of gold. Her smile washed away the heavy atmosphere of the Seaside Café, clearing the stagnant air in a surge of light.

The girl didn't ask again; instead she smiled—brilliantly— and pulled up a chair. As she flopped down on the vinyl-covered seat, Alice had a sensation of a pirouetting, tumbling butterfly: soft yellow skirts, a vivid tie-dyed blouse, a loose string of amber beads, brass bracelets. It was a comfortable feeling, like catching the sight of a favorite childhood book on a shelf, comfortable memories springing right to mind.

"So how ya doin'?" the girl said, helping herself to a fat slab of chip, chewing with fast, energetic slides of her narrow jaw. "You hanging in there?"

Alice was…speechless. She didn't know how to respond. It seemed a long minute before she could summon the will to speak, and then speech came in isolated syllables, choppy and fast: "Fine, I…I guess. I mean…" *Who the fuck do you think you are? Get the fuck away from me, bitch.* "Look, I'd really like to eat my lunch—"

"Good for you! I was hoping you'd say something like that. I was starting to worry you'd just sit there and watch me eat your fries or something." That smile. It wasn't so much a flash of white as a flicking glow, and not just from her rows of imperfect teeth. There seemed to be something natural and luminous about her, as if she *were* light: bright and floating.

"It's OK," Alice said, still shocked, still trapped in the narrow rut she'd carved for herself. *It's not OK. It's not! Go away, leave me alone, go bother someone else.*

"God, Alice, you used to be such a riot. Fuck, look at you now: When does the library close anyway? Still got those dirty books on the shelves?" the girl said with a slow-motion, lascivious wink.

"Do I know you?" Alice flicked through her memory, shuffling years in a mad flurry of schools, jobs, activities—nothing from New York State; nothing from afternoons skating through the Cloisters with her Gorilla Art Hag buddies; nothing from the summer as a watsu intern at Harbin Hot Springs; nothing from those hot and frightening three months in Costa Rica; nothing from standing proudly naked on a Hawaiian beach, feeling the hot sun and the distant cameras of the tour boat on her skin; nothing from the bad-good-and-everything-in-between with that steel-plated, riveting diesel dyke in Florida; and nothing, nothing at all in the years upon years in that little town, her years with Deborah.

Shyness burned behind Alice's eyes without recollection, but wasn't it worse having to ask, having the truth come out— "That summer in L.A.!" or "You said you loved me!" or "After the pain you caused me!"—or smiling and nodding, as she'd spent so many days doing? Besides, there was something about this girl. Alice searched her body, her face, her eyes, her tone, her words' frequency for the flutter of speed, the haziness of acid, the collapse of booze—and found nothing of the sort. Same for the unfocused stare of mental chaos and its too-close sister, fixation. The girl was light and breezy; her atmosphere wasn't needles and bubbling spoons, but rather feather beds and staring up at clouds on a hot summer day, melting them into bunnies, leopards, and fluffy elephants.

She was lovely. But that didn't keep the stammer out of Alice's voice. "I mean, I can't seem to remember—"

The girl smiled, brilliantly, and waved her slim hand in dismissal. "It's OK. I'm sure it'll come to you." She picked up the ketchup bottle and knocked a hefty blob on top of the chips. Snatching a red, dripping one from the pile, she neatly popped it into her mouth. Chewing: "It's been a while, after all."

The girl was like a memory you firmly believe in, only to find that it's an illusion. She was where you knew you'd put your car keys, but when you looked—no matter how many times—they just weren't there. The girl *was* real enough, though; despite the flicking hole in Alice's memory, her presence was something else. There was something else about her: a warm, human aura—something Alice realized she'd been missing.

Deborah's allergies made their house clean by necessity, and while Alice had never left food to evolve into something of voting age, she'd never been one to embrace a cool (in more irritable moments, "inhuman") sterility. When she'd lived in New York, the village flat she'd shared with the rest of the Gorillas had been soft, warm, and comfortable. There'd been dozens of pillows on the furnitureless floors, billowing sheets making the ceiling an undulating, inverted sea of crimson and washed-thin blues. Every cup was cracked and muddy from generations of java, every plate was nicked or chipped, every fork slightly bent, but everything seemed to just taste better that way back then.

The girl looked like a billowing ceiling of old tie-dyes, like a room of nothing but deliciously mushy pillows. She wasn't dirty, but she was all too human. You knew, looking at her, that her legs were not shaved, her pits were wild, her thatch was bushy and curly—but that she'd be warm and soft in bed, earthy and musky between the sheets.

The girl...had Alice seen her frown? In the years with Deborah, Alice had been well trained by that slight change in tone, a firmness around the lips. A frown back home could mean Deborah was upset, Deborah was irritable. Not bad, never that bad, but enough that the rest of the day would be spent trying to remove it, by whatever means necessary. Only then would the tension be able to leave Alice's own face.

"What's worse is that you really do love her, don't you?" the girl said, seriousness playing across her large brown eyes. The frown didn't drop, but the words still held sympathy: pain for Alice's pain. "If she was really bad it'd be easy, wouldn't it? Zap! Off you'd go, babe. But she's not. She's kind and she's good to you—that is, when she's in a good mood herself—helpful, supportive, and hot enough in the sack. But she's not it, is she? Close, maybe, but not really there. So why the fuck do you stay with her?"

"I really don't see why I have to—" Alice started, indignation flushing away her fantasies and her lingering look in one quick, hot flash.

"Just let me finish, doll: I'm just letting you know that I've got at least some of this figured out. Stop me if I'm off-base, OK?"

She gestured with a slab of potato, and Alice was momentarily hypnotized by the suspense of whether or not the ketchup would go flying. Her anger, though, pulled her away from the delight the pattern of red might make on Alice's blue cotton dress. "I don't see why I should sit here— " but she did. She should have stood up and walked out. But she didn't. At the time she didn't know why. Later, she guessed that at some level she really did need to hear this, especially from her.

"You love her, like I said. Really do. But she's not the only one. You sit here, a place she can't touch, and you stare out the window. Dreaming. Now, dreaming's good, but not when you live only to dream, when you're only sitting here in this little grease spot staring out the window or reading your crappy books. That's not good. Your dilemma is that you hate it, but it's also good—but not good enough to make you happy, and not bad enough to make you haul luggage."

Ketchup flew, making red teardrops on the plastic table-top. As far as Alice could tell, she'd been spared the splatter, but she didn't look to see.

"You're a wonderful babe. Damned smart, fuckin' sexy, wild-ass, but never a mean bitch, never irresponsible. You're a great girl. But you're stuck here and you're dying off, bit by bit. You can't walk because you don't want to hurt her, but you can't stay there anymore either. Every damned day you kick at the girl you want to be. You're dyin' by habit, girl. You're better than that. I know you are. More than anyone, anywhere, I know that."

There, that heaviness she recognized. Knew it all too well. Sometimes in the mornings, after Deborah had gone off to work and it was just Alice in their polished and buffed house, she'd feel the weight on her lids, feel the dragging deep down. At first she just thought it was tiredness, lethargy from too-vivid dreams, a restless night's sleep, but then when the tears started to flow she finally recognized the sadness.

The girl, still nameless, stopped her words and just looked...just looked at her. Her eyes, brown like Alice's, were almost bottomless, very soothing.

When Alice had first started to cry those early mornings, she'd been shaken, disturbed by the upwell of darkness. She'd thrown herself into cleaning, shopping, playing in the garden. She'd tried to bring it up with Deborah, but that was the sum-mer her mother was dying, so Alice had pushed it down, held her lover's hand, and tried to still Deborah's own salty descents.

In August, Deborah's mother passed, but Alice still couldn't give voice to her despair. And so it twisted in, became a steaming hatred. Weak, she thought of herself, weak. Couldn't face a little adversity, couldn't deal with a few months of hard times. *Buck up,* she told herself in the stern voice of her father. *Buck up and deal with it. It's not the end of the world. No one's dying.*

"That's very bad for you," the girl said suddenly, seemingly in narration to Alice's thoughts—but she couldn't have. No, she was smiling again, bright and wide, and pointing down at the pile of greasy fries between them.

"A little indulgence—" Alice said, for no reason at all. Just for something to say. She wanted this girl, and the emotions she'd pulled up, to go away. Leave. Now. Go. Away. She wanted to be with her bad book and her greasy food. She wanted to go back to her secret time, her time away from the house and Deborah.

"Thank God, girl. It's the little things like this that keep me going, you know? Get rid of too many of them and—poof—I'm gone. Here's to greasy fries, doll; the little things that keep us alive."

Alice had learned to be careful. Deborah's frown was too easy to bring, too hard to work away. She'd started finding places to relax. The day started when her lover went away to work and ended with her lover walking in the door. The other times were good, just not as good as when she could breathe. Her reflexes became avoidance, fight became flight.

"You're scared," the girl said suddenly, and her warm hand found the top of Alice's tightly closed fist. The contact was electric, a voltage touch. The flight instinct told her to pull away; the fear of breaking down the bricks she'd put around herself was very strong. But...she didn't.

"No, it's just—I..." Alice wanted to say that she didn't know this girl from Eve, suspected track marks down her arms, suspected *Single White Female,* suspected flying china, hysterical 2 A.M. phone calls. But somewhere down where the masonry was cracking, where flight was walking, not running, she realized she did know her. The memory tickled at the back of her brain. It was faint but persistent.

Memory wasn't the only thing tickling the base of her skull. Alice should have dismissed her, pushed her aside as someone not good for her—for dependable, supportive Alice—but she didn't. Simply, Alice liked her. The girl was fast, smart, funny, and—even though she'd done most of the talking—she was actually *there* for her.

"That's OK," the girl said in a low whisper. "You're freaked. You've been walkin' the wrong way for too long. You're in unfamiliar territory—and me, doll, I'm your signpost. And the fact that you haven't, like, gone zoom out of here says to me that you're not completely lost yet."

The memory still tickled but stronger. She did know this girl, knew her well, but the context was weird, twisted. They hadn't dated, hadn't fucked, even though a good part of her wanted to taste her lips, to feel the muscles in her thighs, to see the pinkness of her nipples. They hadn't even talked. The girl's voice was unfamiliar. But Alice knew her, nonetheless. She'd seen her, looked at her almost daily. Where, where, where?

"Do you love me, girl?"

Alice stared at her. Alice stared for a long minute. She vaguely remembered her, but the memory was fogged, thin. This girl had come from out of nowhere, had invaded her space, eaten her fries, read Alice the riot act, and then popped off the big "L" word. Alice stared. This was important, too important to be thought about. She'd done a lot of thinking these last few years, too many thoughts, too much caution. She knew that, and so she stopped the stream of thoughts, the bad images of what might happen, and instead said what she knew she had to say: "Yes."

The girl beamed. Her smile was more than brilliant. Her cheeks rounded, and her wide, expressive eyes narrowed. She started to speak, then stopped herself. Alice watched tears bead in the corners of the girl's eyes. Alice watched as the girl reached up and rubbed the salt streaks away with the heel of one hand.

Red. Where was that red coming from? Alice looked, distracted by something she knew must have been there all along. A square of bright red on the girl's blouse. But then the world shook, and she realized the red was not a pattern on the fabric, not a reflection of crimson from outside the Seaside Café. It was the back of the chair, the back of the chair glowing sharper and clearer with each moment, as with each moment the girl in front of her faded away.

Soon she was just a suggestion, a hint of what she'd been. But before she washed away to nothing but a sense of presence, Alice knew who she was, and then where she'd come from: Sometimes ghosts are just the nearly dead—vanishing after being brought back to life.

When her heart stopped hammering, when her breathing came slow and steady, Alice teetered to her feet and stumbled out the door. The air outside was painfully brisk, clear as ice— but she was warm, comfortable despite the cold. Warm because she was in love with someone she thought she'd lost, someone who'd nearly passed away from neglect.

Hugging herself—and herself—Alice walked down the street, maybe back to the house, or maybe somewhere else. Smiling.

The Diary of a Performative Self
Aja Couchois Duncan

EARLY SIGNS...

The situation comedy was first born in my living room. Being without a father, we had to re-create one nightly from scratch. I always chose Thursdays.

I liked to start small, with a flick of my wrist or the unmistakable shuffling of feet. I was a forgetful father, never able to tell one child from the next; their names were my greatest test. I started with the A's—Allison, Alexandra, Alfia, Annette—never sure whether propensity was familiarity or desperation a mirroring of contempt. *You never should have had so many children,* I complained to my wife. She ignored me, so I had to get her attention with my nails and the scruff of her neck.

I liked to stretch out my legs, to chart the perimeter of my domain. I started pacing. *You're taking too long,* my sister complained. She was a generous father, bringing presents from beneath her nightgown, trinkets she had gathered during the week. We were only allowed to keep them for the evening, then, like all gifts in our house, they had to be given back.

My sister was the only one who remembered our father. My mother swore not to, and who could blame her; they knew each other just nine short years. So my sister was free to criticize my characterizations. I am an artist, I told her; it is not the man but the essence of paternity I am striving to re-create. I spent hours in my room before each performance. There was the wood stage at the end of my bed that I used for rehearsals and the magician's kit my father left after he had learned all of the tricks of the trade.

THEN AND NOW...

Eight years after my mother's death, I still struggle with her body, its placement, the exact position of the urn. It is there on the table next to the front door, right where I put it that afternoon two weeks ago when I returned with the small iron box, the rectangular metal container embossed with grape veins and a strangling of leaves, with what remained of my mother inside—her bone and hair and flesh burned to rattling ash. It is not something one can easily share with her sister. It is not something my sister and I have been able to share.

Stealing it took me several months. Or I planned it for months, but it only took a weekend in Tucson to slip out of my sister's house with my mother's ashes in my suitcase, sure my sister would never contact me again. *It takes longer to make ties than to break them,* I told her within the first three hours of our visit. She was more stubborn than I'd expected. I had to empty the kitchen trash on her living-room rug. I had to wake her every hour on the hour during that first long night to ensure her distaste for my presence. Still, the next morning she forgave me. *Forgive yourself,* I told her, *forgive your horrible taste in porcelain.* That afternoon I found the ashes in a ceramic butter dish, a white-and-black cow-shaped affair. I emptied my mother into the locking metal box and left.

But even before the crime there were irreconcilable differences.

Sharing a mother is hard on any family; there are only so many people one woman can love. Then there is the additional complication of living together, something the human animal seems unable to do. Perhaps this will be the source of our species' extinction; my mother is already dead.

There are theories about hard women without mothers.

This is something women throw at me when I turn my back. The last one fumed for two hours behind me before finally slamming the door. She was a loud woman, with sharp elbows and a crooked thumb. I had not loved her, but I had forgotten myself in her. Time would not be so easily eluded again. It was that day she left that I knew I had to have my mother near me. I procured her, not without some nicks and scratches, but we all do what we have to. Now I have her, and it is up to me to figure out what the final arrangement will be.

POSSIBLE CAUSES…

It all started with the hair on Dr. Looper's arm. Or you could say it all started with my mother's douche bag, hospital-blue; after the divorce it showed up weekly, hanging over the shower-curtain rod. Being single meant chronic yeast infections, so my mother began an intimate relationship with the field of gynecology. It was this more than anything that sealed my fate, that lead me to Dr. Looper. Or you could say anything as a beginning; we all have to start someplace. So I started with Dr. Looper and his hairy arms. He swung into my life as I swung down from my mother's womb, or her douche bag, as the case may be.

I was ten, an adolescent, which means I was subject to a different gravity, another rotational force not bound by the rules of the third planet from the sun. I was a girl with an early menstruation and the promise of a brilliant bust. Or at least I promised myself and the birdcage I hid in when I said my incantation, my potion for love.

The birds had been my father's idea—caging birds, clipping their wings. My mother got rid of them that first morning he left. She opened the cage and lifted the garage door, but the birds had spent so many years in the dark that they were suspicious of the bright, limitless air. My mother was without mercy. Taking a broom, she swept the birds from the corners of the cage, forcing them blindly into the light.

Not wanting to be shed of all fatherly constraint, I begged to keep the cage. Mother refused. But time, as I'd suspected, was against her, and within hours she had forgotten that its unwelcome presence marred the almost perfect eradication of Dad. The cage became my secret weapon, and nothing would come between me and the world beyond.

This was before the witch trials, before America had learned not to share any of its secrets. This was before a box of tampons was $4.99.

So I was ten, and there was Dr. Looper's arm hair and his medicinal white coat; the furry brown skin and the white cotton foreground, the contrast of textures and the distribution of light. He could have been a painting, or we all could have been more intimate than our surroundings. I chose to believe in disparate but intersecting realities, as it was the only option for an impressionable youth.

I was sure that I loved him, sure that he was subject to the magic of my newly shed uterus. The bristly hair on his arm told me so as he ran his hands from my barely shaped hips to the ticklish skin in the pit of my arm. *You are perfect,* he said, his lips molded wax and smiling. *You are perfect,* I reminded myself.

I believed Dr. Looper understood the difficulties of a girl's first menstruation, of her fondness for his thick hairy arms. It was perhaps one of the drawbacks of pediatrics, so many young girls and the soft down just beginning to grow on those parts now wanting the warmth of fur, the warmth of Dr. Looper and his hairy arms.

MYTHOLOGIES...

There is the story about my aunt, the story of Auntie as a girl-child and the passionflowers that grew beneath the arbor. She was my mother's third sister and not the one she remembered liking most, so it wasn't until they were 30 that they spoke of their emigration from heterosexuals and celebrated the vulva as their heirloom.

My aunt was a small, furry child. "Rodent" some called her, quiet to themselves, never sure enough of their place in heaven to say such things out loud. Defiant, my aunt used to stroke herself, rub the sun on her skin like affection. In the darkness there were other ways to accommodate her need. She shaped caverns in the backyard, a den she dug out of the soil between the fence and the neighbor's doghouse. During the summer she'd crawl out her bedroom window and sleep the entire night in the cool earth. So she told me years later, when it was clear that my face was the mirror of her claims and my mother had given me over to family history.

But it is the passionflowers that still call me, she said, the pernicious crown of thorns. A bondage of stamens and the five wounds of Christ surrounded by the virginal white flower, a marker of the discordance between body morphology and the variables of sex. The flowering homosexual in a Christian garden, the first passion as sin and the tangling, spreading vine.

MY 46TH LOVER...

She had ambitypic genital differentiation: heavy breasts and thick masculine wrists, narrow hips and fiercely muscular thighs. Her dark curls were slicked back and cut close to her head, but her lips were the lushness of August, a swollen fruit my teeth ached to bite.

She was practiced in the art of evasion and perhaps even a cruelty that was well worth the pain. She would rush me with her heady scent, the sweet and almost nauseating heat of her cunt filling the room, and then elude me all evening, her heavy strides just beyond my grasp. But hours later, at that exact moment in which I had succumbed to the solitary stupor of unfulfilled desire, she would turn toward me, and with the slightest parting of lips, she would kiss me, moving past my open mouth to suck the air out of each nostril, first the left then the right.

She was not the first to part me open, but when she left, everything inside me closed.

A LESSON...

Death is taught through disappearance. Something lives with you, next to you, or around the block, then next week it is gone. I, for one, disappeared for a week when I was seven, and my family pronounced me dead. They had a doctor fill out the certificate and had already drawn up elaborate plans for a planetarium in my room. That was when I was first introduced to the stars. I followed them nightly in my imagination until later, when my father left, I lost their brightly lit contours to other distractions of peripheral vision. Still, there was that brief time of independence, the celestial mind welcoming a child with a sense of adventure. But I was born of small minds and swollen genitalia. It was decided; I was better off dead.

GIRLS...

Some of the nights that I was performing father, I took things one more step. There were five bars alone on the two-block stretch of shops we called downtown. Normally, of course, I was not allowed, but as my father, there were few things anyone could deny me.

I had already tired of the girls who sat perched on the stools in their nude pantyhose, the olive sticks clenched between their worn rows of teeth, the unmistakable swelling of their big toes. They smelled of feminine deodorant spray, of too much time sitting down. It was the bartender I craved, the one I waited for until 3 A.M. She was the one who smelled of motor oil and gasoline, of alcohol and toothpaste, a woman who drank whiskey in the hope of blurring the faces of the unlucky customers hovering over the bar five minutes before closing, but still hoping to get laid.

I took her home with me and let her sleep. I took her home and kept her up all night long. I hid her bike behind the neighbors' back fence so in the morning she had to wait for me, she had to wake me to escape from me. *I may only be a girl,* I told her, *but I am the spell of your imagination. Conjure me. I will wait in the birdcage, in the darkness of the garage.*

THE LESBIAN BOOK OF RULES…

Older, but not taller, my sister's body fit perfectly against mine. This discovery was made after one of my mother's monstrous dates, a mustached woman with thin lips who scowled across the dinner table for an hour at my sister and me, dark pieces of partially chewed meat dangling from our perfectly demure smiles, before my mother whisked us into my sister's room and asked that we pretend there wasn't a door. In the light of her adolescent bedroom, we pretended other things as well. *Imagine we are the ocean swimming beneath the floor,* my sister said, and I joined her there, our arms and legs pressed against the blue horizon of shag carpeting. It was not hard to imagine our bodies rushing as water rushed against the wrist of my mother washing dishes while Madame Sergeant rubbed her legs against the lavender, silk-covered flesh of my mother's ass. We had both seen Mother's various seductive positions, and even as her daughters we were not beyond their lascivious grasp.

It wasn't until several years later that we found Mother's copy of *The Lesbian Book of Rules* and proceeded to make a list to remind ourselves of the proper way in which desire was supposed to unfold.

1) Women are not a sex; they have a sex, a soft furry hole meant to be stroked, to be pleased and perused.

2) Do not be overly redundant in your feminine signifiers.

3) A predator will only wait so long for its prey.

4) Lesbian desire does not mirror the desire for one's mother or sister. Lesbian sex is not a returning to the womb.

5) Men will still want to fuck you. You may occasionally oblige them.

6) Suffering is neither desirable nor natural.

7) See rule number 1.

My sister was never able to follow rule number 2; she was too deeply bound by the allure of lipstick and high-heeled shoes. I always struggled with rule number 4. In truth, neither of us could follow the course that had been laid out for us; we sprung too rapidly from fantasy to its fulfillment, and rule number 1 was an invitation we would never be able to turn down.

THE BEGINNING OF THE END...

When the summer came, our imagination flailed. My mother, a native to the thick Atlantic heat, took over the father routine. She attempted a pastiche of our interpretations, a representational summary. She started with my sister's gifts and then moved quickly to my frustrated father's voice. He is not like that, we told her; tired of the old dialogue, we were forced to interrupt her or change the channel. This so angered my mother that she slipped into recessive mnemonic aphasia, or at least that was how the doctors explained it before they read the cancer in her eyes.

She became Daddy morning, noon, and night. She threw down the newspaper during breakfast and demanded to know how our small, miserable lives could compare, could ever be as important as the lives of people depicted in the world news. *Look,* she would shout, pointing to a grainy photograph of a young boy, his abdomen swollen with malnutrition, his starved younger sister caught in the crook of his unspeakably thin arm. I told her, *Forty-five percent of American children are starving for affection. The rates are higher in the suburbs.*

This went on for several weeks. My sister and I moved in with the next-door neighbors. A doctor was called. He prescribed rest and abstaining from any interaction with children. He prescribed radiation and pruning the tumor from the frontal lobe.

After the surgery, we moved back in—though the way her illness bore down on us, forcing us to creep silently from room to room, my mother may have never noticed our return. The doctor sent a hospital van over for her each morning. Twisted on the couch, she would wait, a reluctant and dutiful bride newly married to disease. When the driver came slowly up the street, she would have two full minutes to get up and drag her feet to the door.

The mornings were marked by the arrival and departure of the van. Afterward, my sister and I had our days to ourselves. For the remaining summer vacation, we picked up whatever we could find. The most profitable was the liquidation of irradiated bicycle tires. We set up a corner shop and gave each customer a glass of fresh lemonade. We sold 125 tires the first two weeks and would have been able to finance part of our college education if our neighbor, Mrs. Strange, had not gotten wise. *They're selling damaged goods,* she warned potential customers from her bathroom window. *Psst,* she called, *do you know what those two girls have done?* Without the distraction of a blossoming business, there was nothing else for us to do but concentrate on the early signs of my mother's mutation and wait for the first day of school to arrive.

HER BODY AND THE SPACE ITS ABSENCE MADE...

Time passed, but its movement was imperceptible until my mother died. Even then we were reticent to make adjustments. They had removed her body, but we made her breakfast and lunch just in case. That was where Auntie found us the day of the funeral, two girls in the kitchen, a third plate of waffles in front of Mother's empty chair.

It was hours before the funeral, and the church was empty, so we had Mother all to ourselves. My sister, the high school dropout turned cosmetologist, was quick to repart her hair. I was more interested in her hands. The mortician had tilted her palms away from her body, swollen wings anxious for flight. Our aunt had decided on her clothes, white and pink ruffled with long sleeves like a Sunday-school dress. *This is how God remembers her,* she told us.

Auntie told us the story of her first girlfriend. *She looked just like your mother,* she said. I knew better, knew girls were nothing like each other, knew that their hands were slippery fish. I recognized the sound of each finger unfurling. The whisper of hunger between them. *Mother was nothing like any of us,* I said.

PROGENY...

My sister laid eggs daily until she was 14. Of course, my mother and I both knew about the 5 A.M. delivery from the neighborhood grocer, but Mother was fearful of collapsing my sister's hard-worked fantasy. So we suffered my sister's daily trips to the bathroom at exactly 8 A.M., following a strict policy of bathroom use in the mornings. Had we a father he could have built us a second bathroom, but our mother refused to let us improvise with hammers or any other tools. *They are instruments of death,* she said.

On her 14th birthday, my sister called us all into the bathroom. She held up a cracked eggshell in one hand and a mess of egg yolk and white in the other. *It came out of my body already divided,* she said.

MOURNING...

After the cremation, things between my sister and me really went awry. She turned against the unspoken alliance of women in our family and began to seek out the company of men. Her first betrayal was a 17-year-old boy living two blocks from us, whom she lured to her bedroom with the promise of crystal meth and a bootleg Metallica recording. The thread that had barely held us together began to unravel quickly.

It became impossible for us to sit across from each other in the mornings, and frequently her overnight guests would have to negotiate the passage of milk between us, would have to address each of us as if they were the diplomatic representative of the grudge that had grown between us, a fungus spreading beneath our skin.

HOW SHE BETRAYED ME...

Tucson is something like Disneyland, only the desert is Main Street and there are no men in animal suits sweating in the ubiquitous Southern California sun. Instead there are shopping plazas and miniature-golf courses and a dry heat that envelops everyone in its path.

My sister's house was easy enough to find, a lavender stucco amidst the usual Spanish terra-cotta and adobe white that lined the streets like freshly laundered shirts hanging from an endless clothesline. She was waiting for me on the porch in her nightgown, the evening wear of our childhood. This was how we used to find each other after Mother fell asleep; we would slip down the hall and into the other's room, wrap our bodies around each other, our thighs mingling with the dampness between our legs.

Father, you are late again, she told me. *Stop it,* I said, *you know the reasons for my delay.* I rushed up the steps and wrapped my arms around her, surprised by my own longing and the warmth I found there. But it was nothing more than the practiced warmth of family, I reminded myself, lifting my palms from the sticky flesh of her arms and back.

The boyfriend she followed to Arizona was long gone, but

there were other traces of men in her house: The coatrack shouldered a satin sports coat and worn baseball caps too large for her small head to bear. *How can you have learned so little,* I asked her, already knowing the answer was clear from that moment in her bedroom, the egg cracked and yolking, the frustrated desire of the uterus making its claims. *She will never be one of us,* my mother had often warned me. *One of what,* I had wanted to ask.

NOW AND THEN...

My mother cried every night we were separated, even the first few years when I was too angry to hear her. I would wake some nights to a low, dull whine, like the sound of a cat warning off other animals that have come too near. Later I began to recognize her pitch, the cry of a woman too far from home, the cry of a mother separated from her youngest child.

As the oldest, my sister had claimed my mother's body, and as the oldest she had driven the ashes to Tucson six months after Mother's death. At first I welcomed the absence of family; the dark hole of my love sunk into a grave deep enough for the home we all once shared. Later my theatrical nature took over, and I knew I needed my mother beside me. How else could I re-create the heterosexual matrix? Mother and Father lying together at night, side by side.

To Sleep
Laura M. Farmer

I woke up smoking in bed. I couldn't remember how I lit it or how long I had been lying on my back, looking up at the bubbles on the ceiling we painted last summer. Tuesday was silent. I knew she'd wake up soon, ask why it smelled so smoky in here, roll over to give me a kiss, and fall back asleep. The same as always.

I woke up with my eyes already open. I was smoking in bed, lying on my back, staring at the bubbles in the ceiling. I stared at my cigarette, baffled at how I didn't remember lighting the fire, yet here it was, here I was. On schedule. I glanced over at the clock. 8:13. Two more minutes. I took a long drag, my breath increasing the fog over the bed. I inhaled again, wondering if I was really awake this time. 8:15. She rustled awake beside me, asked why it smelled so smoky in here, rolled over to kiss me, and fell asleep.

"So are you going to explain it any more than that?"
"Do you want me to?"
"Yeah…"

But I still fumbled. There wasn't much else to say. It was a great idea and a solid story. It messed with my head and changed my way of thinking, quite possibly for the rest of my days. So I said that. And told her to read it. And then I was silent.

How I despise these ineffable conversations. There are

words, somewhere, that could be said to fill the void and perhaps provide some meaning. But the hope that those words exist is no more. It is extinguished each morning. And all we are left with is words that exist to fill space, to get from bed to the kitchen to the door each morning. They come and go from my mouth like saliva, bitter and bland, oozing out each morning without a second thought until I wake again to open eyes and the pasty taste of stale words and that fear they will never go away. And that I may never sleep again.

"So what's the story about?"

"Oh, it's about this...relationship. Where they just reach this point where there is nothing more to say. All words have been exhausted."

"So what do you write it with?"

Each morning at 8:15. There is nothing more to say. I blink my eyes, knowing I will eat doughnuts, leftover Chinese, for breakfast. That she will wrap her hair above her head in a towel and stand in her bathrobe for seven minutes, deciding what to wear, while the aroma of oranges slinks from the shower to my nose behind the comics. I will eat toast and wonder why this wasn't the morning I got up and made eggs, as I love eggs. And she will put on her slacks and her bra, then turn over to wring out her hair as I finish up Garfield. I will rustle my paper, as if to signal her to start talking. And she will. She will talk from the bathroom, over the sound of her hair-dryer. And I will not be able to understand her. As I am never able to understand her. I will say "what," "uh-huh," and "yeah?" Then she will emerge, her hair a bit frizzy as she scrunches it with her right hand. She will continue this conversation with herself and ask me to put in a piece of toast for her, as she is running late. I will say she is always running late. She will claim this is false.

"Is there a point to the story? I mean, if they don't have anything to talk about..."

"Maybe...maybe there's not." I fumbled. "But those are the things that people never write about, the things and relationships that actually happen."

"But nobody wants to read reality."

Nobody wants to live it either.

I was smoking in bed

when I realized she would ask between bites of toast if the room smelled smoky to me. I will say no and open the porch door a crack. She will close the bathroom door as she finishes her makeup, and I will empty my ashtray over the balcony. I will hear her say something and will stick my head in the room to say, "You're welcome." She will still be in the bathroom as I light a cigarette, taking a long drag as I swing my feet over the railing. The cigarette will be only half-finished before I will have to toss it over. My eyes will watch the orange glow flicker, then fall. I will watch it disappear and wonder how far fire goes before it burns itself into ashes.

I couldn't remember how I lit it

And there will be a bottle of my cologne on the kitchen counter near the patio door. I will spray myself and complete spinning in the aroma before she emerges from the bathroom. Still running late, she will scamper over to me, telling me she loves the way I smell. I will hold her, and she will kiss me goodbye, telling me that tonight she will be home early and we will go out for dinner. And she means it this time. I will smile and agree to be here. She will say she loves me as she shuts the door. I will respond by telling her to have a good day.

"It just sounds boring, I guess."

"What do you mean?"

"I guess they just don't sound very interesting. They're not really in love."

"Not anymore."

"Did they used to be? That might spice it up."

"See, that's just it. She thinks they still are, but the narrator...can't remember if they ever were in love. If they ever were happy. Because everything's so much the same, she can't tell what's a dream and what's real."

"So why's your narrator stickin' around? What's she want?"

"Just to be able to sleep. To know one thing for sure."

"You're so dramatic. I don't know where you come up with this stuff. Listen, I gotta go. I love you."

"Have a good day."

baffled at how I didn't remember lighting the fire, yet here it was, here I was

lying on my back, realizing that I will be in the kitchen at 6:30, hungry, making dinner for two. I inhale, knowing I will make whatever I am hungry for. And she will arrive home, complaining at 7:15 that dinner would have been so much nicer if we had gone out. I will say, "Next time." The food on our plates will be halfway eaten before she asks me how my day was. I will say fine, and that I got a lot of writing done. Regardless of whether I wrote or not. She will look at her plate and say that is great, and ask what I have done with the newspaper. I will point to the

right

on schedule

I will think, *This is the last time I do dishes alone.* The television will be heard as I put away the towel and sit beside her on the couch. She will have the remote in her right hand. I will be reading a book. After 22 minutes she will mute the television and kiss me, taking the book out of my hands. She will pull me on top of her as I struggle to mark my page. We will have sex on the sofa, and she will enjoy it. I will sound like I do.

Tuesday was silent

as I lay on my back, knowing that this evening I will be lying here, beside her still. That she will continue to talk, and I will hold her, with my hands around her waist. Thinking to myself that if I can touch something, it's real. But knowing that it is only
Tuesday, that she doesn't feel me, and that she will turn away to sleep, to silence. Leaving me with empty hands. Again.

I knew she'd wake up soon, ask why it smelled so smoky in here, roll over to give me a kiss, and fall back asleep.

I lay on my back and stare at the bubbles on the ceiling we painted last summer. She rustles awake beside me, asks why it smells so smoky in here, rolls over to kiss me, and falls asleep. 8:15. I am drowsy and expel another dragon's breath into the smoky fog that has enveloped the room. There is the smell of orange shampoo, of newspaper and manuscripts burning. And a cigarette. I was smoking in bed is what they will say. That I didn't remember the fire, yet here it was, here I was. My eyes watch the orange glow flicker, then fall on me, spreading to ashes. The smoke makes her sleep. At last I do as well.

Jacqueline
Jess Wells

In the forests of Provence, France, in the Middle Ages

Marcelle knelt in the dust beside the hut, cutting up a deer she had felled in her most recent hunting trip, piling great bloody chunks of it on the surrounding logs. Jacqueline poked at the fire with a stick and poured morning tea for us all, cats climbing on her lap, her shoulders, winding around her legs.

"How can you stand the screeching of these damn cats in heat?" Marcelle growled to Jacqueline, standing and gesturing at them with her bloody knife. "All night, like the sound of murder. I can't stand these cats."

"You have your job, I have mine," Jacqueline said, offering a cup that Marcelle waved away before returning to her work.

"You're an herbalist," Marcelle scoffed. "Herbs don't scream, and they don't camp out on your body."

"How many plagues would we have if we had no more cats in France?" Jacqueline asked vehemently, as if she were going to charge across the fire and shake Marcelle by the shoulders. I held my cup like treasure, like a talisman against the sight of the cats the Church strung up beside the witches they killed. They killed the cats that hunted the rats until the Black Plague had nearly killed us all.

By noon Marcelle had butchered a wild boar and was stretching the hides of the rabbits, while my godmother Fiona and Jacqueline had set to salting and putting up the meat. We stopped for lunch but Marcelle continued until the entire bounty was cut and she was covered with blood and flies.

Jacqueline set down her empty plate and took Marcelle's hand, so we all followed her into the woods to a hot spring, where she guided Marcelle into the water. Marcelle, pushing Jacqueline's hands away from the top of her pants, splashed water on herself and scrubbed the meat pieces off her hands, then peeled off her shirt and threw it on the bank, trying to hit one of the cats. Jacqueline, still dressed, with the water to her thighs, approached Marcelle again. I am accustomed to women tending out of a sense of duty, scrubbing their husband's back while their minds are thinking of their children or being anxiously attentive to avoid a fist. I was not accustomed to Jacqueline. She laid Marcelle back as if praying, pushing water with a tender hand up Marcelle's belly, between her breasts and around her neck, cradling Marcelle's head with the other hand. Marcelle's breasts were full and firm, areolas and nipples the color of her honeyed skin. Her breasts were rocks in the stream, and the river tumbled around them, as did Jacqueline's hands. Jacqueline started to untie her blouse, but Marcelle stood up, slipped her big hands inside and lifted Jacqueline's blouse over her head, then roughly pulled Jacqueline to her, Jacqueline's little breasts fitting into the space on either side of hers. Finally, with Jacqueline still tight within the circle of her arm, Marcelle stripped off her pants and threw them soaking onto the riverbank.

"Gettin' a woman naked is a very good way to make her family," Fiona said behind me, and she walked into the river and sat down, fully clothed, then stood while the water poured off her with an enormous noise and the smell of algae. She was blocking my view and I craned to see.

"C'mon, little one, come on in here. We stink like the open road. Get yourself in the water here. Have I told you stories of *sprigens* in the forests of Ireland lately?"

"Don't call me little one," I said absently, plodding into the water. Jacqueline and Marcelle had moved down to a bend in the stream, and Jacqueline's skirt was floating, untended, in the current toward them. Marcelle lifted Jacqueline onto the moss-covered roots of a tree that held her like a chair. I could only see her long chestnut hair, and even the cats, who surrounded her day and night, had a hard time climbing to reach her, most of them hanging back and crying on the sheer sides of the bank.

Maybe it was the light. Maybe it was because I had disliked Marcelle when I'd first met her or maybe it really was because her breasts were exceptional, but I watched her touch Jacqueline, watched a streak of light play across Marcelle's breasts, then her shoulders as she leaned into Jacqueline. I wanted to have breasts like that, wanted to know how to touch Jacqueline with that much power, that much tenderness, to be that commanding woman who took her pants off last.

For two weeks Marcelle was hardly seen outside the hut. In the evenings Fiona and I would sit alone at the table on the other side of a curtain that divided Jacqueline's bed from the rest of the hut, while I was transfixed by the moaning, crying, laughing sounds from the other side. Jacqueline had gotten giddy, there were no unkind words between her and Marcelle, and Marcelle walked around with her rope of a braid undone and an incredible smell on her hands. She even occasionally tripped over a cat without swearing.

One morning, Marcelle literally kicked Jacqueline through the curtain. "Ask her," Marcelle called from bed. "You can't let them go any longer."

Jacqueline, clutching her blouse to her, tripped into the room, her skirt on backward. "Antonia, sweet girl, would you help me tend the herbs today?"

"Every day," Marcelle called.

"Come with me today, and see where they are. I'll teach you. You can tend my herbs, it would mean so much to me."

So Jacqueline and I set out through the forest, dropping balls of animal fat and cornmeal for the cats as we walked, legions of them meowing at our heels. They dropped from trees, emerged from burrows, each new litter greeted with joyful congratulations from Jacqueline, a vast herd of fur trailing behind us.

We paced through the forest with great purpose and a small destination. Crampbark, St. John's Wort, motherwort, raspberry in profusion, monk's pepper, and finally, pennyroyal and tansy, each crop more dangerous than the next as we made our way into the woods, the crops secreted behind trees, under a fungus outcropping on the trunk of the fine old pine. They would burn you as a witch for the mere presence of sage, so it was too dangerous to grow medicinal crops in the open, to harvest them in broad daylight. They had to be scattered across the forest, visited at night, especially the aborticides and pain-killing herbs. The only crop that waved bravely in the sun was Jacqueline's field of lavender, which she dashed into like a happy little girl, arms outstretched and knees bouncing high. I followed behind her, alarmed at her display, incredulous at her joy.

"Ah, the sun," she said, falling spread-eagle into the lavender. I lay down beside her. "If I didn't have this lavender in the sun, I would go completely mad living in hiding in the forest all the time. I'm a Gypsy. Bad enough," she said, rolling onto her elbow and looking into my eyes, "that I am stuck here in one place, but it has to be a little hole in the dirt, in the shade, in hiding."

"Why do you stay?" I asked. "You could raise cats elsewhere."

Jacqueline looked at me, sat up, her hair wild and glinting, her blouse open. She picked up a handful of dirt, rich and black, and brought it to her nose: I could smell its peat from my spot beside her. She let it fall through her fingers, then pushed back her hair, the dirt smudging her cheek.

"You have never been in love?" she asked quietly. "Hmm, little one? Are you too young for love? Where is your heart?"

She drew close to me until the air between us hurt my skin. She cupped my face in her hands. "You have never been touched by someone, with hands like bark that cut your skin, but you think if they took their hands away you would die? Someone who loves you doesn't see who you are, my sweet, they see the glow inside you, and it is your honor to live up to the shine. Come," she said, dropping her hands and allowing the air to scald my skin. "We have work to do."

We wove our way through the forest while cats slithered between our feet, Jacqueline describing the layout of her crops, the markings on the trees that I should notice so I would know where they were located, the instructions for the weeding and care.

At night I sat at the table and made up the cornmeal balls for her cats while I listened more closely to her giggle, then suddenly grow silent. My own breath caught in my throat at the sound of her labored breathing, her sense of distress.

"I've made a fire outside," Fiona said, stepping into the house and seizing the bowl off my lap. "You can finish your chores there."

I tended Jacqueline's herbs while she slept late and bathed long. I wandered through the forest haphazardly, trying to find the spot in the lavender where she had fallen in abandon. Coming back to the camp, I crouched in the bushes by the creek to watch Marcelle draw Jacqueline onto her lap.

Three weeks later Fiona and I, accustomed now to sleeping outside the house, were awakened by Jacqueline shrieking as she stumbled outside. Marcelle was several paces in front of her, hair braided, dagger strapped to her side again, a leather sack packed and on her back. Jacqueline clutched her blanket around her, tripping over its hem and the cats that were disoriented from the commotion.

"There is still plenty," Jacqueline wailed. "Stay a few more days!"

"If I tell you three days before I leave, we fight for three days," Marcelle grumbled, kicking a cat out of the way. "If I tell you two days, we fight for two days. At least this way we fight for one hour."

"I hate you. I hate you when you go," Jacqueline said, but Marcelle gathered her in her arms and kissed her as if she could breakfast on her mouth. Jacqueline's blanket started to fall, but Marcelle gathered her to her and dug one hand into her hair. When she finally let Jacqueline go, she turned, nodded to Fiona and me, and walked off toward the forest.

"I am the Gypsy," Jacqueline shouted after her. "I am the one who should be on the road. But no, it is always you. You don't hunt. You just go." I stepped up beside her, inhaling her smell of blanket and warm bed.

"We won't go," I said with as much firmness as I could muster, and clumsily put my arm around Jacqueline's waist.

"That's right," she said, surprised at my closeness. "At least I have you, Antonia. I have you, don't I?"

At Jacqueline's side, I became a farmer, taller, stronger, with a sickle in one hand and the memory of her waist in the other. My skin darkened in the sun, my hands grew callused and rough. I cut and bound lavender, beat enormous batches of stalks to dislodge the fragrant heads. I slashed fungus from the trees, dug for tubers, chopped the raspberry bush, and harvested the fenugreek. One noon she brought a beaker of water for me, and as I raised it to my lips she reached out and touched my sweat-soaked shirt, touched my breast. With the water still clinging to my lips, she pulled me to her and kissed me, then she lay down in the lavender field, descending as if the falling had taken hours, her blouse open, her skirt rumpled, hair mingling with the lavender, and I followed her, filled with the smell of my own sweat and the blood pounding in my ears. My hands slid over her little breasts, but she took my wrist, slid it into the waistband of her skirt, and taught me to navigate. She taught me to play her, and when she rolled me over and spread herself on me, I humbly took another lesson. Jacqueline taught me to command her with my hand and lose myself in her reaction, taught me to send myself into my fingers and let the brain and heart of me float around us, and in the days that followed—the time of her naked in the moss, the time of her on my lap in the peat, the morning of her pressed against a tree—I learned to stalk her climax, needing it more than she, needing it far more than my own, sweet though mine was. I needed to hold her face in my hands and feel her grow utterly still, this vibrant, moving, luscious woman who gobbled her life, who grabbed it double-fisted, flailing about in it, my Jacqueline with more fire in her cat-eyes than most have seen in a church of souls. I would take her chin in my hand and her parted lips would be impatient for my tongue. I needed the right to make her wait, to pin her arms back and drag my teeth across the musky softness of her rib cage, to make her descend from her full-of-life, mistress-of-the-manor position to a state of whimpering patience, moving with the journey of my fingers. Then she would be up again, chirping, this time cheeks flushed, eyes glazed over, nipples shining with my spit, dancing around in some silly little skirt or a necklace, spouting an odd story, and she would be ravenously hungry, as if she'd hiked the forest for a week, desperate over cheese and bits of meat that would fall out of her mouth when she laughed at her own hunger. At the fire in the evening, Jacqueline cooked not for Marcelle, but for me, hovering over my shoulders, attentive and tender, serving me enormous plates of venison, pork, and fennel.

Fiona, meanwhile, had taken to ordering her life around visits to the hot springs and to setting in a store of fermented spirits. Pears when they were in season became pear beer, pear wine, pear brandy, then on to apples and berries. She made wine and beer from anything she could get her hands on, and stumbled around the camp sometimes so drunk she slept in the dirt by the well.

Side by side, Jacqueline and I gathered and dried, pounded and sealed the herbs in clay pots, wrapped them and hung them and stitched them into little bags. I sat by Jacqueline's fire, filled with loving her and feeling at home, feeling while at her side a harmonic, our tempos in syncopation. Fiona slowed her drinking and increased her spiritmaking, bottling enough to sell. We built another hut that was half filled with herbs and beer and half with our sleeping cots. The cats grew in profusion, and Jacqueline danced around the fire at Fiona's offer to carry Jacqueline's cats, her own wine, and our herbs on a route throughout Europe. Gypsy cats, Jacqueline said, on the road as she should be. Fiona planned a route and readied a wagon.

The following morning, Marcelle stepped into the clearing, festooned with a string of rabbits on her left and fish on her right. She called to Jacqueline, who was sleeping soundly beside me, and I covered her ear with her pillow and stepped outside, topless, cinching my pants, with my hair crumpled from the bed.

Marcelle looked at me from under her eyebrows.

"Welcome back, Marcelle," I said, crossing my arms over my chest and planting my feet firmly, my eyes directly on hers but keeping tabs on her dagger.

She dropped her catch into the dust and slowly walked around me, bumping into my shoulder. She stepped wordlessly into Jacqueline's room and was greeted with a shriek. Despite what I wanted to hear as I stood with my back to the cottage—the sound of protest, the emergence of Jacqueline—I had to admit it had been a joyful shriek and that it was now silent inside. The morning air was acid on my skin.

Fiona came out of our hut and tossed me a shirt. "Care to make deliveries?"

I couldn't stay to hear Jacqueline climax, so I grabbed a

cloak and a boda of water and, glancing back at the cottage, set off with Fiona.

What can be said of glorious days? Of days so full of sunshine and quiet that they make you lift your head, finally aware of how stooped you had become? Days of love, days of certainty that make you know, for this instant, that life is good and so are you. When I returned, Marcelle had been gone for three days and Jacqueline greeted me as her savior. I asked her to join me on my trek once, become the roving Gypsy she longed to be again, but she stood outside the cottage wrapped in her blanket, knowing that in a life as good as this, the best of the road was coming back to her.

I traveled when Marcelle returned, and she left to hunt when the time was right. When there was overlap, there was trouble. Marcelle was surly and confrontational, and I admit that I lost all my confidence, so she was even more aggressive. Marcelle refused to share her meat with me, and I made a point of displaying how much money and goods the herbs had brought us. Rabbit entrails wound up under my pillow, and Marcelle developed a mysterious rash that had a very unpleasant odor. We didn't speak. Jacqueline, unable to pamper either of us without incurring the wrath of the other, stormed off to fetch her hooded cape and threatened to leave for good. Since both of us realized she meant it, that our ability to make her come was more important to us than her coming was to her, we made a pact. Unspoken, but made nonetheless. Neither of us had the heart to deprive her of her desires, even if they didn't come from our own hands. So we tolerated each other, Marcelle and I, supplicants to Jacqueline. Jacqueline, now feted at all times, was radiant and joyful, cooked with abandon and farmed as if the dirt on her arms and the shade of her hidden house were one rung south of heaven.

We plied a quiet trade, building a route through Europe: bags of herbs, a manuscript, a few cats, a few barrels of beer. It had been 20 years since I had seen a witch burning, though it had been only five since the church had rounded up hundreds and set them ablaze. We did our part and life was good. The cats and the herbs were taken north, and Fiona and I introduced them to Simone Albi, our compatriot who had a shipping business throughout France. She carefully incorporated them into her routes. Once, after five years, we brought Simone back to our encampment, and she sat by the fire and got drunk with Fiona as if she'd never tasted spirits in her life. The herbs were taken to the hospitals where Simone's daughters worked as nurses, their requests for more brought back to Jacqueline, and we wove the intricate threads of a life, scores of us, entwined. We met midwives on back deer trails and packed bundles for late-night exchanges, hiding the bunches of plants or the linen bags of seeds within the straws of a broom. We looked for women with brooms—it was the mark of an herbalist—and we greeted others in dark night cloaks, carrying brooms with their own herbs. Fenugreek seed for regulating periods, St. John's Wort for anxiety, and tansy for too much fertility.

One spring, Fiona and I had set out to make deliveries, leaving just as the bushes parted and Marcelle stepped into the clearing. Fiona bade her welcome, but I turned my back and headed out, unwilling to see the look on Jacqueline's face. We were only a few hours' ride away from the encampment when Fiona started twitching with one of the seizures that had been plaguing her for years. Her shaking made her horse skittish. I pulled my horse beside hers, hauled her onto the back of my saddle, bound her wrists around my waist so she wouldn't fall off when the shaking grew worse, and, tying the other horse to the horn of my saddle, turned us back toward home. Marcelle and Jacqueline, lunching in front of a small fire, had not even had time to duck into the house yet when I rode up. I jumped down, and the three of us helped Fiona into bed, where Marcelle held Fiona's hands at her side. Jacqueline and I ducked back out of the hut. The routine for Fiona was clear: We had a potion that wasn't terribly effective, and a system for keeping her cool and comfortable, but time was the only thing that eventually quelled the shaking. Looking at Jacqueline, so recently in my bed and now poised to enter Marcelle's embrace, I surprised myself by mounting my horse again and bringing the second horse to Jacqueline. What surprised me more, however, was that Jacqueline mounted the animal and left the encampment.

She rode as if fleeing a fire, oblivious to the bottles of wine, the brooms, and the bags of herbs that were tied to the saddle and hidden within the blanket roll. And I sailed after her, laughing at her delight in her freedom, in her choice to join me, in my success at keeping her from Marcelle. It was one of the first times I had seen her without cats surrounding her, without the shade falling across her face, and she was splendid, her hair wild and cheeks flushed, and when she dismounted at a crossroads she laughed so deep she doubled over.

This was the gift of Jacqueline, not just her beauty, her body, the sense of purpose she gave me. The real gift of Jacqueline was joy. Unfettered, unrestrained joy that pealed out of her without suspicion or defense. I can't remember knowing anyone who didn't constantly look over their shoulder. Even Fiona, one of the happiest people I knew, seemed draped in sadness compared to Jacqueline. With every bud, every clump of dirt, every moment the air poured into her lungs, she was fully immersed in life. When she fought with Marcelle, she did it with all of her claws. She held nothing back, ever. Not when she laughed, not when she argued, not when she came in my arms.

So when Jacqueline mounted the horse again and took the left fork of the road rather than the right fork that I had planned to take, I followed without hesitation. We wound across the hills, then ducked into a section of the forest that I hadn't seen before. I assumed that Jacqueline was just moving with abandon.

Instead she took me deep into the forest for a late-night meeting—cauldrons set up in the middle of the forest, elaborate mixtures that challenged my nose. Inspecting the procedures and the complexity of the operations, I realized these were the best alchemists I had encountered, and it infuriated me that they should be reduced to working in the woods instead of presiding over a fine laboratory like the ones in my hometown at the University of Salerno, Italy. Witches, they called us, wicca, the wise ones. Jacqueline kept to the fire circle, eating goat that had just been on the spit, but I wandered through the crowd, peeking into cloth bags, examining herbs laid out for trade. They introduced me to mushrooms that made my head spin, made me see the wicca floating through the air. We were healers and criminals, as the fire is both cooking circle and pyre.

On one of our many subsequent jaunts into the deep woods, I heard them chanting her name in the bushes...*Joan,* they intoned, *Joan.* She was plodding through France in men's armor, shorn-headed, the light in her eyes, followed by massive men, and women who could wield a stick. They cut their way into the body of English power, and I was glad of it but suspicious. One noose tightens like another, after all. The medicine women flocked to her, ostensibly to repair the Army but in reality hoping to ride into safety—the wicca within the ranks of the armored lady. To no avail, though, and the din rose up from the forest floor again, from the encampment circle. When they burned Joan of Arc, the air above us shuddered, and a pallor fell all around.

But these were glory days, the wet and the sweat and the sound of Jacqueline riding my thigh, of greeting the morning with her face between my legs and the cats climbing over us, the hungry sound of her task much more welcome than the birds.

They were grand and peaceful days, when to have breasts, a stream full of fish, and a loving family by the fire was all that one should ever ask for. I had lived my life chasing endless streets and highways, always en route. With Jacqueline I learned to live happily within the confines of her beautiful patch of France, cradled within the surety of it, moving from vegetable garden to herb patch to swimming hole to bed. I learned to trust again, to shut away my suspicious eyes, and to live for the lavender harvest, the grain crush in the village, the trout stream, and the eating fire, with Fiona, even with Marcelle smelling of offal and wildness. And Jacqueline, my Jacqueline, who taught me joy, letting me live with my face in her lap.

We had reached a peace, and Marcelle and I were her happy clan, leaving her just enough time between us to cleanse the vision of one from her skin, to make way in her turbulent, ebullient heart for someone new. Yet we rarely coincided. One spring day we did, though, and we must have been both so elated over the end of the rain, so pleased to be riding or walking with sun on our faces, that there wasn't any room for what at this point wasn't true jealousy or even competitiveness, just a ritualized separation. Instead we threw our arms around each other's shoulders, comrades for a moment. Jacqueline, thrilled at our arrival, astounded at our togetherness, pivoted and ran forward, daring us to chase her into the forest. We took up the challenge and even though she was now a rosy woman of 40, she sprinted forward, then whirled back to see us, and flung out her arms with joy. But she kept her eyes on us—so unique to find us side by side that she couldn't remove her eyes fast enough. She stepped backward before she turned, then, with her eyes still on us, spun around and sprinted forward. We heard the sound of a bough cracking, but it was Jacqueline, who had run straight into a mature birch that broke her collarbone and delivered a severe blow to her head.

We carried her, speechless, breathless, back to the hut,

united again in our tending of her, and she put some semblance of a body back together in the weeks that followed. When she could walk again, she had a defensive, caved-in quality to her body. A timidity had entered her, and I think the fear she exhibited was even more painful to Marcelle and me than the damage to her body. We fell over each other tending her, and then sat silently together with Fiona by the fire circle drinking too much pear brandy, while Jacqueline, who had entertained us all with her fanciful stories and her pealing laughter, slept in the cottage. The silence held us, bugs in pinesap. When the winter came, the cold settled in Jacqueline's damaged lungs and the three of us sat around her bed while she coughed and laughed and tried to die beautifully, always with cats inhabiting her shoulders and her lap. Marcelle and I were frantic: Marcelle screamed at the cats who covered Jacqueline as if they owned her, and she incurred Jacqueline's wrath for hurling more than one of them across the cottage. Fiona and I struggled with tinctures and mixtures, and I even fled into the forest to ask the wicca at the cauldrons what to do. In the end I brewed St. John's Wort for the four of us and outlawed the brandy. I had wallowed in the joy of her, had worshiped her optimism as if she were a bird that sang in the dark. That I was allowed to love her every day of our coexistence was a gift that sustained me. That she died in my arms was one of the greatest honors of my life. The cats sent up a din the afternoon she passed away, and Marcelle pulled a side of pork from the cellar and hacked it to bits with her knife. Fiona, sweet Fiona, wrinkled and gray, limping and now not prone to seizures as much as to relentless, small tremors, rocked me in her arms as if I were a child of eight.

The death of Jacqueline left us—the old lady Fiona and two middle-aged adversaries—as spokes no hub, clan no matriarch, rattling around uneasily in our lives, jostling for position. Fiona stepped over me for several days while I sat listlessly in the dust of the encampment, and Marcelle wept in the bed. Fiona, still taller than the rest of us even though she was stooped over and shaking with her ailment, took a walking stick and prodded me up off the ground. She beat the covers until Marcelle came out of the bed.

We were leaving, Fiona pronounced.

Every move we made to leave cut us—taking down Jacqueline's shawls, gathering in one last crop, carting cats to the edge of the village and setting them out, bundling others to drop off as we traveled. But at least we were doing something. We packed and hitched up a wagon and helped Fiona into the passenger seat. "North," she said, pulling her cape around her shaking legs and waving us on with her stick.

We arrived at Simone's village just as she was lumbering out of a barn with a oak barrel on her shoulder. She tossed it to the ground, and it cut a three-inch scar into the dirt at her feet. Hands on hips, then crossing herself, she regarded the rag-taggle group of us and took charge. Food was laid out, and we slept as if hoping to wake in another country. The following morning, Marcelle and I offered to tear down an outbuilding that was leaning over, and we flung ourselves at it furiously, as if the building were the constraint of time that had framed Jacqueline's life, her bones that had broken, the shell of her lungs that had collapsed, the structure of our lives that had been destroyed. We yanked them off with our bare hands and our raging muscles, while the stable hands leaned on their pitchforks in surprise. We hurled the boards, broke them under our feet, and Marcelle stormed into a barn, returned with an axe, and chopped the building up.

But her fury turned into blood lust, and whirling around, she looked at me and snarled, as if I had been responsible for Jacqueline's death. I could have stepped aside or cooled her down, but when she lunged at me I took her on, full fist, drawing blood. If we hadn't been so selfish, I thought as my fist knocked her head back, if we hadn't both insisted on being with her or if we had been more generous, I growled as I grabbed her hair and threw her to the ground. If we had been willing to be in the same place at the same time—not a tacit but an actual agreement—Jacqueline wouldn't have been surprised, would have seen the tree, wouldn't have crashed and crumpled and died. We had killed her with our vanity, and it was justice to draw each other's blood.

Simone and her daughters, Helene and Monique, ran to us, all billowing skirts and flapping hands, to pull us away from each other. Simone shoved Marcelle, who flew back several feet before hitting the ground.

"What have you done?" Simone screamed. "No one said you could turn it into firewood, for the love of God. These boards were going to be used in another building! Look at the waste. The waste of my property," she bellowed. She whirled around to me and put her hands on her hips. "What could possibly make you two fight like that?"

She had met Jacqueline, had been in our encampment, but women who have husbands don't see love beyond a beard. There was no way to tell her of Jacqueline and our love. Marcelle stood up and spit blood into the dust. She charged across the distance between us and the women who had encircled us flinched, at the ready, but Marcelle threw a muscled arm around my shoulders and drew me into her, leaning her head on my shoulder. No one in the world knew her pain but me. She cupped my head with one of her strong hands and I gripped her with all the power in my arms. It was our guilt, our love. Her blood was mine—I felt it on my lips as she spat again onto the ground.

Kiss of Death, Inc.
Kathy Anderson

They hang on every wall of my photography studio waiting room. Lesbian couples everywhere you look. Floor-to-ceiling lesbian couples. There are stocky older ladies with gray helmet-cap hairdos, just barely able to put their arms around each other in public, and beaming couples with babies in their laps. There are young couples photographed in arty poses, all naked shoulders and tattooed backs. There are lesbian wedding photographs—both brides in white, cutting cakes, and butch-femme couples in tux and gown. There are biracial couples, May-December couples, and my favorite—the bodybuilder and the librarian.

Ah, domestic tranquillity. Ah, support against a homophobic, hostile world. Come to KD Studio and bask in the reflection of our community. Diverse, proud, joyful partners—that's what you see here. Ha!

It's my private joke that every couple on my waiting-room walls is no more. Some lasted decades, some lasted months. They trooped in here for pictures at some point before the end, when they were still loving and hopeful and feeling indestructible. Or I went to them to record their weddings and anniversary parties.

It's sick, I know, to take a twisted pleasure in this waiting room being a monument to failure, to the death of love. And a slap in the face to every hope-filled couple that comes in to capture the full bloom of their new love. I see them looking around all blushing and pointing shyly to portraits they like.

I want to shake them by the shoulders until their teeth rattle, all the couples in my waiting-room seats. I want to shout in their faces, "It won't work, do you hear me? Enjoy it for now, but whatever you do, don't think it's permanent. Don't build a big castle on a bed of quicksand. Do you see that sign in the window? KD STUDIO: PHOTOGRAPHY FOR OUR COMMUNITY. It stands for 'Kiss of Death,' you idiots."

Most people think KD is named after me, Karen Donahue, but since my second year in business, I've privately called it Kiss of Death, Inc., as I watched many of the couples I was so taken with in the first year go down in flames.

I've watched spectacular breakups, with kidnappings of children and attempted arson and dramatic suicide attempts. I've known breakups of the "she went out for a pack of cigarettes and never came back" variety. There have been a few bloodless breakups, where the couple continued to live together but merrily began to date others. I've seen protracted breakups, years of moving in and out and endless counseling sessions before the final death rattle got so loud that even the couple heard it.

The cumulative effect could have been devastating to me. I started out as naïve and hopeful as my clients. I thought I could make a living in a meaningful way, working for the lesbian community and creating a safe, comfortable place for couples. After the second year I started to feel like the grim reaper of lesbian relationships.

I had two choices: Quit specializing in lesbian photography or develop a sense of humor about it. I chose the latter. I started making bets with myself as to how long a couple would last. I cultivated a keen observation instinct, watching couples when they thought they were alone. I carefully arranged the waiting-room photos to reflect my macabre joke. And I stopped dating once and for all.

My business isn't hurt one bit by all this breaking up. It's a big city, Philadelphia, with a constant stream of college girls, transferred business executives, formerly straight women coming out, and country gals moving into the city to keep the lesbian pot boiling.

Not dating is the best thing I could have done for myself. Unconventional, I know, but it works. If you tell a woman you're not looking for a relationship, she will nod respectfully and totally ignore you. So if someone asks me for a date, I just say, "I don't date." I sound so resolute that they give up quickly. Or maybe they don't really want to date me all that much. I'm not much to look at, with my freckled Irish peasant face and long red ponytail.

My friends give me a hard time about not dating. But most of them have only been through a few breakups. I feel the weight of a thousand breakups in my soul, watching couples and following their stories through the grapevine. I spend my days looking at the happy, doomed eyes on my waiting-room walls. There isn't a woman on earth who could tempt me over that bridge of pain.

I've been there once already, with my college girlfriend. Honey Beth, who opened me up all the way down. Honey Beth, who couldn't keep away from me. Honey Beth, who left after graduation for Illinois and never came back. Honey Beth, who married. A Man. Honey Beth, whose desire for me died as instantly as the ink dried on her diploma.

"She was a LUG (Lesbian Until Graduation)," my friends said with derision.

My friend Addie says I never got over Honey Beth. "You're like an old maimed dog, dragging a dead Honey Beth leg through your life," she says. But I did get over Honey Beth. It's been ten years, after all. What I didn't get over, because it plays itself out over and over again in my studio, is the way couples form, build lives together full of children and pets and houses and businesses, and then their love vanishes.

Not that this process is unique to lesbians, by any means. Straight people have their own version of this sad dance.

You can have it all—the whole endless cycle of desire and distance, of coming together and coming unglued. I want more for my life. I want it to be different.

Addie, the ultimate romantic, tells me the universe will pay me back for my bad attitude. She warns me to take down my gruesome gallery before something bad happens to my studio. I tell her she is superstitious, a typical woo-woo lesbian looking for portents to enforce her own viewpoints. "This gallery is educational," I say to her. "Read these signs and turn back, couples. Maybe I'll hold an illustrated lecture series in my waiting room."

I don't believe the universe cares about my bad attitude toward coupling. Although some strange things have been happening lately.

Three weeks ago I heard a crackling sound and then the picture of the bodybuilder and the librarian fell off the wall facedown, hitting a coffee table hard. Broken glass and pieces of the frame flew everywhere, into the edges of the chairs and deep into the rug. As I was cleaning up, I noticed how dirty the rug was and called the carpet cleaners. They came the next day, which happened to be the hottest, most humid day of the summer. The rugs looked great, but the air conditioner broke right after the cleaning and those stupid rugs would not dry. It took two days before the air conditioning was back on. The waiting room was smelling damp and bad. I just hoped it would go away with time.

At work last week a woman walked in. Now, if I were dating, she's someone I would chase. She had great muscled arms and was quick-moving and her eyes were full of fun.

"I'll give you $50 for that picture," she said, pointing to a wedding picture with a whole party, bridesmaids and ushers and parents and flower girls.

"Only if you tell me why," I said.

"Let's just say I need it."

"Which one are you?" I asked, pointing to the picture.

"I'm not there. I'm not a part of this scene." She shook her head. "Two, four, six, eight...Dykes should not assimilate," she chanted. "That's my motto."

I couldn't imagine why she wanted it. "I can't sell it to you unless I know what you're going to do with it."

"If I tell you, you won't give it to me, " she said, smiling like she'd just told a joke.

I was getting a little mad and very curious. "If you don't tell me, I won't give it to you either. So you might as well."

She sighed. "I'm a lesbian performance artist, and I'm working on a piece against lesbian marriage. It's called *Better to Marry Than to Burn?* I'm going to burn the picture as the grand finale."

"Subtle," I said. I thought it sounded great. "I shouldn't give it to you, but I will. But you have to put black ink splotches over all the faces." Instead of taking money, I gave her my card and said to call me when she was performing so I could get free tickets. I felt a little bad at the thought of the happy couple going up in flames.

It was an unsettling encounter, and my wall was starting to look empty without the bodybuilder and the librarian and now the wedding party. And I was getting a major headache from the smell of the rugs. I called the rug cleaning company to complain. They transferred me until I ended up talking to a morose guy named Albert who sounded like his nose had been stopped up since around 1962. "Sounds like mold," he pronounced. He acted like mold was a personal friend of his. "Mold likes it when it's humid and wet. Mold is very, very hard to get rid of when you leave a rug wet on a hot day like that." He offered to send a mold expert to evaluate.

So Mold Man came yesterday, and the news was very bad. He poked and tested and sniffed and finally said I had to replace the rug, but that wasn't the worst part. He advised me to take every photograph off the wall and get rid of them, saying that they were infected too. I have to repaint the walls when they're empty and start all over again.

My gallery to the folly of coupling to be destroyed! My daily companions who kept me strong against the temptations of dating to vanish! How would I stay centered and firm in my desire to make a different kind of life, without the upheaval of relationships? I was very low as I contemplated my waiting room and pictured the insidious mold multiplying every minute.

The door opened and a woman's head poked in. It was the performance artist.

"It stinks in here," she said, wrinkling her nose.

"I don't smell anything," I snarled. "I'm closed. Go away." I felt like crying. Maybe I had brought this on myself with my perverse gallery. I kept thinking of Addie hissing and pointing her finger at me, saying, "Ooh, you're going to get it. You set yourself up against love, the greatest force in the universe, and you're going to be sorry."

The artist came in and sat beside me. "I came to invite you out with me tonight," she said shyly. "I thought we could talk about art and photography and stuff. I'm new in town."

I hadn't had an offer that interesting in quite a few years. Something inside me started to jump up and down, an internal pogo stick. I looked at her, then around the room at the beaming couples on my walls.

"I don't date," I snapped, avoiding her eyes.

"Cool!" she said. "I don't date either. I hate that couple shit." And she held up her hand for a high-five.

My head was spinning and throbbing. I didn't know if meeting her and not dating her was a good thing or a bad thing. I didn't know if the Universe had sent her to me, my own personal Kiss of Death, who would break my heart into a million pieces and leave me wounded on the floor, a punishment for my perverse obsession. I didn't know if this was sticking to my rule or breaking it. I felt like the mold had attacked my brain.

I did know I had to get out of the studio right then and there. As I locked the door, all eyes were on me for one last time. They just hung there, placid as cows, grinning away. They looked so dear, so familiar, like grandmothers and aunts and sisters.

I couldn't wait to destroy them and start over.

Winnie's Wake
Julie Auer

Winnie always said she was for living. She told me I could spend my life one of two ways: I could live it or I could bear it. She knew Abel Withers too and had since they were both young and decided to stay in town. She was always throwing Abel's name up to me. He stayed because he was scared to leave, though he never got over his fear. He's still here, of course, and that's the hell of it. I guess Winnie was right. It takes longer to bear life than it does to live it. She ought to know.

My name is Lenora, but Winnie always called me Len. Winnie was what my grandmother used to call the "force of the family." So Len stuck. Winnie was not a force in the sense that she had any clout or say-so in the family. On the contrary, she embarrassed most of them. She just had a way of calling attention to herself, but I'll get to that later. Anyway, she was my great-aunt up until three days ago, when a bubble shot up one of the veins in her neck and shut her brain down. They say she lasted a few hours after that.

I've been thinking about her for these past three days, mainly because she's dead, of course, and we all think about the dead when the corpse is fresh and the spirit has drifted on to wherever spirits go. But to be honest, I've been thinking about Winnie because of who she was and what we shared.

God, she hated funeral parlors. I'm sitting in a folding chair watching people pass by her closed casket and whisper about why she wouldn't have it open for her wake. A few more people than I'd expected, but then I traveled 400 miles to...I don't know. Say goodbye? Pay my respects? It's deeper than that. I suppose when the only woman who ever understood you dies, you go the distance to sit at her wake or at least make sure she gets one. And there's the other matter she wanted me to take care of.

Abel Withers is in his element. I have to smile, and I wish I could see Winnie's white dead face too, and trade glances. She said it was fitting he became an undertaker. He was such a morbid, miserable fool. Me, I feel kind of sorry for him. He's standing at the head of the receiving line with my mother, uncle, and grandmother, and he's the picture of grim commiseration. I wonder if that little sparkle to his sad smile isn't really a gleam of triumph that he outlived her. Surely he's thought of that.

I know one thing: If this dead pressure cooker of a mortuary doesn't perk up pretty soon, I'm going to pop open the whiskey jug in my backpack and do Winnie proud. Sometime in the last 20 years or so, Southerners started turning wakes into what they call "a receiving of friends." No music, no whiskey, no storytelling—hell, we're Catholic, more or less, not beholden to the Baptist funereal gloom Winnie always despised. She'll get her wake if I have to suffer excommunication for it.

Baleful screams descend on us from the house next door. Nobody's surprised, though. "Dear God, close that door," Grandmother says. "And pull that window shut. Verla Dean's at it again."

Abel's cheeks turn crimson, and one big purple vein in his neck starts to throb, and for a minute I wonder if Winnie's stroke is catching. After all these years he can't get used to Verla Dean. She lives in an attic apartment in the house next door. Abel's flat-roofed white stucco house pales beneath the pompous Victorian turrets of the Dean mansion. Verla Dean's sisters have confined her there for years, and her only known interest is the occasional stream of mourners meandering in and out of Withers's Mortuary. For as long as anyone can recall, Verla Dean has taken the window seat of her turret and railed against Abel's repository of the dead. The door still hangs open, and I can't help thinking the mourners want to hear her, just once, because it ain't a funeral at Withers's without the hysterical ritual of Verla Dean's ranting.

"Abel Withers! You son of a bitch!" I hear her screaming now. She has a deep bellow, and I slide out of my seat and make for the door before some party pooper tries to shut it. I look up at her robust upper body, leaning weightily out of that tiny turret window, her flabby arms flailing this way and that. What a gloriously mad woman! "Abel Withers! You son of a bitch! You're dead and don't know it! Dead and don't know it! Hear me?" Now for the traffic directions. Don't ask me. Who can speculate on what yokes the ravings of a lunatic? "Traffic to Hades, move to the left! Traffic to Heaven, move to the right!" I can't make out her face from here, but I can't take my eyes off her either, until the final assault. "Abel Withers, you son of a bitch, you're dead and don't know it! Dead and don't know it!"

My uncle slams the door and gives me a snotty look. He's a pious man, my uncle, trapped in delusions of dignity.

I smile at him. "Can't believe Verla's still around, Uncle Wilt. Seems like the longer I stay away from home, the more things stay the same around here."

"No one asked you to leave, Len," he drones.

No indeed. They didn't have to ask. I sometimes wonder if Winnie thought I was taking the coward's way out by leaving. Despite her encouragement, telling me I had a mind to make useful and a will to change the world around me, I wonder. I gather she was glad I left, though I know for a fact she never regretted staying. Lyda had been reason enough for her.

I was 19 and having a hard time. A lot of girls that age

have a hard time, but I daresay I surpassed most of my peers in the sexual angst of youth. Now, I'm not going to sprinkle any scented potpourri on the facts as they were. Fact is, I never had a date, let alone a kiss from a boy. I thought it was my big brain taking hold of my body, and I thanked St. Thomas Aquinas for imbuing my spirit with the strength to overcome carnal distractions with intellect. It didn't occur to me then that I had no carnal distractions to overcome...not just yet.

It was the year I took my first lover, which worried me in part because it was a mortal sin to give over the body without benefit of marriage. It worried me because I realized my motives had less to do with love than, well, carnal distraction. It happened by the side of a dry creek bed under a moonless sky, with only the glow of a battery-charged lantern to outline the edges of a blanket, or the curve of a cheek. We both knew what we were doing when we hid among the pines. We were ravenous, unfettered, and impenitent. We had been acquainted a week.

"Rosa says you are to dispose of the ashes," he says quietly, but it snaps me up out of my daydream like a cold cloth in the face.

I nod my head and wait for Uncle Wilt to say something serene.

"We are all pleased you have taken such an interest in the occasion, Len," he says.

"You know how it was with me and Winnie," I reply.

"I trust you will dispose of them in accordance with the Church's policy."

"Oh, yeah, Wilt. Gotta bury the ashes, urn and all. No scattering." I wish he would leave me the hell alone. "Look, it was in her will that I take the urn, and that's why I'm here. I'll get a priest lined up, and we'll have a burial. Let's do this thing her way. Respect for the dead, right?"

That gets rid of him. The mourners shuffle through an

archway to what was once a dining room. Thank God Grandmother knew her sister well enough to spread the casseroles, pot pies, and pastries decorously about the buffet table. Now we can eat. One of Winnie's old friends has slipped a swing CD into a boom box. I pull the whiskey bottle out of my backpack and head for the table. If somebody doesn't laugh soon, she'll come back and haunt us all.

I never got around to taking Winnie out for a drink, though I've heard she was a hellraiser in her day. Back at the funeral parlor they say she ruled the roadhouses. When I was 19 there weren't any roadhouses, just tame little taverns like Poor Eddie's. I haven't been here in years, but it hasn't changed much. I used to stop by after work during the summers I was home from college. It was a good place to find old friends from high school, compare notes on how drunk we got our sophomore years and how many broken hearts we had endured. I would lie about boys I had dated and parties I had been thrown out of, just to keep up. I wanted to be normal, like any girl that age. If only one of them would walk in right now. Bet I could burn a few ears. Instead I'm sitting at Poor Eddie's, sipping a beer and tapping on Winnie's wooden box. That's what they put her ashes in, it turns out. A box, not an urn.

I don't see anyone I know. They're all kids, like I was then. It's just as well. There's only one person I'd be curious about seeing again, and after 15 years it's barely a passing interest. Funny, though, that night is etched in my mind right next to the first time I rode a bike and the day I took my First Communion. I'm not corny enough to sit at that table now, though it's empty. But I was sitting there, occupied with a novel and a hoagie, when she introduced herself.

"I'm Valerie," she said. "Need another beer?"

I thought it odd for her to wait on me, since Poor Eddie's didn't have table service. If you wanted a beer, you went to the bar and got it yourself. Still do. "No, thanks," I said, but she sat down anyway.

"How do you read in here?" she asked. "It's noisy as hell. Is the library closed?"

I told her I liked the noise. Too much peace and quiet made me nervous. She grinned and leaned back in her chair. She asked a lot of questions, and I guess she could tell I didn't mind having somebody to talk to. I gathered by the way she talked that she was from up north, that she was a few years older than I, and that she managed the place. I also gathered she'd had her eye on me for a while.

She wasn't pretty. Some women don't need to be, and Val was one of them. She kept her wild, dark hair pulled back, and she looked sulky. But she was a tall, busty girl who could spread one hand over the small of my back and nearly touch thumb and pinkie to each side of my waistline. That night we just talked, and she had this smart-ass sense of humor that kept me laughing. I stayed till close because she never got up until close, and it took her that long to ask for my number.

She called the next day and the day after that. We spent a week bearing decency and discretion, and on the seventh day, we roosted high on a hill with a bottle of cheap wine and a blanket and a view of the last remaining drive-in theater in the county. The feature was *Billy Jack,* and I choked from laughing at her ad-libbing of the lines, and it was during one of those wide-mouthed guffaws that I felt that hand sprawl across the small of my back, and if I was surprised by the suddenness of her kiss, it sure as hell didn't show. I felt like I was out of body, though it was more like out of sorts, and sure enough, I soared straight up and out as a funnel of white light appeared out of the stars, and for a split second I thought I had died from excitement.

I hadn't. The deputy's flashlight nearly blinded us both. "Y'all ort not to be doing that here," he grumbled, and spit a brown stream of chaw out one corner of his mouth.

It was a moment of crystallized terror. We lay before the Redneck of Judgment, and lo, he released us with a warning. I felt weak as I scuttled to Val's car, my legs trembling from what could have been passion or fear or both. I thought about running down the hill to a pay phone. But I didn't know who to call, and I didn't want to run away. Val was ahead of me, waiting in the driver's seat, yet I still felt her grip. I noticed her grin as she started the ignition, and her shoulders began to rock, and she threw her head back and nearly passed out from laughing. I waited for the deputy's taillights to disappear down the path, and then I laughed with her.

I find myself patting Winnie's box as I recall that night. I almost ask it—her—do you remember me then? I was mortified the next day. To whom should I confess? I was raised on confession. You never got something for nothing. So I went crying to Winnie.

She called me a horse's ass.

"How could you say that to me?" I bawled. "I thought you of all people would understand."

She stared at me, took a drag off her cigarillo, and told me to sit down. "Understand what?" she asked.

"What's happening to me," I whined. I was pitiful.

"Hell, Len, I understand clearly. You've gone in for a woman. Must run in the family. Live with it."

"How do I live with it when it's a mortal sin?" I wailed.

Winnie pursed her lips and crushed out the cigarillo like she was crushing somebody's head. "Fear is a sin, honey. Lying to yourself is an even graver sin. It kills your soul. Anyway, what's so damn sinful about what you did? Where's the shame in it?"

I sulked in my seat and wouldn't look at her.

"I never fit in here. You never will either," she said calmly. "I stayed for Lyda, and I guess people figured that out after 40 years of me living with one woman. It wasn't easy, but that's life. I guess we were the only queers in town besides Abel Withers, and look at him. A chaste, tight-ass model of propriety. And people still laugh behind his back. What did he get out of denying himself? He's a lonely, dead soul if ever one walked the hollow streets of this town.

"Look at me," she demanded, and when Winnie said do something, you did it. "You know what they say in church. You can't love God unless you love yourself. Well, you can't do that and worry all the time about what everybody else is thinking. Life is hard enough to bear. And honey, I'm not about bearing other people's judgment. To hell with 'em. I'm for living."

Easy for her to say, I thought. Even as a child, I had spotted in Winnie a zeal for defying the order of life in the South. She frightened me then and had probably meant to. All I knew was that I was never permitted to visit her house, where, according to the tactless remarks of my schoolmates, all manner of vice and depravity reigned. "My daddy says your aunt is the Whore of Babylon," a boy told me one time. I was so terrified by the revelation, I dared not raise it to my mother.

I saw Winnie rarely in my childhood. She made appearances for the family gatherings at Faber Farm, on the odd Christmas or Thanksgiving. Lyda occasionally joined her, and the two of them turned heads up and down Grandmother's heart pine veranda. They were both striking women in late middle age, always dressed to the nines in suits they bought on trips to Atlanta or Washington. They smoked, they drank, and there always came the point when Grandmother would order the children upstairs. We knew that was when Winnie had knocked back enough whiskey to start one of her shaggy dog stories. Filthy and funny enough to make the grown Faber men weep and howl, and there we children were, straining our ears from the darkened upstairs hallway as Winnie's husky whisper drowned amid peals of exhausted laughter.

Winnie and I became friends the first time I spoke to her out of turn. Children did not speak except to say "please" or "thank you." My first unsolicited words to Winnie popped out of my mouth as I sat uncomfortably alone with her. She crept into the room and sat down next to me on the bench as I poked at Grandmother's upright piano.

"Do you read music?" she asked.

I shook my head, unable to move my welded jaws.

"Well, that's a shame," she said. "I used to be a music teacher."

To this day I cannot imagine where I got the nerve to say it, but curiosity had always been my most powerful agent. I blurted out, "Are you really the Whore of Babylon?"

Her smile was immediate and precipitated great gulps of laughter. "Sugar," she said, pulling me warmly to her, "I've never even been to Babylon!"

At 15 I defied orders and visited her home. Winnie's house seemed less like a den of iniquity than an oasis of culture in that crass little world around it. Adolescence had isolated and confused me to the point of desperation, and I took to her books and records like a stray dog to water. Mostly I looked forward to our conversations, and they were rarely light. We sat up late in evenings, and I sipped brandy with her and felt like an adult. Winnie always wanted to know what I *thought*. I had never known anybody who wondered what a woman thought.

She rarely asked me about my feelings, though. The news about Valerie was the first time Winnie heard me talk about sex or love, and I think even she was surprised. I mean, that was a hell of a coincidence, and it no doubt crossed her mind that her influence would be the object of blame and condemnation from that day forward. So as vehemently as she urged me to live it out, she cautioned me about what she called "brazen balls."

"Now, I don't want you be like Abel," she said the next time she saw me. She had had time to think it over. "You need to have passion in your life, and this girl sounds like the stuff. Anyway, I don't want to hear details. But just keep in mind, you're young, you've got a lot of figuring out to do. Don't go making any public broadcasts until you're damn sure you know what you're doing. And trust me, sugar. You won't be that smart until your heart's been broken a few times."

I repeated Winnie's advice word for word that night as I lay next to Val.

"That's bullshit," she mumbled. "I thought you said Winnie was cool."

"I said she's brilliant. She's too old to be cool."

"So I guess I'm an experiment. A guinea pig for your fucked-up Southern family. That's great." Her voice trembled as it dawned on her that love might not be in the bargain.

I think I had told her I loved her, but she was smarter than that. It doesn't usually count during lovemaking, when you'll say anything to justify your desire. I doubt she really loved me either, but she wanted to. She was hungry for it. She had followed a woman all the way from New Jersey to a hick town in Tennessee, just on the hunch that it was all for love. That affair ended, and here Val was, marooned in the Bible Belt and living on hope.

"It isn't like that," I said softly. "I guess it's like waking up suddenly in the middle of the night. That's what it felt like the first time we were together. There's a little panic feeling at first. Then I have to get my bearings, figure out where I am." I tried soothing her with a kiss and added, "Stretch out, adjust my eyes, and wait for the dawn."

"Or go back to sleep," she said flatly, and rolled over. "And that's exactly what you'll end up doing."

"Hey."

"What?"

"Wanna hear a funny story about Winnie and Lyda?"

"No."

"Come on."

She turned over and faced me again. She looked unhappy. "It'd better be good."

I looked past her face and out the window to a magnolia branch rustling in the late summer breeze of night, and followed its shadow across the ceiling. "Well, Lyda died a couple of years ago..."

"Oh, for Christ's sake! Why are all your funny stories about death and dying? Is that another one of those Southern things? I don't get you people." Then she laughed and said, "All right. What really hilarious thing happened when the love of Winnie's life dropped dead?"

"It's what happened just before she died. She had cancer."

"I may split my sides. This just gets better and better."

"Hush. Well, she was in the last hours. Now, Winnie and Lyda weren't the most religious people on earth, but they were both raised Catholic and always said they planned to die Catholic. Lyda had wanted to die at home, and poor Winnie was so worn out from taking care of her that Grandmother and a few of my cousins and I took turns helping out. So Grandmother had me call for the priest.

"Winnie just sat in an armchair next to Lyda's bedside and held her little hand. It's an awful thing to watch someone try to breathe when they're in that much pain. I don't see how Winnie stood it. Hell, I don't see how Lyda stood it. But she made us prop her up on her pillows when the priest arrived, and everyone in the room fell so grim and silent as he began the anointing. Have you ever heard the litany of the last rites?"

"Len, I'm Italian."

"Oh, yeah. Anyway, you know that part when the priest asks you if you accept Christ as the Son of God? And the Holy Spirit? And the forgiveness of sins?"

"Yeah."

"Well, then he asks, 'Do you reject Satan?'"

"Yes," Val replied, somewhat earnestly.

"'And all his evil works?'"

"Yes."

"You follow me? Or are you answering the litany?"

"I follow you, already. Move on."

"Lyda just lay there in a yellow mask of death, with just the faintest whisper of life left in her breath. When the priest asked her if she rejected Satan, Lyda smiled, and she said, 'Father, I haven't had a man since 1939.'"

"No fucking way!" Val laughed. "Nobody has the nerve to say that ten minutes before they die!"

"She was just funning. Anyway, we all laughed so hard it nearly killed us too. Even the priest had to struggle to get through the rest of the litany. And Winnie cried for the first and only time, releasing every emotion Lyda had ever conjured in her. Joy, sorrow, love, anger. Mainly love. She laughed and wept so violently that the room seemed to radiate her whole passion, and nobody could move. She was letting part of herself go, and we were witnesses, right there in that cozy bedroom, to the wake of Winnie's love for Lyda."

Val didn't say anything. But I spotted her smile, gleaming a little in the moonlight. Even if she was disappointed in me, it was a good story.

I have to get back on the road. It's Sunday, and I've been agonizing all weekend about what to do with the ashes. Winnie's will specified that I was to dispose of them as I saw fit. Burial is out of the question as far as I'm concerned, the Church notwithstanding. They wouldn't let her have a grave next to Lyda's, owing to the cemetery's policy of "decorum."

Before I leave I have to pay a visit to Lyda's grave. I haven't been here since her funeral. Winnie rarely came here, I'm told, and that fits with what she thought of people who dwell in grief. She thought "grave worshipers" had misplaced notions of where to find the spirit of the beloved. For her, Lyda remained in every bright corner of their sunny bungalow on Iris Street.

She never asked me what happened to Val. I returned to college at the summer's end, and true to my lover's prediction, fell quietly back into the slumber of a secure reputation. Val called me a few times. I was polite and cheerful. The last time she called, I made up some excuse about studying for an exam and cut her off with the promise of calling her back soon. I never did. I heard she moved to Oregon.

I hope she found what she was looking for. I hope someday that I will too. I think about Winnie's life and love. I want my life to be as rich and full. So I'll live it. I open the box, and a thin dust of ash blows into the air. Lyda's headstone peers up from the grass, and I just do it. Dump that heavy pile of ashen Winnie all over the grave, and I'm down on all fours, smoothing it over with my bare hands, kneading it into the earth. Winnie never dreamed I would do that, I'm sure. But she would have thought it was funny.

Reply
Jenie Pak

Maybe you've seen me before—on the street, at a bar, waiting in line for a 99¢ hot dog at The Neighbor's Dog. Maybe I've seen you, searching frantically for a book of poetry, chasing down a cab, riding your bike alongside me— glancing—just for a second. Maybe we haven't met yet but are about to—you reading these words and thinking of the words you are about to write me. Let's not waste any more time. Send me a message, tell me something real about yourself, and make sure it doesn't include candlelit dinners or walks on the beach (though I love the beach!). Cliché will get you nowhere. Just be you—I'm waiting on this end.

I wasn't a dyke until I had a girlfriend. That's what I told myself, that's what I believed. Only a boy's hands had entered me, his thick body against my own like a twin who doesn't want to part. I would meet that girl, that butch, and win her heart. We would understand each other, walk silently in the streets of New York City, finally happy.

It wasn't easy. There were many girls, many smiles, many smells—I wanted them all. Who was I to say no to any of them? My ad had meant something to each one. We were lonely and unsure—surely we could find a way to comfort each other.

But it wasn't like that. She had to be the right one. This was serious. I was in it for good. Don't get me wrong—I wasn't looking for commitment. But fun with the wrong girl is no fun at all. I wrote various ads and posted them on the Web under "Women Seeking Women." I knew this was a risk, that I was risking something, but I wasn't sure what that was.

You should tell me your name. You should tell me why you are alone or looking and you should ask me why I am sitting in the dark looking at the colors of the street outside. Out there, something is changing. Do you feel it too? Everything is moving, and I am searching—I'll admit it—maybe for you. So you should sit close, press your thigh against mine. I should smell your skin, your breath, and feel comforted. You should write, words that come to you and won't stop, make you happy, confuse you, make you who you are. You should share this with me.

One of the women who responded was Russian. Her name was Vita. It may have been something longer, something more complicated, but I'll never know. She wasn't quite my type, I'll tell you right off. Her lipstick was brighter than mine, she carried a purse, her shoes were black dowdy ones that reminded me of the ones my sister liked to wear.

She made me laugh, though. And her eyes were blue, a deep blue like the warm ocean, not cold like the earth after a long spring rain. She was valiant; she made me realize you didn't have to walk with a swagger or slick your hair back to charm the woman walking next to you. *It's not working out,* I told her on the phone. *You're just not my type. You're sweet, Vita, but you're just not the one.* Vita had been in love with her best friend (I know you've heard that one before) in Russia. They had fooled around, but now that friend was married. The last time I saw Vita, before we knew things would end, we were at a diner near Hunter College. She kept making jokes, bad jokes, and I laughed at all of them. I ate all of her fries and pickles and stared at her the whole time, thinking, *I should like this girl more than I do.* But she wasn't the one, though I'd catch her eye now and then, surprised each time how still and perfect her eyes looked, though I could see her mind racing behind them.

Be my first date. I'll be yours. The world sucks, doesn't it? Every day is like diving underwater when I don't know how to swim. You could teach me. I could show you how to dream in patterns and in music. That's just as real as the unreality of other people's dreams. Sometimes I sit on my fire escape on the sixth floor and watch all the cars go by. White lights, lost bodies, one just like the one before it, and after. They could be fish or children leaving school. I don't want to be down there. That's why I'm up here, with the buildings and their smooth faces and deep, protected hearts. Maybe you're like that. Maybe no one knows you, except your name and how you dress and the way you walk. Maybe you can't sleep at night and your body feels like a hundred thousand pounds, or half a pound. Maybe you don't remember your dreams anymore, and morning comes like a shock, then sinks its teeth into your room and you have to enter the world, this world that I'm in and opening the door to.

My ads started getting stranger—you know, out there. I mean, they made sense to me but probably to no one else. That was my hope, though. That my words would reach out when I couldn't. That these women would know me rather than see me—an Asian chick with short hair and shimmery color on her lips.

One girl tried to break me. She stuck her foot in my door and wouldn't come in. I had to either stay in or push her to get out. She always wore a cap and peered out from under its brim. I couldn't figure out if she was hiding from the world— from something she knew existed that was waiting to snatch her up when she least expected it—or if she was playing a game she had invented for herself. It was hard trying to hold a conversation with this one, but I was hooked. I believed her when she said she might be dying of breast cancer and was waiting for the test results. I went out into the winter snow and lifted my chin to the amazingly white sky—you know, when the sky is reflecting off the snow or it's like there's a huge gorgeous bulb lighting up all the ends of the earth. I said a silent prayer for her, and in the middle of thanking the god I felt so distant from, I realized I was barefoot and shivering.

Deena was black and Chinese, and while most people would see the color of her skin, I studied the shape of her eyes—how the left one rose higher at the outer edge than the right one. "Deena, what are you going to do if the tests come back bad?" I'd ask, lifting a forkful of linguine with red clam sauce into my mouth. "That's just how it goes," she'd shrug, and smile a lopsided smile from under her cap. "If they have to cut my breasts off, I don't care that much," she'd say, and look out the restaurant window and shout, "Hey, there's Carrot Top, you know, the whacked-out comedian?"

I remember Deena always talking, but never talking to me. She seemed to throw her words out into the world for anyone to catch, to claim. And if those same words were jumbled into something like nonsense, that was just fine with her. The problem with Deena was that she was a pathological liar. I don't know what had happened to her when she was a kid, or what was going on in her life, but I knew not to ask. Instead I said things like "Hey, you ever go around without that cap?" or "Deena, can't you seena, I'm your hyena?" Sure, I had no idea what I was saying half the time, and the other half of what I said made no sense. Nothing seemed to make sense, though—not the parents we hardly could communicate with, not the strangers on the street with their cardboard bodies shuffling down the streets.

I broke it off with Deena, whatever it was we had. She

would stand me up and make excuses: "I'm sick. I threw up all morning." I'd take the hour bus ride back to New Jersey and warm my feet under my bedcovers. I wanted to believe her, each time, but finally it was enough. "Don't call me, don't E-mail me, don't even think about me," I told her. "Give me one more chance," she pleaded. "I don't know why I lied about the cancer and about that girl who called me the other day. I'm messed up, I know that, but I want you to help me." I hung up the phone and lay in my bed, staring at the room that seemed different all of a sudden. I knew everything was the same, but it felt different—the mustard-colored carpet had always been atrocious, but now it seemed colorless, the way a lover's eyes might after looking into them for so long. The windows appeared to be sewn-on squares on the patchwork quilt of my room, and me an unlucky pattern with no discernible shape, color, design.

If you're out there, I want to meet you—just once. Every girl is different from the next. Every voice, every bone struc-ture, every walk. I want to see you, I need to tell you about the first time I didn't care about the men on the street, about the dream of women crowding my room until it burst in pieces to the street outside, to a forest, to the long, deep ocean that was the wake from the dream and everything that would come after. If you're reading this, help me out. I don't have ESP. I can't break into your house and make you love me. It's not even love that I want.

Let me end by telling you about Beth, the only girl I dated for more than a month. I could tell you about the others: Ji Sun, the Korean girl whose waist-length hair reminded me of the time I almost drowned when I was ten, and her nervous-ness that charmed me but also drove me away. I could tell you about Nancy, the short Chinese butch who wore tank tops tucked into baggy Levi's held up with braided leather belts even though it was the middle of winter. She made me mixes and told me she would be a rock star someday. When my dog died she called from the Chinese restaurant her father owned and said, "I keep wishing every customer was you." I could tell you about the one who tried to get me to move in with her and the one who ran from me after a week, saying I was the type who deserved to be alone in the world.

But instead I'll tell you about Beth. She had big brown eyes I wanted to take photos of and paste onto pictures of myself. She didn't have many friends, and she took karate and kickboxing—it made the loneliness into something good, she said. We made out all the time, hardly spoke about anything that seemed to matter. What kind of a relationship is that, you ask? Let me tell you. It was the perfect one for both of us for where we were in our lives. We knew from the start this would never last, but we were willing to enter each other's lives. I brought her a bagel, poppy seed with cream cheese, and some Pocky—a Korean snack of biscuit sticks you dip into melted chocolate. These were strange gifts, but I thought this would be better than nothing. Beth gave me the book she was reading, *Sexing the Cherry* by Jeanette Winterson. Never mind that I had read it three times.

Her kisses were warm and slow, and I promised myself I would never rush things, but I always did. Since you know we didn't work out, I won't bother mentioning how it ended. Instead I'll tell you about the time she didn't want me to see her naked and was close to tears. I held her big, beautiful body against my own and told her the story of how I used to wet the bed every night when I was eight and nine, and would perform a dance before bed to ward off the evil bed-wetting spirits. "Let me show you," I said, and got up and started walking fast in circles, all the while chanting in Korean the spell I thought would cure me. Let me tell you about the sound of her laughter, so unburdened I imagined a bird flying out of her mouth and out the half-opened window. Let me tell you about her body on the bed, no longer ashamed, saddened by the past, fearful of the future, and my own, now racing around in circles to a dance I performed from memory, from the desire to face whatever was waiting for me, whole, willing, free.

Penny a Point
Karen X. Tulchinsky

"I know, Mrs. Goldstein. I know. Here, have some tea."

She places a Styrofoam cup of lukewarm weak tea in my hand. God forbid it should be hot. She walks down the line of plastic-covered chairs and gives out paper cups of apple juice to the other residents. They're all *mishugena*. The others. Crazy. They lost their minds years ago. Not me. I still got all my marbles. Go ahead. Ask me anything. Go on. What's the capital city? Toronto, of course. Who's the prime minister? What's his name? Oh...you know...that French boy...what's his name? He had a stroke when he was young. You can tell by his lopsided mouth. Ach. What's his name? I know it. Wait. Don't tell me. John Chre-chan. Am I right? I know. So I'm a little forgetful. What's so terrible? At my age? It happens. But listen, I still got all my marbles. That's one thing I can tell you. Thank God for that.

I only moved here last year. I don't need to be here. It's because of my husband, Avram, may he rest in peace, that we came here. He had the Old Timers' Disease. Couldn't even remember his own name. It was such a shame to see him that way. My Avram. Such a good man he was. The best. The grandchildren loved him. Everybody loved him. He made a good living. In the wire business. How do I know what he made? Did I go to work in the factory? Of course not. I stayed home. I raised our children. Two boys and a girl. Beverly, Morris, and Irving. Poor Irving. *Olev hashalom.* Dropped dead from a heart attack at 55. I told him not to work so hard.

That wife of his—the first one. Always demanding the higher matrimonial whaddyacallit payments. He had to go to court all the time with a lawyer. Fighting over money. She took him for every cent he had. I never liked that girl—Mona. Never liked her. Anyway, it killed him, my Irving. All the time fighting in court. Like a criminal. It tore him apart. And it killed him. It's not right. A son shouldn't die before his mother. Not right. I'm sorry. You'll forgive me. See? Even after all this time I break down. I'm sorry. I can't help it. Such a nice boy he was. My Irving.

Did I mention I shouldn't be here? We had our own apartment. Avram and me. A nice one-bedroom on the fourth floor. With a balcony. What more did we need? I didn't mind when Avram got so forgetful. Calling me Shayna. That's his older sister, *olev hashalom*. She died 20 years ago. Big deal. He wants to call me by his sister's name? OK. Never mind. Worse things could happen.

I didn't mind when he left the water running in the bath. Flooded the whole apartment. Thank God we had insurance. They wanted to charge us the damage. Water everywhere. Right through to the third floor. It came through the lights in the ceiling. What a mess. But did I complain? Did I throw him out? No. Live and let live. That's what I say. You should only live to see another day.

Did I complain when Avram left the kettle boiling and started a fire on the stove? No. I didn't say a word. Thank God Evy my granddaughter was visiting. Such a cool head on that girl. She put the fire out. One, two, three. Opened all the windows. We didn't have to tell the super. Or the insurance. She fixed everything back up nice. You wouldn't even know there was a fire.

After that I had to follow him around, make sure he didn't leave the stove on or the water running. Or God knows what. But we managed. Listen, after 62 years of marriage what am I going to do? Throw him out? Divorce him maybe? Ridiculous. At my age? No matter what happens, you stay together. You cope. What else could I do?

I'm only saying this now because he's gone. *Olev Hashalom.* Otherwise the only person I could tell was Morris, my youngest son, and my daughter, Beverly. He hit me, my Avram. Only once. But it was enough. He didn't mean it, I know. But what could I do? He was like a little boy with a temper tantrum. I don't know who he thought I was. His mother maybe. Who knows? I had to call Morris on the telephone. He came right over. With his wife, Leah.

"You'll have to move into a home," Morris said.

"A home?" Oy. I never thought it would come to that. Always I thought when we got too old, Morris or Beverly would take us in. Why not? They got plenty of room. Their kids are all grown up with lives of their own. How much trouble would we be? I'd help with the cooking. The cleaning. The great-grandchildren. But what can you do? They didn't offer. A burden we'd be, maybe? They have their own lives. My daughter and her fancy-schmancy husband-the-doctor—every night they go out. To the show. The ballet. The opera. Opera schmopera. Who can keep track already? Who needs to go out every single night? And Morris? Who knows why he didn't take us in. A son you can't depend on for that. I'd be living in my daughter-in-law's kitchen. Maybe she didn't want me.

So? Avram and me would be a burden. And that's it. What can you do? The old aren't wanted. We aren't needed anymore. Not in this world. So, we moved in here. Into this place. I couldn't manage Avram. In the end he was like a baby. That's what happens with the Old Timers' Disease. At the end. A big baby was my husband. Who knew he would die so fast? We gave up the apartment. All the furniture. My dishes. Even my good pots and pans my mother brought over from the old country. My beauty-ful soup pot. Such a pot you'd never buy in America. Not for a million dollars. My daughter didn't even want it. She said it was old and stained. So? I threw it in the garbage. My good pot. I had that pot my whole life. Such a nice soup you could make in that pot. Like heaven. Everything else went to my children and grandchildren. This one took a lamp. That one took a rug. Everything was gone. So after Avram died, Morris said I might as well stay here. I had nothing to go back to and nobody to take me in. So? Here I am. In an old folks' home.

All the other residents are *mishugena*. They don't know from nothing. They cry like babies. They talk nonsense. They drool. Some are in diapers even. Can you believe it? They don't remember how to control themselves no more. A shame. When I get to that stage, I hope God will put me out of my misery. You wanna know why there's plastic on the sofas? Well. There's your answer.

I only have one friend here. Miss Frieda Birmbaum. She turned 83 last month. Two years older than me. A lovely woman, Frieda. She lives in the next room to me. One of the only other residents who still has all her marbles. At least I can talk to somebody. It passes the time. Otherwise, what am I gonna do? Sit in the lobby and stare into space? I used to embroider. Oy. You should have seen my tablecloths. Like artwork, my Avram used to say. I gave tablecloths to all my kids. To my grandchildren. My friends. I donated to the Hadassah so they could sell them for charity. Beverly says my tablecloths always sold first. Right away. For a good price. So? Why shouldn't I be proud? But meantime, I can't do it no more. Why? My eyes. I can't see. It's no good anymore. I went back to the eye doctor. Maybe I need stronger glasses. He said it's the whaddyacallit? The catamatracks. I need an operation. I said he could just forget about that. I'm scared maybe he would slip and the knife goes into my eye, and boom! I wouldn't see at all. Like Mrs. Krausman I used to know from the neighborhood. Went in for an operation. Came out blind. Not me. I said forget that. So, the world's a little cloudy? That I can live with. Beverly says I'm *mishugena*. I should trust him. He's a doctor. He does these kind of operations all the time. So? I told her she could go ahead and let him take a knife to her eye if she's so excited. And that's the end of the story.

Frieda says I should have the operation too, but I told her the same thing I told Beverly. She laughed.

"Sometimes in this life," she said, "you gotta take a risk."

"How do you know, Miss Birmbaum?" I asked.

"Listen, Mrs. Goldstein. Plenty of risks I've taken."

"You?"

"Sure."

"Like what?"

"Like plenty." She opened her handbag and pulled out a deck of cards. "Now, let's play gin. A penny a point."

"I can't see."

"I'll help you."

"How do I know you won't cheat?"

She got quiet for a minute. Then she leaned in real close. She smelled nice. I couldn't describe it. Like some beauty-ful perfume. From Paris, France, I think—it was so beauty-ful.

"I don't cheat my friends," she said in a serious voice. Like it was life and death. And I knew I could trust her with anything.

"OK," I said. "So deal already. What's the hold-up?"

Such a grin Frieda gave to me as she shuffled the cards and laid them out.

Frieda never married. Can you believe that? I asked her, "How come?"

Her eyes looked sad. I thought maybe she was gonna cry, and I was sorry I even asked.

"I was engaged once. When I was young," she said.

"Oh." I didn't know what to do. I felt bad, making her sad.

"To someone…very special…"

"But it didn't work out?"

"This...person...loved me. I know they did. But at the last minute, they got cold feet, I guess."

"He ran out on you before the wedding?" I asked.

"I guess you could say that."

"And you never went out with other fellas after that?"

"I dated some...people. But I was never in love like that again."

"Weren't you lonely, Frieda?" I couldn't help asking. A whole life time alone. Imagine.

"I had friends. Lots of girlfriends." She winked at me then, and I felt a strange feeling in my heart. I never felt closer to anybody in my life as I did to Frieda in that moment. She was so sad and...what's the word I'm looking for? Lovely. She was lovely. For the first time I was glad to be in the home, so I could meet Frieda Birmbaum.

Beverly came by today. Sat with me in the day room. Not a bad room. It's bright. Sliding doors open to an outside patio. Beauty-ful flowered wallpaper. There are sofas and chairs, covered in plastic of course. And bridge tables with hard chairs for playing cards. We always sit at a table. Let the *mishugenas* sit on the plastic, not me.

Beverly *chacked* me a *chinick* from the moment she got here. You know what that means? It means she drove me crazy. Again with the operation. Can't she think about something else? All right. I know she means well. But listen. How many times can I hear about the same thing?

"Stop already with the eyes. Please," I begged. "Let's talk about something else."

"OK, Ma. Fine."

"Good."

"So? What's new?" she asked.

"What could be new here? Maybe if I lived by you something

would be new. With the great-grandchildren maybe. Or the cousins. But no. I live in a home. What's gonna be new? Mr. Feldman drooled again? Big news."

"Ma. Don't you have any friends?"

"Friends I should have? In here?"

"All right. I'm just asking." She looks around. "There's lots of people here. Isn't there somebody you like?"

"What'll we talk about? They're all *mishugena*."

"Everyone?"

"As far as I know."

"Oh, Ma. Are you sure?"

"I'm sure," I say. Then who should turn up but Frieda Birmbaum.

"Mrs. Goldstein," she says, all smiles like I'm her best friend, "you didn't tell me you had company. Who's the lovely lady? Hello. I'm Frieda Birmbaum." Frieda sticks out her hand for my daughter to shake. "You can call me Frieda."

"Hello. I'm Beverly. Sophie's daughter. Ma, you didn't tell me you had such a nice friend."

All right. So all of the sudden I'm a criminal. This one didn't know I had a daughter. That one didn't know I had a friend. Is my life an open book? Am I under investigation all of the sudden?

"Won't you sit down and join us?" Beverly says to Frieda.

"Thank you, dear."

Frieda gives me a look. I pretend I don't see nothing. Why does she get to me the way she does? Right to the heart. Like love and pain at the same time. Like heartsick. I never felt something like this before.

Next thing I know Frieda pulls out her deck of cards and we're playing gin. Even Bev. My "I never gamble" daughter agrees to a penny a point.

"That's the one I'm waiting for," Frieda winks at Bev, as she picks up the jack of spades. "Thank you."

"Don't mention it," Bev smiles.

Frieda grins back.

Then Frieda's telling Bev a joke, and my daughter's laughing and giggling at everything Frieda says and I'm jealous. Why isn't Frieda paying attention to me? What am I? Chopped liver?

"Gin!" Frieda says.

Big deal. Another winner. "I don't feel good." I say. And I push up from the sides of the chair. Real slow and shaky. "I'm going to my room."

"Ma! Where you going?"

"What's a matter?" I say. "I don't feel good. That's it." I push so hard on my chair it knocks against the bridge table and the cards go flying, but I don't care. I want them to. I shuffle slowly across the lobby. I can feel my daughter and Frieda watching me.

The next day I stay in my room. I ain't hungry. I don't wanna see nobody. Everyone else can go jump in the lake for all I care. I don't feel good. So don't bother me. I hear a knocking at my door after lunch. "Go away!" I yell.

"Sophie, it's me. Frieda. Open the door."

"Go away."

"Sophie."

Part of me wants to open the door, but I just pull the pillow over my head so I can't hear the banging and I drift off to sleep.

I dream and I dream. I'm in a beauty-ful ballroom. In a beauty-ful dress. A gown. With purple sequins and beauty-ful silver shoes that sparkle and shimmer. I'm the belle of the ball. I ain't 81 years old in the dream. I'm 25. And I can see perfectly—20/20. My hair's done like a princess. And I'm all dolled up. With lipstick and eye shadow. I look like a movie star. All the men—they can't take their eyes offa me. I glide across the dance floor and stand at the side waiting. A handsome gentleman comes over to me. He's all decked out. In tuxedo and tails and top hat. Like Fred Astaire. He dances to me. He has a white carnation in his lapel. He looks like a million bucks. Better than Avram ever did, may he rest in peace—and may I be struck dead a thousand times over for being unfaithful even in a dream. But Avram is dead and I ain't. So? What am I gonna do? Lay down and die when a handsome gentleman comes calling?

I smile at him. Excited. I haven't felt like this since I don't know when. All prickly. And sharp. Like the whole world is bright and brilliant with color, and sounds are separate and sweet and beauty-ful. My heart flutters like the young girl I am. And the handsome man comes closer and he's young and tall and strong and his eyes are Frieda's eyes. Dark and brooding and mischievous. They make my belly turn inside out. Frieda holds out a white-gloved hand and I take it. She leads me to the dance floor. Her strong hand against the small of my back is a *michaya*. An unexpected pleasure. A miracle. The world is in its rightful place. I feel happy and scared and excited and safe. All at once. I throw my arm around her neck and she smells like that beauty-ful perfume from Paris she wears. We waltz around the room like Fred and Ginger. All eyes are on us. I'm a princess and Frieda is my prince. I feel proud to my toes. Then I feel Frieda's *shmeckalah* growing inside her trousers. Pushing up against me urgently. I push closer into her. I haven't felt like this since I was young and me and Avram were first courting. We were so young and innocent we didn't know what was what. Frieda pushes harder, and I want to go to bed with her, but I feel ashamed. Why can't she just be a gentleman? And dance nice? Always they gotta start pushing their hard *shmeckalahs* into you. Without my permission. But even I gotta admit, it feels good, so I pretend I don't notice nothing, and Frieda pushes and pushes and she's saying, "Sophie, I love you. Sophie, open the door. I love you. Open."

And I wake up. Someone's banging on the door.

"Sophie!"

It's Frieda. The real Frieda. She's banging at the door. I can't answer the door. Not after a dream like that. I feel so ashamed. I pull up the covers. And I hide.

The next day I go downstairs for breakfast. I'm sick of hiding in my room. And Wednesday is pancake day and I don't wanna miss out. Pancakes are my favorite breakfast. I don't wanna see Frieda either. Not after a dream like that. So I go and sit way in the back of the dining hall. Maybe she won't see me. I squeeze in between Mr. Feldman, who is senile, and Mrs. Schwartz who can't see and can't hear. That way I'm safe. I don't gotta talk to nobody.

I eat my pancakes, minding my own business. Usually I like pancakes. But today they taste like lead in my throat. Even with lots of maple syrup. I can hardly swallow it down. Everything's getting stirred up in my throat, like there's already a big lump there, blocking the way.

"There you are." I hear Frieda's voice before I see her. "What are you doing way back here, Mrs. Goldstein?"

It feels like my *kishkas* are turning over inside me. Like I'm on a roller coaster ride at the amusement park. I can't look up.

"So? What's the difference where I sit?" I stare at my cold pancakes.

"What's the difference? Because you always sit with me."

"Well, today I'm sitting with Mrs. Schwartz."

"She can't hear a word. She don't even know you're there. What are you talking?"

"So? Doesn't she deserve a little company too?"

"And you can't stand Mr. Feldman."

"Shah. You want him to hear you?"

"Sophie, what's the matter with you? Is it because I won?"

"What?" I look up for the first time.

"At cards yesterday."

Frieda's big brown eyes are looking back at me, and all I can think about is her hard *shmeckalah* pushing into me and my heart starts pounding and I feel like maybe I'm gonna have a heart attack. I push up from the table and run away.

"Sophie?"

I stay in my room again, all morning and afternoon. By dinner I'm hungry, and in this place if you don't make it to the dining hall, you don't eat. So I wash up a little, comb my hair, put on a little lipstick. Even at my age, you wanna look nice when you leave your room. And I venture downstairs. I already decided I ain't talking to Frieda. No matter what. I can't. Look what happens when I look in her eyes. I don't wanna have a heart attack. Then what good will I be? If I ignore her, she'll go away. And that's it. I go and sit beside Mr. Feldman again. Mrs. Cohen the communist is on my other side. When she was young, she was in the labor movement. Now every day after dinner she stands up by her table and makes a speech about socialism. What can you do? She used to be a big shot. She's still trying to educate the masses. Even here. What do I care? Do I have to listen? I can tune her out just as easy.

While Mrs. Cohen's making her speech, I glance around the room. My eyes go to my usual table. Strange. Frieda's not there. I check all the other tables. I can't see her anywhere. That's not like her. Frieda loves dinnertime. She loves to eat, and even more she loves to socialize. What if something happened to her? What if she took sick? My heart pounds again inside my chest. I feel a little sick. With worry. I push back my chair and stand. Walk over to the nurse's desk in the lobby.

"Yes, Mrs. Goldstein?" asks Ann, the nurse.

"Yes, dear. Can you tell me, is there something wrong with Miss Frieda Birmbaum?"

"Miss Birmbaum?" She looks at her list on a clipboard. "Frieda."

"Oh, Frieda. Her sister picked her up this morning. She's gone out for the day."

"Sister?" I didn't know she had a sister. First time I've heard.

"Yes, Mrs. Goldstein, her sister." Ann enunciates the words very carefully, as if I'm deaf. I can hear just fine. I'm just surprised. I didn't know Frieda had a sister. I walk away, head for my room.

I want to wait up for Frieda. Sure I will hear her open her door when she arrives back home. But it's getting late and I'm sleepy, so I stretch out on my bed and close my eyes. Just for a minute or two.

I wake the next morning at 5, still in my clothes. I feel exhausted, like I never really slept. I wash up, put on a little lipstick, comb my hair, and leave my room. Frieda isn't at breakfast. I'm starting to get worried. I ask the desk nurse again.

"Hmm. Frieda Birmbaum..." she says as she looks up the name. "Oh yes, she's leaving us. She's moving to Florida with her sister."

"Florida?" Oh my God. What have I done? I've driven her away. Now maybe I'll never see her again. My Frieda. The tears come to my eyes. I can't stop them. I feel like I'm gonna faint. I see black spots. I can't catch my breath. My knees feel weak. The black grows bigger and bigger. Then it is everything.

I wake up in a hospital bed. Clean white sheets. Bright lights. Smell of antiseptic and bleach. They got one of those whaddyacallit? Intervenious wires in my arm. What for? I'm not sick. What happened? Oy, I must have fainted. Frieda. Now I remember. My Frieda is moving to Florida. Oy. And it's all my fault. I never should have sat with Mr. Feldman. She probably got jealous. Maybe she thinks I'm sweet on him. Ridiculous. He don't know his forearm from a loaf of bread. Why would I be sweet on him? Oy, what have I done? What a mess I've made of everything. I was so afraid of getting a heart attack. And look. I landed up in the hospital anyway. My throat is so dry. Maybe a nurse will come along. I need a drink of water.

I hear footsteps at the door. Beverly. She smiles, walks over, sits in the chair by my bed, leans over, kisses my forehead.

"Hi, Ma. You're awake. Feeling better? You sure gave us a scare."

"I'm fine. I'm thirsty."

"Here, have some water." She pours a glass of water from a blue plastic pitcher on the night table.

The water feels so good going down my parched throat.

"Ma, there's someone who wants to see you." Beverly says, with a strange look on her face.

"What are you talking?"

"Only she thinks you don't want to see her."

"Who? What?"

"Just wait here." Beverly stands.

"Where am I gonna go?"

"I'll go get her."

What's she talking about? I sip on the water and wait. I almost faint all over again when Frieda walks into the room. Her eyes have the same effect on me as always. My belly does a little dance. Only this time I'm not so afraid. I like the feeling. It feels nice.

"So? Aren't you gonna sit down already?" I ask.

"You want me to?"

"Of course I do."

She sits. "How are you feeling?"

"I'm fine. I fainted, that's all. What's the big deal?"

"I thought maybe it was your heart," she says.

Oy, is it ever my heart. "I hear you're moving to Florida."

"Where did you hear that?" She seems surprised.

"The home. The nurse told me."

"Oh. I was. But…"

"But…?"

"It's not going to work out."

"I didn't know you had a sister."

"Sister?" Again she seems surprised.

"They said you were moving to Florida with your sister."

"My sister?" She laughs. "Ruth's not my sister… she's…well, an old dear friend." Something about the way she says "dear friend" is strange. Like she's trying to tell me something. But I don't know what it is.

"So you're not going?"

"No."

"You're staying?"

"I'm staying."

"You'll stay next door to me?"

"Why would I move?"

"Frieda…" I don't know what I want to say. "I'm sorry" is all I can think of.

"For what?"

"I thought I was gonna have a heart attack." I try to explain. I don't know the right words for what I'm feeling, so I look deep into her eyes. Maybe she can read my mind. I reach over and take her hand. So soft. And small. I squeeze her hand and bring it to my face.

"Because of me?" She understands.

I smile and shrug a little.

"Oh, Mrs. Goldstein, I think maybe I'm gonna have a heart attack too."

"That would be a big mess, if we do. We could have side-by-side hospital beds." Frieda laughs. And I laugh too. Her hand feels nice against my face. So right. Just where it should be.

"How about a game of gin?" she says.

A warm sweet sensation floods me. "Penny a point?" It feels good just to be with her.

"Is there any other way?" She slowly releases her hand from my grasp and reaches in her bag for the deck of cards.

I miss her hand terribly; it's like part of me has been torn off. I watch as she deals, never taking my eyes from her hands. As if she knows what I'm thinking, she picks up her cards with one hand and reaches for mine with the other. I squeeze her hand tightly, to let her know I'll never let go again.

After I get released from here, I know I'm gonna ask Frieda to move into my room with me. After all, it's expensive to have your own room at the home. Why pay two rents when we could get by with one? Am I right? We could play gin anytime we wanted. Even after everyone else has gone to bed. And other games. To pass the time. When you're with a good friend, the time passes faster.

"Gin," says Frieda, plunking down her cards.

I smile at her with all my heart. I don't even care that she won. Again. As long as she's here.

"Your deal, Mrs. Goldstein," she says, her eyes sparkling like a teenage boy. Like Fred Astaire. In top hat and tails.

I pick up the cards with my free hand, squeeze Frieda's tightly, and shuffle the deck one-handed. Fancy schmancy. Like a real dealer. A real pro. Happier than I've ever been. In all my 81 years.

Her Clear Voice Undid Me
Carol Guess

After high school, while my I'm-not-gay girlfriend Madi was juggling community college and denial, I got a job at Low Cost Cart, a discount grocery in Norfolk. It was a 30-minute drive each way, but no one in my hometown was hiring. The distance ended up being a good thing because I found a second life at Low Cost.

In my new life I was a spy.

"Congratulations, Miss Cooper," my boss smiled as he shuffled my tax forms under the cereal samples littering his desk. "You've just been hired as the World's Slowest Shopper." Dorrit stayed smiling the whole time I knew him, which unnerved me until I realized his teeth were the wrong size and probably hurt his mouth. Frowning wasn't an option, though he sometimes barked commands or pinched.

His huge teeth must've needed filing, like Madi's rabbit Cindy Crawford, because Dorrit ate constantly—mostly cereal, but occasionally raw pasta. Grapenuts was his favorite. He'd scoop handfuls from a box on his desk, dribble them onto his tongue, then crunch. We could hear him coming from aisles away. Rumor had it that Boosey Ballard had been hired specifically to pick up after Dorrit's habit, but Boosey went mute when asked point-blank.

Me, I was security. Low Cost had terrible theft problems. There were shoplifters with bulky sweaters, but just as often folks piled carts to the ceiling and sailed past the cashiers. I figured the name of the store was misleading;

probably people realized mid-shop they couldn't pay and decided to risk arrest rather than go hungry another day.

It was my job to observe them and rat to Dorrit. My official title was Adviser to the Manager on Strategic Uses of Confirmed Security; basically I was a human hidden camera. I pretended to shop all day, putting things in and out of carts and baskets, ostensibly reading labels and contemplating calories, while all along spying on suspicious sorts.

"Women with children are the biggest risk," Dorrit said when I asked what to watch for. "Infants are easily stuffed with expensive merchandise."

Dorrit's lessons on Suspicion and Sneaking required me to adjust my interpretation of "store." I lived in Pine Manor, a modular park with no pines anywhere and tiny boxes for manor houses. Just as "pine" and "manor" demanded that I use my imagination, so too "store" required an imagination. Like an imaginary income. And I imagined income for every shoplifter who looked even remotely desperate. Goof-offs or pathological creeps or men who hadn't stolen anything but kept putting their fingers down their pants I reported as a matter of course. Justice had to start somewhere. But mostly I stayed on the side of the shoplifters, who were enormously creative. Got to where I admired their schemes and shenanigans so much I stopped doing my job and started absorbing. You could say I went to college too—Petty Crime School. The lessons were invaluable.

Mostly I spent time in Baked Goods, where the view scanned several aisles and the smell reminded me of women. First thing in the morning I'd stop by Pastry and ask Constance Mulvey which treats were fresh. She was a smiler, very "Have a nice day." Somehow, though, you knew she meant it. I always asked her to set something aside for me to eat on break with Low Cost coffee.

I'd known Constance some years back, before her dad got transferred and they moved to Norfolk. I remember she cheated at flash cards in math, was the first to wear a bra in fifth, and punched some boy in the face a couple weeks before she left. The punch didn't make sense to me until a few years later. He'd called her queer, which I thought meant unique.

Constance had dropped out of Norfolk High. She never said, but I knew why she'd quit. The baby that meant the end of her time at Norfolk was a toddler now, with thick black hair. Every payday Constance stopped by for her check covered in applesauce and carrots, tugging the kid on a short blue leash.

The leash was too weird, but Constance was something. Her ways were ways I loved to watch. She wanted folks to find some comfort—so different from Madi that I felt refreshed. Got to where, when she saw me coming, she'd smile like she'd been baking secrets. Got to where, when I saw her smiling, I'd smile back and she'd look down.

Till then I'd used the intercom sparsely. Folks rarely paged me but meant business if they did. Once in a while I had to call the all-alert: "Tom Thomas to checkout," meaning "Something freaky is happening and I need help." Then everyone who could leave their stations was supposed to casually meander toward danger, pretending not to look while keeping hawk eyes open. Usually we fucked up Tom Thomas big time. People were so glad to stop working they'd swoop, sometimes at high speed, and then form a buzzy circle. We caught a couple of shoplifters this way, permanently damaging their psyches, since the buzzy circle looked like a village militia armed with brooms and bags of flour.

Mostly I filled and unfilled my basket, or practiced steering a cart with my toes. Sometimes I'd challenge myself to shop under restriction. I'd do a vegetarian basket, then food from Nebraska farms, then colors—all green, say, or (harder) purple. My purple basket was mostly eggplant. And so my days went, putting back what I'd picked up, eyeing customers, playing both jury and judge in my mind. I got my thrills letting folks take home bread and milk for free. "Robin Hood," Madi called me; that was how I bore boredom.

That, and smiling at Constance.

When I first heard "Cooper to the freezer," I thought I'd forgotten to reshelve some meat. I left my basket in the middle of the aisle ("obstacle course" was another staff favorite) and trotted to the back of the store. Rubber mats marked a maze through spilled milk and sponges. Beyond was storage, dank as a cave. Maybe in another century it had been well lit, but in this one half the bulbs hung scarred. The dim room echoed with the box-cruncher's metallic chewing, the freezer's low hum, and the radio's complacent wheeze.

There were always at least two stockers frantically running a treacherous, wheeled ladder back and forth along endless rows of vertical shelves, climbing like monkeys, backing down hugging boxes of jam or juice to their chests. The stockers had the hugest arms I'd ever seen. Three months of working at Low Cost could transform a wuss into Goliath. It was hard to tell male from female; everyone was sinewy, with bright green aprons flattening their fronts. I wanted very much to be a stock clerk, but I made better security, Dorrit explained, because I lived outside the city limits and thus was close to anonymous.

Two of the more agile monkeys were scaling the shelves while their ladder-holder fussed with his apron. The radio was tuned to prom-type songs; for a moment I thought of Madi making out with some dude. "For cover," she always said. "If you were a boy, we'd be engaged." It was hard to tell what was true and what was lying when lying was always a part of our day.

"Cooper." It was Constance, standing by the freezer door. I hadn't recognized her voice over the intercom. "Help me unload." She gestured toward a dolly stacked with plastic buckets of frozen dough.

We were always encouraged to ask for help lifting. Dorrit

was terrified someone would slip. Low Cost had been sued, sure, and would be again. There were morbid posters everywhere, with pictures of bloody cut-off thumbs and neon lists of rules nobody followed. We couldn't, actually; following store policy would've shut down shop. Like the rule on tools: No one 17 or under could operate machinery. This included box-cutters, which the stock clerks, mostly high schoolers, needed, logically enough, to slit open boxes.

I figured Constance needed a tough girl like me to unload. The fact that I could only lug one bucket from the dolly to the freezer at a time, while she could do two, make small talk, and scratch her nose didn't deter me from believing I was truly helping.

"Thanks so much," she said. Then, "Isn't it nice outside today?" The small talk went on for several minutes while the monkeys climbed higher and our fingers froze. "C'mere," Constance said, gesturing toward the freezer. As I stepped inside, she shut the door.

Beyond the storage part of the freezer was Dairy. The dairy room wasn't quite so cold. Constance hustled me in and made a big production of looking around, even peeking through the knee-high slots behind sliding glass doors that opened onto the dairy display inside the store.

"Milk's low," I said. "Yogurt too, and butter. Where are Lyle and Marian?"

"Meth," she said, as if drugs were geography. I thought about the Ghostly Hands—how sometimes when I passed the dairy display, Lyle or Marian's gloved hands would poke through from the back room where Constance and I now stood, only not arranging stock but wiggling. Once two hands free-floated over the margarine, playing cat's cradle with neon string.

"I have a question for you, Cooper. But you have to promise never to tell."

As if I hadn't been frozen already, I froze. All that was

about being a good girl stopped. Onto the table Constance tossed every card. And it seemed to me that the cards she held were nothing like the deck Madi bought me: "Old Maid," illustrated as boredom and gray. Constance was showing what her fingers could do, and it wasn't knitting, dominoes, or pricing. She showed, without words, what she wanted from me. Whatever I saw, it was the thing others missed.

"Listen." She put my hands on her chest. "What do you hear?"

"Heart beating."

"For you."

"I figured."

"And you?"

The freezer got warmer. Over the next several days we sold spoiled milk. I said yes to the heat and the secret. It was barely private; I learned that I liked that. Liked almost being caught, liked tension and timing. And so I came to understand that the intercom, seemingly an instrument of authoritarian control, had been appropriated by the staff for schemes, stealing, and sexual favors. I learned who paged who, and why. "Annette to Poultry" was Larry in Produce. "Matthew to Condiments" was Eileen from Front End. Soup hated Deli, and would page Deli to the loading dock when the weather was awful. Deli was a little dull, and would stand outside dutifully, gazing into the storm for a truck that never came.

"Cooper to the freezer." Her clear voice undid me. She'd wait by the door with those buckets of dough. On the rare days that Lyle and Marian were actually working, we'd steal a cold kiss in the freezer itself. Oh, the romance of it—frost on frozen dinners melting as our chests met through our aprons and our hands slowly went numb.

Once Marian walked in on us. "Wow," she said. "Trippy." Then she vanished in a cloud of weedy breath. Later she told

Constance she'd dreamed about us. "You were stealing stuff," she said, which felt true.

My time in the freezer seemed so detached from the life Madi and I carved out in secret. Sometimes I worried that I meant nothing to either girl, that they were just users. Maybe I was destined to be the first stop on the road to out, and the road not a road but a circus high wire, clowns everywhere, no net anywhere.

But guilt.

The first time Constance kissed me I went home to Madi. "What'd you do, Cooper, rub air freshener in your hair?"

"Spilled a box of detergent."

"Must've been a mess. Will you look over this essay? The topic is supposed to be "Why I Like to Read and Write," but I don't, and I think I say that maybe too many times."

Why I Lie and Cheat on Madi.

Because it doesn't feel like something bad.

Kissing Constance was a shield of a lie. With my small, tight secret in front of my chest, Madi's jabs hurt less than they might've. The way my grandma Mookie wound gold ribbon around my annual Xmas undies was the way I wound dreams of my trysts in the freezer around ordinary Low Cost days. It wasn't love; I was glad to know this. Glad to understand the difference, and me still young. I knew I'd never fall in love with Constance, never get past her small talk, her ditziness. She'd whine if I didn't drop everything to seek her, sometimes paging me four or five times. I kept worrying Dorrit would catch on to us, but with Constance it was the same as with Madi: No one saw what was in front of them. Our obviousness was invisibility to them.

I made jokes about this to Madi. "Whaddya call two girls having sex in the middle of a store?"

She'd raise one eyebrow.

"Playing checkers."

Madi never laughed, but I thought it was funny. Not funny *ha ha* but funny *yeah, right*. Of course, Madi objected to my use of the word "sex" since, according to her, like according to almost everybody, girls didn't have sex together. They had practice, or friendship, or comfort. And lies: If girls couldn't have sex, then Constance and I were just defrosting the freezer. But Constance came scented, like no defroster ever. She had three smells to her: girly, pastry, baby. I usually took home two out of three.

At first Madi believed that I was terribly clumsy and spending all my time in Cleaning Supplies. But as the weeks wore on and I always smelled like the same non-Cooper combination, she started raising her eyebrow when I said I was tired.

One day she snapped when we were driving around. "Maybe if you spent a little less time with your fingers in the laundry detergent, you'd have more energy."

"What does laundry detergent have to do with energy?"

"Nothing. That's exactly my point."

"What are you trying to say? I mean, just say it. I mean, if you're implying something, I mean, just say what you're saying, if you want to say it, Madi. I mean, Madi, Jesus, I have no idea what you're talking about."

"You smell funny."

"I bathe regularly."

"That's not what I mean. Are you cheating on me?"

If we're not having sex, how can I cheat? I felt my breath weave through my ribs, over and under till I could only say "No."

"I am so relieved. Like, I totally thought you were cheating on me with some girl at Low Cost." Madi grabbed my thigh, practically steering us into a ditch. "Let's find someplace to fuck."

How can we fuck if we aren't lovers? It was strange, how Madi's mind worked, but mine had started to work in strange ways too. However did I explain to the part of my mind that's full of logic that I wasn't lying? Lies were everywhere, and not even good ones. Not *I'm lying to protect my aged grandmother who needs a loaf of bread*, but *I'm lying because it's easy and I feel like I can do whatever I want*. Strange, stranger, strangest. I smelled like Constance to Madi and Madi to Constance.

I excused it with a great long list. *I don't fuck Constance. We only kiss. Madi doesn't even believe that we're lovers. Girls don't count, like people say. I'm a good person, so this can't be too terrible. Work is work. Home is home. Nothing I do could be as wrong as wrong.*

I told myself I was just avoiding Madi's anger; still, the lies stopped the wrong way. Constance missed two days, then five. I called, but got no answer. The phone rang and rang, dry cracklings vanishing like echoes on the intercom. On the sixth day Dorrit asked me into his office on a "private matter." My cheekroses froze. I saw Lyle and Marian, dizzy speed freaks, tattling.

"Constance Mulvey won't be coming back."

Selfish Cooper. Thinking only of herself and fucking. Blaming blissed-out Lyle and woozy Marian. Did I care, just then, for Constance—worry what had happened? No, and no. I wasn't worried. Only for myself, mostly missing, already, how wet she got, and quick. Thinking *slick*, thinking *salty*. Thinking *lovely snuggly girly tasty*. And I was thinking *tease her* in the hothouse freezer. And Dorrit was saying Constance was gone.

Pregnant.

This was the private matter. So private everyone was told in a whisper; along with my paycheck I took home deceit. I learned whispers at work and lying at home. Discovering that I could lie and get away with it was like discovering sex. At first lying was just a tool, a way for Madi and me to deny that we were lovers. We lied to others, but mostly ourselves—Madi

129

pretending our touch meant nothing, me pretending love could solve everything. We lied to save ourselves and each other. We lied to survive; there seemed to be no alternative.

Lying about Constance was never pretty. It wasn't revenge on stupid grown-ups or necessary to get by. It was wanting two things and learning to juggle. But the worst part was anger. Anger at Madi.

Madi was love; I'd known this so long. I'd seen through her and liked what she, shining, showed. But her light had its shadow, invisible, not something I saw but something I couldn't. I knew it was there when she asked for Too Much. It was some game, Too Much, only never funny. Too Much meant asking for something she knew I wouldn't want to give, but could. To test. Too Much meant Push, and Misunderstanding, when what I wanted from Madi was Touch and Listening.

What made me crazy was her keeping on. On and on when my hurt showed like stop. I didn't blink red but held steady, my pulse visible through the set of my mouth. And still she'd dissect my language with the bitter tools of suspicion and distance—Cooper, her lover, a frog on a table. Frog, Cooper; Cooper, frog.

Sometimes I questioned why I stayed. But when she sensed me pulling away she'd go stone, forcing me to do the work to pull her back. She turned my emotions all around, making me act the gesture I'd set out to ask for. Things got so tangled. I'd flinch when she hurt me, she'd call my flinch cruelty, I'd flinch, she'd call me harsh. Then I'd be a puddle and not Cooper. Usually it got smoothed over with Madi hugging me, saying she forgave me to my saying sorry.

When all I wanted was for Madi to need me. To want touch, to want talk, to be a voice in my head. Sometimes when we'd pass on the street, I'd hold up both hands *hello*.

Meaning *ten fingers*.

But she never, not once, believed I was faithful. And so I wasn't, and the cycle droned on.

The GirlsClub
Sally Bellerose

I'm depressed. My girlfriend left me. Then I got cancer of the colon, so I had to have my large intestine removed, cut out, the whole thing, gone.

I'm a lesbian alone with no large bowel and an ostomy bag hanging off the front of my abdomen. Who's going to love me now?

OK, so my girlfriend left me four years ago, long before my ostomy, for reasons that have nothing to do with cancer. That doesn't make it any easier. It was hard enough trying to find someone to love me before this damn bag of shit took over my life.

I don't have the kind of family that talks things out, but they're all being nice to me, because I'm depressed. My family never talked to me about having a girlfriend when I had a girlfriend. They never talked to me about her after she left. My family never talked to me about having a colon. Now that I don't have a large intestine, they don't talk to me about the fact that it's gone.

I go to my parents' house for dinner. I'm not quite ready for solid food yet. My mother cooks a special meal for me. No one complains about all the vegetables being mashed or the lasagna being bland. Except my sister Jane. "This is stupid. Why are we all eating mush?" she asks. My brother's wife shushes her. Jane leans over to me and whispers, "If you were still on intravenous feedings, we'd stick needles and tubes in each other's arms and Ma would hook us up to I.V. bags to eat."

After I mope around for a few months, Jane decides that it's time for me to start getting out more often. She says nobody who matters is going to care if I have an ostomy or not. If they do, to hell with them. She says dinner once a week with the parents doesn't count as getting out. My sister Jane is married. She's happy. She thinks I should be happy too. She thinks I should work a little harder at it. She thinks I should avenge myself on the cancer and my ex–large intestines by being happy. I think she should back off and let me wallow in depression until I'm damned good and ready to be happy.

Jane loves to dance. I used to love to dance too. She harasses me until I agree to go dancing with her. I'm afraid she's going to take me to that place with the phones, where she met her first husband. You sit in a booth with a number on it and hope somebody thinks you're cute and gives you a call. I don't ask where we're going. I just want to get it over with. I'm asleep in a chair in my living room, dressed in my best T-shirt and the only jeans I own that fit over the ostomy bag, when she blows the horn for me.

She drives straight to the parking lot of the GirlsClub, the only lesbian bar in town. She jumps out of the car like she's here every Saturday night. "Come on," says happily married heterosexual Jane. "I haven't been here in 20 years."

We were in high school the only other time Jane had been to the GirlsClub. We were on our way home from a basketball game. My father let Jane drive his car. I made the honor roll, and she convinced him that I deserved a ride in a '67 Buick. She claimed that the GirlsClub was the bar where all the dykes hung out. The place was taboo, so Jane wanted to be there. I told her she was full of shit—how would she know where dykes hang out? I should have known better than to challenge her. She drove into the parking lot with her ponytail swinging like she owned the place, same as tonight except now the ponytail is gone. That night we got carded and thrown out at the door, but we got an eyeful. It made a bigger impression on me than it did on Jane.

It's after 10 o'clock and the place is filling up. Women are joking around, checking each other out, making noise. Jane grabs the only table left and makes herself comfortable. She cranes her neck to get a good look around the room, paying no attention to me. I'm happy to be left alone. Finally she gets her fill and asks me what I'm drinking. "Bud," I say. I shouldn't be drinking beer. Yeast. It's going to bubble up and make noise when it empties into my ostomy bag.

She walks up to the bar. I take a good look at her. She's wearing tight acid-wash jeans and a French-cut T-shirt. I'm used to taking good looks at her. She's my sister. I've spent all my life helping her decide which jeans make her ass look good and which color blouse shows off her blue eyes best. Usually when I look at her it's like looking at myself in the mirror. You get so used to yourself that you never really know what you look like. You never really get the big picture. Now I'm looking at her saddled up to the bar of the GirlsClub. What I see wakes me up. Sister Jane is pretty good to look at. It never really hit me before.

I must be seeing what other people see when they first look at her. She's a sexy, plump, ripe-looking white woman. All curve in tight clothes, but that isn't what gets my attention. What amazes me is that you can see her personality in the way she moves, the way she carries herself. I always knew she had guts, but I never knew you could actually tell by looking at her. I'm sure of it. You can see who she is by the way she moves around the bar. It's all over her. She's hot shit and she knows it. I'm sure the other women in the bar see what I see. I keep watching her. She's older, she's smaller, and she's got on tighter clothes, but she looks a lot like me. She looks the way I used to feel.

"Quit staring." She plunks down two Buds.

"You look pretty good," I say.

"Pick out a nice woman who's not your sister to stare at and tell her how good she looks."

"Shut up. Since when are you afraid of a compliment?"

"See anybody you like?" Jane asks loudly, then turns around in her chair and takes in every woman in the place.

"Jesus. Will you shut up?"

"Why? You're in a bar and you wouldn't mind meeting somebody nice. Big deal."

"No. You're in a bar and you'd like me to meet somebody nice."

"What's the point of going through all the trouble of being q-u-e-e-r if you can't even look at women in a bar? Pitiful."

I decide to sulk. She's being an asshole. What would she know about how much trouble it is to be a lesbian? What does she know about how it feels to have an ostomy? She's never depressed. She's too busy poking her nose in other people's lives to get depressed about her own. She keeps looking around. Watching women on the dance floor. She doesn't even notice that I'm sulking.

Suddenly I've got all her attention again. "Let's dance," she says.

"Dance?"

"Dance. See all those women shaking around? They're dancing."

"I'm worried about my ostomy," I lie. I'm not particularly worried about it. I had a light supper, and I emptied it before I left. It hasn't come loose, fallen off, or leaked in months. I don't want to dance. I don't want to dance with Jane.

"You're afraid to dance in a room full of lesbians," she grins.

"You don't know a damn thing about it." I want to hit her. "I've danced here hundreds of times."

"When?" she says. "When was the last time you danced? Even alone in your apartment. Or at Ma's. We used to dance with the kids at Ma's."

She stands up and takes my hand, dancing with me still seated. "Up," she says. She should be struck dead by the look I'm giving her. I'm depressed enough without dancing with my straight sister in a dyke bar. She knows I'm pissed, but she ignores it. She dances around me even though I'm planted in my chair. She won't let go of my hand. It's getting embarrassing. She's making a scene. I get up and move around a little on the dance floor. They're playing some whiny New Age music with no beat. I'm making plans to kill her as soon as this dance is over.

Then a miracle happens. Without so much as a fraction of a second between songs, Aretha Franklin comes booming over the speakers. Aretha R-E-S-P-E-C-T Franklin. No two white girls have ever danced to Aretha Franklin as well, as often, or as devoutly as my sister Jane and me. We danced to Aretha at both of Jane's weddings. Jane brought Aretha and headphones to the hospital after my operation. I can move to R-E-S-P-E-C-T. I wonder if my ostomy bag can move to R-E-S-P-E-C-T.

Jane squeals "R-E-S-P-E-C-T, find out what it means to me" and pulls me to the middle of the floor. She dances and shakes her sisterly ass at me. I try to stay pissed off, but my ass shakes back. It takes no effort at all. I can do it without a girlfriend. I can do it without a colon. I can do it depressed or not. Our asses shake back at us from three mirrored walls. We admire ourselves. I gain new respect for the lighting and mirror arrangement at the GirlsClub. I'm sure that women of good taste are admiring us. We display ourselves generously. We know when to shake our shoulders. We know when to grind our hips. She knows how many steps I'll take to the left. I know how many steps she'll take to the right. We meet in the middle, shake our asses some more, then step back, the same way we've been doing since it 1964.

Jane wipes the sweat off the back of her neck, then onto the back of my jeans, and laughs. I'm sure someone in the room must be admiring me. If I weren't depressed, I'd wish that it was the cute redheaded woman sitting at the table across the room. I walk up to the bar and order a Bud and an orange juice. I try leaning on the bar with my butt sticking out, but the bar cuts into my ostomy bag. I sit on the stool and hear a gurgling noise. My ostomy bag is beginning to fill. My hand slips inside my jeans. I know I'm all right, but I can't help checking. A woman on the stool next to me says, "You OK?"

"Adjusting my ostomy bag," I answer.

I can tell she has no idea what an ostomy is but she isn't asking. She plays with a big silver ring on her baby finger. After a minute she turns to me again. "Wanna dance?" she asks.

"An ostomy bag is an appliance you wear on your abdomen," I say. No response. "It's kind of a heavy-duty plastic bag that catches your waste." She looks at me blankly. "You know, your feces, if your bowel can't do the job." She gives me a weak smile. "I don't have a large intestine," I say. It feels so good to say it out loud that I decide to repeat myself. "My whole large intestine was removed."

"Oh," she says. "You sure can dance. So can your girl-friend."

She's ruining my big moment. I'm coming out to her and she's not taking notice. I don't correct her about the girlfriend. Maybe I will, if she starts paying better attention. But Aretha is churning out "Chain, Chain, Chain...Chain of fools," so I say, "Thanks, I'd love to dance."

Illuminated Crypts
by Dorothy Lane (Sunlight)

Denise is sitting across from me only inches—or centi-meters—away at a sidewalk table of the café Deux Magots. She has put my bouquet of lilies of the valley in a glass of Perrier, where their fragrance floats in the circle of our meet-ing. Around us the morning sparkles with Paris spring, sun warming after weeks of drizzle. Everyone is out. Voices hum, people stroll along the sidewalk absorbing the sweet air, or hurry to Saturday errands, swinging their string bags. How can she leave on a day like this? Without me?

The bitter, dark coffee burns my tongue—is that what makes it hard to speak? Smoke from her Gauloise hovers between us, stinging my nose and veiling the sharpness of her features: her triangular face, high cheekbones, piercing brown eyes. I love to watch her face, animated, vibrant. As I do her hands, sculptor's hands, which mirror each word as though shaping them from clay, adding an emphasis that makes her statements impossible to refute.

"Think about it? Why? I know I must go. It's my life. You know, Julie, I explained that to you before." She closes her eyes and blows a wisp of smoke into the air, then follows it—herself a wisp of smoke—beyond the chestnut trees into that blue sky and soon on to Provence, to her new studio between the hills and the sea.

Already I feel she has gone. I order another coffee and drink half of it before she comes backs, snuffs out her cigarette, and looks at me.

I reach for her hands. Small hands, but strong enough to wield the mallet and chisel and sensitive enough to read the shape of a smile. Those hands have touched me everywhere and made me feel that I'd never been touched before. I can't imagine time stretching on and on, days and nights without her. "If you have to go somewhere, come to New York with me."

"I can't take my work. Without that I don't exist."

She gets up to leave. I stand up too and surround her with my arms, but they don't hold her back. She kisses me and slips between the tables, out to the street and on.

Slumping into the chair, I watch her disappear. A crack rips through me like a clay figure dropped from the tower of the church across the square. Crumbling, I stare at Saint-Germain-des-Prés, patched with the alterations of a thousand years, while the past 12 months slip through my mind and down the street.

This was the sidewalk café where we first met. I was discovering Paris, with no idea that Denise would be my most precious discovery. I was here to study the Romanesque frescoes of central France, but hadn't gotten beyond Paris; I was so enchanted with the city. One day while I was lingering over an aperitif, watching people come and go, two women arrived and sat at a table next to mine. Attractive, as French women are—whatever their age or station—keen, human, vitally alive. Their conversation was too fast for me to follow, although I tried, but it was clear they were having an argument. As they drank their Pernod, the quarrel accelerated. It had the ring of an old theme warmed over.

When the taller woman left, the other began to cry. Was it anger, I wondered, or sadness? She searched for a handkerchief but found none. An American woman, I'd stuffed my bag with little packets of tissues and everything else I thought I might need in a foreign land a decade after the war. I offered her one, and without a word she accepted.

She haunted my thoughts as I wandered the old streets of the city, the markets, galleries, book stalls on the quays along the Seine. Each stone drew me into its history and led me to the next in search of something I couldn't name. Visiting the Rodin Museum one afternoon, I was overwhelmed by the marble skin of *The Kiss,* the anguish of the *Burghers of Calais,* studies of Balzac nude and bathrobed, belly bulging, arrogant. In the chapel I felt a pull and looked up into the balcony, where *The Thinker* sat leaning forward, staring down. At that same moment, I felt someone else watching me and I turned. I hadn't noticed her there before—though I would have recognized her anywhere, I'd seen her in my mind so many times. Indeed I half wondered if I'd been looking for her as I explored the faces of the city. She was wearing a thick red turtleneck under an open, rather tattered mackintosh. Pencil in hand, she was looking at me, drawing.

"I hope you don't mind," she said and returned to her sketchbook. It was hard for me to focus on the sculpture then; between the pieces, I glanced back. The artist had gotten up and turned her attention to a study of *The Kiss,* running her hands over the form like a blind person caressing her beloved. I wished suddenly that it was me.

When I stopped to buy postcards, she came over, tore a sheet from her pad, and handed it to me. "For the paper hand-kerchief," she laughed.

The drawing of me was a good likeness, more than an image, for it contained a passion I didn't know I had. A signature at the bottom read "Denise."

When I thanked her, she shrugged and asked, "You like Rodin?"

"Oh, yes. And being here where he worked, to see his sketches. And the finished pieces. I feel like I know them…from inside." I stumbled along, embarrassment withering my French.

"This is the first time for you?" she said.

"The museum? Yes."

"Paris. La Ville Lumière." Her words floated in the air for a moment, glittering.

I nodded. "It's beautiful, magical. It's like a dream, except it's so real. It's hard to leave."

"Then stay."

We walked along the Rue de Varenne toward the Métro, passed the station, and continued. Passed Invalides and on to the bridge where, as though in agreement, we stopped. A barge was floating languidly down the Seine, laundry flapping from a clothesline on its deck.

"That's how I'd like to travel," I told her. "Through all the rivers of France."

"You will visit the provinces?"

"Yes. If I manage to leave here."

"Let me show you Paris first," Denise said, sparkling. "Corners of the city you might miss by yourself."

We shopped in the crowded stalls of the Foire de Ferraille, sat in the sun at the Arènes de Lutèce while children played on the ancient stones. We listened to Bach and flamenco in a cellar of the École de Guitar and to a chanteuse in a cabaret on the Rue Jacob, stopped to absorb the soft light of the Square Furstemberg. Even places I had been before had more facets when I went there with Denise.

Above all, she showed me what it is to love a woman. We had gone to dinner in a little restaurant in her neighborhood and talked pros and cons of restoring medieval statues to their original painted colors. She invited me to her room to continue the discussion. Behind her, slowly I climbed the seven flights, and with each irreversible step emotions churned inside me, fear warring with my fascination.

Finally, we reached the top. She took out a giant key and inserted it in the door. In those years it seemed as though half of Paris lived in garrets, rooms for maids who no longer existed.

The room was tiny, with a bed, a table, a chair, an armoire, and a window level with the chimney pots of the Marais. I stood there for a long time looking out at the narrow streets below, too scared to face Denise. But with ease she brought me back to the room, handed me a glass of cognac, and resumed our conversation. We talked through centuries, past midnight, past the last subway train. She invited me to stay and I said yes.

She gave me a nightgown and an hour later slipped it off and roamed my surfaces—my thighs, stomach, breasts, each rib, the tendons in my neck, and arteries that pulsed like hammers even when I held my breath. She followed each indentation to its source, each projection to its peak as my tension grew, like waves swelling beyond fullness then erupting to roll toward the shore.

I felt as though she was molding me into a new shape of myself. By her touch, she taught me how to touch. "My first time," I told her, opening my eyes to watch the liquid movements of her face.

"What?" Her voice was a whisper in my ear.

"The first time I've slept with a woman, the first time I haven't run from the thought—back to the safety of my boyfriend."

"Ah, good." She smiled. "It won't be the last."

We made love all night, and by the time morning had reached the chimney pots I was a different woman. We curled into each other's arms and fell asleep.

Denise wasn't the first woman I'd been in love with, though I'd never had the imagination or courage to name it before. But the feeling was the same—the high, the longing to be with her—I'd known that for years. Winona, my high school locker partner. Mrs. Wilson, my 10th grade English teacher. Janet, a friend I'd slept beside at a pajama party. There were a dozen of us on the floor, mattresses spread wall to wall. Janet had put her arm around my waist and drawn me toward her. Every cell in my body quivered, and I didn't sleep that night, even after the last giggle had rippled through the room. But the models and expectations engraved into my mind left no clue for that confusing pleasure. Obediently, I kept following the rules.

A grant to work in France was an invitation to be free, a chance to discover myself as I discovered a world that, however old, was new to me. On the ship going over, I stood on deck and stared at the ocean and the sky—an infinity where anything seemed possible. Every wave washed away my limits and left me naked, open, ready for a new life. Whatever shape it might take.

The weeks that followed were ecstatic, but my time was ticking away and, except for some trips to the Bibleothèque Nationale perusing illuminated manuscripts, I hadn't begun my project. The reproductions in the Musée des Monuments Français urged me on to the real frescoes on real walls. Denise too had returned to the studio and her teacher. Loving a woman was not new for her.

In central France, I traveled the route of medieval pilgrims from town to village, from church to abbey. Auxerre, Tavant, Saint-Savin, their crypts glowed with colors of the land—yellow, mauve, chestnut, green. In the countryside, oxen pulled the plows, women washed clothes in the river, life was still lived much as the art on the cathedrals showed 800 years before. I was immersed in the past all day, but that world of saints and seasons was not my own, and I longed for Denise at the bistros where I ate, in the rooms where I wrote and slept.

Some weekends I went back to Paris. It wasn't far; the distance of spirit was greater, making it hard to return to my solitary work. One morning at breakfast Denise said, "I'm going to the south, there's a sculptor there—"

"Great. I'll go with you. There are wonderful Romanesque cloisters I'd love to visit."

"No." The word cracked in the air. "I have to work."

My silence filled the room, and Denise added gently, "This is important to me."

"I'm not important to you?"

"Yes, of course." She smoothed her hand over my face. "But I can't think when you're there."

I drew her fingers to my lips. One kiss and she pulled back. Something in her had closed, leaving me on the other side. "When are you going?" I asked.

"In May."

"That's only a month away. We'll miss spring. I want to be with you in spring."

"Come back before I leave." She turned toward the window, watched the rain course down the glass.

I got up, grabbed my coat, and ran down the stairs into the street. Now I didn't see the rain watering the chestnut trees, glistening the cobblestones. It felt lifeless, gray, dreary, dissolving my dreams of time with Denise, her laughter and her touch.

On and on I walked through the drizzle, not knowing, not caring where I was. As though from a great distance, I heard horns blowing at me, angry drivers shouting, felt cars rushing past as I blindly crossed the boulevards and streets.

I don't know how long I walked. Eventually the rain, cold against my face, revived me. Looking around, I saw I was on the banks of the Seine, across from the Ile de la Cité, the spire of the cathedral reaching up into the clouds. I crossed the bridge and went in. The arch of the nave soared above me, the stained-glass windows concentrated light, and I felt a moment's peace. I couldn't take Denise with me any more than I could take Notre Dame. But I would see her again in May before both of us left for our separate worlds. May Day, when the fragrance of lilies of the valley fill the streets of Paris. Then later, when the pain had healed, I'd still have the love. And a new life and passion she had opened in me.

Bessie and Sweet Colleen
Ta'Shia Asanti

It was a funky Friday. Funky 'cause it was 94 degrees and sticky as hell. Nevertheless, the energy at Charlie Baker's Jazz and Supper Club was high. Folks clad in their weekend finest were lined up at the ticket booth, laughing and smoking, arms draped around their cackling dates. There were as many Whites in line as there were Blacks. That was a switch. Crackers had driven across town, through the garbage-lined streets and the stinking ghettos of Harlem, to hear Bessie sing tonight. The sight of them standing outside in their starched suits and alligator shoes made Bessie grin as Colleen gently ushered her through the side door into the club. *They're here for me*, she thought proudly, easing by Deano, the backstage security guard.

The band was playing the warm-up set, and they were cooking! The jingle of ice cubes on thin glass played a sweet melody of hefty bar business and fat tips for the girls. The club managers were being extra friendly tonight. Charlie, the owner, stood at the front, offering the male patrons free cigars as they entered the main floor. Benny, the co-owner, walked around lighting the cigarettes of all the single ladies. Chile, the money and the bullshit was flowing from every corner of the lounge. And that ain't no lie.

As Bessie entered her dressing room, she sunk into the customary conversation that accompanied her to every performance. This was the time when she psyched herself up. The time when she silently reaffirmed her talent, attempted to crush her personal doubts. But tonight old Mr. Doubt was playing a cruel trick on her mind as she stood in the mirror applying last-minute touches to her makeup.

Where was she gonna get a voice tonight? Were they tired of listening to the same old songs? Was she really as good as everybody said?

She smoothed down the edges of her hair with a little bergamot pressing oil and adjusted the straps on her dress one last time. The dress's aquamarine chiffon felt good as it rubbed against her hips and thighs. It reminded her of the greatness sleeping inside her soul, the gift God had chosen to give her. Bessie. Lil Black girl from the ghetto. Now a famous singer, known all over the world. She exhaled and walked toward the curtain that led to the main stage. She took one small step onto the floor, then another, then another. She felt the heels of her shoes sink into the heat of the rubbery stage.

Forget that sorry shit. I am Bessie. Jazz singer of all time. I cut a record and sang in the swankiest joints in Harlem when colored folks were barely able to sit at the bar beside Whites.

But the loneliness was like a vacuum. And the doubt was like an ocean driving her to the middle of the sea, where she would surely drown. If only she had some people she could talk to. The people who had been her friends since she was a baby girl riding a tricycle said she had become uppity. Uppity? Shit, didn't they know she'd just spent the last of the emergency food stamps she kept in her desk drawer? Sure, the royalty checks were coming in regular now, but so were the bills. The bills. The goddamned bills never stopped.

She could see the microphone now. She inched across the stage past the drummer, around the saxophonist, by the keyboard player. Sparkling beads of sweat erupted across the top of her forehead. She could smell the audience. Taste their perfume. Hear their whispers. A cloud of smoke encircled the spotlight that awaited her in the center of her pulpit. She felt the hairs on her arm warm and curl. She could see the crowd now, and they her. As she took the microphone in between her brown-sugar fingers, a roar of applause exploded into the thickness. The first note of her opening song, "Tell Me the Truth," was better than perfect; it was utopia swimming on vocal chords.

After 45 minutes of belting blues, sultry ballads, and heel-tapping jazz renditions, Bessie was rewarded with a standing ovation and applause that flowed like a river. The press bombarded the stage with continuous flashes from the large contraptions they held in the palm of their hands. Skeeter, her bass player, escorted her offstage to the safety of the green room, where there was no one waiting to tell her what a good show she'd put on. No one, until Colleen came bellowing through the door.

"Girl, you were badddddd! Did you know there was a promoter in the audience? I was sitting at the table right next to him. He said he wants you to come to Paris and sing at one of his clubs. Bessie! Hey! You hear me, girl? You 'bout to be rich!"

Colleen had a way of making her feel so damn good. When the world had walked out on her, Colleen had been standing right there, like a brick underneath a sagging bed. When everybody was doubting her, telling her not to quit her day job, Colleen said, "Sang, Bessie! God put you here to sang. If he didn't, my name ain't Colleen Loleetha Rumpkins."

Bessie Is Reborn in Harlem

I remember the night we went to the *Jerry Davis Talent Show*. Colleen had heard about this talent competition on Fridays by way of her cousin Jasper. She talked me into going. That's where I met Claude Perkins, the talent scout from Washhouse Records, who later signed me to my first recording contract. The people were out of their seats screaming and throwing money on the stage by the time I got to the second verse of my song. Yup, that was the beginning for me. My first single sold over 500,000 copies. Claude took half my money, but I didn't care. The world knew my name. I bought Mama a house and bought my brother Derrick and his wife, Sue, a new car to cart around them six babies and the bun in the oven they was 'bout to drop any minute. They were so dang-gone happy to get rid of that beat-up jalopy that passed out every other corner that they didn't know what to do.

Donny, the slick-head saxophone player I was in love with, took $2,000 of my money and put it into some investment wheel. Two weeks later the investors skipped town with my dough. Donny showed up to the house with some skinny bimbo in the car talking 'bout, "Bessie, I like my women thin. You too bulky. You sho 'nuff understand, don't you?"

"Niggah, what ain't to understand 'bout you and your buckhead little waynch? Get on off my driveway—and don't ever come back 'round here!" I said, and slammed the door.

I acted tough, but when I closed that door, I swear the tears just flooded my brain. God, why everybody got to leave me? What's wrong with me, Lord? What I do wrong? I'm a mistake—that's what it is. I'm a dang-gone mistake.

Every man I ever loved either hit me, cursed me, or left me. I was a good girl. I cooked, cleaned, made good long love to them like the lovin' never was gon' end. They still left. Every single one of 'em. Finally I just start expecting them to leave.

Donny leaving was the last straw. It almost destroyed me. I couldn't eat or sleep for days. That Sunday morning after his little fiasco, I was sitting there in the kitchen, eyes all swollen, mascara running down the center of my cheeks, when in walked Sweet Colleen. "Bessie, girl, what you crying for?"

"Donny said I'm too fat to love."

Colleen busted out laughing. The insensitive cow! How she gon' laugh when I'm sitting here crying? "What's so funny?"

"Oh, honey, I ain't laughing at you. I'm laughing at that loser's sorry-ass excuse for being a pimp and a user. Ain't nothing wrong with you, girl. Nothing at all. You's a fine healthy sistah with thunder for thighs and a chunk of chocolate for a be-hind. Don't you let that man or no other make you doubt yourself."

"Then why they all leave, Colleen? Every man I try to love leave me."

"That's 'cause you always picks the leaving kind. You pick the hip, slick, cool niggahs. Niggahs with wood swinging 'tween their legs. You need you somebody that love you just as much as you love them."

"Where he at? Huh? Where is the man? I done looked all over the world."

"Maybe you looking for the wrong person. Maybe you shouldn't even look. Let him come, baby. In the meantime, sang! Sang your black ass off! He'll hear you. He'll hear you and come."

I sang like I never sang before the next night at the Copa Lounge. Then I sang again at the Palace in Hollywood, hoping he'd show up, whoever he was. He still didn't come. Colleen was right there clapping and hollering like I was singing brand-new songs every night. I decided to make her my official manager. She was handling everything for me anyway. She had my bathwater ran for me when I got back to the hotel and hot tea waiting on a pretty silver tray to soothe my throat. I felt good when I was with Colleen. Safe. Protected. Loved. Just plain old good.

Bessie Finds Love in Gay Paree

Just like Colleen told me, some rich White folks flew me, the band, and Colleen to Paris so I could sang at some big nightclub. But when I got there, they wouldn't let me sang. The real owners of the club said niggahs couldn't sang in the Bowlegged Club. I cried like a baby. Cried till my eyes were swollen and red. My first trip outside the United States, and racism kept me from showing them crackers what a real jazz singer sounded like.

"Them crackers don't know what they missing, Bessie. It's their loss," Colleen said.

That made me feel a little better. Some Black folks found out what happened and invited us down to their little supper club. Do you know them White folks had the nerve to sneak in there to hear Bessie sang? Yep, Jimmy Ray's was packed wall to wall with people. I gave 'em something to talk about. Yes, I did. I sang so good my picture was in the paper the next day. They even wrote a story about me. But I couldn't read it 'cause it was in French. I kept a copy to show everybody back at home anyway. My picture was right on the front page. After signing autographs for over an hour, I hopped into a long white limousine with Colleen. We were feeling real good—so good that we didn't get back to the hotel until 2 in the morning.

I changed into my robe and slippers. Colleen was in the bathtub relaxing, steam rising off her legs, her feet propped up on the edge of the tub.

"But I still haven't found him, Colleen," I said. "I done sang all around the world and he still ain't come. I stopped looking and he still ain't come. I'm supposed to be a nun. God meant for me to be a nun, Colleen."

"You fool. God ain't meant for your hell-raising ass to be no nun. He'll be here. He'll be here tonight. You watch and see. Why don't you order some of that nasty-ass French food? They need to get a soul food restaurant in Paris so us Negroes don't starve to death. Where's my towel?"

"On the rail behind the shower curtain. I'll see what I can figure out on the menu. It's all in French!" I fell out laughing at that. I stretched out across the bed and laughed until I couldn't laugh no more. It felt good to my soul to laugh. I mean, I laughed from down in my gut, up through my nose and out my ears.

After a dinner of something or other in a bowl and lots of bread and butter, I leaned back on the fluffy pillow on the huge king-size bed in our plush suite at La Rue's Chateau.

Before I knew it I'd dozed off. When I woke up there was somebody standing in front of my bed. I thought I was dreaming, then I heard the traffic outside the window. I tried to focus my eyes, but I'd had a little too much wine and things looked hazy. He was wearing a gray pin-striped suit, white shirt, black bow tie, and a black brim. I rubbed my eyes so I could see him better. Was the man wearing lipstick? Lord, don't tell me my husband gonna be a queer. Now things were coming in better and he was...what...Colleen? "Girl, what the hell you doing all dressed up like a man?"

"I felt bad for you, Bessie. I was tired of hearing you suffer, wanting love, needing love, wanting a man so bad. So here I am. I'll be your man tonight."

"Lord, you sho done lost your mind, Miss Colleen. I—"

I was getting ready to tell her how she'd gone totally out of her mind, but then her lips were on top of mine. Her sweet honeysuckle smell flowing through my nostrils. She caressed my face and gently raked her long cinnamon fingers through my hair. I found myself kissing her back. I felt her hand slide over my breast, down my stomach, and to my crotch. It felt so good. I didn't—or rather, couldn't—stop her. Miss Sweet Colleen climbed on top of me, and she loved me right into the next morning. I canceled my luncheon with the Ladies Circle in Amsterdam. She loved me into the afternoon. I never asked another question about it. I wasn't gay. This wasn't about being gay. This was love. It was a soul finding a home. It was destiny meeting me at the door of life. She was the answer to my prayers, walking and talking. I never went back to the fear and doubt that plagued my past. Sweet Colleen was right: The Lord had brought me a man. And I didn't give a damn if he lived in a woman's body. Thank you, Lord. Thank you for my voice, thank you for the heartbreaks, and most of all, thank you for Sweet Colleen.

Lovingkindness
Kelly Barth

At 12, the age of spiritual accountability, the age at which Jesus debated Talmud with the teachers in the temple, I couldn't have given an account for a great number of things. I lied about having periods so I could be excused from taking showers in gym class. I masturbated and then lost sleep worrying about it. I did not defend my frail best friend, Margaret Sapper, from the daily attacks of a la\rge-breasted bully, Frannie Daniels, because I feared Frannie would turn her abuse on me. I was small and homely and beset with worry. There was no mistaking the disparity between Jesus and me, no risk I'd become delusional.

Like Jesus, however, I wanted to go to church as often as possible, especially on Wednesdays. Wednesdays meant youth group meetings and Mary Ellen Adams, the pastor's daughter. She inspired in me the zeal and abandon of Saint John, of Saint Peter even. I would have dropped everything to follow her.

I loved her the first time I met her, at age nine, even though my parents had suggested the two of us play Barbies while they and her father discussed the possibility of his becoming our pastor. I played Barbies with no one but my best friend, Margaret, who, like me, involved her Barbie—and the Sunshine Family, '70s hippie Barbie rip-offs—in tense hostage situations. I loved Mary Ellen even though her Barbie played Mommy. Her dialogue was flat, her plot dismal. From my hiding place behind the Barbie 747, I peered at Mary Ellen

151

bouncing Barbie up and down and asking Ken what he wanted for dinner, telling him how nice he looked. I waited to be filled with the disgust that never manifested.

So desperately did I want to go to Mary Ellen (that's what church had become to me) that one Wednesday night, when our sky-blue Ford XL was in the shop and my mother had no way to take me to youth group, I had a textbook pubescent event. I yelled. I rolled across my bed into my bedroom wall, which was wallpapered with tiny clowns.

Wearing nothing but her panties and bra, my mother took breaks from fixing potato-hamburger patties to stand in my bedroom door and monitor my condition. She herself was going through, as I heard her tell people on the phone, "the change." Every so often she would redden and lift her shirt to show us the sweat running down her stomach. "I think we can turn this heat down just a little bit," she'd say to the rest of us bundled in sweaters. Familiarity with the sudden onslaught of her own mood swings must have given her enough empathy to keep from harming me.

She stood at my bedroom door, drying her hands on a dishtowel. "Do you see how silly this is? Do you see a car in the driveway?"

"I'm going," I said. "I'll walk if I have to." I swung my legs over the side of the bed and put my shoes on. That day I had scored a touchdown for the wrong team in flag football, and in retaliation Frannie Daniels tried to wring my hand off my arm. In junior high school, I and others like me were deformed chickens that the other birds eventually peck to death. At youth group, everything changed. People, especially Mary Ellen, liked me because I could make them laugh.

"You're not walking," my mother said. "There are no sidewalks on Chrysler. Someone will hit you. It's ten miles away."

I'd had no intention of walking to church. But I had a way with my mother. For instance, she had believed me even when

I told her my first grade teacher's father loaned her his farm animals—horses, cows, pigs—to bring to our class. At a parent-teacher conference my mother told my teacher to thank her father for his generosity. My teacher's father sold insurance.

"I'm certainly not walking with you," my mother said and left the doorway. The elastic had given out on one leg of her underwear, and this made me feel sorry for her for a minute.

I resumed my tirade.

"I like the Bible studies," I said, pulling out the big guns.

"The patties are sticking," my mother said.

I threw myself against the wall again, imagining the youth group in the church kitchen without me. First, we cooked dinner together under the supervision of Sharon Taylor, a short, heavy woman with a small mustache who worked part-time as youth minister to defray the costs of divinity school. I imagined them making spaghetti and meatballs, and Mary Ellen dipping her fingers in the jar of sauce, smearing it across someone else's cheek instead of mine.

The telephone rang.

"Your sister Kathy's getting her hair cut over by the church. She heard you, all the way in here, and asked if you wanted a ride. After all that, I don't know if I should let you go."

Mary Ellen missed youth group that night. She had cheerleading tryouts.

On Wednesday youth group meetings during Lent, those of us who would be 12 by Easter met in the Colonial Room—a long, carpeted room filled with Early American furniture and heavy green drapes—for confirmation commissioning class. By the end of the eight-week course, we would, ideally, become Christians. We would take our First Communion at the Maundy Thursday service, to commemorate Jesus's last supper with his disciples.

After our communal supper on the first Wednesday of

Lent, our confirmation commissioning class teachers, Sharon Taylor and Pastor Adams, Mary Ellen's father, handed out workbooks called "Serendipity." The Presbyterians didn't like to scare people with too much unadulterated talk of Jesus. Instead, the workbooks had lots of innocuous cartoons and blank lines sprinkled throughout, designed for penciling in answers to questions such as "Martin Luther wrote the _____ and nailed them to the door of the _____."

A question on the first page read, "In your own words describe what it means to be a Presbyterian." I had only a rudimentary understanding of the faith, handed down to me from my parents. From a cup Sharon passed around, I took a pencil badly in need of sharpening and wrote, "It means trying to be a good person. You are sprinkled instead of dunked. *Presbyterian* is hard to spell; maybe Presbyterians are smart. Our cross looks funny. It doesn't really look like a cross. We are not Catholics. We are not Baptists." Then I ran out of lines.

To foster group cohesion, "Serendipity" also included sections called "rap sessions." Rap sessions went out of the vernacular in the 1960s, but being a frugal church, Trinity Presbyterian had purchased the workbooks in large quantities at a discount in the 1960s. They sat in a box in a sunless room in the basement, and so, aside from a slight smell of mold, each fresh workbook gave the illusion of being current. One rap session question said, "If the group were a car, I would be its (a) gas tank, (b) engine, (c) battery, (d) wheels, (e) windshield wipers, (f) exhaust pipe, or (g) spark plug." I knew very little about cars, so I just picked the battery because I knew that it had no moving parts, was square, and had to be recharged occasionally.

Mary Ellen pointed at me and said, "I think this one's a spark plug. She makes us all crack up all of the sudden, like we'd stuck our finger in a light socket." Mary Ellen had chipping red fingernail polish, dark eyes, and a smell of clean clothes, Bonnie Bell lip gloss, and tobacco, from a cigarette falling apart in the bottom of her suede purse.

I know how Mary Ellen smelled, and I know how her skin felt because once after confirmation commissioning class she and I were the last two people left roaming the halls of the dark church playing Sardines, the youth group version of hide-and-seek. The rules said that the seekers each crawled into the hiding place with the hider until only those straggling seekers who had not yet found the group must wander the tile hallways alone with only the occasional light through the church's stern 16-paned windows to guide them. You could not end Sardines by calling out, "I quit." You had to keep looking until you found everyone waiting somewhere in the dark for you.

Mary Ellen and I found each other by the half-door to the crawl space in the wall of the fellowship hall where they stored folding tables between church suppers—a favorite hiding place because it could hold so many people. She touched my sleeve, and I swatted at her hand in the dark, like you would a june bug trying to hang on.

"Shit! Sorry. Oh, my God," she said. "Who is this?"

"Kelly," I said. I did not need to ask her. I had her voice memorized.

"Thank God it's you."

"Have you seen anybody else?"

"Not for a long time," she said, whimpering a little.

"Shhh," I said, taking charge. We stood still, Mary Ellen squeezing my arm. "That's it. They've all found each other," she said.

Another rule said you couldn't pair off to search. It unfairly minimized the fear and shock upon hearing the collective rustle of clothing rising to greet you in the dark.

"I'm not letting go of your arm," Mary Ellen said. "Rule or no rule."

She pulled me into the crawl space. "Are we sure they aren't in here?"

We both felt into the darkness, touching spider webs, exposed cement blocks, the bowels of the church. On what felt like a tabletop, I touched what I hoped was jelly. Aside from each other's, we felt no clothing or skin. "They aren't here," she said. She sat and pulled me down next to her. She put her fingers between mine.

"Whatever happens, don't let go of me," she said.

"I won't."

For different reasons, neither of us wanted to start seeking again.

"I refuse to keep looking," Mary Ellen said. "I've had a hard day. When we find them, I'll have a heart attack. You won't leave me, will you?"

"I wouldn't leave you," I said, and then added, "I'm not going out there alone," so she wouldn't know that I longed to stay there in the crawl space with her. We hid like that for what seemed like half an hour. For a while, she nervously rubbed her thumb back and forth over my hand. I tried to count the number of times just to keep myself from touching her with my own thumb. If I had touched her, Mary Ellen would have known I hadn't done so out of fear.

When Mary Ellen felt good and ready, we found the others, in the chancel area, under the massive church organ. One of the boys lay camouflaged across its pedals in a black-and-white rugby shirt. Before someone turned on the lights, Mary Ellen squeezed my hand and then turned it loose.

In confirmation commissioning class, we learned creeds: the Apostles Creed, the Nicene Creed. We memorized and recited them as proof that we understood what it meant to eat the flesh and drink the blood of the Lord at Maundy Thursday service. I believed in God the Father Almighty, maker of heaven and earth and in Jesus Christ His only Son our Lord, who was conceived by the Holy Ghost, born of the Virgin Mary, suffered under Pontius Pilate, was crucified, dead, and buried; He descended into Hell; on the third day he rose again from the dead; He ascended into heaven, and sitteth on the right hand of God the Father Almighty. From thence he shall come to judge the quick and the dead. I believe in the Holy Ghost, the Holy Catholic church, the communion of saints, the forgiveness of sins, the resurrection of the body, and the life everlasting. Amen. Very God from Very God, begotten not made, the pink plastic baby wrapped in felt in our manger scene, a tiny tiny man who lived everywhere, in pockets, and canyons, in lemonade, in the tip of a conch shell, between Mary Ellen's teeth. I recited these creeds, as familiar and as yet without meaning as the Pledge of Allegiance, but wearing their own groove into my brain after having heard them every Sunday for 12 years. I learned and promptly forgot many things about John Knox, the founder of the Presbyterian church. I looked at maps of the Holy Land pulled like window shades from a metal scroll on the wall of the Colonial Room and followed dotted lines representing Jesus's movements on earth.

At the end of the eight weeks I received a certificate from the Presbyterian Church USA with my name on it, saying I was a Christian. Sharon Taylor gave me a mustard seed trapped in a little ball of blown glass fastened to a necklace. The boys got tie clips. If I had faith even as small as a mustard seed, I could move mountains, Sharon said Jesus said. I imagined breaking my necklace like I was tempted to break the glass panel over the fire alarm outside my algebra class when I needed Jesus in a big fat hurry. I didn't wear the necklace but kept it snapped in my coin purse, where I also kept a few hairs I gleaned from the rug after my dog died of cancer. In algebra class I took the mustard seed and the hairs out and hoped they would do something, anything to take me away from junior high.

Sometimes, if I concentrated, I could conjure up a vision of Jesus, a calm, thin, ineffectual vision. Sensing my confusion about things, my mother took me to Zondervan Music and Gift, where I bought a pocket mirror with the perfect picture of white Jesus in striped clothes, knocking on a heavy wooden door of a stone house with a porch light. "Behold I stand at the door and knock. If anyone hear my voice and answer, I will enter in and sup with him, and he with me." I kept the mirror in the bottom of my purse. When things got bad, I felt around in my purse until I found Jesus and pulled him out and held him tight in my palm where no one else could see. I told Jesus I had faith that he could take me away from the school bus, the smell of stale vomit, hot vinyl, and teenage boys. I had faith that my parents would have money to buy me pants at the middle of the school year to replace the ones I had grown out of at the beginning. Over time, though, I became annoyed by Jesus's persistent silence.

"I asked a boy who goes to your school, Pat Pernice, if he knew you. He said your name sounded familiar, but he couldn't remember you," Mary Ellen said the Wednesday before Easter. She went to a different school than I did. "I met him at a party."

"I know who he is," I said. "We're not friends or anything."

Pat Pernice rode my school bus and every day he blocked the aisle and called Margaret and me "faggots." "He thinks we're girlfriends or something," Margaret said. "Why would he think that?" Every day, a good girl with Jesus in my purse, I waited there until Pat Pernice chose to let me pass. "It is not right to hate," my mother always said. For an hour or so every day after school, I hated myself instead.

"You know why you and Pat aren't friends?" Mary Ellen

said. "You don't smoke and that's why you don't know people who smoke. He's a nice boy."

"It wouldn't help if I smoked," I said. I was too afraid to smoke. According to the scriptures that describe him eating and drinking with tax collectors and sinners, if he'd come in the 1980s Jesus would have hung out with people who did.

"No," she said. "That's right. You couldn't smoke. You're one of those people who's going to live a long time. I don't know anyone else like you."

She was probably right, I thought. I would live a long time, but whatever for?

"Lissa has decided she doesn't feel comfortable graduating from confirmation commissioning class," Sharon Taylor said at the last meeting before Maundy Thursday communion. Lissa didn't want to be rushed into becoming a Christian. None of us said anything. I suddenly doubted everything anyone had ever told me about Jesus. What if Lissa knew better? What if it was all an elaborate hoax? What if he was just a picture on a pocket mirror?

"Does anyone want to ask any questions about Lissa's decision?" Sharon said. I felt sorry for her and Pastor Adams. They had lost a recruit. Mrs. Baker, Lissa's mother, had jet-black hair cut like Marlo Thomas's and had divorced her husband and gone back to college. My mother didn't like Mrs. Baker and her highfalutin' ways.

"Did she decide on her own?" I finally said.

"Yes, Lissa came to us on her own. It was a difficult thing for her to do."

"Well, how do we all know we're ready?" Mary Ellen asked.

Pastor Adams and Sharon had no ready-made answer, so they left the remaining six of us in the Colonial Room to rap about it without adults present.

It would never have occurred to me that I had the option of refusing the Lord's supper, let alone the creeds, maps, group cohesion exercises, John Knox, or church governance. For crying out loud, I had already signed a piece of paper saying I believed in Jesus.

After a while, Sharon and Pastor Adams came back into the room.

I tried to believe in Jesus, as much as you can believe in a person you hope is really there.

"Any questions?" Sharon said. "No?"

All six of us came to church early on Maundy Thursday, on the night of Jesus's betrayal, to walk through our part of the evening.

"All right," Pastor Adams said. "After 'Let Us Break Bread Together on Our Knees,' I will come down like this and offer you bread, and you'll take one of the cubes. You hold it until you hear me say, 'Take, eat, this is my body broken for you. Do this in remembrance of me.' Then you can eat your cube, and everyone else will too." He stopped and smiled.

"How do you break bread on your knees?" I asked. Despite the solemnity of the moment, I felt I couldn't live without the laugh I knew I would get from Mary Ellen.

Other more substantive questions hadn't yet formed in my brain. Take a cube of the creator of the universe? Sure. I could do that, whether Lissa could or not. So could the rest of my fellow confirmands. I had never been allowed to before, and that, if no other reason, made me look the slightest bit forward to communion. We all knew the drill. During moments of intense boredom, all of us had inevitably stumbled across the extra communion service leaflet glued to the inside back cover of our hymnals by the Women's Circle. Leader's words in red, People's words in black. I had begged for even a crumb of my mother's piece of the Lord's body, but she never once relented. Most of what I knew about the Lord's supper was that for the past 12 years I hadn't been invited, but had been made to sit among the those who had, watching them chew and swallow.

"Now you'll stay seated, and I'll hand the person on the end the tray of cups," Pastor Adams said.

I winced. I feared the tray of cups more than the idea that Jesus wasn't real. Made of solid brass and filled with four tiers of tiny glass cups filled with grape juice, the tray weighed about 50 pounds. Once Mrs. Andrews, the palsied church librarian, dropped the tray. It made a sound I'll never forget. I remember the puddle of juice and broken glass under Mrs. Andrews's chair, and the long purple stains down her legs. I remember the collective gasp and how, aside from the lady with blue wavy hair in the chair next to Mrs. Andrews attempting to put shards of the little cups back in the holes in the brass, everyone acted as if nothing had happened.

"Is is really blood?" Mary Ellen said and then grabbed my thigh, snickering. As always, I had to try so hard to pretend I didn't like it more than I should.

Pastor Adams then offered Mary Ellen a serious explanation of transubstantiation, a belief that at a certain point during the mass, the wine—or, in our case, juice—did indeed become the blood of Christ.

Throughout the evening, Lissa Baker's refusal of Christianity hung in the air above us. Did anyone know Jesus well enough for all of this? Nevertheless, I and the six remaining confirmands each took our first sip of the Lord. I had expected to feel something.

Easter Sunday morning, I hunted for foil-covered chocolate eggs my parents had hidden in the ruffles of lamp shades, under couch cushions, inside my father's Romeo slippers. My mother said that the Bakers thought too much anyway when I brought up Lissa that sunny afternoon. "Don't you worry about her."

After Easter services—He is risen; He is risen indeed—we ate ham with cherries. That Sunday night, with the first smell of wind and dirt and spring blowing through the window screens, I watched Charlton Heston part the Red Sea, and that was enough for a 12-year-old to believe in one day.

Sometime later that year I stepped out of the shower onto an orange shag bath rug and said to the ceramic cherubs hanging on the wall with plastic flowers coming out of their heads that I was a lesbian. People had started to notice. A prayer grew in my head that Jesus might make me stop being a lesbian. In fact, I told him I had the faith that He could make me act like everyone else.

I read *Invisible Man* and came to believe that if you want to hide badly enough, you can always find a safe enough place.

So well did I hide my real self that by the time I turned 14, Kurt Dreiling, an older boy in the youth group, mistook me for a girl who liked boys. I saw in him an opportunity to appear normal for a short time. Nearly everyone in the youth group had at some time or another paired off in the few weeks before the annual mission work trip. Potential couples watched each other during sermons like they would look at a pair of loafers through a shop window, imagining how they might look in them.

Because I loved Mary Ellen only, I never concerned myself with pre–work trip courtship displays. All I cared about was that she didn't like church boys and always left her current boyfriend at home, carrying a postage-stamp-size picture of him in a plastic sleeve of her wallet. Without attachments, she remained at my complete disposal. We rode together, ate together, slept in adjoining bunks.

The week before the work trip, while Kurt, Sharon Taylor, Mary Ellen, and I stood on the church steps in the darkness after youth group meeting, Kurt's fingers, with their bitten-off nails, pushed their way into my balled-up hand. Reluctantly, I opened my fist. He never said a word to me.

That year we went to the Presbyterian camp at Flathead Lake, Mont., to clean up ash from an eruption of Mount Saint Helens. On our way there, at a truck stop in Scott's Bluff, Neb., Kurt decided to leave me and sit at the back of the bus, next to Jodie Hamilton, who he'd found out had broken up with her boyfriend before she left. He never returned to the seat I saved for him. At about 2 in the morning, somewhere in the west, Mary Ellen wobbled to the empty seat beside me, the light from a passing truck revealing the look of concern on her face.

"Are you all right?" she said.

She sat with me all the rest of that night, past dark hills and radio towers, until we saw the first light in the sky in Wyoming. She did not sleep, but she asked permission to lay her pillow on my shoulder. She leaned against me, telling me why Kurt might have left me for Jodie Hamilton. It took concerted effort to pretend to mourn. I looked out the window, hoping she could not see my look of contentment reflected in the glass.

"He never liked me anyway," I said, taking advantage of the situation. Mary Ellen worried about my self-esteem, a concept discussed in our "Serendipity" workbooks.

"I like you," she said, milking my upper arm like an udder. "If I was a boy I'd like you, or if you were a boy—you know what I mean."

The bus broke down somewhere in Wyoming. The Presbyterian church that had planned to host us only one night graciously let us sleep on the floors of their Sunday school classrooms for an indeterminate amount of time. While driving the only backup vehicle into Laramie to pick up a mechanic, our bus driver pulled to the side of the road and had an aneurysm. Mary Ellen's mother, Joan, who had ridden with him, called from the hospital to tell us of their helicopter ride.

Every afternoon, about 3 o'clock, an older boy, Kevin, took a baggie of pot from inside one of his tube socks. Everyone, including Mary Ellen, left to smoke it—everyone, that is, except a quiet boy named Paul, a fat girl named Debbie Jones, and me. The only thing the three of us had in common was that we hadn't been invited.

An Eagle Scout, Paul sketched plants in a spiral notebook. I followed him through the dirt and sagebrush, squatting when he squatted. Debbie sat on the ground next to us. She loved Jesus with a fervor unknown to any other youth. She carried a white leather King James Bible with a zipper, given to her by her father, who had been so fed up with the Presbyterian hesitancy to go full out for Jesus he'd become a Baptist. She also wore a pin with a picture of a goose beneath the words HONK IF YOU LOVE JESUS. No one had the heart to point out to her that her mother was having a poorly concealed affair with another of the adult sponsors.

Over our heads, the blue sky stretched taut as the lid of a jar.

"Where is everybody?" Debbie said on the third day, standing to her feet. Neither of us answered her. She had a lima bean–shaped patch of dirt pressed into her shorts. I hated her for not being Mary Ellen. Eventually, a line of the smokers reappeared on the crest of a foothill. For a few hours after smoking, Mary Ellen either took a nap or said things that didn't make any sense. "I'm sorry," she said every day. "You wouldn't want to come anyway. It isn't fun." She did not permit me to follow her.

Our fourth night of sleeping on the floor of the K–3 classroom, I walked in my sleep. Mary Ellen found me digging in a bucket of crayons, searching for a doorknob. When I took a sip of the water she brought me, I awoke to an entire room of youth group girls, blinking, irritated.

"How far do you think you'd have gone if I hadn't found you?" Mary Ellen whispered before we fell asleep.

"Not far enough," I said.

A mechanic fixed the bus, and we made it to Flathead Lake Presbyterian Camp. The first day after cleaning volcanic ash, I stepped on a field mouse on my way out of the mess hall, where I spent my break times reading *The Hobbit* while Mary Ellen smoked pot in the pine trees. I saw the mouse fly off the sole of one of my huge new hiking boots and lie on its side gasping. I cupped it in my hands until one of the adults took it away from me and killed it behind a cabin.

After dinner I went to my bunk and wrote on a piece of paper: "I want to go someplace else." I folded up this prayer and carried it in my coat pocket.

A few nights before we went home, I tried to remember what my mother always said: "You have to make yourself part of the group. Get back on that horse." During devotions, we sang "Pass It On."

"It only takes a spark / To get a fire going / And soon all those around / Will warm up to its glowing / That's how it is with God's love / Once you experience it / You want to sing / It's fresh like spring / You want to pass it on."

By the end of the song I had determined to pass it on, whatever it was, so I volunteered to play the ugly person in a group initiation game called "The Ugliest Person in the World." I shouldn't have done this. By participating I hoped to rise in the youth group's social strata and gain further access to Mary Ellen's presence. Those in the know about initiation games belonged to an exclusive group of only the most fearless, robust teenagers.

"OK," Joan said, "you remember what you're supposed to do?"

"Yes," I said. I'd watched The Ugliest Person in the World

before. I laughed and took several mincing steps into the kitchen, where Joan wrapped me in a green army blanket and led me back into the center of the mess hall.

"OK," she whispered, "have fun."

"Under this blanket," Joan said in a sideshow voice, "is the ugliest person in the world. Is anyone here brave enough to look?"

I lay on the floor chuckling quietly to myself. The two volunteers who knew the score each lifted the corner of the blanket, looked at me, screamed, and fell down on the floor near me, as if dead.

"Anyone else?" Joan said.

An inkling of worry crept into my brain. I was supposed to do something when the third person, one who did not know the joke, lifted the blanket. But what was it? Maybe I'd never known at all.

It was really very simple. I was supposed to have screamed when the uninitiated person lifted the blanket, making them even uglier than me, the ugliest person in the world.

"I am ugly-and stupid," I thought, lying there. I imagined I looked like a turd someone had laid a blanket over. I considered creeping away, blanket and all, into the adjoining kitchen.

Joan handpicked Mr. Bradish as someone who enjoyed being laughed at. He lifted the blanket and peeked under.

I smiled and waved at him. He lifted it again, waiting for the punch line he knew must be coming.

I heard everyone laugh, then I felt Joan's foot slide under the blanket and hunt for me. "Oh my, someone survived," she said and whispered something down to me that I couldn't quite hear.

"Ugly person," Joan said, "I'm sending Mrs. Bradish over to look at you." She said this loud and slow just in case I had missed the reminder that neither of the Bradishes knew the score. Mrs. Bradish also looked at me and lived to tell about it.

"Who is it?" I heard people whispering to each other and giggling.

Finally, I heard the floorboards squeaking near me and Mary Ellen's whisper, "You're supposed to scream," she said. "I'll take care of it. Scream when I look at you."

"Not my only daughter, Mary Ellen. Are you going to look? Brave girl, brave, brave girl."

Afterward, I spent the closing hymn, "For Those Tears I Died," in the bathroom looking at myself in the cracked mirror over the toilet saying "idiot." When I did not follow everyone to the cabins Mary Ellen came in after me. Instead of moving away from the spreading pool of embarrassment around me, she stepped right into it, associating with it, with me. She sat on my bunk and asked me to tell her stories about my Uncle Sam. They made her laugh. She sat on my bunk until she thought I had fallen asleep.

While the youth group was away cleaning volcanic ash, the church voted to remove Pastor Adams from his position. At general assembly he had voted in favor of allowing gays and lesbians to become full, voting members of the church.

As soon as Joan and Mary Ellen returned from the work trip, the family packed all their things into boxes and moved out of the manse. I never saw Mary Ellen again. My mother said she didn't know where to take me to find her. When I asked why they had left, my parents told me the half-truth that Pastor Adams had had to leave because no one wanted to give money to the church anymore. Had I known the whole story, I would have known that I, not Lissa Baker, should have dropped out of confirmation commissioning class. I would have believed that I had no right to eat the flesh of the Lord or to become a Presbyterian. I might also have thought, however,

Kelly Barth

that maybe Pastor Adams knew something about gays and lesbians and God that other people did not. Surely, though, I
would have thought that I had no right to love Mary Ellen,
through whom, though I was not yet aware of it, elusive Jesus
Himself had poured out His lovingkindness to me.

Invisible
Mary Sharratt

We were school friends, going on 16, always in each other's company—arm in arm and laughing down the street, finishing each other's sentences. When her parents began to fear we were too close, she used her magic to make me invisible.

So I could be with her always.

So no one could separate us.

We had the wildest escapades, my lover and I. Imagine what it would be like to have an invisible girlfriend pleasuring you during algebra class or in the dentist's waiting room or on a crowded streetcar. No one looking at her would be the wiser. They would see a modestly dressed girl from a good family (her father was an orthodontist) with a smooth auburn ponytail, her face flushed, her lips parted as if she were lost in some fantastical daydream. I used to tell her she looked like Saint Theresa of Avila in the midst of a vision.

My lover and I lived in an anonymous city in Central Europe where the narrow streets were lined with smog-stained stucco buildings painted in dull pastels. Behind each boxy building was a labyrinth of alleys and inner courtyards full of overflowing recycling containers and sighing pigeons. The only green places were prim little parks where it was forbidden to sit on the grass. But I could sit wherever I wanted. The invisible have that advantage.

Being invisible, it hardly mattered that I was a runaway with no money. I could dress in silk curtains pilfered from the State Opera House. I could walk naked. I could sleep with my lover in her virginal twin bed or sneak myself into the executive suite of the Imperial Hotel. When my stomach was empty, I wandered from shop to shop, helping myself to quail eggs and chocolate-covered ginger.

I could also fly. It was simple. I'd leap out of a tenth-floor window and instead of plummeting to my death I would soar. I had to move my arms and legs in a slow, rhythmic breaststroke—swimming through air. My lover was jealous that she couldn't fly with me. Those who are visible are chained to the earth by Newton's cruel laws. Maybe her jealousy made her grow tired of me.

"You bore me," she said as I described the aerial view of our city, how I could see into every hidden courtyard. *"You are not real."*

She wanted a lover she could show off when she dressed in her evening gown of claret velvet and wore her mother's choker of heirloom pearls. She wanted a lover whose arms she could dance in all night during Carnival, swaying under chandeliers with crystal teardrops fragmenting the light into a thousand rainbows. I was something childish she had invented, something she was on the brink of outgrowing.

To celebrate her 18th birthday, her parents held a fete in their spacious apartment on the ninth floor of a mustard-colored stucco building. There was beluga caviar and Dom Perignon. Tuxedoed manservants bore trays of Godiva chocolates. My lover wore a white silk minidress reminiscent of an ancient Greek tunic. Her legs were bare, but her feet were shod in silver pumps. "You look like Artemis," I murmured, but she ignored me and wandered away. It's not difficult to ignore someone who is invisible.

My sense of betrayal was so palpable that it seemed like a living entity. My aura flashed around me in fire-engine red and bruised purple. I ran through the room clutching myself and weeping until I was heaving and choking. And then I was surrounded by eyes: a room full of piercing, unbelieving eyes. My emotion had broken through the spell of my invisibility. No longer a phantom, no longer a shade—I was just a gawky 17-year-old girl in a maroon sweatshirt and ripped-up jeans. In the sea of cold staring faces, the coldest one was hers.

Staggering out of the room, I parted the overdressed assembly, went to one of the tuxedoed caterers, and began stuffing my mouth with the Godiva chocolates he held out on his silver tray. "Take some home with you," he whispered. "These assholes can afford it." So I filled the pockets of my jeans with nougat pralines that would melt there, staining the denim forever, leaking through to my pelvis.

I headed to the balcony. The air was filled with the kind of golden evening light they photograph our city in for the tourist brochures. Sucking on dark chocolate, I straddled the balcony's cement railing. All the while I thought how absurd it was that such a pretentious apartment would have such a hideous balcony of bare concrete, no different from those of the slapdash social-welfare apartments they had put up right after the war when they were rebuilding our city from the ruins. *"Ruins,"* I spat, balancing on that cement edge, teetering on the brink.

I thought I might have caught her eye with my flamboyant show. The trouble was, no longer invisible, I caught everyone's eye. They all came rushing out of the French doors to drag me from my perch and restrain me—for my own good, of course. But I danced back and forth on the concrete wall, evading their grasping hands and scanning their glaring faces for her face. By all logic she must be moved to feel something. She must be afraid for me. What if my ability to fly had disappeared along with my invisibility? What if I were now just as mortal and breakable as everyone else? I waited for her to come forward, so I could see worry or tenderness or apology on her face. Finally, I spotted her on the far edge of the crowd. Our eyes locked, but hers were contemptuous and hard. She was giving me the kind of look you'd give a pathetically bad actress.

And so I jumped.

Don't get me wrong. I'm no Ophelia, no Sylvia Plath. I'm not going to destroy myself for love or poetry or anything else. My will, you see, was too strong to let me fall. Maybe I fell a few meters, but then I stretched my arms like a falcon stretching her wings and glided through the evening sky, as golden as Tokay.

My lover clung to the edge of the balcony and stared through the empty air to the street below, searching for my body, but I had escaped her vision. I was invisible again, completely invisible, even to her. She had lost me forever. I was the scar she would carry with her through her string of broken marriages, her memory of me like a ghost following her always. But I was flying. I was soaring, rising in circles, in spirals, in that honeyed evening sky, until her apartment building shrank to the size of a marble and disappeared.

My Dead Aunt's Vodka
Lori Horvitz

When I watched relatives pick through Aunt Thelma's belongings—her clothes, camera equipment, dishes, sculptures from all over the world—I couldn't help thinking about the story I'd just seen on the local news. Sanitation workers had set off sticks of dynamite to scare seagulls away from the garbage dump, but after the smoke cleared they'd return. One official compared the birds to kids at the mall. "Just gotta keep movin' them along," he said. I personally took offense at that analogy—I hang out there plenty with my friend Mindy; we usually sit in the food court and look at people and make up stories about them. No harm in that, right? Nonetheless, if I had a stick of dynamite, I might have thrown it right smack in the middle of Aunt Thelma's living room.

Overlooking the Long Island Expressway and the Watchtower building in Queens, Aunt Thelma's apartment was perfect for watching cars, trucks, and trains zoom by. And that's what I tried to do. Then I noticed my mother clutching a balalaika, an iron trivet, and a bottle of vodka. She didn't even drink, but my Aunt Harriet said that particular bottle was worth a lot of money—you could only get it in Russia. I imagined Aunt Thelma carrying the bottle through the customs gate at Kennedy Airport and, when she got home, carefully storing it alongside her vintage wine, saving it for a special occasion.

Unfortunately, she brought that bottle halfway around the world for nothing. Aunt Thelma died of an eye disease that ate at her brain and turned her into a vegetable. It all happened so quickly I didn't even get a chance to say good-bye, and the next thing I knew, I was sitting in her apartment watching relatives grab her stuff like people who loot supermarkets during blackouts.

The last time I saw her, Aunt Thelma was singing, "Those were the days, my friend, I thought they'd never end..." But they did.

Amid the ransacking, I heard murmurs of her free spirit, her travels, her beauty. "What a pity. Hundreds of men proposed to her, but she never found the right one," my grandmother said.

Even while clutching her ivory chess set from Mozambique, my father wasn't as kindhearted: "No one was good enough, and look what happened."

That year, for my 15th birthday, my mother gave me Aunt Thelma's camera. At first I didn't want it; why would I want my dead aunt's camera? What if I caught that terrible eye disease when I pressed my eye against the camera's viewfinder? But I gave in. She'd probably want me to have it, and it sure beat the crappy Instamatic I'd been using. Along with the camera, I got a bag full of Aunt Thelma's slides. Slides of palm trees and foreign billboards and exotic-looking people in straw hats clinking glasses together. One day, I thought, I'm going to travel the world and drink expensive vodka and clink cups with strangers. And take pictures of it all.

But in the meantime I took pictures of my poodle, Jennifer. During one session I shot a whole roll of her chewing up a Barbie doll. In the last photo, Barbie's decapitated, mostly bald head lay next to a sleeping black poodle. I brought the series into my photography class, thinking I had produced a profound piece about women and oppression and all, but my teacher, Miss Sweeney, who'd praised the sunset series I'd taken before, sent me to the school counselor to talk about "anger management."

I didn't think I was angry, but when the counselor started to get on my case about my subject choice, I just shook my knees and refused to speak. Finally, I spewed off the statistics I'd read about anorexia and bulimia. "Look what happened to Karen Carpenter!" I said. But the counselor wouldn't go for that. She called my mother and wrote out a Prozac prescription for me. All because of a decapitated Barbie head.

But I wasn't going to let those stupid ladies get in the way of my art. A week later I bought a GI Joe for Jennifer to devour. At first she didn't take to Joe, but when I rubbed chicken fat on his hairless, muscular torso, she was all over it. I got a great shot of her fangs clasped down on the doll, just his feet sliding out of her mouth. Reminded me of the food-chain charts I'd seen with the whale eating the fish eating the algae. Yes, this was survival of the fittest, and Jennifer proved to be more fit than GI Joe. Who needs soldiers? Picture a troop of poodles on the battlefield, slowly moving into enemy territory.

Only my best friend, Mindy, saw those photos, and she loved them. In her parents' backyard pop-up camper (Mindy slept there for a month since her grandmother was staying in her room during that time), she flipped through the stack. "These are the bomb!" she said. "But if your mother sees them, won't she make you take Prozac?"

"She already thinks I'm taking it," I whispered. "Instead I'm breaking up the capsules and sprinkling them into my father's dessert every night. In the Jell-O, chocolate pudding, fruit salad. And since I volunteered to be dessert queen at home, no one suspects a thing. And he's been much calmer."

Mindy's mouth fell open and her eyes popped from her head. "You're shitting me!"

I smirked, shook my head from shoulder to shoulder.

"Nope. It's the truth. Haven't you noticed that now when he asks questions, he *listens* to your answers?"

"Now that you mention it," she said, "he does seem nicer."

"Here's to Jennifer!"

We gave each other high-fives and laughed until we just about fainted. That's the great thing about Mindy. She rolls with the punches. And not just with my punches. Just two days before, she had invited me out with her friend Eugene, who'd just gotten a new Saturn for his 17th birthday. He drove us to the corner of an empty church parking lot, and from his pocket he pulled out a funny-looking fluorescent-red pipe and a baggie with "the best fuckin' ganja this side of the Mississippi." Mindy and I had never smoked before, but she acted like she was a regular stoner. Not me. I choked and coughed and felt like I was going to die in that damn Saturn. Five minutes later I breathed in a combination of new car, marijuana, and Eugene's musty sweat. We stared at the tree in front of us for a good ten minutes. That's when I noticed Eugene put his hand on Mindy's leg. She just sat there, didn't flinch, until he moved his hand down to her kneecap. Why was she letting him? Was she so high she couldn't respond? Thank God she finally laughed and jerked her leg up.

"That tickles!" she said.

"Sorry," he responded, not knowing what to do but start up the car and drive.

At the first stoplight I inched closer to Mindy, still a little baffled as to why she let Eugene touch her. After all, she told me time and time again she thought he was a big nerd, "but a cool nerd."

I didn't want to go home just yet; I was pretty out there, but Eugene said he had to get home and dropped me off first. Of course, I couldn't help thinking he'd try to make another move on Mindy and that I wouldn't be there to protect her. I guess she could've protected herself, but would she? In my house, my parents sat in the living room watching 20/20, something about a jilted lover—a doctor who had injected his former mistress with blood infected with AIDS and Hepatitis B.

Before anyone noticed my bloodshot eyes, I ran into my room. Jennifer followed and snuggled under the covers beside me. From my night-table drawer I reached for Aunt Thelma's bag of slides, gathered a handful, held them up to the light. In one I'd never seen before, she looked like a brunette Marilyn Monroe standing in front of a big old '60s Chevy, arm in arm with a tall, skinny woman who had a short pixie cut. They both wore chinos and leather jackets, and they were way cool, cooler than any of those models posing for Banana Republic or Ralph Lauren. Written on the slide frame: "Daytona Beach, 1972." I stared at that slide for so long that Jennifer figured it was worthy of a sniff and an almost-lick.

The next morning, right outside of homeroom, Mindy blabbed and laughed with Eugene. Maybe they had started going out. I felt a little nauseous and walked straight into the classroom. Five minutes later (why did she take so long?) Mindy stuck her head in and asked if I was OK.

"Got some killer cramps," I said, even though I'd finished my period the day before. "And I've got a big geometry test to study for." That was on a Friday, and that weekend I had to go to my cousin's bar mitzvah in Baltimore.

While the band played the hora and "Macarena," I couldn't stop thinking about Mindy and Eugene. How they were together and laughing and sharing secrets and how everything would be different when I got back. And then, to make things worse, a big fat boy at the bar mitzvah asked me to dance to "That's the Way—aha aha—I Like It," and I said yes. Halfway through the song, his body came to a standstill. "Forget it," he said—as if it were me who couldn't keep up. Dissed by a fat boy at a bar mitzvah!

On Monday after school, I called Mindy and asked if I could come over. "I aced the geometry test and the cramps are gone. Let's celebrate!"

In Mindy's camper I opened my knapsack and tugged out two plastic cups, a jar of orange juice, and Aunt Thelma's vodka.

"Where'd you get the booze?" Mindy asked.

"Can't get it in America." I poured the orange juice into the cups, added a shot of vodka, then mixed the drinks with my finger. "It's my dead aunt's vodka." On the count of three, we each swigged down an entire cup.

"Yuck!" Mindy said.

"I could hardly taste it."

Mindy didn't want anymore, but I fixed myself another, this time adding more vodka. We played two rounds of Spit while listening to the shrieks of Björk.

"Are you going out with Eugene?" I said, as if asking about her favorite kind of chicken: broiled, fried, baked, or barbecued.

"Are you crazy?"

As Mindy shuffled the cards, I stared at her pale blue eyes, the two freckles on the tip of her pointy nose. My body started to feel like Play-Doh.

"He kissed me the other night, but..." she said, shuffling cards then separating them into four piles. Still looking down, she scrunched up her face and stuck out her tongue, as if she'd just stepped into a pile of dog turds.

To make sure my arm was still there, I touched my silver-spoon bracelet, fingered the little nugget of amber in its center. At that point I was riding on a Björk wail, a giant wave that pulled me into dangerous waters. "You kissed him?" Was I just jealous? I studied Mindy's lips, the tiny crevices running across her lips that had brushed up against Eugene's. Gross. "Did you like it?"

I put my cup down. I was drunk. I didn't even want to hear the answer. I lay down on Mindy's bed, my head staring at the Johnny Depp poster on her ceiling, but Johnny was making me dizzy. I shut my eyes. Usually I loved Björk, but now I wanted her to shut the hell up.

Mindy poured a cup of orange juice and made me drink it. "Did you really think I'd go out with Eugene?" she said.

I didn't say a thing. Didn't even open my eyes. Why did she kiss him? Next thing I remember is Mindy stepping out of the camper, telling me she'd be back in a minute. What seemed like hours went by. Probably only the equivalent of two songs.

When Mindy returned, she set up a plate of saltines and peanut butter. "Maybe if you eat something you'll feel better."

I didn't respond, not because I couldn't but because I felt that Mindy had betrayed me. She kissed Eugene.

"Beth! Are you OK?" I felt her move closer to me. She opened one of my eyelids. Then the other. "Bethy...say something!" Then she lay next to me.

Finally, I opened my eyes and stared at Mindy's forehead, the thin blond wisps bursting from her hairline. I extended my arm and brushed my finger through her bob. Why do they call it a bob? "Bob," I said. "Bob...bob...bob—"

"What about Bob?" Mindy asked.

"Great movie...you know, with Bill Murray." I laughed, thinking I was so fucking clever.

She moved closer, until she wrapped her arms around my shoulders.

Mindy lifted her head and kissed me, the softest velvet kiss, my first tender kiss with anyone besides Jennifer. Suddenly Björk sounded like smooth lake ripples.

"Better," Mindy said.

"Better?" I asked.

"Much better than Eugene."

We weren't in Tahiti or Moscow or Havana, but inside Mindy's pop-up camper with tinted plastic windows that zippered open and shut, I wandered through foreign territory. Aunt Thelma hadn't carried that vodka bottle halfway around the world for nothing.

Groundwater
Amy J. Boyer

The first picture is of Hannah. She is reclining in our bath-tub, her breasts small pale islands in the bathwater. It's her one vice, the love of gallons and gallons of hot water. I am folded onto the lid of the toilet, staring down at my long, broad hands. I am nearly a foot taller than she is, and I feel too big around her when she is naked, but I am glad to be with her in the rose-scent-ed steam that makes her hair curl so tightly and so dark. "We had to call the cops on one of the guys—assaulted one of the others," she tells me. "Wasn't taking his meds. I thought I was past believ-ing you could rescue people, but I could just strangle him."

I take one damp hand. It seems half the size of mine. "I worry about you. Bunch of strung-out guys who can't handle their tempers..." In my head the men shout, shove one another, try to punch.

"Right," she says. "So I'm stronger than they are." She looks at me so hard I forget how small she is. She becomes as large as me, which is why I love her.

The next picture is how I see myself, Cass. I'm in the weight room. There's no particularity to my surroundings, just the smell of stale sweat, which comforts me with its familiarity. I am doing lat pulls, because they are easy and satisfying, and I am by myself with the creaking pulley and the clashing weights.

Always I see my father. He fills the hallway, tugs his belt out of the loops. "Biting the hand that feeds you!" he hisses. "That crack about me making all the smog in California." He works at a refinery for Shell. He beats the worthiness of chemical engineering into the backs of my thighs.

The day after that belting I sat down with the football boys in my high school weight room. I didn't care if they called me dyke or bitch or what, because I didn't care anymore if the names were true, if anything were true, I just wanted the strength to pin my father. In the fight one of us broke a chair; neither of us knows who did it, though he blamed me. And my mother, finally, left.

The nexus is the map of the town that is now home to me. A gray area, shaped like a dog's tongue curled to lap water, shows a toxic plume, slowly broadening through gravel 250 feet down. In City Hall, on a high dais, men and women debate whether the university and the Department of Energy are cleaning up the plume in timely fashion, 40 years after their laboratory began irradiating hundreds of beagles. After that, it provided the beagles with coal fly ash to breathe, and went on to "toxic gas-particle mechanistic aerosol studies." Ever since, the waste has leached through soil; now it has reached the water we bathe in. The university spokesman shows slides of mechanical waterfalls, airing the poisons away. The consultant for the Citizen's Oversight Committee shows slides of ditches lined with weeds and calls the university a "recalcitrant polluter."

This is my university. First, the town became mine, as I cast away my childhood: See? My lover. See? My bachelor's degree, earned six years late, but earned. I want to fight the mass of the university. I want to defend the virtue of my academy. My heel beats upon the floor. A few seats to my right, a woman taps softly, constantly, on her laptop keys. Her asymmetrical haircut and expensive suit are arranged to draw admiration. I am not sure whether I want to bed her or be her, the woman with an unconfused half-smile and tranquil shoes.

As I bicycle home, I pass men and women under lights, running after a Frisbee. What's a degree but a Frisbee? I'm staying on for a master's, maybe a doctorate, my excuse to keep running on the groomed fields of academe. On my right is a line of drought-accustomed olive trees. On my left are arcs of water falling onto an empty soccer field. In my head is my father: "Biting the hand that feeds you!"

Tonight, in the rose-scented steam, I tell Hannah about the meeting. "You could do your thesis on it!" she says. "Stop shouting at the newspaper all the time." I look down at my hands. I was planning to work on mountain streams, with no oil in them, no chemistry except what granite and fir give them.

After her bath, in bed, Hannah rolls onto her side, and I press against her warm naked back. I kiss the back of her neck. She lies very still. "Sorry," I say, and roll onto my back again. It's been a month and a half of her lying still, and before that it was a month. As soon as she got her job at the shelter this started. If it could improve my life I'd drive those homeless people back out under the bushes.

She says into the darkness, "I'm sorry too, Cass," and rolls back toward me. Now I'm the one immobile. I feel my father uncoil in my chest. My ribs hurt from squeezing him down. I know he never imagined me grown. He hit me as if I would never be someone who could hit people too.

When I finished my bachelor's, I was planning to hammer at the arid cliffs of the Great Basin, tracking sea beds from the time before petroleum was formed. Today I stare at a gaudy soils map above the shoulder of the man who convinced me to study the movements of water in the here and now. He skims a report from the meeting: high levels of mercury in the creek near the university. My leg jerks, a substitute for running away from his blunt hands as they turn the pages.

He hands me the report. "The Coast Range is full of mercury, and it leaches right into that creek. Hardly the university's fault. But go for it. We have half a dozen people working on mercury transport, upstream, or up in the Sierras. They're working with agency people. You could make contacts." He's got his hands behind his head, his legs stretched out; my leg calms down.

"What about the groundwater toxins?" I ask.

He laughs. "I wouldn't touch it. There's university politics, there's town politics. Either will damp your idealism real fast. I can think of half a dozen projects that would be more fun and get you out into way better scenery." He looks at me, expecting assent. I nod, feeling my face grow stubborn.

Then he does the thing that makes him my adviser: "What the hell, somebody ought to do it. Now, if I had to pick a fight with someone so you could get your research done, who would I piss off?" He glances at the surrounding buildings, breathes out, plants his feet. "That's what tenure's for. I'd go to bat for you."

Before I leave I say, "I didn't know there were mercury deposits in the Sierras."

"Not deposits. Leachate from gold mining. Mercury was part of the processing."

There are no Sierran streams without our waste?

Myself, throwing stones into saltwater. Behind me a standpipe flames at my father's refinery. I hate the oil washing onto the beach.

"So the pristine stream's a myth," I say.

His hands say, *I don't know.* "You could try Alaska."

In the weight room I'm lying prone, doing leg curls. In the mirror that I'm supposed to watch for form, I see a woman walk in: the unconfused woman. Today she wears a pricey brand of sports bra and stretch shorts that show off her thighs. I have a bowl cut, and I work out in a ragged T-shirt and old jogging shorts. As she begins her stretches, I watch the mirror for her carefully exposed abs. Her body is so well tended; I'm sure it's not for me. But her gaze is not drawn to the broad shoulders of the men in the room. It's my ass she eyes, as my thighs bunch and lengthen.

She walks up to me as I finish. "Spot me on the bench?" she asks.

I stand behind her head, looking down at her as she pushes the weights up from her chest. She's not beautiful on the bench. No one is. I get let into something sweaty and struggling. I watch her breasts, her mouth.

She tells me her name is Elena, asks if I want to go for a beer.

In the shower I watch the water swirling into the drain, going to the treatment plant near the landfill that the university used to bury dogs and beakers. Does the water from my shower drain underground or into the creek? Does my shower push the toxic plume any farther? I don't know.

One day in the shower, washing my hair, I daydreamed of Hannah saying, "You have nice hands, actually," and rising onto her toes and pulling my head toward hers. When I first saw Hannah I saw someone I didn't need: a little woman in a paisley skirt, buying lunch at the campus coffeehouse. I wanted only my degree, proof I could do something besides spray weed killer on dandelions and run a stinking two-stroke leaf-blower. But the little woman was saying to a stoop-shouldered blond, "Don't put up with her talking like that. You don't call *her* a bitch." I had never known I wanted fierce kindness until I saw Hannah's eyes.

After that I saw her everywhere, across the street, in the library, at the grocery. I imagined taking her out. It always turned into my offending her, until the daydream in the shower. That day I took my hands out of the lather and looked at them and thought, I have planted a lot of flowers. Roses. Irises. Icelandic poppies with petals like tissue paper. Maybe I could do this.

Tonight Elena laughs at me as I call Hannah: "Bumped

into a friend at the gym, thought I'd eat with her."

"I'll miss you, but I wouldn't be great company," Hannah says.

"Yeah? Another bad day?"

Elena moves away discreetly.

Hannah exhales her exasperation. "A client stashed a bottle of Everclear under his bed, and first he blamed his roommate even though he stank, and then it was my fault I went snooping, and out of the kindness of my heart I put him on warning instead of kicking him out, so he's pissed at me. Fabulous fun."

"Shee-it, honey. Being good to people who can't appreciate it."

"Eh, well. Enough do," Hannah says, and I argue with her a little as I watch Elena amuse herself with our bickering.

I watch Elena's perfect, clipped fingernails dip up a guacamole-covered chip. She's in University Relations. "You know the newsletter that Citizen's Oversight guy said was misleading? I just got hired to write it." She bites into the chip. Her teeth are perfect too, and white.

I ask, "So *are* you misleading the public?"

She shrugs, one-shouldered. "Everything I say is the truth."

I laugh. "You haven't answered my question."

"Close enough for me," Elena says. "I don't worry about things like that. I have a good life, OK money. There's few enough happy people in the world. I'm one of them— that's enough."

Every moment of happiness I get is an achievement, bigger than my degree. What would it mean to be simply happy, without having to be good?

In the darkness I pull Hannah toward me, press harder and harder, wanting downy belly, adamant bone, delicate hands on me, proving I am not my father, proving even the scars he gave me deserve to be caressed. I kiss her cheek, her neck, her lips. She is still, then stiff.

"Oh, hell," I say. "What can I do? When does this stop?" I lurch out of bed, drag jeans over my T-shirt, stumble out of the house. Instead of the lit street I see only my ex-lover Jeannine, coming around her kitchen table, shouting, "What do you want from me?" She grabs my hair, rabbit-punches me, and I feel the dull thud in the back of my kidneys and the hard quick pain from my jab to her chin, joy in that pain, in seeing her shocked eyes, oh, I wanted to jab again and again but I ran away, hundreds of miles away to here, and now I am here: myself limping along the line of olives, the arcs of water hissing next to me.

At the farmer's market, Hannah and I buy eggplant striped purple and white, peppers from banks of orange, red, green, yellow. Every week a haggard man at one of the booths presses a free basket of cherry tomatoes on us, his gift for Hannah's getting him out of the shelter and into a job. We buy organic, my rich penance for the smog from years of leaf-blowing, pesticide residues from weed killer, nitrate runoff from fertilizer carried by sprinkler water into storm drains. Nitrates are in the toxic plume.

It is still warm enough for the children to play in the fountain. I love to sit with Hannah and watch them running through the water: They look like no one has ever hurt them. I can smell the water's chlorine. Chlorine becomes chloroform. We absorb it through our skins. Chloroform is also in the toxic plume.

Hannah chats with friends as I lie drowsing in the grass. She seems to know the whole city from her internships on the way to her social work degree. I like just to listen to her voice dip and crest. Then someone says, "Hi...did I see you at the Superfund meeting?" I look up into the sun: It's a heavy little blond woman. I nod.

"Michelle, Cass," Hannah says, grinning at us. "Cass is

thinking of doing her thesis on the Superfund groundwater," she tells Michelle.

"*Thinking* about it," I say. "My adviser's not sure."

"Of course not," Michelle says. "The university doesn't have a lick of integrity."

I am surprised into saying, "Well, he hasn't said no…"

"I could tell you all kinds of things if you decided to do it," she says. "All *kinds* of things." She walks off to the playground and calls one of the kids off the jungle gym, a redhead with a ponytail, perhaps four years old. As they walk back past us Michelle waves, and so does her daughter, happily. I wave back, surprised how pleased I am.

I dig through the university phone book. I try a number and get handed off from one person to another. Finally I reach a man shouting over machine noises, "No independent investigation allowed! Superfund regs!" The back of my thigh shakes against my chair. His machines sound like my father's turbines. My father, shouting at me, over noise, over anything.

"Independent? I'm in the university!" I shout at him in our quiet kitchen.

"Not a site employee! You got a beef, talk to your congressman!"

"Fine," I say and hang up.

In the weight room Elena and I stand over each other in case of failure, lift with our fingertips the extra ten pounds that allow struggling arms to bring the weight up, away from the body, when failure occurs. As we are putting weights on a barbell I realize she and I are exactly the same height. Something relaxes in me: a slight strain I have always felt with Hannah and never known was there.

In the bar I tell Elena about the man on the phone. She

laughs at me. "What do you expect? Your Alaska idea's a lot better. Or would you miss your honey too much?"

I picture an Alaskan stream, glinting under the night sun, how clear and spacious and quiet it would be. My chest tightens. "Eh...maybe we could use a rest from each other. Lesbian bed death hit hard a few months ago...not for me. For her."

Elena raises the immaculate lines of her eyebrows. "What's her problem? You're cute, you're smart, you're strong. She's lucky to have you."

I try to laugh, not very successfully. I want to believe Elena. I can feel the exact weight of her breasts without yet having touched them. To feel my nakedness relax against her skin, forgetting the strain of holding a body small enough to break—that would be belief.

At home, Hannah is already in bed. When I switch on the lamp to undress she rolls toward me, mumbles, "Hey, you." She smiles sleepily. She is so unguarded that my throat hurts. When I slide in under the covers she puts her arm over me. I turn to her, pull her against me, harder, harder. I can't distinguish the strain from my love for her; it's how I know I love her. I smell the beer on my own breath. How can I be good enough for this?

I talk to my adviser, who mentions, in specific, the half-dozen projects with better scenery, but he makes some phone calls for me. In the library I read about hexavalent chromium, bromodichloromethane, cesium 139, hydrostratigraphic units, groundwater movement of dissolved volatile organic chemicals. When people glance at me angrily I realize my heel is drubbing the floor. I think of Alaska, of salmon running shoulder to shoulder up undammed streams, and relax.

At the farmer's market the Citizen's Oversight Committee has a table. As I pass I hear one of the people from the town hall meeting. "Well, you just worry," she says. "We fenced off our section of the creek so people couldn't come onto our property and catch those fish and get loaded up with mercury." I've seen people fishing as I've biked along the creek. They are often darker than the typical people in this very pale town, and they usually drive much older cars. I wonder what protection the fence is really meant to give.

I go to the site where the beagles lived, just over the levee from the creek. I have heard that salmon still run in this creek, that otters swim half a mile upstream; I myself have seen hawks rise heavily from the branches of cottonwoods. Today the creek is green with summer algae, narrow and muddy within a thistle-covered floodplain. Before me are two layers of cyclone fence, the outer ones bearing small yellow signs: RADIOACTIVE MATERIAL. Beyond the signs are gravel rectangles outlined in concrete, partially dug out. I think of opened graves. Past the rectangles are row upon row of metal boxes the size of kennels, but sealed. They must be containers for some sort of remains. The yellow boxes and gray rectangles march for a quarter mile, then give way to baked earth covered in the brown stalks of star thistle. In a corner of the lot sit rows of smaller, shrouded boxes.

What does it mean to be good, if it means immersing myself in this?

Hannah sets down a dish of eggplant sprinkled with oregano from our backyard. Her face is loose with fatigue. I look at her blank black eyes and think of my desire, how clean and bright it felt at first, how muddy it's become. I begin the ritual: "How was your day?"

"This time it's a woman, got some history on her— homeless women, they get raped, you know..." She looks at me, grief-stricken. "But either she's cowering in a corner or she's attacking you.... I don't know if we can keep her. It's fucked."

We're silent a while. "You go work with all these people you can't help and then come home and I can't help you," I say. I try to spear a cherry tomato in my salad.

She smiles at me, a little. "I'm sorry."

"Yeah, well," I say. My chest tightens so hard I feel stabbed. "I hate being helpless!" and the sound of the smack tells me I've hit the table.

"Honey," she says.

"Don't soothe me. I'm not one of your clients."

"Thank God," she says.

"Lot of good it does me. At least they get you for the day. When you're not too tired for anything."

"You'd have a lot of competition," she says.

I want to stop shouting. My chest stabs. I have to shout. "I do have a lot of competition. Every goddamn drunk in town! Maybe if I were one of them you'd fuck me."

Her eyes are fierce, and they are not kind. "People give me shit all day. Are you going to start?"

"Might as well. Being good isn't getting me anywhere." I'm breathing hard, not shouting. She gets up, begins sweeping onion skins and bits of lettuce off the counter.

"Damn it, don't go away from me!" I'm up now too, coming around the table. "I'm not one of them! Goddamn it, why won't you touch me!"

Her eyes flicker into fear, out again. *Not the first one she's faced down.*

My chest cracks open. Sharp relief. I have no choice now: My arms uncoil.

Her fierce eyes.

I slam the cabinet. The panel punches out. The door pops open. Our cups and glasses arc to the floor and I can see each one, the beautiful half-parabolas as they go down and then the spray of glass as they shatter against each other and still she stands there and I run for the door and it's only when I can't open it that I know how much my hand hurts.

But my left hand works and I'm gone.

My first memory is of red tulips. I don't know where I saw them, but they are the picture I carry of love. As soon as Hannah could find them in the store, she came home with a bag of bulbs. I protested: They used too much water. She said they would flower in the spring rains, and she made me show her how to plant them. Next spring I won't see them bloom. Realizing this, I become very calm. Strange to be so calm out here, where the wind is whipping the trees, colder and damper than it has been since April.

Sometimes after my father had left cuts, I felt just this calm. I love this feeling, because it's the only time I am not afraid. Elena seems that calm. I think of us calm together. Is that having happiness, without having to be good?

Elena's furniture is too expensive and too sparse for the apartment. Next to the door is an antique mirror, full-length. She says, "OK, yeah, I used to be a model and I haven't totally let it go.... Really. Want to see pictures?"

"Sure."

She leaves the room. I glance at the mirror. I don't want to see myself. I wonder what life Elena left, what life she sees in the mirror now. I think of her sleek body, how just being an animal next to it will redeem me. *She's lucky to have you.* My broken hand throbs, dissipating my calm.

I leave the mirror and go into her kitchen. There's one pan on the stove, clean, steel-clad aluminum with a thick bottom. A food processor sits in the corner. Good, maybe I won't be living on food from cans. A bulletin board full of photos hangs on the wall. Hannah and I have a bulletin board too: Hannah's parents, my mother, Hannah's sister and brother, her grandmother, my brother from one of our good times, Hannah's baby niece, the friend who helped me leave Jeannine.... Elena is in all her photos: Elena at a lake, Elena on a beach, Elena in front of a restaurant, Elena, Elena, Elena. There is no one else in them.

I hear her behind me. She holds her portfolio. I say, "I can't do this."

Her smile changes a little, not much. "I'm only giving you this one chance."

I nod.

She walks me out into the sharp metallic smell of the first rain of fall.

Outside the city the rain seeps through acres of tomatoes and sunflowers, carrying nitrates and atrazine into the groundwater. It falls on the reliquiae of the university's poisoned dogs, carrying chloroform and cesium. It loosens all the oil of summer from the roads, and it will run, newly slicked, into ditches and storm drains, into the creek, into river and ocean. As I walk under the olive trees, the hard rain soaks through my clothes to my skin. I hold my cracked fist to my mouth, weeping, and the rain carries my salt as I walk through my home, to my home, the home that holds me though I don't know how to live here.

My Son Jake
Marnie Webb

My defroster didn't work, so Jake and I played tick-tack-toe on the inside of the windshield as I drove up the Pacific Coast Highway.

We were in the part of Malibu I hate because the ocean is in the wrong place, and I'd put a napkin over the compass on the dashboard since it gave me a headache to think the Pacific is north of me and not west where it belongs.

I get Jake Thursday after school and every other weekend. His father has him the rest of the time.

My mother thinks this means there's something wrong with me. No woman should give up her child, she always says, then looks at me with her schoolteacher eyes over the tops of her glasses. It's a good effect, but I know it means she can't see me, since she's nearsighted.

That weekend Jake and I were driving to Big Sur.

"Why can't we take the regular road?" he asked when we'd hit the traffic circle in Long Beach. "This way takes too long."

But there was no reason to get to Big Sur in a hurry. It was November and too cold for us to hike, and once there—in the cabin I had to rent for three nights even though we could only stay for two—Jake would watch TV or play with the Nintendo 64 his dad had bought him for his birthday, which he'd insisted on bringing. In the car, on PCH, with its turns and stoplights, I had Jake and what we saw out the windows and that's all.

We ran out of space to play tick-tack-toe, and besides Jake wanted to stop because he didn't think it was safe.

"You can't see," he said, and took the napkin off the compass and wiped the window. "Why do we always have to drive?"

"Because then you can get used to the idea of being someplace new. Look," I said and pushed one of the radio buttons. "We have to find a new station. It's one way of telling where we are."

"Dad says you just make that up because you're afraid to fly." His father has told me that too.

And it is true. I am afraid of airplanes. I don't understand the whole heavier-than-air flight concept, and I'm convinced planes only stay up because of mass hypnosis. All the people on board believe in flight, but what happens when I step on? I'm a disbeliever.

"I really do like the drive," I said, and reached over and tapped Jake's chest. "I like being with you."

"Dad says you used to drive up to San Francisco and just turn around and drive home."

I couldn't possibly imagine why Doug would have told him this. It's true, but it didn't have anything to with Jake. It didn't even have anything to do with Doug. It was just that for a while those short little trips were the only way I could stay in one place.

"I like to drive," was all I said to Jake.

He tapped on the windows and I said, "Let's play the alphabet game." He didn't say anything and at *G* I said, "Give up."

My mom said she didn't think I was grown-up enough to raise a child and I told her, "Well, then, shouldn't I leave him with Doug?" She just blew air out of her nose in a harsh blast and said that wasn't the answer. The answer was for me to grow up.

At Carpenteria I pointed at a beach house and said, "That used to belong to your grandpa, but his grandma was crazy and sold it and hid the money, so well no one was ever able to find it."

"You point to a different house every time," Jake said.

"What?"

"You tell the same story, but every time you point to a different house," which I didn't doubt since I didn't know which house it had actually been. I liked the story, though, and couldn't believe Jake remembered which house I'd pointed to the last time we drove through.

I wished he were still so little that all I had to do to distract him was tickle his stomach.

"Do you want to marry Mrs. Nelson?" he asked a mile and a half later. How did he know to say that? I hadn't told anyone about Maddie. Not even Doug. Especially not Doug.

Maddie taught kindergarten at Jake's school, and the day she touched my elbow and introduced herself I stayed quiet, trying to remember if I'd talked too loudly in front of her classroom, but then I remembered that her class had gone home by the time I got to school to pick Jake up from third grade.

"I've met your husband but not you," she said as Jake walked up to us, his backpack on both shoulders and his sweatshirt tied around his waist, and I knew why she was talking to me. To meet the woman who gave up custody of her kid.

"People will think there's something wrong with you," my mom had said the day I told her I wasn't going to fight Doug. "He's a better parent," I said.

"But you gave birth to that boy," my mother said and then walked away, which was a good thing because I didn't have anything to say next.

"He's not my husband," I'd said to Maddie Nelson. She must be another one of the gossipy women in this place who just wanted to get close enough to touch the monster mother, I'd thought. "He's not my husband; he's Jake's father." I wasn't sure why she smiled and touched my shoulder before she walked away.

Maddie Nelson talked to me the next week and the week after that, and I still couldn't figure out why.

"Well?" Jake brought me back to the car. I reached across and tickled his knee. "Stop it, Mom." He moved his legs away.

"Why are you asking?"

I started showing up ten, 15, 20 minutes before school let out and Maddie was always in her classroom and we talked until Jake pulled on my arm and said, "C'mon, Mom, let's go."

Finally, two months ago last Thursday, she asked what I did for a living and I said systems analyst and she asked what that meant and I said, "It means I think about every possible implication and every possible consequence and imagine them as far off in time as I can and then I make something for people to use to get their job done."

I was still thinking about how to describe my work when she said, "Will you go out to dinner with me?" I wrote my home number on the back of my business card and didn't understand why she was red or why she said "I'm not usually this forward."

The first night Maddie and I went to dinner, I didn't know it was a date. I picked her up at the school and she was waiting for me in a window with no screen and she walked to my side of the car and said, "Let me just go inside and get my jacket."

I watched her walk away and step through the window, and even then I wasn't quite sure why I was there except that she had the calmest voice I'd ever heard on a woman and when she talked to me she looked right at my face.

She said I could pick the restaurant, so I drove south for half an hour until I got to El Patios and while I ate the number 4, which I was able to order without even looking at the menu, I told her I used to eat there with my parents every other Friday night. Later I drove her past the house I'd lived in when I'd been in elementary school and she put her hand on my knee as I told her that the summer between second and third grade, my brother and I argued about whether Mutual of Omaha's Wild Kingdom was in South America or Africa and we'd both been disappointed when we found out Mutual of Omaha was a company, not a country. I smiled when she laughed, and I don't remember thinking she had her hand on my leg still and made no sign of moving it. Despite what I did for a living, the implications of that did not cross my mind.

When we stopped in front of her house, I left the engine idling until Maddie reached over and turned the key. She touched my cheek and leaned forward and kissed me and then her seat was back and my shirt was open and she asked if I wanted to come inside and I said no, not yet, as if there would be other nights and I licked her ear and then she was walking into the house and I had two thoughts at the exact same moment: I'd never licked Doug's ear, and I couldn't believe I'd been necking with a kindergarten teacher.

I looked at Jake, still waiting for my answer to his question. Doug and I had settled our divorce two and a half years before the first time I even talked to Maddie.

"Why are you asking?" I said again. Since Doug couldn't have known, I tried to decide how my mom had found out and why in the world she had told Jake.

"You always talk to her," he said.

"I talk to a lot of people, bubba." I was relieved that this was going to be easy to get out of. We were at Pismo Beach, and I knew an all-night restaurant and asked Jake if he wanted dinner.

I ordered calamari and let the legs of the tiny squid dangle out of my mouth and wiggled them.

"Stop it." Jake slumped in his chair, and I pulled all of the squid into my mouth.

"Are you going to marry her?" and the waitress looked at me as she poured me more coffee.

I drank it fast and paid the bill.

"Are you?"

I kept thinking time meant he forgot the question, but I should have known better. Jake remembered the circle jigsaw puzzles of garden flowers I put together when he was too young to talk.

I decided to go for a technically correct answer to the Mrs. Nelson question.

"Women can't marry each other," I said, which didn't address the issue of desire.

I did not tell Maddie she was the first woman I'd been with until after we'd made love. I pushed my face into her breast, and she kept having to ask me to repeat myself, and she ran her fingers through my hair in a way that made me feel safe and sexy at the same time.

"It's OK, baby," Maddie said when I finished talking. "You'll be OK."

It was two days later, when Doug and I met for dinner to talk about Jake's problem with homework, before I understood what she meant.

"You don't have to hear it every night," Doug said. "He argues and fights and then spends hours sharpening his pencil. He says you don't make him do it."

I shrugged. "He's in third grade. What homework should he have to do?"

"It's going to make a difference when he's in high school. You of all people should be able to think this through."

And when he said that, Doug was talking about Maddie, not Jake, even though he didn't realize it. Until that moment I'd made no effort to picture Maddie and me in any future. I'd just been captured in the humid present-tense of her bed.

"Well," Doug said.

"You're right," I said, but I was talking about Maddie and had completely forgotten Jake's homework.

It was almost 2 in the morning, and Jake asked if we could

stop so he could go to the bathroom. We'd both been quiet for miles, but I knew he was still waiting for the answer, and I knew too, as I stood outside the men's room at a Mobil station in I-don't-know-where, that no one had told him about Maddie. He had stood there Thursday after Thursday, watching me fall in love with her.

"You only touch Mrs. Nelson and Dad," he said when we got back in the car. "Only you don't touch Dad anymore."

"I touch you," I said, and put my hand flat on his stomach.

"Oh, Mom. I'm a kid. I don't count." He didn't squirm back from my hand and instead hugged my arm, and I didn't move so there was no reason for him to stop. "I just want to know," he said, and rested his cheek on my arm. I felt his warm breath on my elbow.

After that dinner with Doug, I'd called Maddie and asked her if she was a lesbian. Somehow the word had never come up in any of our conversations.

She laughed. "Well, let's see. I haven't slept with a man since prom night, and I don't think that counted. And I'm interested in you for more than just sex, so yes. Yes, I guess I'd say I'm a lesbian."

Which I'd figured. That was just the warm-up question.

"So does that mean I'm one too?" And I didn't know why I was so frightened of the answer because I was sure I wasn't prejudiced against gay people, even though I couldn't name any that were more than nodding acquaintances.

"Well," Maddie said and she wasn't laughing anymore and I counted her breaths until I got to seven and she answered, "that's something you have to decide."

That seemed like a cop-out to me, and I said so. "You know more about this than I do. I want to know what you think. I already know what I think." I had no idea what I thought.

"I think you like making love to me."

The first time I was inside Maddie I closed my eyes and imagined all of me was swallowed into her.

"But that doesn't have to mean you're a lesbian." And when she said that, I could tell she was as afraid of saying it as I was. Only I didn't know what she had to be scared of.

"What do you think, Maddie?" My voice broke on her name, and I felt like I was having an out-of-body experience.

"I think so. I want to think so."

And when she said that, even though I hate the cold, I would have been a penguin if she'd wanted it.

Then suddenly I had visions of having to tell my mother, who already didn't think I was a real woman, and telling Doug, who would start to think that was the real reason we'd broken up, even though it had nothing at all to do with it.

Actually, I wasn't quite sure why Doug and I had broken up. I know that one night Doug had asked me if I loved him more or differently than I loved the rest of the world, and I said I hoped not, that I thought everyone deserved the same level of caring and respect, and when I looked at him I realized that wasn't the right answer, so I said I loved him more specifically than I loved the rest of the world because I knew him better, but that didn't seem to help either, so I said I picked up his laundry and nobody else's and he said that was only because the dry cleaner was on my way home from work and no one else had ever asked me to do that for them.

When I asked Jake if he knew why Dad and I weren't living together anymore, he said it was because I didn't cheer at soccer games, which wasn't the answer I was expecting. I don't know what I was expecting.

"What?"

"Dad thinks you should cheer at my soccer games. He gets mad because you don't clap or anything."

And so when my mom asked why Doug and I were getting divorced even though we seemed to get along and even if we didn't we had a son and so should learn to stay together, my generation wasn't prepared to work at anything, I said, "Because I pick up his laundry and don't yell at Jake's soccer games," and she thought I was being flip and then said that she never understood what I saw in him in the first place, and I told her again, Doug was leaving me, I wasn't leaving him, but I didn't point out that I wasn't doing anything to stop him.

When Jake and I pulled into the gravel driveway at the cabin, he was still hugging my arm and I felt the in-and-out of his breath and I turned off the car and thought, If only Maddie were inside waiting for us, I would need nothing more than this moment.

"Are you ever going to answer me, Mom?"

The stars were bright and I could see the traces of X's and O's on our windshield. They were all cat's games.

I rolled down the window, and the air was cold. I could smell the ocean, mixed with pine.

And I told him I would marry Mrs. Nelson if I could, then I waited.

Jake nodded. "Can we go in now? I'm cold."

I got out of the car and picked up my son, his feet dangling past my knees, and I hugged him the whole way into the cabin.

Ghetto Anthem
R. Gay

1. *O Say Can You See*

The girls are in the backseat giggling as I try to maneuver the baby's seat between them. They're talking about sex, how 32 days without it is an eternity, and Amber adds that once her boyfriend André gets out of jail, they're going to have sex every day. Of course, the baby is only a month old, and I'm thinking that she should never have sex again. Well, she should at least wait a few months for her body to heal. I'm fuzzy on what the standard is in this sort of situation, but Amber is only 14, and in general the thought of her having sex horrifies me. As I wait for my girlfriend to lock up the house, I turn to the girls. "When y'all grow up, you'll realize there's more to life than sex and no one has sex every day forever."

Amber rolls her eyes.

Lola, my girlfriend's 16-year-old daughter, André's sister, smirks and mutters, "You're so old, and maybe it's different for dykes."

"I'm only 25, and no, it isn't," I snap.

"When my man gets out of jail, we're going to get married, and I can promise you, we'll be kicking it more than once a day," Amber says.

Lola gives her a high-five. Her boyfriend is in jail too, so clearly the two of them can relate on a level I'm unable to reach. I nod slowly, staring at them in the rearview mirror, knowing full well that neither of them will marry their boyfriends or have sex every day forever.

We're on our way to the Lincoln Correctional Facility. André is in jail for a month or so, sitting out fines; he was caught driving on a suspended license in a car without plates. I've tried to impart to him the importance of obeying laws, but it's more fun for him to cruise the streets with his homeboys. He's at that age. Now he calls us every night, crying, talking about how he should have done things differently, how he should be there for his baby. I bite my tongue, but really I'm thinking he should have thought about all that. I'm thinking that even when he gets out of jail he'll never be the father this baby needs.

At the jail we have to show identification. We lie about Amber's age, since you need to be 16 to visit inmates. The visiting area is full, so we have about ten minutes to wait. The tiles on the waiting-room floor are dingy, and no amount of cleaning will ever make them white again. The seats are hard, plastic, too small. A stack of mini-lockers rests against one wall. Tamara, my girlfriend, refuses to sit and paces back and forth across the waiting room. She hates jails. Her ex-husband is in one, and she swore she'd never visit one again, but here we are. I take the baby from her carrier, and she stares at me with her wide gray eyes. She's the most beautiful creature I've ever seen. Some nights, when I'm studying, I'll hold her in my lap and end up staring at her more than the pages of whatever book I'm reading. She recognizes me, I'm sure of it, and as we sit here I run my fingers along the hem of her outfit, a tiny pink dress with white lace ruffles. She looks confused, and I'm thinking she shouldn't be here…this isn't right. Babies don't belong in jails.

* * *

Tamara and I met five years ago at the adult bookstore where we both worked. I was paying my way through school. She was taking a mental vacation from the traditional work-force. The first time I saw her, she was holding two huge plastic vibrators. "What are you staring at?" she asked. "Nothing," I said, to which she replied, "That's what I thought." I remember thinking she was really quite attractive to be working in a place like this for no good reason: skin the color of roasted almonds; sad, light-brown eyes; and hands that told the story of several lifetimes. Working on the long and lonely graveyard shifts, we became friends. I told her about my less-than-exciting life; only so much can happen to you when you've spent the past 20 years in school. She told me about hers: her ex-boyfriend, ex-husband, and most recently, her ex-girlfriend of six years. I quickly learned that in relationships we pay for the sins of past lovers. When you make a mistake, every piece of scar tissue around your lover's heart seems to peel away, exposing an open wound.

We have always realized that we are nothing alike. I'm often afraid that we are so different that we won't be able to stay together. She is ten years older than I am. I am from the suburbs and act too white to really be black (according to her). I try to explain that black people aren't all from the hood, that being black means different things for different people, but sometimes I have to accept that her world is a lot smaller than mine. She has three kids, and she is (again, according to her) a classy ghetto bitch. She is also loud, bossy, moody, and a control freak. But there's something about her I still can't resist, despite my friends telling me she's wrong for me, that I'm just looking to rescue her from an impossible life. At first, that may have been what we were about, but I can't imagine my life without her. I'd like to think that I understand her.

* * *

Between the waiting room and the actual jail is a glassed-in room of sorts where the guards sit. From where we sit, we see inmates pass back and forth from their cells to the visiting area. As they go by, they pause, hoping to see someone here for them. They pose, make silly faces, give us the finger until a guard prods them on their way. Finally, we see André. He looks tired, his clothes are wrinkled, but when he sees us he smiles and jumps up and down, pointing, blowing kisses to Amber. He wants us to move closer to the glass so he can see the baby, and I stand and turn the baby toward him. She stares ahead blankly then starts whimpering, which soon turns into a high-pitched wail. Turning her around, I rest her against my shoulder, softly patting her back, and quickly her tears subside. The waiting room is too cold. I feel awkward, out of place, like there's a code of behavior I'm not following properly.

A few minutes later a bored voice over the intercom says we can go into the visiting room. We pick up the baby carrier, her diaper bag, our coats, the baby's blanket, the stuff the girls brought for André, and our caravan of misfits heads to the visiting area. As we pass through the narrow hallway, I catch a glimpse of the waiting room from the other side of the glass, and I realize I would never want to be in here.

✳ ✳ ✳

The more time I spend with Tamara, the more I learn about life. She showed me my first food stamp, how doctors treat you when you're on Medicare, what it's like not to have anyone to fall back on. And I often ask myself what I've shown her, beyond what life is like for a graduate student: comfortable, detached. "I've always had to hustle," she often tells me, by way of explanation. "I had André when I was 16 years old. I had to take care of me and my baby, because no one else would." The first time we go on a drug run together, I am driving, she is sitting next to me. Our friend Irene is in the backseat. "You always take three people," she says. "One to drive, one to inspect the merchandise, and one to hand over the money." It all seems rather cumbersome to me, but I nod as if I understand perfectly.

We're in North Omaha because Tamara says, "The niggas up here are less paranoid. They're used to seeing other black people." Again I nod, and follow her cryptic directions to a guy named Buster's house. On the drive up, she and Irene have instructed me on the many fine nuances of drug transactions: how to package, create a customer base, and avoid the cops. "Don't you ever feel guilty about selling dope to other black people?" I ask, and they laugh, as if it's an absurd question. "We don't sell to our family members, but other niggas are fair game." "That's a shitty attitude," I say. "Whatever happened to hard work and perseverance? That's how my parents made it. It's how I'm making it." Tamara shakes her head. "Some people are lucky, but you have to understand that no matter how hard black people work, white people will never let us have what they have." It all seems so hopeless. They are truly convinced that this is the best way. "Everybody has a little hustle," they assure me.

At Buster's house I sit in the car, gripping the steering wheel until my hands, sweaty, seem stuck in that position. I keep looking in the rearview mirror and the side windows to check for cops. I don't like this feeling of being a breath away from going to jail. If this is an adrenaline-producing risk, it's doing nothing for me. When Tamara and Irene return to the car, they both say "Drive" at the same time, and I make my way out of Omaha. They show me the dope, because I've never seen it before. I'm disappointed when I see the cream-colored pebbles. All that fuss, over this. I quickly realize this will be my last run.

* * *

I've never been inside a jail before. There's a smell: It's heavy and bitter and makes your skin crawl. It's loud. The walls echo with coarse voices and cruel language. A few of the inmates leer at the girls as we make our way to the empty table where André is waiting. I want to cover them with my coat, the baby's blanket, anything to shield them from their eyes. And I want to run out of this room full of scary people and never look back. When we reach the table, André pulls Amber into a passionate embrace and, blushing, I look away.

Tamara smacks André in the back of the head. "Try and remember that I'm your mother and I don't need to see that shit."

Chastised, André sits down, pulling Amber onto his lap. "Sorry, Ma," he says.

I nod to André. He nods back. We have an understanding.

"How's the baby?" he asks.

I smile softly, still patting her back. "She's fine, a little fussy."

"I've missed her," he says. "But I know you and Ma are taking good care of her."

I hand him the baby, and as he takes her into his arms my hands are still on her. I'm afraid she'll fall. It's as if her tiny hands are holding onto the veins leading into my heart, and I can't let go, because if I do my heart will be torn from my chest.

"I've got her," he says. "I know how to hold a baby."

Nodding, I sit next to Tamara, and we exchange a look. My chest feels tight. I keep blinking, reminding myself to breathe. I can't hear a word anyone is saying.

2. *By the Dawn's Early Light*

The day the baby was born, we were up at 6 in the morning, when Amber's water broke. We rushed to the hospital, but it was hours before anything interesting began to happen. When the labor pains really kicked in, André freaked out. He started jumping up and down, which I have to admit looked rather funny, because he always sags his jeans, and they ended up around his knees. There he was, his girlfriend sweaty and panting heavily, and his boxers were showing.

"Pull up your pants," I told him, laughing under my breath.

"Women are amazing," he kept saying. "What am I going to do? I'm going to be a daddy."

Between these statements he'd walk toward the bed and touch Amber but immediately back away, as if he were afraid of hurting her.

"André, will you sit still? You're working my nerves," Tamara said, flashing him an irritated look.

The nurse, who was studying the baby monitors, eyed André with disapproval and said, "If he can't calm down and remain quiet, he's going to have to leave."

Tamara snapped her neck and stared the nurse down with a glare. "You may do this every day, but this is his first baby. Why don't you leave until we need you?"

The nurse stormed out in a huff, and we fell out laughing.

"White people always gotta ruin a moment," Tamara said, a growl in her voice.

I nodded toward the doorway, and Tamara sat on the stool next to the bed, taking Amber's hand in hers, wiping her face with a cool cloth. André and I headed down the hallway and stopped in front of the nursery to look at the newborns.

"They're so small," he said. "I can't believe I'm going to have a little person soon."

I squeezed his hand. We heard a high-pitched scream, and André started jumping again. Placing my hands on his shoulders, I forced him to sit down and took a seat next to him on the floor. For a while we sat in silence, then I started rambling about the birth of my nephew, how gross and cool it was to watch, how I'd never forget it for the rest of my life. He sat quietly, fidgeting with his pants every now and then.

"I don't have kids of my own," I told him. "I mean, you guys aren't my kids...but you're as close as I'm ever going to get. I want you to know that means a lot to me."

"It's cool," he said.

"Right now you need to be there for Amber. This is hard, this having-a-baby thing, and she needs you to be strong. I know you're scared, but you're not alone. I'm here. Your mother's here, and we're all going to be here for each other."

"Right, right," he said, rubbing his forehead.

"So are we ready to go back in there?"

Slowly, he stood up. "Yeah," he said. "But you're right. It is kind of gross."

I grinned, then shuddered as Amber screamed again. We rushed back to the room in time to witness Amber in the throes of yet another contraction. André paled, but I flashed him a stern look, and he straightened his shoulders and lightly stroked Amber's sweaty face. When it came time for the final push, I had to leave the delivery room. Only immediate family allowed. Amber wanted her privacy. I was disappointed, but I left. I understood how these things worked. There was a small alcove a few feet away from the delivery room, and I sat on the couch there, staring at the muted television, the empty coffeemaker, the torn magazines in a pile on a small table.

When I heard the baby's first cry, my heart fluttered. Then I heard crying…Tamara crying, saying, "She's so beautiful. My baby is so beautiful." Pacing the hallway, I felt like one of those expectant fathers on TV. Eventually Tamara emerged, her eyes and face red, streaked with mascara, and she looked so happy that I wanted to take the moment and put it in a safe place, a memory to be retrieved when needed. Silently she came toward me and, opening my arms, I wrapped myself around her. We didn't speak. We didn't need to.

* * *

Looking around the visiting room, I'm struck by the poor dental health of many of the inmates. Some are missing teeth;

some have gold teeth, yellow teeth, crooked teeth. I find it all repulsive, because I have this thing about bad teeth. I just can't deal with them. Surrounded by this disturbing display, I'm momentarily distracted from the fact that this is my first time in a jail, with a newborn baby, visiting my stepson who is a baby himself.

Tamara brushes her hand across my cheek. "You're quiet," she says.

"The teeth."

She laughs, because she knows how I am. "Are you OK?"

I realize that my left leg is shaking as her hand wraps around my knee to steady it. "I'm fine."

But my arms feel empty. I want the baby back. I want to take her home, where she'll sleep warm and safe between Tamara and me, cooing occasionally in that soft, gurgly way.

"How are you holding up?" I ask André.

He wrinkles his nose and tries to look tough. "I'm a man. It ain't no thing being up in here."

Next time he calls I'll remind him of that, but now I smile politely. "That's good. Need anything?"

"Could you put some money on my book?"

I stare blankly, and Tamara whispers in my ear, "You can put money on his book to go toward his fines and to pay for stamps and whatever."

I nod. "I'm sure we can do something. Let me see where things stand after we pay the bills."

"Cool," he says. "Did y'all bring me any blacks?"

Amber reaches into her blouse and proffers a pack of Black and Mild cigars she had hidden in her bra. André isn't allowed to smoke them at home because their sweet stench makes me nauseous, so there is a bright side to this situation.

"That's my baby," he says, excitedly. "I've been fiending for these."

Again, I'm biting my tongue, because I'm wondering if he calls his *other* girlfriend "baby" when she comes to visit.

After an hour, the baby is hungry and needs changing, and I'm tired. After I look pointedly at my watch, Tamara stands up, hugs André, and tells him we'll be back next week.

We're all quiet on the drive home. I'm crabby. Amber is crying. Lola is crying because she misses Jarell, her boyfriend, who's in a different facility. Tamara is trying not to cry, which makes me want to cry. The only one not crying or on the verge of tears is the baby, who I am convinced understands the situation perfectly.

Tamara reaches across and starts playing with my hair. "Thanks for coming with us. I know you didn't want to."

I shake my head. "It's fine. I know it was important to you, and I wanted to see him too."

Later, in bed, she is spooned against me, and her body is so warm and soft that for an instant I think our lives are perfect.

After I reach over and turn off the light, Tamara whispers, "I wanted better for my kids, you know."

Though she can't see me, I nod. "André's a good kid. He'll straighten out. And Lola and Thomas are doing well...it's definitely not too late for them."

She sniffles. "Sometimes I'm not sure. I don't know how to save them."

"From what?"

"From this. From having to visit all their relatives in jail. From being less than a paycheck from the streets. From living like me."

I kiss her shoulder and hold her tight. "We're doing pretty well."

"Yeah, *we* are, but things happen. You could get tired of all this."

"I didn't say all that."

"No, I did.... I'm not stupid, you know. I know I frustrate you. I know you think I'm too ghetto," she says.

"I've never said that about you, and I'm not trying to change you. Besides which, you could get tired of me. I'm square. I'm too quiet. I always have to be right."

"Your friends think it," Tamara whispers.

"It is none of their business."

She sighs. "You say that now, but sooner or later you'll leave. Everyone always does."

"After five years I'd say it's a little late for me to be having doubts. I knew what I was getting into from the start."

Tamara rolls over, and I feel her staring at me in the darkness. "Are you sure?"

* * *

The first time I introduced Tamara to my parents, I was a nervous wreck. They're sort of snobby and have all these preconceived Haitian immigrant notions about Americans that aren't terribly flattering, so I spent hours coaching Tamara on how to act and drank a bottle of Pepto-Bismol before I finally gave up, hoping that nothing too traumatic would occur.

It went remarkably well because, like my mother, Tamara is a lady MacGyver with a dash of Martha Stewart thrown in for variety. While my dad and I tried a new brand of rum he had brought back from Haiti, they were in the kitchen yukking it up about KitchenAids and bathroom grout. Over dinner, my parents' eyebrows flew into their hairlines a few times as Tamara talked about the kids, but it was an uneventful, almost pleasant evening. On the drive home Tamara said, "That wasn't so bad, now, was it?" And I had to agree, it wasn't, so we started visiting them every other weekend, sometimes bringing the kids, whom my parents were more than delighted to spoil. At this point they were willing to take grandchildren anywhere they could get them.

3. *What So Proudly We Hailed*

I've always known that Tamara has secrets, drifting like silent spaces between us. Even after all this time there's a part of her life she refuses to share with me. It's almost as if she's afraid I'll change if I know what she thinks I don't know. Some nights she disappears for hours at a time and returns home in a panic, quickly locking the door behind her. Tonight is one of those nights. I'm in bed, reading a book, with the baby sleeping on my chest. The light rise and fall of her chest against mine comforts me and, like a silent metronome, sets the pace for my reading. I'm trying not to look at the alarm clock, because if I do I'll realize it has been five hours since Tamara said she would be home. And then I'll have to begin my routine of worrying and wondering if she's been in an accident, or worse. I'll have to get angry that she always does this, that I let her get away with it. And then I'll have to resign myself to the fact that this is the way things are. So instead I wait and read and pretend everything is OK.

* * *

Sometimes there's no definite time or place where things go wrong. Sometimes things have always been wrong, and sometimes things just are the way they are...neither right nor wrong, resting in an uncomfortable void. I wake to the sound of someone retching in the bathroom so, putting the baby in her crib, I stumble out of bed, wincing as I bang my knee against the end table. Only a thin sliver of light interrupts the darkness of the hallway. Quietly I tiptoe to the slightly ajar bathroom door and stand watching Tamara vomit into the toilet; her hands, the right darker than the left, gripping the basin so tightly that her knuckles have turned white.

I knock on the door and push it open. "Are you OK?"

"Get out of here!" she screams, turning toward me, before retching again.

I'm frightened by the look of her, eyes red, tears staining her cheeks. I back away and return to bed, my stomach tying itself into knots. I don't want to cry, because I cry too much, but I find myself heaving deep, hoarse sobs into my pillow, tears falling faster than I can wipe them away. I ask myself how many more nights of this I can take, how many more nights she can take. A while later I hear her at the foot of the bed, undressing. She crawls in carefully, but we both know she knows I am awake. I feel the silent spaces drifting between us. They are cold, with a heavy bitter smell, like the air in the jail.

"Are you OK?" I ask again, my voice breaking.

Tamara inches her body toward me, burying her head beneath my chin. While she says nothing, I feel her tears falling onto my neck, trickling between my breasts. I shiver.

"Whatever you're doing, it's not worth it."

"I know," she whispers, "and the whole night I thought of you. I could hear you telling me it wasn't right. But I'm a hustler. It's the ghetto in me."

I crack my jaw. "That answer isn't good enough. It's what you always say, and I'm not stupid. I do have some idea of what you're doing."

"I'm not cheating on you, if that's what you think."

"I almost wish you were. It would be safer."

She's silent for a moment, then sighs. "I'm handling my business. Sometimes you have to do what you have to do."

"There are better ways."

Tamara pulls away, turning to face the other direction. "You aren't running me, do you understand? Joyce tried to pull that shit."

"Baby, I'm not trying to run you. You know me better than that. But I do know there's a better way to get by, whether or not you can see it."

"All I know is my way."

"Why won't you let me show you a different way?"

She reaches back and fumbles through the sheets for my hand. "It doesn't work like that."

I hold my breath, listening to the night sounds of the house. There's a leak in the sink in the laundry room, and I can hear the tiny drops of water falling against the plastic basin in a steady rhythm. Thomas, Tamara's youngest son, falls asleep with his radio on, and I can hear the faint strains of the local Top 40 station. The ceiling fan in the living room is humming and rattling a bit because some of the screws are loose. The baby is snoring gently in her crib. I want to say something more to her, but I don't. Like I said, there are secrets between us, and I see them, like shadows living in our walls. They scare me because I can't make them go away and I can never forget they are there.

In the morning Tamara gives me a brief sketch of what happened the night before: a deal gone wrong, cops coming on the scene, her swallowing the merchandise, or the evidence, as it were. She looks terrible, the skin around her eyes and mouth is gray, almost a sickly white, and her entire body is shaking. It's hard for me to look at her, so I kiss her forehead and read to her until she falls asleep. I'm missing class, but I need to be here right now. I want to believe I can protect her.

4. *At Twilight's Last Gleaming*

I fell in love with Tamara the day I had my first cavity filled. We had been dating for five or six months; things were casual, or so I would tell myself, unable to think of anything but her. I left the dentist's office, and my mouth, lips, and tongue were numb. I felt dizzy and tried to keep the car moving in a forward direction but ran up on the curb a time or two and kept giggling for no reason. I went directly to her apartment and parked the car at an awkward angle in the gravel parking lot, tripping over the small stones as I made my way to her door. After another giggle I knocked and waited, leaning against the railing behind me.

"Who is it?" she asked from behind the door.

"Police! Open up!"

There was a pause, and when she opened the door she scowled up at me. "Don't play like that."

I giggled again, trying to look apologetic.

"What happened to you?" she asked, pulling me into the apartment after taking a quick look around, as if to make sure the cops really weren't there.

"Dentist," I mumbled, but it came out sounding like "Dumb fish."

"Oh, my poor baby," she said. "Sit down."

I fell into the couch and tried to hold my head up. Tamara sat next to me and gently cupped my face with her hands, placing tiny kisses along my jawline.

"I'm going to be so good to you today," she said, brushing her lips across mine.

I pouted. "I can't kith you back."

"You don't need to."

And the look she gave me, the tenderness of her touch, I fell for her. I could literally feel myself falling. A voice inside me told me to back away, protect myself, keep things cool, and I fell anyway, and in my mind I was watching myself, thinking, *Here we go.*

*   *   *

When I come home from school that night, Tamara is sitting at the kitchen table with Thomas, helping him with his homework. She follows me into my study, perching herself on the edge of my desk as I do my nightly ritual of emptying my book bag, sorting my students' papers from my own.

"How was your day?" she asks.

I can tell we're going to pretend last night didn't happen. "Like any other. Yours?"

She frowns. "I'll tell you about it later. You know me. There's always drama. You want to do something tonight?"

I nod. "Primetime?" I say, suggesting a local nightclub where all the black people hang out.

"Right. Listen, I need a hundred dollars."

Instantly I'm irritated. "Why?"

"You can say no if that's how you feel."

I dig my fingernails into my desk. "I haven't said how I feel. I'm just asking you why you need that much money."

"I have business to handle."

"I don't have it."

"Fine," she says angrily, leaving the room.

"So that's how it is?" I call after her.

Minutes later she's standing in the doorway. I'm sitting in my chair rubbing my forehead, kicking at a stack of books against the wall.

"I really need it."

I don't say anything.

"Do you trust me? I promise I'll give it back."

"This isn't about trust."

"Just say yes or no. I can get it somewhere else if I have to."

I want to say no because I know her scheme won't end well, but I'm more frightened by the thought of that *somewhere else.* So I agree, and five minutes later she's out the front door.

When she comes home, hours later, she looks defeated almost. I'm watching television, talking on the phone to my mother, whom I promise to call later.

"What's wrong?"

"I lost it," she says, sitting next to me.

"Lost what?"

"The money."

I try to keep my voice steady. "How did you lose a hundred dollars?"

"Are you raising your voice?"

My eyes widen. "No. I'm just wondering how you lost that much money in a few hours."

"I don't want to get into it."

"More stuff that's none of my business, I suppose."

"Pretty much."

"I see," I say, standing up. "I don't feel like going out anymore. I'm going to bed."

"So now you're mad at me?"

I stop and turn around. "How should I feel?"

"I'm sorry..."

"And I'm tired."

I lay in bed, fully dressed, staring at the ceiling. I knew this would happen. It's not the first time. It won't be the last.

* * *

When we first started dating, Tamara refused to spend the night at my apartment. She hated all the white people living in my building; she felt they stared at her when she came to visit. But I'm black too, I'd tell her. You're different, she'd remind me. And she preferred to sleep in her own bed, she didn't want to leave the kids alone. Instead, after walking Thomas and Lola to the bus stop in the morning, she'd come over and crawl into bed with me, still in her pajamas. Most times I was barely awake. I'd simply roll over and slide my arm around her, only to wake up later surprised to find her lying there. Other times she'd be over watching a movie or hanging out, only to fall asleep with me but leave before I woke up the next morning. I wasn't allowed to sleep at her place. "The kids aren't ready," she'd say, and I could understand that, but really she wasn't ready. She said that sleeping with someone the whole night was far more intimate than just having sex. Sometimes I think she still feels that way, as if opening up to me is a line she won't allow herself to cross.

* * *

A few weeks later I'm watching Tamara clean the house. I've offered to help, but everything has to be done her way. She's meticulous—some might say anal—about cleaning. There's something extremely sexy about watching her, the way she pays attention to the little details: dusting the pewter figurines on the entertainment center or arranging the couch pillows just so. I often say she's so strange about cleaning because it's the one thing in her life she can control. Tamara says she doesn't like a nasty house. She watches me out of the corner of her eye, and she knows I know she knows how much I enjoy these moments, these moments when our life feels normal.

"What are you looking at?" she asks, running a feather duster under the couch.

"Nothing." I blush and look away.

"How could I tell?"

I grin. "You know I like watching you clean. Leave me alone."

She shakes her head. "You're very strange, but I like it."

"Besides which, the sexist in me likes the thought of the little woman at home keeping thangs clean."

"I can be butch," she says.

I roll my eyes. "I can't seriously consider you butch when your fingernails are that long, particularly as you straighten the doilies on the coffee table."

"Fuck you," she says, laughing.

I smile and sit quietly, wishing this afternoon would never

end. The baby is sleeping. The kids are happy. We're happy. Things should always be this way. I think of the movie *Say Anything* and how John Cusack tells Ione Skye's father that he's realized what he wants to do with his life. He wants to love Ione, because he's good at it. That's how I feel about Tamara, but we aren't two kids just out of high school, on our way to London. At this point in our lives being good at loving each other may not be enough.

* * *

We're in the car on our way to get André, who's just been released. We're both looking forward to having him home. He grows on you after a while. Jay-Z is on the radio. *It's the hard knock life (uh-huh) for us. It's the hard knock life, for us! 'Stead of treated, we get tricked. 'Stead of kisses, we get kicked. It's the hard knock life.* I tap my fingers against the steering wheel, bob my head from side to side.

"This song is the story of my life," Tamara says.

I stop tapping. "You think?"

"I know."

I chew on my lower lip. "It won't always be that way."

I want to tell her I love her enough to do everything in my power to make things different. I want to tell her she's the most amazing person I know; that with or without me, she's going to come out on top. I want to fill the silent spaces between us. But instead I turn up the volume, because this isn't about what I want.

Waiting for Claudette
Jamie Joy Gatto

I watch the translucent red candy as she pulls it in and out of her lips, slowly turning the sucker around in her mouth, wagging it between her teeth, allowing the gummy white stick to fall languorously between her lips, now tinged a watercolored, cherry-pop rouge from the sweet, sticky confection.

She's reading the paper, one hand over her eyes as shade from the summer sun's glare. She's completely unaware of my lustful gaze, seemingly more mesmerized by Ann Landers than I am by her beauty: a portrait framed in the grassy green of my backyard. When she finally spies my stare, she wrinkles up her nose at me and sticks out her tongue, painted too ruby red from dye #40.

"You won't *believe* what Hag Two has to say about porn..." Claudette rambles on, beginning to read aloud the daily column. In our world, one of a sisterhood that spawned as neighbors at the age of five, "Hag One" is Dear Abby, "Hag Two" is Ann Landers.

"What?" I say, transfixed by her lips, wanting her to speak more, wanting to watch her mouth perform more tricks for my amusement. As she speaks, the words fall into blossoms, blur into roses, and I have no idea what it all means, other than Claudette is in the same place and time with me, and this makes me happy, unfailingly happy. I pretend to hear her say she loves me. I pretend to watch her pull the lollipop from her mouth and place it into mine. I pretend to watch her lean in, as if to kiss me. I pretend she...

"So what do you think?" she asks. Plump cheeks smile at

me in their own strange, crooked way. Head cocked, her pony-tail flips at an odd angle.

"I think she's an old hag!" I laugh, hoping it's the appropriate response, and knowing Claude so well, I know she'd at least agree to that.

"Yeah! And what's with the ancient 'do? Her hair looks like it's made of plaster," Claude laughs. "How could she possibly think up anything that makes sense with that helmet head?"

And I watch her body jiggle and her breasts move like ripples on water, like Venus on a platter, like cool, cherry Jell-O, wanting to dip my face between her breasts and bury my head in the softness of her belly, to hide in her forever, but the sun lets me know it's too bright out and way too hot. And she's back to reading the paper silently, chewing on her candy.

Claudette twirls a piece of her flyaway hair, having ditched the spent sucker stick under a brown leaf. She's deep into the features section. Every once in a while she moves her lips as she reads, as if to purposefully emphasize the intensity of her expression. Her brow furrows now and then, and I want to lean over and touch her, to comfort her in a small gesture, but I realize now, more than ever, that I'll never be able to share anything but a token gesture of friendship, the kind between old friends, exclusively meant for sisters. No deep lingering caresses, no passionate embraces, not a teasing touch on the tip of her nose to make her smile. I'll never be able to unbutton her pink blouse—one button by one by one—to take her voluminous areolas between my teeth and suckle them like a spring lamb...to let my tongue glide smoothly over the soft folds of her belly, lingering in the hollow of her navel, tasting the sweet, salty taste of young pink maiden, to place my nose into the delicate, downy blond essence of her sex, to taste the sugary tang of her wet, ripe clit...to take my cherry girl, my Claudette, to shivering heights of happiness with my lips, to that blissful place I feel when I touch myself alone in bed, thinking of her, but always, always alone without Claudette.

* * *

At 44 she is lovelier still; the hint of fine lines around the contours of her face reminds me how often she smiles with her eyes. I see the same color blue, mixed with a splash of dove gray reflected in the eyes of Sara and little Jim. They are like two fat cherubs sprung forth from the songs of Erato, little cookie-cutter cupids made wholly human and nurtured by the sweet mother's milk of Claudette. Sara climbs into my lap and presses my cheeks together, squishing my face, calling me "Little Mommy," a name I suppose she's given me because of the contrast of my gangly limbs and spindly fingers to her mother's full body and huge, encompassing embrace. I love Sara as if she's my own daughter, and I wonder if the gods had granted me the seed of life, could I have made children as lovely as these with my Claude, and if the gods were so benevolent would I have also had the power to tell her I loved her so, that I wanted her so?

Claudette has her hair in curlers, the old-fashioned, spiky kind, secured with thin pink plastic rods. Why she still tries to curl her straight, silky hair, I'll never know. They say women always want more of whatever it is they can't have. Sara squirms in my lap, eager to have her hair curled too. I take her little tufts of blond silk between my long fingers and try to wrap them in the smallest curlers. She wiggles so hard that each downy puff I curl wanders out, uncurling as fast as I can get the next one in. As I play with the child's hair, Claude dresses before her vanity, fussing with her face and squinting into the magnifying mirror.

"Do I look old, Mare?" she says.

"Like a shriveled prune."

Claude sticks out her tongue at me in the mirror as Sara slithers out of my lap and squeals, chasing after the cat. "You know how weddings are," she says, her mouth hanging wide open as she dabs mascara on her lower lashes. "They always make you feel like maybe you could be more in love, like you could start again, like maybe *you* could be that bride." She uncurls her hair. "Hey! Maybe you'll catch the bouquet," she giggles, a curler stick wedged between her teeth.

"Yeah. Maybe. I'll be the world's oldest bride."

"And I'll be the world's pruniest maid of honor. We'll be Hag One and Hag Two!" she practically yells, laughing as her face blushes red roses.

I think of Claude on her wedding day, and I remember every fold in her satin gown, every pearl in the lace of her sleeves...the fluid, translucent wisps of tulle that fell around her face, framing her lush cheeks, covering them with her blusher veil. I know what it feels like to dress her, to prepare a goddess. I recall the honor of dressing her in the white brocade corset, pulling tight each of the laces into smart, even X's, and how her breasts spilled from the top of the garment, hovering as if they popped from their invulnerable security...and how her legs looked ripe and smelled of musk and green tea, lilac and jasmine as I pulled the blue satin garter over her plump thigh, sliding it up the transparent hosiery, lingering right above her knee, my hands upon her legs as I looked longingly into her eyes, trembling, knowing my left hand was just a few more inches from the sacred place between her thighs. And how I wanted to keep my hands on her body as the photographer took our photo, to be cherished forever, matted in gold, stored for decades in a white, leather-bound, gilt-inscribed book: "Maid of Honor Dresses the Bride-to-Be."

Claude is still chattering on about new beginnings and love renewed and how maybe she'll renew her vows with Jim on their tenth, when she turns and says, "Mare, I gotta ask you something, and I'm serious." She takes both my hands and holds them tightly. She looks right into my eyes, my heart is in my throat, and I want to tell her now, and seeing her again as that bride, *my* bride, if only in my mind's eye, has awakened my strength, revitalized my will. All the urgency I once felt for Claudette feels as if it has been finally buoyed, made lighter by the gods, and with all abandon I open my lips, and I start to speak, but she shushes me—plump, manicured fingers on my lips—and says, "Mare, will you be my maid of honor when Jim and I renew our vows? I wouldn't have it any other way."

And I smile, grasping her hands even more tightly; a tear wells in my eye, and I nod. "Of course," I whisper. "Claude, of course."

A Preference for the Moment
Ronna Magy

October

We are walking down that California winter road. A fine
spray of dust lifts off each step, airy footprints marking themselves in fading light like skywriting—there, then gone. We are
walking away from our little cottage. On the right a Christmas
hedge of red roses still blossoms. A light glows from inside a
house window; it is not quite dark outside.

A few more footprints along the road, an opening into a
clearing, and you are gone. I watch your steps, follow you
down. Slowly, from a pomegranate tree you pick off the red
ornaments one by one and place them inside your black jacket
until they bulge out and you become a many-breasted woman.

You crack one fruit open and for just a moment expose its
red eyes to the purpling horizon. Like berries so sweet they
could never last long outside the mouth, the red seeds are
taken in and sucked one by one.

The next morning by the lake, a few brown maple leaves
float on the surface. Curled yellow and red ones cover the cobblestones outside our cottage window. I awoke early, at 6. Sit
in the window reading, writing, and sipping tea. A cream-
colored candle burns in a silver holder on the table. A few
brown leaves rest against the glass where I placed them after
our walk.

Under a paisley comforter in the next room you lay in
bed reading *The New Yorker*. You flip the pages one by one.
You are a reader; I like this about you. I like that you love

words, get lost in words, search for words in your dictionary, and use them in our talks. I like that you tell stories the way my father did when I was young. I like the feel of you next to me in bed. The way your hands caress the length of me. The way your mouth feels on my breasts. There is a comfort in this love with you.

On the stove rests a basket of last night's pomegranates. For me they are foreign fruit. I am fascinated by their lack of modernity. How difficult they are to eat. How tough their crusty skins. How sweet the seeds.

You are a connoisseur of pomegranates. For you, in your realm, there would be pomegranates. And I would spread the red seeds along your body and eat them off you one by one, licking a red trail across your stomach and down to your hips. There would be pomegranates and my caresses and a few cinnamon buns and morning things like good coffee and your long gray robe. We would spend our days licking sugary cinnamon morsels off our fingertips and rubbing fingers around each other's lips like children, feeling old sensations again for the first time.

November

One night I stand in front of you, purple towel around my waist, breasts exposed. You like my breasts. I am your model, and you my camera's eye. Slowly I move from right to front so you can see their fullness. So you can imagine caressing them, sliding your fingers along them, circling each nipple with your tongue, putting each in your mouth. I stand, and your camera eye clicks, picture after picture. I want you to remember me. Remember each pose. The slope of my right breast. It is close to a mango. Has the texture of ripe, the color of warm, full flesh.

When we are apart and I am at my house, I take out my album of you. Spread the pages of your shoulders, neck, breasts, legs, one by one in front of me. Imagine your hands between my legs. Wait for your fingers to pull on my lips, walk between the folds, rub on my clitoris until the moans begin and for you to say in one ear, "Come, honey. I want you to come."

When we are apart, I have to remember all this to stay connected to you. I must remember the way you slick back your hair, the way your nipples rise when I rub your back and place small kisses on the insides of your legs. I become the photographer and you the model. We change sides of the camera. The model and the trained eye interchange. As if the model remembers the photographer's way of standing, sitting, posing, viewing, clicking, smiling, talking, being. The lines blur, the black and white of old photos become gray. Photographer-model, model-photographer, camera eye–naked eye, photo–real life. There is no I and other. The you is me. I am yours.

From the end of the bed I move toward you. You throw back the comforter, exposing a thigh to the light. I have not spent enough time with these legs. I feel them strong around my hips but don't yet know them. Leg to leg we move across the surface of the bed, as if it is water and the legs are paddles. Back and forth. It is liquid, we are solid. It is fluid, we are porous. The white bedsheet water laps across our legs. Steadily we navigate the mattress, sheets, comforter. You lay me down on a blanket rock in the middle of the bed, saying, "Let me look at you." On your face, the look of one who has waited but is no longer searching.

In my album you will be on page 1, 2, 3, 4, 5, all the way up to 100. Under the plastic will be your picture, some notes about each trip, each place, each fruit, each flower, each experience. Turning the pages I will remember you, but I prefer you to the memory, the taste to the afterthought, the experience to the idea, you to the cells of my brain that retain and recall.

January

Your French mother sits with us on the green couch in your living room while dimming light darkens to the color of your

English tea. I do not see her as you plunge Kalamata olives and pieces of dry salty cheese onto the back of your tongue and swallow hard. I am immersed in your brown eyes and soft lips. Early on I do not know your mother to be present, or her signs. She is not visible, but she is there.

In October at the lake you told stories of growing up, how she never wanted you, left you alone, didn't listen when you cried, called you bad. You tell those stories and I am sad for the child you were and the childhood you didn't have. You paint a girl in a brown wool jumper, schoolgirl pleats, hair cut short, lips sucked in. There is a plainness about you, invisibility.

You deny your mother's presence as we drive the long return back from the lake, empty desert mountains twirling through miles of sand and leafless shrubs. I ask if it is she who moves through your coldness, but you say no, she is not what makes you pull away, and drive on in silence. "There is," you tell me, "nothing to say."

I met your mother once at a Rosh Hashanah. She wore a white Chanel sweater piped around in black. The kind some women might have worn in the '50s, but not those I knew. She wore the white sweater and matching pants—Saint Tropez vacation wear, European—and did not smile. Inside the sanctuary tightness, the corners of her mouth pulled in, the schoolmaster's rod held her shoulders back. She said "Hello"; that was all. She did not look my way again, sat down the row, deliberately leaving empty seats between herself and me. Perhaps she hated me because I, your lover, was a woman, and she could no longer possess you the way she had when you, as a child, were hers.

Recently, shedding old angers, you invited her for Hanukkah, asked her to light the candles and say the blessings. She talked of your divorce, repeating, "When are you going to remarry? You need a man. You can't have only women as friends." At you she threw the words "man" and "marriage," watched as they passed from her mouth into you, rose up red along your face, throat, and arms. She is the only woman she wants you to love.

After this incident you dispelled her from your house the way she forced you, unwanted, from the womb. Locked the front door, left her outside pounding, wanting to come in, and you did not open the door. You did not let her in as she screamed, just as she turned from you when you were a child. That one day you kept her out, thought the closing of a door would keep her away. Before, when you tried to lock her from your mind, she came back in dreams and in our making of love.

After being with you for three or four months, I realize she lies with us in bed, watching you, commanding you, talking to me through your voice.

I do not know this at first. All is new and fresh, your touch, my arousal, my hands on you caressing, finding the right spots. I do not see her until during lovemaking you begin to want more. "This is good," you say, but still you want more touch, sex, intimacy, and love. "Not enough," you say and demand loving when I am tired and in need of sleep. "Not enough," you say. You want more.

At first I think I have been selfish, but after days of love-making insatiability still dances in our bed, lies between the sheets, and lodges in your words. Each time you are with me, each time we make love, this woman appears. You cry out for me and my love, but it is she for whom you long.

From childhood she has groomed you, last daughter, to care for her. She tells you it is the way of women, expecting you to strip away the years, your breaking away at 20, crossing borders to find a new life. There is the expectation that you will come home and again be hers. You are to be silent, not think. You are to not feel, not care. Only to wait on and care for her as she gets old. You, who craved her love like scarce water. She, who gave you barely enough to sustain life.

The clothes lay below us on the wooden floor. My black jeans and sweater. Your silk stockings and lace bra that curves low on your breasts, revealing the place where I rest my hand. Your mother's presence stands next to the couch in back of me. Your mouth forms the words "Love me." You look through my eyes and back at her.

Recycled
Kristin Steele

The bite of the alarm clock breaks the morning's skin as Kate opens one eye to meet the red glow across the room. She keeps her clock on the dresser by the door to force herself to put her feet on the cold hardwood floor. Vertical positions urge her toward the shower instead of allowing her to hit the sleep button and duck back under the covers. But no matter how many mornings in a row she performs the task of lugging out of sleep, 3 A.M. is still an ungodly hour. She vaguely hears the coffeepot start as she gently bounces off the hallway walls, rubbing her half-mast eyes, feeling her way to the bathroom. Her tabby, Jones, follows her, jumping from one throw rug to another to invite her to fill his bowl.

Kate's heavy boots sound louder on the front porch's steps than she'd like. She skips every other one on her way down, leaving size-10 marks on the dew-covered pavement. What her boots don't wake, the roar of her '74 Volkswagen will, so she's gotten in the habit of putting it in neutral and releasing the emergency brake, allowing her car to roll down the mild slope she lives on. When the car glides closer to the main road and farther away from her neighbors, she encourages her baby to wake. There's nothing like the first hit of engine exhaust coming through the vents to finally draw her into her surroundings. The drive to the truck yard is long enough for her mind to wander to the dull drone of the engine behind her, coffee steam opening the pores above her lip and across her nose as she reels in the cup for a long pull. Today there's no one else on the road, and she knows she can hit green at all of the intersections along Sandy Boulevard if she travels at a constant 32 miles an hour, each light coaxed from red to green as the first bit of tire tread hits the crosswalk.

What Kate likes most about driving a recycling truck is standing on the sideboard as she maneuvers it down the street, her foot hanging out over the rolling asphalt. She closes one eye, and the retreating ground blurs underneath her boot, giving her a momentary sense of traveling much faster then she actually is.

Recycling is a more invasive job than she'd expected—discovering private bits of information about the people living on these parceled Portland streets. She gets a firsthand glimpse of what they discard. Sometimes it's just trash, but often secrets are buried deep in the curbside bins. Newspapers and the orange juice cartons that got used up while reading them. Mrs. Alegheny's weekly stash of vodka bottles with the labels ripped off. Their powerful fumes give them away every time.

Crisp mornings on the truck are something none of Kate's friends understand. Her early workday allows her to spend afternoons in her shop, making wire figures and sculpting, or hours in the kitchen cooking and inventing new recipes. But there's something else about the job that she loves: Every morning, with the rumble of the truck beneath her, she gets to watch the slow-rising sun, dogs on their morning rounds, kids running off to school. In her hooded sweatshirt and too-big gloves that keep the grooves of the tin cans a mystery, her almost-six-foot frame and well-used arms allow her to swing the recycling boxes up and over her head onto the truck bins in one swift motion. As the sounds of crashing glass disturb the silence of a sleepy street, she jumps back up in the truck and ashes one of her too many Marlboros into the rusty can she keeps on the dashboard. She has a freedom outside the walled boundaries of these homes, which she gets a clear picture of as she makes her rounds.

* * *

Morgan can always sense when the alarm is just about to go off. This morning she wakes with a start exactly two minutes before the set time. She's found that this morning shot of adrenaline is better than any cup of coffee, and those two minutes allow her exactly enough time to stretch, wipe the sleep from her eyes, and roll over and switch the clock radio to NPR before the annoying buzz. She lies staring at the white-plastered ceiling while news stories filter through the air around her. In recent weeks, the hours between 5 and 7 have come to be her favorite time of day. Her mother, no matter how insistent, still will not call any earlier than 7. For these two hours Morgan is alone and unscathed. She listens to her furnace start its morning tug-of-war with the brisk morning air that has crept in through the gaps around the doors and windows of her house.

The rumbling of the recycling truck pours in, indicating another Monday. Morgan peels back the covers and saunters into the kitchen. She puts the teapot on the stove, absently standing in front of the refrigerator while she waits for it to whistle. She notices a photo of her and her father from last Thanksgiving under a magnet on the freezer: He's wearing a crazy hat, wielding a turkey knife like a madman for the camera; Morgan stands next to him in mock horror, hands on her cheeks, eyes wide and bright. She traces the outlines of the two figures, slides her finger down the slope of her father's cheek. The ringing of the phone pierces her reverie.

"Hello," she states, more as custom than statement, knowing her mother will announce herself on the other end. It's 7:03.

"Did I wake you?" her mother, Sharon, asks.

For the past six weeks since the funeral, every morning has started this way. Morgan understands her mother's newfound loneliness and need, but Sharon has left her daughter little time for her own grieving. Morgan's brothers have been left out of this by virtue of geography, simply flying in for the funeral then quickly departing. All of them are long-distance calls; Morgan is a local one. For a frugal mother there's really no question between dialing seven numbers or 11.

"No, Mom. How are things?"

"Well…" and she starts the daily litany of lost sleep, bad dreams, diminished appetite, constant housecleaning. Morgan listens with one ear but lets the other wander around the house and out into the street. She hears a sudden blast of smashing glass and moves to the living-room window facing the street. She sees the recycler carefully setting empty bins back on the grass median between the sidewalk and street; the guy before usually just threw them on her lawn. She watches the recycler jump back on the truck and cruise down the street. The cardboard pile that should have been picked up is still on the grass. With her mother meandering on the other end, Morgan slides into her boots and takes the cordless phone out with her to check on the cardboard. As she approaches the misshapen pile, she spots a note on top:

> "We're sorry that all of your recyclables could
> not be collected today. Cardboard must be flat-
> tened and bound in a stack no larger than 24 by
> 36 inches. Thank you for your cooperation."

"Morgan, are you listening to me?" Sharon asks, more tired than angry.

"Yeah, Mom, I'm here." Morgan takes the note and crumples it into a ball as she heads into the house, where the teapot whistles full force.

* * *

Kate jumps off the truck at 1229 to find the cardboard pile she left last week. It hasn't moved an inch. At the top she sees an envelope with the words "To whom it may concern..." She picks it off the pile, noticing DAD'S STUFF written in marker on the box underneath. Inside the envelope she finds the note she left last week, ripped into tiny pieces. Kate laughs; this is the first time she's seen this kind of response. Usually customers come out and scream at her or just make the correction and that's the end of it. Today, though, she appreciates the originality and slides the envelope into her back pocket. But the pile still isn't flattened or bound. She knows that if she starts to let one thing slide, everything curbside will go haphazard. So she goes to the truck and retrieves another notice detailing the cardboard specifications and fastens it back on top of the pile, wondering what the reaction might be this time. Kate turns to jump on the truck when she hears the front door behind her slam shut, heavy footsteps hitting the walkway.

"Sir? Excuse me, sir?" Morgan bellows from mid lawn.

Kate doesn't respond; instead she takes a long pull from her cigarette and reaches for the truck's gearshift. She turns to look at Morgan, who's huffing and lining up argument points on the cuff of her sleeve. Kate notices Morgan's shirt is misbuttoned, the left side riding one buttonhole higher than the right.

"Oh, wow. I'm sorry," says Morgan, realizing her error.

"It's OK. I get that a lot. Are you here to chat about the cardboard?"

"Yeah...I...um," Morgan stammers, unable to regain her composure after looking Kate in the eye.

"Look, it's easy. All you gotta do is flatten it and wrap either tape or string around it. OK?"

"What difference does it make?" Morgan spits out, regaining her composure and remembering why she ran out into the yard in the first place.

"That's simply the way it needs to be done. I'm just the poor messenger. Give it a shot—stomping on cardboard boxes can be a lot of fun," Kate offers with a smile.

Morgan almost smiles but instead looks at the boxes, sees DAD'S STUFF scrawled across the top, and suddenly turns. "Just get them out of here and stop leaving me all these damn notes," she yells, plucking the piece of paper off the pile and tossing it toward Kate.

With that she storms back into the house. When Kate hears the door latch, she chuckles, picks the note off the ground, and puts it back on top of the pile. *It was worth getting up this morning,* she thinks. She guides the truck quietly and easily from the curb and down the street, replaying the pretty girl's tantrum over and over in her head.

That afternoon, Kate slides out of the shower and into her faded, stained overalls. She pulls on a pair of tattered Converses and grabs the boom box on her way out to the detached garage that doubles as her studio. She notices Morgan's envelope on the counter as she passes through the kitchen. Smiling again at it, she takes it out to the studio, propping it against the lamp on her table. "To whom it may concern." Kate looks at the words, written hastily in green ink, and appreciates the formality Morgan attempted with a curbside recycler. It didn't say, "Hey, you in the hat" or "Stupid fuck who won't take my cardboard." Kate zooms in on the word *concern,* thinking of the gentle sweep of Morgan's brown hair across her brow; remembers how Morgan quickly broke when she looked at the lettering on the box. Kate wonders why those boxes *concerned* Morgan—not really the boxes themselves, but what they once contained. She wonders whether Morgan's concern might actually be a need for someone. She clicks on the radio, and an old Fleetwood Mac tune pushes itself out of the blown speaker, creating a baseline hum absent in the original recording. She picks up her spool of wire and winds and bends it around and over itself, a small figure slowly emerging from the twists and turns.

Morgan, on all fours in the corner of her kitchen, is sweating, fueled by this morning's altercation—though she's hesitant to call it that, since that implies both parties were involved in the argument. She was the one who had screamed. The woman was just doing her job, right? Armed with a toothbrush and a bottle of soap mix, Morgan is certain the grout between the floor tiles shouldn't be this dark. The whole thing this morning probably shouldn't have gone down the way it did, but there was little she could do to mask her embarrassment about calling that woman "sir." Instead of giving in, though, Morgan once again decided to take the higher ground—to which she wasn't really entitled. Of course the boxes should be flattened, but she just can't look at them anymore.

What started as a simple musing about the color beneath the gray grout is now an obsession, each toothbrush bristle turning back on itself. Morgan wipes away the foam to find a lighter and cleaner color. Relieved, she smiles, but then realizes that now that she has discovered the true color underneath, she won't be able to rest until the whole floor is spotless. She takes a big breath, drags her sleeved arm across her forehead like a windshield wiper pulling sweat away from her line of vision, and takes on the whole floor, limiting her vision to one tile at a time.

* * *

The following week, Kate swings Morgan's newspaper bin

up over her head to load onto the truck. But her right foot slips off the curb, and she drops the box before it's completely empty. A stack of newspapers falls to the ground with a defiant thud. She lowers the box and reaches for the pile to throw into the truck. As she slaps her glove on top of the stack, she realizes that every newspaper is uniformly folded in its original fashion and that instead of being ten different editions, they're ten copies from the same day: September 15. It looks like someone put 35 cents into a newspaper machine, pulled out the entire stack of *Oregonian*s, and dumped them into the recycling bin.

As she lifts the stack, one of the newspapers slides out and hits the curb, cleaving into its separate parts. Annoyed, Kate throws the stack back on the ground and scrambles to pick up the loose sections. She notices that the back page of the "Living" section is missing a square in its bottom left-hand corner— home, ironically, to the obituaries. Curious, she checks the other newspapers and finds them all dissected, with a surgeon's accuracy, in the same fashion. Kate heaves the stack into the truck, turning to grab the other items on the curb. There, for the third week in a row, are the cardboard boxes, unchanged. No ripped-up note. No note at all. Just the ominous unchanged stack that speaks volumes. Kate hesitates a moment, then pitches the boxes into the truck. She considers leaving another reminder, but when she looks at the house and sees a small light in an upstairs window behind horizontal blinds, she decides that the war is over and slowly navigates down the street.

* * *

The next Monday, instead of spending the last minutes before 7 tucked under the covers listening to the news, Morgan gets up at 6 and showers. She felt suffocated under the covers and had to get out. She makes a 6:30 run to the neighborhood coffee shop and orders an extra coffee and scone, then rushes home, relieved to find the recycling still on the curb. She places the coffee and small brown paper bag on the cement in front of the bins, cautiously looks up and down the street, and heads into the house. She opens all the blinds and dashes into the bathroom to check her hair in a quick and seeming-not-to-care way. She paces until she hears the telltale engine barreling down the street, then perches herself in the living-room window. Steam rises from the hole in the cup's lid like a smoke signal from a lost hiker hoping to be spotted by passing planes.

Morgan watches the street, body tucked behind the curtain, head sticking out. She sees Kate pull up, brake, and jump off the truck in one fluid motion. As she bends for the first bin, knees expertly positioned to cushion the blow of the weight to the back, Kate halts at the sight of the offerings. As she opens the sack, Morgan glimpses a flash of white in a smile. Morgan waits for her to look up, and when she does she peeks out from behind the curtain and waves. Kate offers a bigger smile and stands on the curb, alternately sipping the coffee and slowly breaking off pieces of scone, chewing and nodding in Morgan's direction. When the phone rings, Morgan lets the machine pick up.

"Are you there? Hello? It's your mother. I don't know where you could be at this hour. Call me as soon as you get in."

Morgan continues to watch as Kate sets her gifts on the dash of the truck and turns to finish what she came for. Her motions are graceful to Morgan, as if she were in slow motion. As Kate jumps on the truck and turns to go, she raises a gloved hand, allowing it to linger in the air between them as she drives away. Smiling, Morgan goes to the phone to check in on her mother.

* * *

The wire figure sits nimbly on the dash as the truck bounces down the street. A surge of adrenaline shoots through Kate as she turns the corner and comes up on the now-familiar

1229. There are no bins out front; no real reason to stop. She attempts to lower the volume of the truck's boisterous brakes by slowing down half a house away, gliding to a stop just past Morgan's front door. The blinds are shut, the light off. Kate grabs the figure and jumps to the sidewalk. Instead of crossing the dew-topped lawn, she steps around it to the walkway and advances to the porch, careful not to step on the wooden stairs; her heavy boots would give her away. As she bends down to leave the figure on the porch, a raised voice filters through the window to her left.

"Mom, I don't want to keep going over and over it. I'm doing the best I can."

Long silence.

"I lost him too. So did everyone else in this family. We're all dealing with his death."

Silence.

Kate quickly rises and moves away from the porch so as not to be caught listening. She backs away from the house, noticing the flaking paint along the trim and the just-too-long grass. Weeds weave in and out of the shrubs. She looks at the pile of wire on the porch; from the street it appears small against the house. The gold and brass wire gleams in the early morning light. She nods, turns, and goes.

* * *

Morgan knows this will definitely be a decisive move. Preparing a meal for someone is a weighty prospect. Does she eat meat? White or wheat bread? Not everyone is a mustard fan. For an entire week she debated the contents of the brown sack but finally settled on peanut butter and honey, hoping to tap into a kindred nostalgia and circumvent the whole animal product issue. Wheat, not white. But not a chunky wheat with all kinds of twigs and berries and things—just something simple.

She waits until 6:45 to apply the honey so that it won't soak too far into the bread. She adds a plastic bag of carrot sticks, carefully cut into bite-size pieces. Bottled water and chocolate chip cookies. From scratch. Nothing too presumptuous or fancy; she's never believed in false advertising. Homegrown before gourmet any day. But it's the finishing touch, the reason for the whole endeavor, that's proving to be the most trouble: the offering of the phone number. Should she write something cute on a napkin? Leave a note at the bottom of the bag? No one on the face of the planet could make this graceful, she thought. But her indecision is immediately broken by the clamor of the truck coming down the street. She scribbles something quickly on the bag and runs out to plant the bait. Instead of taking it out to the curb, she decides to split the difference, placing it halfway down the walk, and dashes back into the house.

Kate, running late, abruptly stops the truck and has both of the recycling bins dumped before she even realizes where she is. For some reason she feels like she's being watched and quickly turns to see, out of the corner of her eye, the curtains being shoved back into place. Letting out a laugh, she scans the front of the house for more movement, when she spots the brown bag on the walk and approaches, kneeling to its level. The words on the front seem hurried and unsure:

> "So there's no unclumsy way for me to do this, really. Two left feet, two left hands, two left brains. Consider this a gesture. The intent is up for debate."

Followed by a phone number.

Kate nods her head in flattery, looks up to see the curtain over the oval glass on the front door pulled back and Morgan behind it anxious for response. Kate simply smiles, reaches for the bag, and unfolds the top. The sweet smell spills out, and right away she knows it's peanut butter and honey. She giggles, wondering how someone could get it right on the first try. She pulls the sandwich from the bag and, facing Morgan, places the sandwich over her heart and bows in front of her master chef. Kate returns to full height from the bow in time to see Morgan throw her head back, her laugh audible through the door's thin glass. Their eyes meet and hold. Both are satisfied, and Kate walks backward to the truck, her steps sure without even looking.

* * *

The sun's last rays stream through the back window, making the accumulated dust all too visible on the tops of counters and picture frames and unburned candles. Morgan, in the middle of the room with a rag in her hand, is debating whether to dust or go to a movie when the phone rings. She does a mental tally on the first ring: Her mother has already called five times today, the last being less than an hour ago, so she should be fairly safe now. She picks up the phone—*Please, don't be Mom* written in the air in front of her—and takes a deep breath. "Hello?"

A slight pause on the other end, then, "How could you possibly have known that peanut butter and honey is my favorite?"

Morgan smiles, takes another breath, and traces patterns in the dust.

The Fall
Helen Vozenilek

"I was looking for warmth and companionship, and instead I found you," I tell her during one of our last discussions, just so she knows how worthless I think she is. I have not been at all gracious about our break-up. But I figure that's not the role of the one getting dumped. Our purpose is to vilify, slander, and plot divine forms of retribution.

Suddenly newspaper accounts of spurned lovers committing outrageously desperate acts captivate me. I pore eagerly over the morning paper. Cars driven off cliffs, multiple tire slashings, kitchen knives stabbed into front doors, sharp projectiles launched through windows, drunken fits of self-immolation. I am that spurned lover, crazy with grief. My vision is sharp like shards of broken glass. Pushing my own cart down the now-widened aisles, I see the broken hearts that topple from the shopping cart annals of criminal behavior. That an unrequited love affair may have caused the Unabomber to take up his particular form of mail delivery makes him so much more understandable to me.

It's not that I'm happy being so miserable. There are few places I can think of where I wouldn't rather be. I feel like I'm at a blackjack table in Vegas and the dealer's got 21—showing. Still I keep betting more and more chips, either not believing the cards laid out in front of me or somehow thinking that the rules of the game are going to change. All the while, my stack of chips gets lower and lower. And I wonder when I'll finally decide either to declare bankruptcy or, at least, to look for a game with better odds.

I bought a bunch of those drippy self-help books and plastered my walls with "One Day at a Time" stickers. Clearly I was the bottomed-out, life-is-unmanageable, powerless-to-do-shit, contorted lost soul these books were written for. After all, I was desperate enough to buy the books. A physicist friend explained her own General Theory of Relationships: the time it takes to get over somebody is equal to the time you were with them. This idea made me feel badly for my friend because she had been married 15 years and 15 years is a long time to anguish over someone or something. The thought cheered me personally, though: I figured I'd be able to pick myself up off the streets within a year's time. And I rather looked forward to a change in my musical interests. I mean, how much longer could I possibly listen to "Cry Me a River"?

Listening to a spiritual talk show, I learned of a candle ritual for soul cleansing. It really was quite elaborate. The first night you light three candles, the second night you move them around, Ouija-board-like, and so on through the week. And on that seventh day, if everything goes as planned, release should be yours. Excitedly, I wrote everything down so I'd be sure to do it just right. But then I couldn't find any candles. So instead I made the biggest goddamn bonfire in my backyard, gathered all the cards, letters, and photos that had anything to do with her, and threw them en masse into the flames. The searing heat left me with an oddly reassuring glow. Then I started in on burning the clothing she'd given me. But halfway through the first polypropylene shirt I stopped myself. For one, I was worried about the toxins these "natural" synthetics were emitting. And also, the ex had pretty good taste in clothes, and I had to ask myself who was losing out in the conflagration.

Believing in the madness of saints and in pain being one of creativity's prickly spurs, I pursued various art forms. I bought a special journal I christened *The Dumping Diaries*. One week I wrote nasty, hateful, you-make-me-sick letters. The next I penned beautiful poetry of fate, love's ineluctability, and the partnering of our souls. When I showed some pieces to writing friends, they talked about how the writer often needs a certain distance from her subject. My paintings during this time were streaked and turbulent. All unfinished. The little clay figurines I made cracked and, with one swing of the hammer, were quickly reduced to dust. I finally realized I was stuck in that land of paralysis between pain and psychosis.

Once I realized it didn't have anything to do with Patty Hearst, I went to an SLA—Sex and Love Addicts—meeting. If nothing else, I heard it was a good way to meet somebody. But I only made it through two sessions. For one thing, I couldn't even open my mouth without sobbing. All the eagerly seated SLAers would be trying to welcome me, and I'd be all loud and doubled over in hysteria. I embarrassed myself. And then, listening to people's stories, I thought I really needed to be in a healthier environment. It made about as much sense as visiting a cancer ward when you aren't feeling well. But more than anything, I wasn't into examining my behavior patterns. After all, she was the one who was screwed up....

At first I raced furiously from one project to another. I was finally going to be able to do all the things I hadn't had time for when I was in a relationship. Paint the house, travel to distant countries, get an advanced degree in something or other. I woke up every day with a new design of how to get on with my life. My plans spewed forth like hot volcanic ash. But then they laid around solid and unmoving as molten rock. I never got around to finishing anything. Taking the garbage out was about all the detail and execution I could muster. Maybe someday I'll get around to returning the gallons of paint stored in the garage...

Now I've finally just stopped making plans altogether. I figure why set things up so that I'll feel like even more of a failure?

At the beginning, friends would invite me out for wine and

tears. Everyone's a seamstress when it comes to mending a broken heart. But after a while the invitations dwindled. I picked up a certain impatience: the barely concealed rolling eyes, the exaggerated "Anything new?" Other times, the more blunt "Move on," as though I were a cow stuck on the highway, unable to cross over the hand-painted grates.

This past Easter I went to church after a ten-year hiatus. I thought if I could just mobilize around the idea of renewal, I would be able to ascend from my sorrow. Kind of like Jesus did, leaving behind only a few earthly vestments so the angels would know he'd been there. Only the rungs of my ascent would be different. And I'd give the three-headed hound a swift kick as I rose from my hellish domain.

But try as I might, sitting there in the pew, I couldn't really get behind the whole Jesus thing. To be denounced, betrayed, and forsaken by your buddies, and then to forgive them, seemed borderline. Like, they have programs for people like that. And forgiving the ex really wasn't anywhere on my list of priorities. At least not in this lifetime.

Not that I have any business comparing my pain to that of Jesus. And although I've been thinking a lot about how this reminds me of feeling rejected by my mother, truth is there's no comparison. To know that his father set up the whole deal must have been pretty devastating to Jesus's self-esteem. Even if he *was* able to turn things around at the end. But who knows, maybe I too will get a good book out of it.

Actually, comparing myself to others does help. When you're in pain, it's important to remember how much more pain you could be in. And surely on that neon spectrum of heartbreak and abandonment, my loss keys in at the lower end. You hear about people who come home from work and find that their spouse of 25 years has simply packed up and gone. Disappeared. Finito. No note, nothing, just an empty closet. At least the ex talks to me, or says she will in a few months. And I know where I can usually find her. A few nights back I sat outside her darkened windows draining the last of a six-pack, and hoped that the next day when she saw the empties strewn all over the yard, she would at least think of me.

But even with all my sprinting, memories found my feet firmly locked into the starting blocks. Late nights and early mornings were the hardest. Though I'd rearranged my bedroom furniture three times, I still couldn't get rid of her. I'd lie awake restaging our missed lines, dropped cues, poorly timed exits and entrances. In that thin curtain hour between what has come to pass and what has not, I prayed aloud for guidance. And deliverance. And tried to understand—if faith could move mountains into the sea, why wasn't mine strong enough to bring her back to me? Finally I'd drop off to sleep, waking with a start to her imagined knock at the door, her voice calling through the echoing night.

Eventually I perfected the right mixture of beer and Benadryl, so I now make it through the nights with only a slight hangover of what might have been.

Now summer has finally cast off its cheerful facade and the days have lost their boastful insouciance. Gazing out my window into the early gathering night, I'm trying to believe in the compassion of time. I'm trying to find the sanity born from the season's inexorable change. I'm trying to remember that after the dead and decaying foliage, after the blinding, naked coldness, there will come another season. There will come another time. A time to laugh, a time to dance, a time to gather oneself together again.

I'll be ready.

Goombay Smash
Jane Eaton Hamilton

The hotel was what your travel agent, a gay man who gave you an itinerary with a 16-hour layover in Toronto, recommended. He showed you an advertisement in *Girlfriends* magazine. Two women sunning in chaise lounges were photographed from the rear; only two tanned, fit arms showed and then, beyond them, the swimming pool, and then, beyond that, some potted palms. It looked like paradise, and you were keen to sign up. Now that you're actually here, you know that the resort is only passable, and the pool is the size of a kitchen sink. Your room is undeniably cramped, with hardly enough space for all your and Marg's luggage, which in very short order open like orifices and ejaculate vibrators and sandals and hemorrhoid cream. In the window the broken air conditioner burbles; the room is as cold as a refrigerator. You spend your first night in the defrost drawer, huddling against Marg like a stick of celery. The good part is that, tossed together under the covers, you and she make love, and if there's a little something missing after five years together, at least she's having sex with you, not someone else.

The room was billed as "poolside," and it does not escape your attention that the puddle they call a pool is down a long hall, through a courtyard, and then through the dining room into a second courtyard. Nor has it gone unnoticed that no one could swim in it, not really, that it's too tiny for more than a single crawl stroke end to end.

The morning stretches out leisurely. There is a breakfast of sorts served in the dining room, with coffee, orange juice, toast, and cereal. As promised in the glossy brochure, there are plenty of women. *Only* women, in fact, and they mostly come in twos, like Ark animals. You and Marg take your plates to the courtyard and sit in partial shade at a white resin table. "Hey, Marg," you say, and when she looks up at you, you send her the visual equivalent of an elbow to her side. You want her to look at all the sets of twins. For instance, the two women who wear the same white serge baseball shirts, with black trim that says KEY WEST as if it's a team. The women are young, probably in their mid 20s. You can't for the life of you imagine what they do when they aren't busy with a tropical vacation: Are they accountants? Historians? This hotel, for all its inadequacies, doesn't come cheap. They have identical blond hair, spiky on top but roping between their shoulder blades in back. Are they perhaps actual twins? No, they smooch. They look longingly across their table at each other and rise to plant wet kisses on each other's lips.

It would be like kissing yourself, you think, and think about how many nights you've been left to do just that.

There is another couple who wear identically styled hair blown poufily back. One is streaked blond and the other is brunette, but that's not what you notice. What you notice is the sameness, and their similar thin lips. When they depart, going off to do you-don't-know-what with their day in paradise, another couple takes their spot. Though different in build, both of these women have masses of curly black hair cascading to their waists.

Maybe this is how American lesbians celebrate their anniversaries, you think. Never mind paper, silver, gold: American lesbians have hair anniversaries. If they make it two years, they part on the same side, five years they spike, ten and they bob. Twenty and they both wear buns in snoods.

"Psst," you say. "Marg, look over there."

Marg says, "What, Joyce?" and looks up at you a little annoyed.

You point out the women with waterfall hair and try and explain about hair anniversaries, and how the two of you should get matching buzz cuts, but Marg just frowns and goes back to scraping out her grapefruit with a stumpy-handled spoon.

You hope if you live to be 90, you never look like anyone's clone. Unless it's Marg's. You would be Marg's clone if she asked. You would—if she asked.

You rented a car in Miami, and when you called your mother to say you were a bit hesitant about renting at the airport because of all the violence toward tourists, she said, "Don't be silly. They only kill Germans." Canadian, you drove down the southern seaboard through the linked group of southern Florida islands called the Keys. Because it was late October, every home or business you passed, just about, was decorated. Americans take their Halloween seriously. In Vancouver, where you live, Halloween is reserved for the few days immediately preceding the end of the month: a simply carved pumpkin on the doorstep, a demure bowl of candy in the foyer. But in Florida porches are massed in white cotton pulled out to resemble spider webs. These are huge, ten or 20 feet across. Black plastic spiders gallumph across the netting. In every second window, convincing fright masks made of rubber are displayed along with white-sheeted ghosts or black-sheeted witches. Maybe it's the tropics. Everything here is ripe and half-rotten, even holidays.

Ways you have debased yourself for her:

1) You have laid nude on your car, a gigantic hood

ornament, in your garage that smells of dirty oil, waiting for her to raise the door with her remote.

2) You have danced naked to girl-group songs in your kitchen.

3) You have served her chocolate birthday cake in your birthday suit, coming to her with your breasts illuminated by candlelight.

There is something disorienting about breakfast. For one thing, you are smack-dab in the middle of a bunch of vacationing lesbians, which means you ought to feel like a hog in heaven. But you don't. Instead you feel pasty-skinned and overweight, as if you carry the heaviness of Canada with you. No one looks at you. No one cruises you. You might as well be a pumpkin.

Vines hang down the sides of the buildings, trailing things that look to you like red licorice ropes. Hibiscus shrubs bloom hot and pink, thrusting up deeply colored stamens. Everything droops and drips. Oranges plump on leafy stems, changing from green to orange. The hot tub gurgles. Although you wish it weren't true, skeletons dangle from some of the palm trees. When you were thinking about taking Marg away somewhere, you researched palm trees and found out there were 3,000 varieties. There are probably ten or 20 varieties around the courtyard. You try to dredge up names: coconut, saw cabbage, Royal.

You are almost positive Marg doesn't want to be here with you. She's made it clear. When you said, "Let's get away," she said, "What? You and me?"

While Marg finishes eating, you go to the office to ask for a room upgrade. You want a suite right beside the pool because, as you tell Camille, you didn't come thousands of miles to stay in a room the size of a closet. "I gave closets up years ago," you say, grinning stupidly. Camille doesn't think you're funny. There is a room you can move to at noon, she says, for an extra $30 U.S. a night; if you pack, Camille will see that your bags are moved. Even if you get back late, someone will be in the office to exchange keys with you. Camille is a strapping blond who wears a white shirt calculated to set off her dark tan. As far as you can see, there is only one of her. For a minute, you think she likes you. For a minute, you think she's moving your luggage as a favor and won't expect a tip. She asks if you and Marg have signed up for tomorrow's women-only sunset champagne cruise. You say, "Should we?" as if Camille will know what's the right move to please Marg, then plunk $80 U.S., which works out to something like $8,000 Canadian, on her desk and wait for a receipt.

Marg and you stroll out to discover Key West. You walk south to where a marker tells you you're at the southernmost tip of the continental U.S.; Cuba, it says, is only 90 miles away. You think of the refugees trying to cover the distance by raft; you shake the thought—a responsible, workaday concern—away and try to concentrate on paradise. Walk to the water's edge. Point at your chest. Say, "These are the southernmost boobs in the continental U.S."

Marg laughs, which you consider such a hopeful sign that you mention hair anniversaries again.

You watch pelicans dive-bomb for food. You love their greedy pouches and how they skim the surface of the waves looking for fish. Florida birds astonish you. In a restaurant parking lot on the way down, you and Marg saw a flock of tall, red-legged white birds you believe were ibis. And you've noticed a white heron too, standing in the ocean shallows by the side of the highway.

It's hot out, so every store becomes a relief, both from the heat and from the street vendors who promise the cheapest T-shirts in America. There's merchandise for sale that you'd never find in Vancouver, and lots of art galleries; while Marg leans on the door frame, assuredly bored, you buy three framed prints and arrange to have them shipped home.

On Duval Street you buy a black ostrich feather, look hard at Marg, and say, "For later."

Marg wants to tour the Hemingway House. Hemingway was never a favorite writer of yours, but because Marg's happiness is paramount and because old houses fascinate you, you agree. Also, you see it as a chance to get off your feet, if only for a minute. Key West is supposedly a walker's paradise, but you can attest firsthand that touring has hardly been like walking on clouds. Asphalt is asphalt, and after a while the balls of your feet ache no matter how pretty the scenery. And there's been some pretty good scenery. Especially the flora, the wild, untamable growth that loops and spirals through people's yards, messy as intestines.

There is a little while before a tour begins, so you and Marg wait, examining a brochure, sitting on the lip of a mosaic tile fountain in the courtyard. The house is a registered historic landmark. It's big and blocky, painted beige, with wonderful oval windows with green shutters, a Spanish Colonial made with local brick. The grounds are perfect; philodendrons mass and climb banana palms, dangling leaves as big as boogie boards.

And in fact the tour is lovely too—the house is warm and sweet. You long to reach out and run your fingers across the spines of the books in the many bookshelves, even though you know most of the books were probably not Hemingway's. But many of the furnishings are genuine, things Hemingway and his wife Pauline accumulated in Spain, Africa, and Cuba. There's a wonderful birthing chair in the master bedroom that belonged to Pauline; Pauline had two kids with Ernest and you wonder if she used the chair. A sign strapped across it says PLEASE DO NOT SIT IN THE CHAIR. You wonder about being a scofflaw and sitting anyhow. You wonder what you would give birth to.

Hemingway built the first pool in Key West. It is filled and blue and beautiful, much nicer than the miserly one at the guesthouse where you're staying. Apparently it about broke Hemingway—even in the late 1930s, the cost was $20,000. That's why he sunk a penny—his last, according to legend—in the wet cement of the patio.

Marg says her favorite thing is the catwalk from his second-story bedroom to his office over the pool house.

"Aren't writers romantic?" she asks dreamily. She taps the brochure on your arm. "It says he wrote *A Farewell to Arms* and *For Whom the Bell Tolls* here."

Marg once booked you into the Sylvia Beach Hotel in Newport, Oregon. The only room left was the Hemingway Room, which had a view of the parking lot and an even better view of the Dempsy Dumpster. Worse, it had a moth-bitten deer head right above the bed. You dreamed that it fell and one of its antlers gored you through your heart.

One of the many six-toed cats slinks around your ankles, its malformed paws flattening on the porch boards. The air smells like jasmine.

Mallory Pier: It's where you end up after a long afternoon of walking, staring the sun in its swollen orange eye as it winks into the Caribbean. Night falls, but all around you are hucksters. An acrobat totters across a wire strung 15 feet above the boardwalk. A sword swallower pushes blades that look black and deadly into his throat. A teenage boy grins while tourists take snaps of the iguana on his shoulder. A bearded man lets his parrot hop on tourists' shoulders then asks for donations. It's busy. It's noisy. It's colorful. It mirrors your mood. All that cacophony, that jostling, that competition for your attention. That's what it's like inside you. There isn't a calm neuron in your entire brain. They're all aroused. They're all snapping and popping to the Latin music of the pier. You could burst into dance any second, something as disjointed and arrhythmic as a wooden puppet.

You're almost positive that she gives the other woman things you've given her.

Where is your watch?
My watch?
The watch I gave you for Christmas.

Where is that ear cuff I gave you?
Ear cuff? I don't know. Did you give me an ear cuff?

This has been going on for months. Something has been going on for months. That's why you're here, why you planned this trip—to have Marg all to yourself, to have her undivided attention. At home, Marg is a very busy chef in a very busy restaurant and, as far as you can tell, also a very busy lover—although not in your bedroom.

At home, you have taken to watching the Discovery Channel while you wait up for Marg. Recently, they had a week's special on sharks. Sharks, researchers contend, are as intriguing as whales and dolphins. But after watching eight specials, you don't agree. You don't see anything interesting about sharks. Not great whites, not whale sharks, not hammerheads. They don't vocalize. They don't breach. They don't even breathe air. They're fish, not mammals, and that's what the researchers seem to forget. The only thing that intrigued you, especially considering the upcoming trip to Key West, was an aerial shot of a man and a woman standing in water just thigh-high. Dotted around them, each within 50 yards, were seven great white sharks. According to the TV, the ocean is like that all the time; the announcer offers up the image to prove that sharks only rarely attack humans. They would only like you kicking on a surfboard so that, from underneath, in their stupid, subterranean brains, you looked like a sea lion. You and Marg together—twin sea lions.

You and Marg recently bought a house together. Naïvely, you assumed this meant that the two of you were seriously committed. Because as a teacher you have summers off, you started to putty and scrape, mostly alone, in July. In early August, when you moved your bed to start painting the walls in there, a note fluttered to the floor from under Marg's pillow: *What am I doing?* it asked. *She's young enough to be my daughter.*

Although you are not personally that young, you know who is. Her name is Emma. She's the new sous chef at Marg's restaurant. She is young, skinny, and married. She wears a lot of black.

When you get back to the guesthouse, your belongings have appeared miraculously in the "suite" beside the pool. At this guesthouse, where the rooms are the size of closets, the suites are the size of rooms. They are only called suites because of the extra amenities, like a foyer two-by-two-feet wide and a candy dish on the bedside table. Some women are having a party just outside your window; you and Marg decide to try the Jacuzzi in the other courtyard, which is abandoned. But someone has sprinkled soap into it and when you turn on the jets it begins to foam. At first it is hard to see the bubbles; in the dark night they make only the ghostliest, Halloween outline, but after a while the bubbles begin to pop against the bottom of your chins, against your lower lips, against your noses. When Marg inhales one she says, "Oh, for pity's sake. I think we should call it a night." You swat bubbles away, cupping them like breasts. You step from the tub after Marg, spilling suds, and pull a towel around yourself while you watch Marg walk away. You tiptoe through the breakfast room. You half hope the partying women will ask you to join them. You wonder if there is something identifiably Canadian about you that causes them not to. Perhaps your pasty skin reminds them of snow. Perhaps they understand that you are the kind of woman on whom your lover would cheat.

You crawl into bed beside Marg. You want to be held in her arms, but she has her shin in her hand. She is dotting After Bite where the mosquitoes have gotten her. Into her leg she says, "First there was nothing, and then there was *A Farewell to Arms*. I'm still trying to get over it."

The women outside hoot and holler. You lean across Marg and empty the candy dish into your palm. You wonder who has stayed in this bed before you, whether they number in the dozens or hundreds, whether they've left pieces of themselves behind in the form of stray hairs or dandruff or stains, whether they were new lovers or old, whether any of them fought. You are not fighting with Marg, of course, and that has to count for something. It is not exactly a honeymoon between you, but not fighting has to count for something. You think about Key West's narrow streets, the small saltbox houses, their gingerbread trim. You walked past a small store with half of its wares on its outside wall. A woman in a yellow dress tended it.

"May I take a picture?" Marg asked and the woman, cackling, waved her hand.

You blinked at each other, trying to decide if that meant yes or no. The hands of an antique clock circled too quickly. A sign said THANK YOU, EMORY. There was a life-size baking mold of C3PO from Star Wars. There were a bunch of plastic bananas, a trombone, a washboard, a coconut monkey's head, and a sign with a Fitzgerald-like character in tennis whites under the word GOOMBAY.

You lie in bed listening to the party from which you are excluded. Marg puts down her After Bite and sighs. "I wish to hell they'd just shut up," she says, and as if in answer you hear an interruption. Marg slides from bed and reports from the window. "It's the police," she whispers. "They've had a complaint. They're breaking it up."

It is after 1 o'clock when you finally slide into sleep.

You wake groggy, as if you were one of the drunks at the party. The sun bakes at the window. Marg is nowhere to be found. You stumble to the bathroom and remember that today is the day the guesthouse moves you back to your old room with the broken air conditioner. This room is booked. This is also the day of the sunset champagne cruise. Tomorrow, leaving Key West, you will visit an alligator swamp before heading to the airport.

Maybe Marg is at breakfast. Yes, yes, she is. When you join her, slipping into a molded booth in the breakfast room, you're aware that people are finally noticing you. But they don't seem very friendly. The twins in the Key West baseball jerseys actually scowl. Marg shrugs. She says, "They think we're the ones who reported them."

Even though you didn't report the revelers, you feel guilty. You feel like a wet blanket, smothering fun. You smothered the twins' fun. You smothered Marg's fun. Marg used to be a happy woman. When you met her, she was happy. She was happy for a while after that. For a year or two.

You wonder if Marg is missing Emma; if she came to breakfast alone because she couldn't stand to be near you another minute. You remember that once upon a time, things were new and fresh between the two of you. Marg's eyes danced the cha-cha when you came into a room. You aren't hungry. You brave the shattering glances and serve yourself a small bowl of unflavored yogurt. It's sour. It puckers your lips.

After thumbing through tourist brochures, Marg has an idea for the day. She wants to rent scooters.

"Scooters? As in motorcycles?" Perhaps you screech, because three sets of twins turn to give you scathing glances. Has Marg seen how Key West drivers drive? Maybe she wants you to die. Maybe she wants the insurance money so that she can open a restaurant with Emma. Or you'll end up a vegetable and Marg, called upon to nurse you the rest of your natural-born days, will smooch a tag team of women while you lie in bed watching, helpless, your back shattered. "I can't ride a motorcycle."

"See?" Marg says, and passes you a brochure. She taps it. "They give you lessons on the spot."

That is how the two of you end up scorching through Old Town like Halloween rockets. The scooters aren't so hard to manage, after all, but you'd prefer to stick to the back roads, where it doesn't matter if you give it too much gas and fly. Marg has an idea. You scooter out through a military base to a public beach. Like twins, you both wear your one-piece black bathing suits under your pants; you park and hotfoot it across the sand to the seaweed-ridden shore. The waves are tall; they slap against the beach and sound like Alka-Seltzer. Marg insists you have to swim since you're here. Marg insists you can't come all this way and not get in any water other than a sabotaged Jacuzzi. So you run in. The water is surprisingly cold, like Canada's. There's an undertow. Seaweed wraps around your neck. You lie back, and before a wave capsizes you Marg snaps your picture. You are wearing flip-flops, and this is mostly what will show up: two sizable blue floating feet.

Suddenly you scream. Something has brushed against your leg. You spring to your feet. There, undulating in the waves, is an alligator. An anaconda. You scramble to shore. Gradually, the thing washes in. It's a severed tail about five or six feet long. The wound is red, ragged, and fresh. The tail tapers off to nothing.

"I think it's a snake," Marg says, captivated.

You look at her. "An anaconda," you say. Once, your brother's girlfriend called your brother's penis "the anaconda of love." You told her you weren't interested in knowing.

"Go figure," Marg says, snapping a photo.

Severed, the tail can't do much. It can't do harm. It can't swim. It can't even scare you.

Marg has another idea. She signals and pulls over to the side of the stumpy road and tells you she wants to visit the graveyard. There's a gravestone she wants to show you.

You ought to have guessed this was coming. In all the places you've vacationed in your years together, Marg has wanted to see the graveyards. You think her interest is macabre. You think there is nothing to learn about the Fijian or Mexican population by looking at what kind of graves they make. Marg disagrees. Marg thinks houses of the dead capture the heartbeat of a nation.

"The dead don't have heartbeats," you mutter as she putters onto the thin asphalt drive snaking through the cemetery. She leaves a sassy plume of blue exhaust behind her. When you pass a high-rise of maybe 40 graves, a condo unit, Marg stops. The graves are indented; they look like cubbyholes for school children. The white stone is blackening with age.

Marg peers at you and says, "You've got me wrong, Joyce."

You are busy trying to knock down the kickstand of your scooter so that you can sidle over to the shade. Your flip-flop bends. You bruise your toe and curse. You look up at Marg, who has produced a hanky and is swiping at her high cheekbones, her upper lip, the back of her neck.

"About Emma," she says. "It's not what you think."

You don't know how to respond. You realize that the suspicion of this affair is central to who you've become over the past year.

"She's just a kid I admire."

You know you have to say something. "I love you" is what comes out.

Marg makes a noise in her throat and revs the throttle on her scooter. The bike surges forward; it's an instant more before Marg's torso follows.

It's very hot, very close, and the sun is beating down. The grass here is all scrubby, not really what, in Canada, you'd label grass at all. Of course, Marg and you live in a rainforest, even given the absence of trees. You listen to the surprisingly loud *put-put* of Marg's scooter fade into the distance before you turn the key on your own and try to catch up.

The grave Marg has been trying to show you has this stone:

I TOLD YOU I WAS SICK
B.P. ROBERTS
MAY 17, 1929 TO JUNE 18, 1979

Marg drags you out for a walking tour of Old Key West. There are dozens of houses on the tour, but it's too hot to last through all of them. You stand on the sidewalk staring up at assorted homes. While you rub your feet, Marg reads the brochure aloud:

"This is the Richard 'Tuggy' Roberts House," she says.

"Is that so?" you say. Emma's just a kid, all right. A kid Marg admires?

"Do you have a problem with that?"

"I don't," you say. "Why would I have a problem with that?" You angle close to Marg and link arms with her. You don't know what you're asking.

Marg shakes loose and suggests you stop at Shell World. They have a vast array of conch shells, black coral, shells made into jewelry, saltwater taffy, and shark jaws. You pick out a conch shell you can hold in your hand; its brown stripes are shiny. You present it to Marg as a token of your trip. All the missing gifts have gone completely out of your head. You can't imagine she would take something you gave her—an emblem of a romantic vacation—and pass it along to a woman with whom, it is clear, she is not having an affair.

It did not occur to you, when you plunked down your money for the sunset cruise, that mostly what you were paying for was the privilege of drinking as much booze as you could pour down your throat in two hours. You are a teetotaler, and while Marg drinks, she doesn't drink when she's on the water because of vicious seasickness. All the twins, with whom you are in close proximity while the sky dazzles, ignore you steadfastly. The baseball twins are today wearing matched purple tank tops with pink triangles in the spot where, ostensibly, their hearts should be.

"Come on," says Camille, the woman who moved your luggage from room to room, the one who talked you into this cruise. "Just one drink. It's on me." She orders at the bar, then passes each of you an orange concoction that looks nearly dangerous. "Goombay Smashes," she says. "An island tradition."

Obediently, the two of you sip.

You stare at a sign advertising an organization called "reef relief." Accidental boat groundings damage the sensitive reef, it says. "Brown, brown, run aground. Blue, blue, sail on through."

A lone dolphin explodes on the starboard side of the boat, leaping and drawing the boat forward.

You haven't dared to reply to what Marg said in the graveyard. It is too much to hope for, that Marg is faithful, and yet you do hope. At night, in your minute, frozen room, you touch her breasts and tell her you feel like you and she are two halves of the same woman. "Two thirds," you correct, because together, it's obvious, you don't add up to one. Really, why don't you admit it? You don't add up to two-thirds. You add up to two.

Marg lifts on her elbow to look at you. She raises her eyebrows. "Good night," she says, and pushes away your hand.

Before you leave Key West, Marg finds a handmade tile store and talks you into blowing most of your leftover money on two coffee mugs. With the exchange, they cost nearly $100 each. But you think it's a good sign. While they don't exactly match, there are two of them. Two of them. Which must mean that Marg envisions a future for the two of you. You also buy a trivet that depicts a woman and a wolf side by side. You don't say anything out loud, but to yourself you nickname the wolf Emma.

The next afternoon you are off to the alligator farm north of Miami. Your rental car is small, slow, red; in your mind, it flashes your tourist status like a beacon. The Keys are navigable, but once you're north of Key Largo, things are dicier. You start to notice hurricane damage—palm trees without fronds, mostly. Your mother told you all about Hurricane Andrew, which she watched on CNN, and now you pass what she said along to Marg.

"One woman was in her bedroom with her six-year-old daughter," you say, "and the hurricane swept under the house, pulled up some floorboards, and stole the sneaker off the child's foot."

Marg signals a lane change. You want her to say something, but she doesn't.

"A lot of people found out their insurance was no good. The government declared it a disaster area. The hurricane did millions of dollars worth of damage."

Marg adjusts the rearview mirror.

You can't seem to get her attention. You say, "Do you love me?"

She says, "What time does the brochure say this place closes?"

You get lost in Homestead. Homestead is supposed to be one of the most dangerous spots in the continental U.S; more people get murdered here than anywhere else. Marg is not impressed with your abilities as a map-reader. You drive up and down country roads that bisect agricultural fields, palm tree nurseries, mostly, but you never find where you're supposed to be going. You say, "Those are Alexandria King Palms they're growing, for your information."

Marg pulls the car over. She reads the map. "This is 192nd Avenue N.W.," she finally says disgustedly. "We're supposed to be looking for S.W. I told you you need reading glasses."

You say, "Oh. S.W. S.W. Right." You twist the map upside-down until S.W. becomes apparent to you.

Marg's patience is being tried. You suggest she let you drive. The only people around are farm workers passing in beat-up vehicles. You get behind the wheel, where her hands have left wet slicks. She directs you and keeps directing you. Finally, you drive into the slippery edges of sunset.

The Everglades Alligator Farm is the alligator farm closest to the airport, from which, about midnight, you'll leave. It's nearly 5. The place closes at 6. The dollar-off coupon in your hand is wrinkled and damp, but it still proclaims that you are about to have "A Gatorific Time!"

"Have you ever been on an airboat?" you ask Marg. Now there are signs that tell you you are getting close: EVERGLADES ALLIGATOR FARM, 10 MILES and an arrow pointing.

It is very, very rural, but not at all what you imagined the Everglades to look like. You thought of water, swamps, men who wrestled alligators with their bare hands. "Unspoiled Florida at its Wildest" says the coupon.

You are very tired, very weary, and very hot when you pull into the Everglades Alligator Farm driveway. But you're happy to have found it. It's only ten after five, so all the hours of travel, all the stress, have been worth it. On the door to the gift shop is a skeleton with blinking green eyes. Marg puts her face in her hands. You say chirpy things like, "We're here, sweetheart. Come on, my little mung bean. Everything is fine now. You'll see. Let's go have our gatorific time."

You try to sound upbeat. How did Marg get so far away from you? Because in this Homestead parking lot, mere feet from thousands of alligators, in a spot not very long ago ravaged by a hurricane more severe than your emotions, you understand that Marg is already gone. She's here, beside you, but she's already gone. If not to Emma, then to whomever her next lover is, to whatever her life holds in store for her future.

Marg looks at you. You try to decipher what's in her eyes. Pity? Her hand reaches for the car door. It swings open to blasting heat. You follow her determined walk into the gift shop. Cold air hits you. There are alligator goods arrayed on many glass shelves and for a fleeting second, you're sorry that you spent all your money on art and ceramics. There are alligator stuffed animals and alligator spoons and vinyl alligators that will swing from key chains.

What you'd really like is a picture of someone an alligator chewed up and spit out.

Marg stands in line at the counter. The clerk snaps bubble gum in an otherworldly shade of blue.

"Two," Marg says.

The clerk says, "We're closed." She does something with her register, which is computerized. A register tape begins to jerk out, trailing longer and longer.

Marg says, "You're open till 6."

"Sure," says the clerk, "but not for airboat rides. Last airboat ride's at 5."

Marg doesn't know what to say. Neither do you. Both of you are imagining this whole insufferable day, the expensive mugs, the cruise, the hot tub, the broken air conditioner, the unending highways, being frightened and lost in Homestead, driving around aimlessly for hours.

"Come back tomorrow," the clerk tells you. Her eyes slide slowly up and down, up and down, first Marg's body then yours. You'd think she'd never seen lesbians before. The cash register tape winds onto the counter and twists there like something alive, like a snake: an anaconda d'amor.

"We can't," Marg says.

You agree. "We're flying out tonight."

"This is it," Marg says. Marg's haircut is nothing like yours. All those years ago, when you met, it should have been a dead giveaway that the relationship couldn't last.

"She's right," you echo. "This is it."

Millie's Girl
Tzivia Gover

It was late in the evening, and I'd never come to Millie's trailer any time but during the day, so what was already a strange situation felt stranger than usual. And I'd never gone there before without Sarah.

As soon as I steered the van into the driveway I could hear a dog's low growl heating up to a fevered bark. "Easy, Dixie," I crooned out the window, though I knew that old border collie probably couldn't hear me. Funny thing about old dogs: They go deaf selectively. They can hear a can opener bite into a can of Alpo, but they can't hear you say "Sit." Dixie heard my van invade the cool stillness of her yard, all right, but she wasn't going to hear any words of consolation.

Millie heard me, though. My headlights caught sight of her silver braid swinging behind the screen door as she turned her head from side to side trying to identify her visitor and, I suppose, the reason for the visit.

"You again," Millie said as I stepped from the van. Dixie was at my knee, transformed now from guard dog to happy hostess. She licked my hand and nuzzled into my legs as I approached the trailer's stoop, which was nothing more than a pile of cement blocks.

Millie, who probably wasn't too far into her 60s but who looked older, the way people do when life's treated them roughly, held the door while I went inside, with Dixie at my heel. On the cramped table in the far corner of the trailer I spotted an open can of beer set on top of the comics page from the newspaper. A song about a young man talking to his father, who was in heaven, played from a crackling transistor radio. It was a Top Ten Country Hits program, as far as I could make out. Soon there'd be songs of cheating wives, and I didn't know if I could bear it.

I unsnapped my bomber jacket and dropped it on a chair. The 75-watt brightness of Millie's kitchen, bordered by the complete dark outside, felt whole and insular. Then Millie's voice broke in like thunder.

"Dog's coat don't grow much in a coupla weeks. With all your education I'd think you'd know that much."

Anyone else would take this as a sign they weren't welcome. But I'd been coming here to groom Dixie—*we'd* been coming here to groom Dixie—for several years now, and I was used to Millie.

Sensing that this visit wasn't on her account, Dixie curled up under the table and let out a clattering sigh. I cleared a couple of cats, Gertie and Bertie, from the bench and sat down.

I tried to make some excuse for my presence—said I wasn't sure we'd remembered to do Dixie's nails last time we'd been around, but Millie quieted me with a grunt.

"Dog's nails are all right," she said, pulling another beer from the refrigerator. She adjusted to unexpected company with the brutal ease with which she seemed to greet every situation. "But you could give me a hand with them packages," she added.

For the first time I made out the particulars of the clutter on the small countertop along the trailer's far wall. Millie's place was always so crammed with things—packages of batteries, empty cans of cat food, magazines, books, a pair of pliers, and a handful of clothespins on top of a pile of laundry—that I had long since stopped taking notice. The packages she was indicating now were grocery sacks filled with boxes of powdered milk, bottles of aspirin, and cartons of cereal.

"See, you're not the only one thinks I'm charity," Millie said.

Millie had recently begun complaining that Sarah and I thought of her as a charity case, and that's why we did Dixie's grooming free of charge. During our last visit it came up because she'd invited us to stick around for a little "Charlie"—Millie's shorthand for a tuna sandwich—but I'd said we had to run. Which we didn't. We had to fight was more like it. While we'd been out in our van—"On the Growl" is what we call our mobile dog grooming business—Sarah had said she'd been "thinking" about things. And it just got worse from there. It was as if Dixie had understood what we were saying that afternoon, because she kept trying to hop down from the metal cutting table. They say animals can sense it when a storm is brewing.

But Millie had stayed in her trailer and didn't see how two women, despite working in such close quarters, could avoid touching—even the casual brush of arm against arm. So when we refused her invitation for lunch, she muttered something about how friends stick around, social workers breeze in and out.

I'm here now, I wanted to say. Instead I just said, "What?"

"My niece comes by once a month with these packages—so I don't start eating the cat food, I figure."

"Your niece? But I thought you didn't have any brothers or sisters."

Millie ignored that. "But I can't get the darned things up into the cabinets. Not fast anyway. She never thinks of that. Just breezes in—" Millie handed me a box of powdered milk. "And out." I took the box and placed it in the high cupboard she'd indicated with her chin.

As far as I knew, Millie had no family. She'd never mentioned a husband or children. And she once told me she'd been an only child, that she'd left home before she turned 20, and that both her parents were "up with God or down with the devil...guess I'll find out which soon enough," is how she put it.

We spent the next five minutes unloading the bags. It was fast work, but Millie insisted it would have gone on all night and into eternity if I hadn't shown up. But that might just have been her own act of charity. Making me feel useful.

Then we went back to the beers. "Where's your partner in crime?" Millie asked. Whenever she said that I pictured Sarah with a painted-on mustache, in a trench coat, carrying a violin case with a machine gun inside. Usually it was an image that made me smile but just then I didn't want to think about Sarah, or where she was. When I did think of her, I felt something burning in my chest—the place where my heart used to be. It wouldn't be the first time I'd been dumped for a guy. But it would be the hardest. No, that's not even close. It would be...impossible. Impossible to even contemplate. I turned to my beer, tested the sharp edge of the can with my tongue. "Sometimes we work separately."

Millie sized me up, like she was looking at me for the first time that night. "It's a little late for you to be working, one way or the other."

I turned away from her gray eyes. Which was hard to do because I love looking at Millie's face. She's old enough to be my mother, and she looks like she could be my grandmother. Her skin is dry and wrinkled, but I always have the urge to touch it. I expect it would feel like suede. She's missing some teeth on the bottom, which gives her mouth a sour-looking pucker. You can see that her life's been hard, but not how. And despite everything she says, you can see that she's kind. I see it, anyway.

That's probably what drew me there that night, though if you'd asked me I wouldn't have known what to answer. It's not like I didn't have friends I could turn to. I had plenty. But I wanted to go someplace where I wouldn't have to explain. Millie wouldn't ask questions. She'd just let me be.

I remember the first time I met Millie. Sarah and I weren't

business partners yet, not life partners either. Technically, you couldn't even say we were in love. Technically.

I was working in a pet store that had a little grooming business on the side. Sarah had been one of my regular customers. She was working as a caterer then, and she always smelled of something different: cilantro or lemon or sugar. She had a poodle-terrier mix, which should have been an awful combination, but this little guy was so cute I thought Sarah should put him in commercials.

The dog was the excuse for our first date. In fact, I think I'd said something really lame, like, "I've been grooming Lucky for a long time now, and I think it might be time to take the next step." I saw a hint of panic in Sarah's eyes, like she thought I might be losing my mind. "I'd like to take your dog for a walk," I said quickly.

Sarah looked down and began to fidget with the dog tag samples that were on the counter; she was running her finger over a red one shaped like a fire hydrant. "Of course," I added, "you could join us if you'd like."

She looked up, in that way she does: the left side of her mouth grinning more enthusiastically than the right. It's a smile that makes her look a little bit cocky and a little bit shy all at once.

It was one of those fall afternoons when it looks like the sky is sagging under its own weight. "How about we take Lucky to the ocean? It looks to me like beach weather."

Sarah looked over her shoulder, past the display of cat scratching posts, and out through the plate-glass window to the darkening sky. "Any weather's beach weather in my book," she said, scooping her dog up under one arm like a purse.

We drove to my favorite beach, where Lucky could run off-leash without anyone bothering us. We had just gotten out of my pickup and were climbing over a dune toward the ocean when this Border collie came limping by. Sarah knelt and called the dog over. It whimpered but obeyed. I was impressed by how she handled this stray, scratching it behind its ears before gently lifting one paw. I was jealous too. In that moment I'd have walked barefoot over a bed of glass to get her to lift my foot that way.

The dog's tag didn't have an address. Just the name Dixie and a phone number. While I was pondering this morsel of information, Sarah caught the green shard between the nails of two fingers and slid it from the dog's paw. It wasn't a serious wound. But I was impressed by Sarah's sureness, her confident movements, and the easy kindness she showed the strange dog.

A mist of rain began to fall and Lucky bent his head. He looked stricken by the turn this day was taking: No one was heading to the ocean, and this interloper of a dog had stolen the spotlight of Sarah's attention. I crouched beside him while his mistress decided on a course of action.

"There was a pay phone in the lot. Why don't we call the owner? Just in case."

We walked back to the parking lot, Dixie staying by our heels as if Sarah's act of kindness had been an invitation to eternal friendship. Which, as it turned out, it was.

Since Sarah had done everything up to this point, I took the phone. She read me the numbers off the dog's tag, and I dialed. The voice on the other end sounded low and strong like the rumble of a semi. It was her dog all right, the woman said, and it was "far enough" from home. I told the owner, who said her name was Millie, that if she'd tell me how to find her, we'd drive the dog home. As Millie barked the directions at me, I repeated them out loud in the hopes that between the two of us, Sarah and I would remember them and find our way. "Go west to the center of town. When you see the high tension wires, that's my road. You'll see an old white truck parked across from where I live."

"Wait," I said, "will the truck be on the right or the left?"

"Right," Millie said. "Trailer's is on the left. Road's down the center. Are we clear on that?"

I wasn't. But by then the rain was starting in earnest, and besides, something in the woman's tone told me the conversation was over.

When we pulled up in front of her place, Millie, wearing a work shirt over a sweatshirt over dungarees, shambled across a stubbly lawn. "So. You found me," she said, and walked inside in a way that commanded that we follow. Coffee was brewing in an angular metal pot that in another context I would call vintage—but hers was just old. There were telephone cords, papers, books, plates, and metal appliances everywhere. I counted five cats, including one sleeping on top of the refrigerator and two curled up on the table.

"Old man like this could be wandering for days," Millie said, folding herself down to an uncomfortable stoop to put out a bowl of food for the dog. "We old ones do that. Wander, that is."

Although I already had enough reasons to fall in love with Sarah, she gave me one more when we walked out to my car. "Let's go back and visit Millie sometime," she said. "I like her."

I'd liked Millie too. "I should make house calls to people like that," I said as I steered the pickup onto the road. "How's she going to care for that dog's coat? And all those cats…"

"People like her trim their dogs themselves," Sarah said. In fact, on later visits I'd discover that Millie did a lot more than that by herself. She'd managed to bring her cat Jo to a clinic to be spayed but snipped the stitches herself when the time came. She pulled them out one by one as I stood protesting.

When Sarah and I started our mobile grooming business a year after meeting Millie, we put her first on our list. We convinced her she was helping us out by letting us work on Dixie in our new van, which we'd outfitted with a "walk-in" blow-dryer, cutting table, and sink. "We need the practice," I told her. After that, our visits weren't questioned. And although these days we have a waiting list of customers who'd like us to drive out and groom their dogs, we always make it a point to get to Millie's.

"You don't have to keep sipping if the beer's all used up," Millie was saying. I'd been trying to look like I was still drinking because I knew the beer cost her dearly. I didn't suppose her niece brought her cases of Bud. But I guess I'd been doing a pretty poor pantomime. I was distracted, after all. All I could think of was where Sarah was, and with whom. Strange thing is, we'd just decided to have a commitment ceremony not one month before. It was her idea to get married, but I was the one who asked.

She'd been hinting for a while about having some kind of ceremony. I wasn't so sure, though. Not about us—as far as I was concerned my life with Sarah was as close to perfect as two people can expect to get. It was the idea of getting up in front of all those people to declare something so intimate that bothered me.

But one day we were driving in the van between clients, and I looked over at Sarah and thought, why not?

Or maybe that's not how it happened. Maybe Sarah was right, and the only reason I asked that day was because we'd just visited her friend Bobbi, who'd left her girlfriend for a premed student. A guy. Looking back, Sarah says I asked her to marry me out of fear. That what I wanted was to tie a knot, literally. To tie her to my side.

Some knot.

Anyway, that day, when we were driving, before Sarah came up with her theory about knots, I just said it. We were happy and the wind was blowing through the window, sending her hair across her forehead—she pushed it away with one hand, and her eyes were sparkling. I said, "Sarah, marry me." And she said, "Yes—I mean no!" I almost drove into the Ford Explorer that had just put on its brakes in front of us. "No?" I couldn't believe it.

"Ask again—the right way, and I'll reconsider," she said. There was that smile again.

"The right way?" As the words came out of my mouth I knew what she meant. "Down on one knee?" I asked.

"And a ring," she answered.

The knee I could manage. I pulled over to the side of the road. We were outside one of those mini-malls, with a few pathetic little stores: videos, liquor, a Laundromat. I ran into a deli and looked around wildly. I found what I needed in the candy aisle. Cracker Jack. Hoping they still put rings inside as prizes, I bought a box and opened it right there at the counter. A rub-on tattoo. I went back to the aisle and filled my arms with boxes of Cracker Jack. The pimple-faced clerk stared at me like I'd lost my mind, but I went through every box. After about six, I found what I needed.

She's been wearing that silly plastic purple ring ever since. Well, maybe she isn't wearing it tonight, I thought.

I heard a crashing noise and looked up to see Millie leaning into the fridge. "For the love of J.C.," she muttered as she righted some fallen bottles and pulled out another beer. She flicked the radio off as she passed and lowered herself into her seat.

Without the radio the night was too quiet. Just a slight *whoosh* of traffic from the highway beyond. Suddenly I wanted to talk. Fill the silence. I nodded toward a picture thumbtacked to the wall. "That must be your niece's mom," I said. It was a picture of two women of about the same age, standing in front of Niagara Falls. I could make Millie out right off the bat. She was much younger here, but I recognized her wide, flat nose and her intense gray eyes. She was wearing a crisp white shirt and a skirt that was all business. I remembered how my father always said, with a note of disgust, that I walked like John Wayne. Then he'd go into a whole speech about how Marilyn Monroe would cut the tip off one of her high heels to make her walk look sexier. As if I might attempt something similar to make my walk more feminine. I wondered if Millie's dad ever said anything like that to her. The woman who I thought was her sister, on the other hand, looked much more feminine. She was wearing a skirt too, but hers hugged her slim hips and drew attention to her well-formed calves.

"Told you, I'm an only child in this world. Seeing how I turned out, my parents didn't dare try again."

I'd heard Millie say this before—in those exact words. Which is why this "niece" was so confusing to me.

"Then you were married once," I said.

"No one in his right mind would marry me," Millie said, elbows dug into the table, two hands gripping her beer. "And the feeling was mutual, thank you very much." She leaned back, sipped her beer.

"Who's this then?" I said, determined now to get an answer.

"We used to tell people we were twin sisters—of different mothers," Millie said, and I heard a deep laugh roll out of her. And for the first time in my presence, Millie looked truly happy.

"When I was, oh, much younger than you are—let's see, musta been 17 years old—I met that lady in the picture there."

She laughed again. Sadder this time. "We need more beers if I'm going to go back that far in time."

I made a move to get up, even though we both had drinks in front of us.

"Stay put, you. I was just talking." Then suddenly she was quiet, and I could have kicked myself for interrupting. But I didn't need to worry. She seemed anxious now to go on.

"Only reason my folks had any baby at all was to prove they were normal. See, they were as queer as you and me put together." I choked on the sip of beer I'd just taken.

"But..." I stammered.

"You wanna know why didn't I come right out and confess the first day you and your little dolly waltzed in here?"

I must have nodded, stupidly, because Millie continued. "In my day we hushed up. Coming out then meant to finally admit to yourself that you're queer. Today it means shouting it from the rooftops, whether people want to hear it or not." She shifted in her seat. "Your generation talks too damn much," she muttered.

But then it was Millie who did all the talking. She said she started running away from home at age six, when she'd get picked up by the police, who'd serve her an ice cream cone at the station while they waited for her parents to come collect her. Later on, she said, she didn't get on quite so well with the police.

"Being gay back then was like an automatic guilty verdict. When they did street sweeps in the '40s and '50s they'd take you to the house of detention and ask if you were guilty or not. They never said what you were charged with and it didn't occur to us to ask what were we guilty of." She told how she'd pay $5 to get back out on the streets. "But now I'm way ahead of myself." She reached across the table and, for a dizzying moment, I thought she was going to take my hand. Instead she moved a wicker basket that was an improbable part of the clutter just to the right of where my hand was resting. She moved the basket slightly, as if there was indeed a precise placement for each item in this impressive disorder. Then she got back to her story.

"Those were happy days, the ones with my lady. Jean was her name." Her face softened then, as if just saying the name *Jean* could soothe away the years. "We met in the office where I worked," Millie went on. "I was in the mail room. She was a secretary, of course, the only job a girl was supposed to have. I'd get my jobs by fudging my name on the application. I'd write M.C. Cooper. That's Millicent Claire, but they didn't have to know that. So at least I'd get an interview with the boss, and I'd get a chance to do something besides just type someone else's letters. It worked too, because I got jobs no woman was supposed to have. I even drove a bus for a time. But then, I was in that mail room. Just a kid, but I'd already dropped out of school—well, they'd thrown me out, really—and I was working for my own paycheck. Still living with my folks, though."

Millie paused, deciding whether to continue. She cocked her head to one side, as if listening for the words she was about to say: "One night, we got ourselves caught." The word *caught* sounded like a slammed door.

"My father stomped into my bedroom and found me stark naked with that very woman." She plucked the picture down from the wall and put it on the table in front of her, studied it like it was a poker hand. "Well, we were girls then."

I looked at the picture instead of at Millie.

"Lickety-split I sent her out the window with my flannel robe. Threw my leather working boots out after her. We were on the first floor, thank the Lord above." Millie laughed again, but it was a smaller, sadder laugh. In the silence that followed I could hear Dixie shifting under the table, readjusting her sleeping body. I wondered if she'd heard this story before.

"It was February, and she must have freezed her behind out there in my robe," Millie said. "Next morning I woke up and heard my mother on the phone with a psychiatrist. Those days you got locked up in a mental ward for what we'd done. So I climbed out that same window and never looked back. Never saw my parents again. Didn't hear word one from or about them either. Case closed."

Millie brushed her hands together, like she was wiping off dirt.

"Oh, Millie, I..." But it was as if I weren't in the room at all. Millie just kept talking.

"I'd read in the papers that the dykes and fags were getting arrested in Greenwich Village. I looked at that headline and said, 'That's the place for me.'"

She went on to tell me about the dark, dingy bars she'd

have to run out of every time the cops came around, but how she loved every inch of New York City anyway. "Except that I couldn't be happy without my lady. So I came back up here and I found her."

Millie thumped her beer can against the table. "Problem was," she said, leaning in as if she were about to tell the punch line to a long joke, "my lady was married now." She folded her thick hands over her chest. "Pregnant too. See, my parents were set to send me to the nuthouse. When her parents got word of our little adventure, they arranged this for her."

"Oh, Millie," I said.

"Don't you 'Oh, Millie' me." It was the closest I'd heard Millie come to real anger. For all her gruffness, she wasn't bitter. I felt rebuffed, and crossed my arms over my chest trying to be tough like her.

"You kids don't know love like we had," Millie said. Her voice was back to normal. Softer, though. "We had it good," she said.

She told me that Jean announced to her new husband that Millie was moving in, or Jean was moving out. Being a Catholic man, scared of divorce, he agreed. They told the neighbors Millie was Jean's cousin, visiting from St. Louis. "That was one long visit," Millie said. "Fifteen years."

I thought of my five years with Sarah. "Then she left you," I said.

"The cancer got her," Millie corrected. We both looked down into our laps for a long moment.

"Shocked you, didn't I?" Millie sounded proud as punch when she said it.

"Yeah. You did," I said. "Why didn't you say something before?"

"You never asked." Millie planted her hands on her thighs and stood up.

I took the hint and nudged Hudson, a calico, off my jacket.

But I didn't want to go home. That would mean finding out whether Sarah had returned from her date—or as she kept calling it, "dinner." "Stop blowing this all out of proportion. It's just dinner," she kept saying. Either way, I still couldn't believe it. She was out. In a dress. With a guy.

She'd gone out with him in high school; he'd taken her to the prom. She still had the picture—the two of them posing in front of a trellis covered with roses. She was gorgeous in that ridiculous green gown. I'd never paid much attention to the guy she was standing next to. He seemed irrelevant.

But when we were making our invitation list for our wedding—commitment ceremony, I mean—she decided to look him up. He'd probably be married with a brood of children now, she said. Wouldn't it be fun to invite him? I didn't think to argue. My high school sweetheart was on the guest list too. She and her husband, that is.

Anyway, Sarah called her old prom date up, and sure enough he was single. "Focusing on his career," was what he told her. Next thing I knew they were like regular phone buddies.

Next thing I knew after that, Sarah was brushing out Dixie's coat while I gave one of the cats a flea dip, and she was telling me she just wants to be normal. She wants a wedding that's legal. In all 50 states. She wants our lives to be validated. This, it seems, was her solution. My friends keep saying she's just got cold feet. That I should let her work it out. Which is probably why I chose to be here tonight with Millie, instead of any of them. Millie makes sense.

"You know," Millie was saying, "I've always wanted to pay you girls for all the work you've done for me and my little menagerie here."

I shook myself out of my brooding. "No, Millie. I won't take money from you. We love Dixie…and the cats…we…"

Now Millie was pulling a stool over in front of the kitchen cabinets. With a determined effort she climbed onto it, rung to seat, then slowly unfolded herself to a standing position. "Millie, don't—" I said.

I could have finished that sentence any number of ways. *Don't climb up there, you'll kill yourself,* I could have said. Or, *Don't try to pay us, please let us give you this gift, because you've given us so much.* Or, *Don't remind me of Sarah and our work together, and of what will happen if we don't work together anymore—if we don't work out.*

Millie had her hand on a teacup that was teetering on a high shelf. I reached for her elbow. "Come down from there, Millie," I said.

For a moment she swayed, and the hand that was reaching for the cup trembled. I stepped closer. Millie handed me whatever it was she'd fished from the cup. I didn't pay attention to what it was, just shoved it in my pocket and reached up for Millie's hands. They were still cool from holding the beer, and she let me help her to the ground.

I was so relieved that she was off that stool that for a moment I forgot about what I had put in my pocket. It wasn't money, I knew that.

"You can put that stool back in the corner there," Millie said, as if nothing at all had happened.

I did as I was told, then touched the outside of my jean pocket, unsure what I should do now.

"Well, go on and take a look, for J.C.'s sake."

I reached in and pulled out a wedding band with a diamond chip in the center.

"That's the ring I gave to my lady. Not worth much in money," Millie said. "But it has value. Believe you me."

"I can't, Millie," I said, trying to hand the ring back.

Millie turned away, making a lot of work of clearing the cans from the table. "I know," she said. "Something's come between you girls."

"But, I didn't say—"

"You don't have to tell me. I know trouble."

Millie's back was still toward me. She kicked open a low cabinet and tossed the cans under the sink.

"Then you'll understand why I can't take this now... Sarah and I..."

Millie walked toward the back of the trailer, as if I'd already left. "Next time I see you I want to see her by your side. And I want that ring on her finger."

She patted her bed, and Dixie looked up from where she'd been curled under the table. The cats sat at attention too. Millie patted the bed a bit harder, and all the creatures moved toward her, climbing one at a time onto the well-worn spread.

As I was leaving I took the ring out of my pocket and was about to lay it on the phone stand by the door. But I was afraid Millie wouldn't find it there. Instead, I put it in my pocket, thinking I'd bring it back next time I came to groom Dixie.

But I never could go against what Millie said. And although by the next time I came back to her trailer Dixie's coat had grown long and matted, I did return with Sarah. The ring was on her finger. And it's still there today.

In all the time I'd been her friend, Millie only ever got one thing wrong. Our generation does know love like she had. At least Sarah and I do.

About the Contributors

Kathy Anderson's poems and short stories have been published in literary magazines and anthologies. She is the 1999 winner of a fellowship from the New Jersey State Council on the Arts and completed a 2000 residency at the Virginia Center for the Creative Arts.

Deborah J. Archer teaches English and women's studies at the University of Nebraska-Lincoln. She grew up in Houston and came out during the glorious hedonism of the disco era. Her work has been published in several literary magazines.

Ta'Shia Asanti is the editor of *Gay Black Female* magazine and a staff writer for *The Lesbian News*. She is the recipient of the Audre Lorde Black Quill Award from the National Black Lesbian and Gay Leadership Forum and the Best Romantic Fiction by a Woman of Color Award from the Literary Exchange in Chicago. She has just completed a collection of short stories titled *Womyn Lover* and a novel, *All the Things Your Man Won't Do.*

Julie Auer is a lawyer and native Southerner. She has won several awards and has a novel in progress.

Kelly Barth earned an MFA in creative writing from the University of Montana, where she was a fiction fellow, and has received grants from the Missouri Arts Council and the Kansas

Arts Commission. One of her stories appears in the anthology *Women on the Verge* (St. Martin's, 2000).

Sally Bellerose quit nursing after 20 years to become a full-time writer. She is working on a novel titled *Legs*.

Amy J. Boyer holds a Master's degree in fiction from UC Davis and has been published in *Lesbian Short Fiction, Mendocino Review,* and *Putah and Cache*. She is writing a novel about love, land, bodies, and redemption.

M. Christian, author of more than 100 published short stories, has been published in *Friction, Best Gay Erotica, Best American Erotica, Best Lesbian Erotica, Set in Stone, Men for All Seasons,* and many other books and magazines. The editor of several anthologies, including *The Burning Pen, Best S/M Erotica,* and *Rough Stuff* (with Simon Sheppard), Christian has also published a collection of short stories, *Dirty Words* (Alyson, 2000).

Aja Couchois Duncan teaches poetry to youth through California Poets in the Schools. Her work has been published in *Clamour, Fourteen Hills, Prosodia, Transfer, MIRAGE/PERI-OD(ICAL), San Jose Manual of Style,* and *Superflux*.

Elana Dykewomon has been a lesbian cultural worker and radical activist for more than 30 years. In 1998, *Beyond the Pale*, her Jewish lesbian historical novel, won both the Lambda Literary Award and the Ferro-Grumley Award for Lesbian Fiction. Living happily with her partner among friends, she tries to make trouble whenever she can.

Laura M. Farmer is a junior at Coe College in Cedar Rapids, Iowa. Her work has appeared in *The Pearl* and *Coe Review*.

Currently she is studying religion and creative writing in Maynooth, Ireland.

Jamie Joy Gatto is a New Orleans writer and bisexual activist whose short fiction has appeared in *Best Bisexual Erotica 2000, The Unmade Bed, Unlimited Desires,* and *Black Sheets,* and is scheduled for a number of upcoming projects. She is editor in chief of the Web 'zine www.MindCaviar.com and its online resource center, A Bi-Friendly Place, and writes an online sex column for www.suspectthoughts.com. Her first collection of short fiction is titled *Melpomene in Ecstasy: Stories of Sex, Death, and Loss.* In addition, she is coediting an anthology with M. Christian, *Villains and Vixens: An Erotic Celebration of the Scoundrel.*

R. Gay is a graduate student in creative writing at the University of Nebraska-Lincoln. Previous and forthcoming publications include short stories in *Scarlet Letters, Best Transgender Erotica, Moxie* magazine, and *Herotica 7.*

Tzivia Gover's work has appeared in various anthologies, including *Love Shook My Heart, Home Fronts, Lesbians Raising Sons, Home Stretch,* and *Family: A Celebration.* She has an MFA in creative nonfiction writing from Columbia University.

Carol Guess is the author of two novels, *Seeing Dell* and *Switch.* Her memoir, *Gaslight: One Writer's Ghosts,* is forthcoming from Odd Girls Press. She teaches creative writing and LGBT studies at Western Washington University.

Jane Eaton Hamilton is the author of four books. Her short work, which has appeared in publications including *The New York Times, Maclean's,* and *Seventeen* as well as a number of anthologies, has won many awards and has appeared in the *Journey Prize Anthology* and *Best Canadian Short Stories*. Her short work has also been cited in *The Pushcart Prize* and *Best American Short Stories*. "Goombay Smash" won the 1998 Prism International Fiction Award and was reprinted in *Best Canadian Short Stories 1999*.

Lori Horvitz's poetry and prose have appeared in numerous literary journals, including *Quarter After Eight, Thirteenth Moon, The Brooklyn Review,* and *California Quarterly*. She teaches literature and writing at UNC at Asheville.

Dorothy Lane (Sunlight) has had work published in *Common Lives/Lesbian Lives, Sojourn, Maize,* and several literary journals as well as anthologies, including *Off the Rag, Mother/Daughter Voices, Alternatives, At Our Core*, and *Saltwater/Sweetwater*. She has been nominated for a Pushcart Prize and an award from the Mendocino Coast Writers' Conference. She is the author of the novels *Womonseed* (Tough Dove Books) and *Being* (Earth Books).

Ronna Magy's work has appeared in *Heatwave, Hers 2*, and *The Bilingual Review*. She lives and writes in Los Angeles.

Jenie Pak received her MFA in poetry from Cornell University. She has poetry published or forthcoming in *Alligator Juniper, Five Fingers Review, Many Mountains Moving,* and *The Oakland Review*. She recently moved to San Francisco and is proud to have her short fiction first published in a dyke anthology.

Ruthann Robson's newest collection of fiction is *The Struggle for Happiness* (St. Martin's Press, 2000). She is also the author of two other collections of short fiction, *Eye of a Hurricane* (1989) and *Cecile* (1991), both published by Firebrand Books, and two novels, *Another Mother* (1995) and *a/k/a* (1997), both published by St. Martin's Press.

Mary Sharratt makes her home in the San Francisco Bay Area, after 12 years of living in various European locations. Her short fiction and essays are published in *Puerto del Sol, Bookwomon, Iris: A Journal for Women, Hurricane Alice,* and elsewhere. Her novel, *Summit Avenue,* is new from Coffeehouse Press. "Invisible," which appears in this anthology, received a 1998 Pushcart Prize nomination.

Kristin Steele just finished witnessing the production of her first play (*To Wed, Divorce, and Bury*) and is trying to survive Los Angeles with her girlfriend and two cats. "Recycled" is her first published story.

Karen X. Tulchinsky is the award-winning author of *Love Ruins Everything,* a novel named one of the top ten books of 1998 by the *Bay Area Reporter,* and *In Her Nature,* short fiction that won the 1996 VanCity Book Prize. She is the editor of numerous anthologies, including the best-selling *Hot & Bothered* series, the Lambda Literary Award finalist *To Be Continued,* and *Friday the Rabbi Wore Lace.* She is currently writing a novel and several screenplays and teaching ongoing writers' workshops. Visit her Web site at www.karenxtulchinsky.com.

Lu Vickers lives in Tallahassee, Fla., with her girlfriend and three sons. She has twice been the recipient of a Florida Arts Council Grant. Her work has most recently been published on Salon.com.

Helen Vozenilek is a full-time electrician and part-time writer who desperately wants to reverse the percentages. She lives in the San Francisco Bay Area.

About the Contributors

Marnie Webb has had work published in print and online literary magazines, including *Blithe House Quarterly, The Belletrist Review,* and *The Blue Moon Review.* She lives and writes in the San Francisco Bay Area.